TALES OF PREHISTORIC SURVIVAL
(CRYPTOFICTION CLASSICS)

TALES OF PREHISTORIC SURVIVAL
(CRYPTOFICTION CLASSICS)

LAST OF THE MAMMOTHS
Raymond Turenne

MEN OF THE MIST
T. C. Bridges

COACHWHIP PUBLICATIONS
Greenville, Ohio

Tales of Prehistoric Survival (Cryptofiction Classics)
© 2020 Coachwhip Publications

Last of the Mammoths published 1907 (trans.)
   Raymond Auzias-Turenne (1861-1940)
Men of the Mist published 1922.
   Thomas Charles Bridges (1868-1944)

No claims made on public domain material.

CoachwhipBooks.com

ISBN 1-61646-491-7
ISBN-13 978-1-61646-491-2

LAST OF THE MAMMOTHS

RAYMOND TURENNE

CHAPTER I
THE THUNDERBOLT

The Hon. John N. Corliss, United. States Senator from New York, was a "self-made man"; that is to say, he had been the architect of his own fortunes. Of course he boasted of the fact to every one whom he met, but from my point of view, I could never congratulate him upon his achievement. Perhaps, a few thousand years ago, when primitive man inhabited the caverns of the Stone Age, it might have been a matter of pride; but in the twentieth century, when one finds free schools even amongst those very queer people amidst whom, thanks to the same Corliss, I nearly lost my life; the talk about being a self-made man is only the blatant boast of the parvenue. Now I, Raoul Le Fort, whose people were well-to-do in Paris, and who without the need to work, won the Grand Prize of Rome at the School of Fine Arts, consider that my success does me more credit than that of Senator J. N. who had to strive or starve from the time he was seven years old.

And what a smell of the Almighty Dollar there was about him! When I met him at the club, I could hear it rustle and hustle in the shape of stocks and bonds and thousand-dollar bills, and upon my word, if he so much as sneezed, I half expected to see a shower of twenty-dollar gold pieces rattle on the floor.

It would not have been so bad if there had been one redeeming point about him in the veriest shadow of the ideal. But he was an utter barbarian, whose sole mission in

the world was to heap up dollars. His great-great-grand-
sons, never having had the pleasure of his acquaintance,
will probably engrave a remarkable list of virtues on his
monument; but I can sum up all that was best in him in
four words. "He was Eva's father."

How such a thing could be was no more to be explained
than a miracle. One could only lose himself in astonishment, as did your humble servant on the day when he first
saw *her* in Central Park, one morning between six and
seven—that most delightful hour of the day when New
York wakes up, stretches itself, and yawns.

She had stopped on the edge of the lake, and was care-
lessly throwing some crumbs of cake to the swans. All at
once the glorious sun rising above the eastern roofs encircled her with a golden nimbus, which grew and grew until
it included both her and her black horse in the same gold-
en aureole, and then rippled over the dancing wavelets
whence the beautiful birds seemed springing to greet her.
It was an admirable vision of light and life, and it nailed
me and my horse Rakib to the spot, uplifting me for a second into a heaven of ecstatic contemplation.

But my shadow must have startled her, for all at once,
raising her head impatiently, she shook her reins and started her Arabian off at a gallop, disappearing along the Mall
and Fifth Avenue. Was there a suspicion of a smile on
those dainty lips? Very likely, for when one is struck dumb
with admiration, and betrays it in his wide-open eyes and
mouth, he looks somewhat of a fool. All the same, whether
she was laughing at me or not, she left me much in her
debt. I had had the pleasure of contemplating the purest
possible type of the American girl of the twentieth century—the adolescent Diana of ages dead and gone—come
to life again, not in cold marble, but in warm flesh and
blood, still palpitating with the life-giving breath of the
Creator.

As a general thing, I never come across a pretty girl
without following her with my eyes as long as possible, to

prolong my aesthetic appreciation. Rakib, my horse, who was educated by a beautiful girl of the tribe of the Haymon, in the Western Sahara, would have followed on the track of the fair unknown at his best speed, and when I forcibly turned his head towards Sixth Avenue, he champed his bit and flecked me with foam as a mild protest.

"What are you thinking of, master?"

"Quick! to my studio," I said; "at your fastest, Rakib! At last I have found my masterpiece. Come, my best of horses, come!"

With a whinny of appreciation, he was off like a whirlwind. He understood me to perfection, because we used to have long, confidential talks every morning. And how I worked that day, from eight to six, ten hours straight on end—for all companionship a pot of black coffee, a locked door, an absolute silence, and always before me a diaphanous vision—intangible, unapproachable—to catch it one must have the palette of a Quentin de la Tour.

At last I tore up all my sketches and dropped despairingly on a camp-stool, and head in hands and pipe in mouth, set myself to becloud my studio and clear my ideas simultaneously. Whereupon the gods came to my rescue in the form of two brilliant ideas.

First, to find out who she was.

Second, on my knees, if need were, to beg from her the favour of a dozen sittings, since she alone in all the world could glorify my canvas with her beautiful eyes, glorious as those of a Byzantine virgin.

Having settled these points, I went to dinner at the Athletic Club, for I knew that if I had the good luck to meet my friend Hamilton, who was a walking directory of New York, I had only to turn over the pages of him.

"Hallo, Freddy!" I said, as I entered the Club, "I was just this moment thinking of you. Can you do me a great favour?"

It was indeed my man, deeply interested in mixing in a metal tumbler the multifarious ingredients of a twentieth-

century cocktail—known as a T.C. Two waiters were looking on in reverential silence.

Let me finish this," said Hamilton, nodding towards
nine open liqueur bottles and a bowl of pounded ice,
where he was compounding some unknown abomination.
"Just imagine, these wretches do not know how to dole out
the Mariani! One drop too much—"

"Don't let me interfere with your horrible chemical
combinations," said I, rather impatiently, "but just answer
a simple question. I have seen this morning, in Central
Park, between six and seven o'clock, the very prettiest girl
who ever galloped across New York. You must know the
name of the delightful vision."

"Well," said Freddy, "there are, in Fifth Avenue alone,
some fifty amazons who are, every one of them, the prettiest
girl in New York. Now put in some crushed strawberries—"

"Hamilton, will you drop your pernicious concoctions
for two minutes and talk sense? I do not want any fooling
or comparisons. My fair unknown has such golden hair,
and such black eyes, that you cannot mistake her."

Freddy, whose little ways I will speak of later, always
remembers animals better than he does people. Hence his
first question, which, for a moment, led me to believe that
he was intoxicated.

"What about the dress?"

"Why, the simplest of riding habits, man."

"I mean to say the coat?"

"The coat?"

"Yes, yes, yes. The horse's coat, stupid!"

"Oh, a thoroughbred Arabian, like mine, only jet black
with a white star on the forehead."

"That's good enough. You're after Eva Corliss. She rides
like a madwoman. Once, out hunting, I said to her, 'Look
out for the sharp corners, Miss Eva.' What do you think
she said? 'Wait till I am sixty, my dear boy.' Believe me,
she is a girl whom it will not be easy to make an impression on."

I felt like punching his head, but curiosity restrained me.

"Eva" (oh, the dear name!), "Eva Corliss? Is that the famous millionaire, President of the Central Railroad, head of the Steel Trust?"

"And of half the companies listed on the Stock Exchange," said Freddy. "Corliss, the Steel King. At fifteen years of age he was a telegraph messenger, jumping over New York gutters. At twenty, as a mining prospector, he ended by 'striking it rich!' At thirty he was 'dead broke!' At forty, Steel King, Railroad Emperor, and United States Senator from New York, and worth a hundred million dollars."

"What, that cigar-shop Indian, hewn out of a block of cross-grained wood with a blunt hatchet, with that horrible squint, with one eye on the steeple of Trinity Church and the other on the Mills Building? The ugliest man on earth!"

"He is worth a hundred million dollars," repeated Hamilton, phlegmatically.

"Devil take the dollars! The daughter is simply perfect, Freddy, perfect!"

"Well?"

"Well, well, well! Here is a problem for you. Given the incarnation of dollar-making materialized in the shape of old Corliss, how to evolve from it an ideal form, one of Raphael's patricians, a second Jeanne of Aragon, more lifelike, more human than that in the gallery of the Louvre."

My voice was drowned by peals of laughter.

"The cocktail! The Le Fort idealized cocktail!"

There were a dozen of them around us, particular chums of Hamilton's, who had come from table, dined, wined, and doubtless intensified by the too potent T.C. I turned and fled. There are certain occasions when the body is a misfit for the mind.

It can be imagined that, from this time on, there was endless gossip about me—amiable suppositions which were far from doing me harm, since they finally reached the ear of my fair apparition, and, I have reason to believe, predisposed her in my favour. In fact, a week later, after an introduction in due form at a five o'clock tea, at the house of my excellent patron and friend, Mrs. General Monroe, she was kind enough to visit my studio with her father.

"What is this thing?" said the Steel King, planting himself before my last production.

I bit my lips not to retort, "It's a chromo"; he irritated me so much from the very first.

"Papa," said Eva, "it is a portrait of Miss Rudy of Philadelphia."

"Rudy—William Rudy—the kerosene man?"

"The Oil King, sir," said I, "as you are the Steel King."

I think my answer pleased him, for, as they left, he shook hands with me cordially, and said—

"Are you too busy to paint a portrait of my daughter!"

Would I paint his daughter? Oh! Margaret, Eva, pearl, flower, and woman!

"I will be glad to pay you to do better than you did for Rudy—twice as much."

The daughter of the Steel King blushed, and placed her little hand over her father's mouth.

I uttered a few incoherent words, and it was arranged that I should work at her house (in America the father lives at his daughter's), where, as it seemed, she had her own studio, and she said good-bye in that haughty manner which suited her style of beauty so well. *Magnificat anima mea*, O Lord.

It is needless to repeat to you that from this thrice-blessed hour I looked on Eva Corliss only with the regard that an artist feels for the most charming model that has ever come before his vision. Three days every week I went to study the secret of her exceptional beauty; and as the portrait grew slowly under my brush, there ensued delightful talks from which I learned to appreciate the charms of her mind. Instinctively she had the most refined taste. Every visit added to the attractions of our first meeting in

Central Park. And during all these too short hours passed above the clouds, the atmosphere of New York, overcharged with steam and electricity, and the mad race for wealth, vibrated around us. Here was heaven, and all around us was hell. What a contrast and what sweet remembrances!

I have never known how long the dream lasted, and I have never tried to find out. I have a perfect horror of figures and memoranda and statistics. But I shall never forget the rude awakening from my dreams.

For my awakening was as horrible as the fall of Icarus from the heavens, on the day when I found before my picture, a hundred times re-painted, my *bête noir,* Corliss, with his hands behind his back and an ominous wrinkle between his thick eyebrows.

"Now, then, Le Fort, let's talk business. Twenty minutes to two? We have ten minutes to spare. Eva will be here directly. Now, sir, as to the portrait. When will you deliver it? It seems as if we had been working on it for a century."

"Senator," said I, "you cannot produce artistic inspiration to order. One day I often undo what I have done the day before."

"Le Fort, you surprise me. Now let us see—"

He pulled out of his pocket his dirty grey note-book, smelling all over of the "business man," which set all my nerves on edge, and turned over the leaves.

"The order—"

I almost jumped. He looked at me in astonishment and went on—

"The order was given on the twentieth of last December. It is now the eighth day of May. That means that you have been at work one hundred and thirty-nine days. Nineteen weeks and a half! See here, Le Fort. In these hundred and thirty-nine days I have driven a tunnel through a mountain."

"That has nothing to do with it," I said. "A single hair of Miss Eva's head—"

"Nonsense! These paltry items are of no account. A hair more or less on a head! Absurd! It's the face, the general result, that I look for."

A paltry item, a hair more or less from the head of Eva, who had the most dazzling Venetian locks that were ever dreamed of! I lost my patience as with one who blasphemed.

"Permit me, sir," I said, "to be judge in this affair. A work of art is not a question of time."

"Really, Le Fort, you surprise me. I cannot understand you. It is for your advantage to be quick about it. I'm not paying you by the day, but for the picture. You cannot postpone a picture in this way indefinitely."

"Senator, a work of art is not a matter of money."

Corliss was silent for a moment, looking towards the door—that is to say, on account of his terrible squint, he was looking me straight in the face. Evidently he was asking himself whether I was as right in my mind as I appeared to be sound in wind and limb. At last he said—

"I would really like to know, my boy, what I am paying you for, and how you would make a living if I did not pay you. It's all a matter of money. What is your painting business good for from your point of view as an artist?"

I could not restrain myself any longer, and I exploded.

"Deuce take the money! What is painting good for? For nothing, sir. What are painting, sculpture, music, literature, good for? Nothing in the world. They are absolutely useless. They do not produce a dollar in any shape or form. You have no need of them in order to sleep, to eat, exist. Service, profit, 'what's it good for,' are words which are at mortal enmity with the word 'Art.' But were there no art in the world, Mr. John N. Corliss, man would be only a brute which did not think, nor dream, nor even know how to weep. The magic glamour of the springtime, always young; the pensive evenings of the long days of autumn; the radiant faces of the virgins who have not yet left behind them their terrestrial paradise—all the intangible and yet most potent beauties of the universe belong to Art. Doubly and trebly accursed is the barbarian who passes them by without seeing them. *Perinde ac cadaver.*"

I do not know if it was the final crushing blow of my Latin, which I do not believe he understood in the least, but never have I seen a more disconcerted countenance than that of the Steel King at this moment, He stood with blank face, eyebrows like exclamation points, mouth as round as an O—a perfect Caran d'Ache caricature—until all at once the clock struck two.

"Two o'clock, and I have lost ten minutes. You are the first man who can boast of having made me lose so much time. Ten whole minutes! Well, attend to me. Live on art and water if you like; it's all the same to me. Forty-five years ago I had scarcely more to eat and drink myself. But, for Heaven's sake, finish the portrait. My daughter is going away soon, and—"

"Going away—she—"

"Why, yes; there's nothing so very extraordinary about that. Next week I believe she is going on a trip to Mexico with some friends. So hurry up; don't use so much paint, and finish it."

Something contracted my throat, my sight became dim, and I leaned against the mantelpiece for support.

"It's impossible," I said. "She must not go like this. I cannot bear it, Senator—I cannot."

Corliss had a heart, although it was not easily come at under its thick crust of dollars.

"Don't worry," he said, rather kindly; "eight days is quite long enough to complete your work. And look here! I will pay the whole price, even if you leave out one or two of Eva's hairs from the portrait." And he laughed heartily.

"It's not a question of portrait or of money," I exclaimed, entirely beside myself. "Can't you understand that I love your daughter so that the idea of her going away drives me mad? That I wish to marry her? That I have the honour, Senator—to ask of you—her hand—in marriage."

The Steel King's smile disappeared between two lips set as if compressed in a vice, and he was as one turned to stone. I had never thought definitely that some day I must finish the interminable picture of Eva, that I could not go on eternally painting her. Fool that I was! If I had only paved the way beforehand with him, perhaps with her. But here, without warning, without any preparation or diplomacy, I had cried out my love, my mad ambition, to this dollar-maker, this tyrant before whom thirty thousand men bent the knee.

"My poor child! A French artist! And I had thought—"

These words, spoken in a low voice, made me raise my head, and for the first time I saw in his face some trace of Eva, perhaps in the firm lines of the mouth, which could not lie. And it was that mouth which had pronounced the words "French artist" with that Anglo-Saxon inflection that I could understand better than anybody, and which summed up to the foreigner all that we Frenchmen endeavour to avoid in ourselves.

My self-respect gave me courage to confront this infernal Yankee.

"Senator—"

At this moment the works of that confounded clock clicked and turned, and two strokes sounded, then one.

"Quarter-past two," cried Corliss. "The Stock Exchange will be closing. You ought, Le Fort, to have spoken of this earlier or later on. I've no time now—it's most annoying. Still, we will look into the matter. My daughter must have returned, for she is always punctual. Sit down and wait for me here."

I believe I would rather die than pass again through such suspense as I endured before he came back. Yet he lost no time, and, as he came rushing in like a mad locomotive, he opened a side-path to safety.

"Have you enough money to support a wife?" he said.

Ye gods! This ogre who talked in this way had an income of four or five million dollars. But a moment's consideration gave me a little hope. I must not say no.

"I earn enough for two, or even three, Senator. Our common friend, Hamilton"— the Senator gave me an odd look—"could give you all the necessary information on the point. It would hardly become me to discuss it with you."

"I do not agree with you. If you wish—I do not say to marry my daughter, for we are yet a long way distant from such a proposition—but if you wish me to make a memorandum of your application"—and out came the dirty-grey note-book—"I must see in you that practical side which alone authorizes a man to undertake the responsibilities of marriage."

Practical! Make a memorandum! Proposition! A real physical nausea rose to my throat. I closed my eyes for an instant, and Eva's image came before me in all the splendour of her beauty. I made a supreme effort to cope with her brute of a father.

"I am twenty-seven years old, Senator. My father was French Consul at New York, and my family is well known in Dauphiny."

"I don't care anything about that. The French Ambassador, or some of my agents abroad, can give me all the necessary information on those points. What I want to know is how much do you make in a year?"

"Seven or eight thousand dollars, Senator, since you wish to know. I might double that if I gave up my four months' vacation in the autumn."

"Why not give it up, then?"

"Because what I earn is enough for me. Eight thousand dollars, Senator, is but a drop in the bucket compared with your millions, but it is enough for happiness when one is in love. What more can I say? I was so taken by surprise that I was mad enough to ask you for your daughter's hand; and here I am."

A voice straight from Paradise echoed behind me.

"And here *we* are, papa."

I turned round, trembling with emotion. How they smiled at me, those beautiful, black eyes with their golden reflections—eyes beyond description by pen or brush. Corliss himself was dazzled. He kissed Eva, made her sit down in his place, and, caressing her blonde head with one hand, began to talk, half to himself.

"I began life with eight thousand times less. Heaven be good to me, what a long struggle it was, what a life of effort and trial. Your mother and I, in failure and in success, always walked together hand in hand. Why must she leave me before the end of the journey? Now she could have helped me so."

I hardly followed his words further. Before my eyes also hovered some vision—come back from that far-away night, where rest all those loved ones whom we have wept for so bitterly and forgotten so quickly.

All at once Corliss, whose reveries were not apt to be of long duration, said—

"Our friend the artist is hot-headed. Monsieur Le Fort, I will give no answer now to your request. It is hardly necessary to say that until further orders the portrait can be considered as finished. But before we part, I will ask you one more question. Money is not necessary for happiness; I am not at all sure that it adds to it, and who should know better than I? On the other hand, I do know that work is indispensable to it. Here in America we gauge it exactly by the money that one makes. Now I seem to have heard at the club that you had rather odd tastes, that your bachelor life was that of a Bohemian. You appear to confirm these reports by your mention of the long vacation that you take every year, and your want of punctuality in your engagements aggravates their serious nature. I have not the least confidence in these fires of straw, these passing inclinations—"

"Papa, it is four months now."

He gently put his great hand over his daughter's beautiful mouth, and went on—

"Which blaze up for a second and then die out, leaving only ashes behind. If you can make twice as much money by working twice as hard, why not do it, were it only to scatter it over Europe afterwards? Can you be lacking in ambition? The freaks that one passes over in a bachelor are inadmissible in a married man."

I considered for a moment before I answered him. It is the hardest thing in the world to graft a new idea of things upon a mind so set and opinionated as his. But Eva's glance gave me courage to try.

"Senator, the great mistake you make is in considering artistic vocations from a business point of view. The business man's first idea is to make money; it is the last thought of the artist. Their ideals are as different as are the means by which they attain them. Take painting, for example. As in any kind of human work there is need of years of labour, the study of designing, the appreciation of colour-values; but above and beyond all, inspiration is necessary; that is to say, for a portrait-painter like me, the power to throw on the canvas, under the reds and whites of a face, that mysterious inward reflection which portrays a woman's soul. That is the whole secret, and no one can put a price on it. Well, the eternal litany of Israel, the adoration of New York around the golden calf, is fatal to such inspiration. When you see every one rushing down town every morning on the hunt for the almighty dollar, when you hear in the street, at the club, even at home through your telephone, nothing but, 'How goes it? How much are you making?' when you live in the midst of a race of madmen who eat, drink, and sleep money, at last your brain turns, and you feel yourself becoming as mad as they. Then, to save my art and to save myself from myself, I fly to the concealment of the woods, near the hidden springs where one hears the very whisper of Nature, where the birds sing without stopping to think what their voices would pay them in the song-market. I listen to them, I get back to Nature's heart, and I renew my artistic spirit. And even from the point of view of 'Does it pay?' Senator, these hours that you call wasted are the most profitable of my life. If I have not been able to make you understand this, your daughter, who received from Heaven at her birth the eighth sense—the aesthetic sense—could explain it to you better than I."

Corliss said not a word; not a muscle quivered in his face of iron. So I was also silent. Then he rose.

"I do not quite follow your reasoning, Le Fort; but there must be something in it, since you have undeniable results to show for it. Come back here day after to-morrow at this time and we will talk about it. Eva will be here, too, and I want to think matters over."

"Senator, my gratitude."

"Do not thank me yet, for I have conceded nothing; there is a condition I have to make."

The eyes of my *fiancée*, for so I already called her to myself, her beautiful eyes grew sorrowful. She said in a pleading tone—

"Papa!"

"That will do, my dear. Wait until Monday. They are waiting for me in Wall Street. Good afternoon, Le Fort. Will you have a cigar?"

His automobile whirled us away, me to the club, him down Broadway. I was in a state of mind that I can hardly define, although Eva had strengthened me with a last glance full of courage and support.

What surprise could the Hon. John N. be concocting for me in that cash-box which served him for a brain?

CHAPTER II
THE SECOND THUNDERBOLT

Eva's portrait is still there in my studio, covered with a cloth, and its glowing mass of Venetian hair still awaits the finishing touches. Will it ever be completed? When I said good-bye to her at the Grand Central Station, she answered, "No, not good-bye—*Au revoir*," holding out both hands to me. Her father looked on in his usual phlegmatic style, while around him were a crowd of idlers, worshipping this statue of a hundred million dollars.

But all that I saw was her dear black eyes, full of love and distress, clouded with tears ready to fall. It was the remembrance of those tears, of her young soul yearning towards mine, which, uplifting me above the world, gave me strength to answer, "Good-bye, and *Au revoir,* but not for long, dearest," instead of seizing her in my arms, jumping into the train, and shouting to Corliss—

"So much the worse for you, my friend. You have driven us to it."

Do not blame me, reader. I am as honest a man as you; but there are some critical moments—but let me tell you.

On the Monday, as agreed, at precisely three o'clock, I met the Steel King and his daughter. His first remark was—

"I have thought over your request, Le Fort, and I see no objection to it, nor, I believe, does my daughter." (On that point, thank God, I was sure.)

"But I must tell you at the start that I will not receive as a son-in-law any one who does not agree to an entirely reasonable and honourable condition."

"Whatever it is, I promise."

"Wait a moment, Le Fort. Sit down and listen to me before you promise anything. It is not very much, but it is all-important. See here. You probably know that I have recently given to my native city of New York, a Museum of Natural History, completely furnished and equipped. Have you seen my Museum?"

"I must confess, Senator—"

"You ought to go and see it. It is very complete, and it cost a lot of money. The first five cents that I earned when I was a youngster were devoted to a visit to the other—the Museum of the University. Mine is free. I have collected in it everything that is to be found in the museums of the Old World, every possible thing, Le Fort. The custodian, Joshua Cavanagh, a very well-informed scientist, to whom I will introduce you, has arranged everything in the best manner in the bottles, cabinets, drawers, and on the walls. Very well. In the Corliss Museum, the museum of all museums, there is one thing lacking which I have never been able to buy."

The Steel King stood up and angrily ran over the leaves of his note-book; although it seemed scarcely credible, he was disturbed by a genuine emotion. Eva was looking at him, also disturbed, almost pleading.

"In my Museum," he said, "there is lacking—a mammoth!" and he fell back into his chair.

I did not understand him in the least, but I thought it was the right thing to answer in a sympathizing tone.

"It is very unfortunate. A mammoth? I assure you I am very sorry."

In the same tone of excitement, Corliss went on—

"Do you know what a mammoth is?"

"Why, yes. A sort of prehistoric elephant."

"It is the main attraction of a museum, Le Fort. There is only one in the world, and that is in St. Petersburg. There is not one in New York, and the Corliss Museum has only a plaster cast that Cavanagh got done. Do you think that John N. Corliss is a man to be contented with a cast? This plaster monster is the shame of my life, and I want a genuine, enormous, colossal mammoth. Now, do you realize the importance of your mission?"

"My mission?"

"I think my meaning is clear," said he, shrugging his shoulders. "I am going to send you up into the polar basin to seek, find, and bring back my mammoth. That is the condition that I spoke of."

Upon my word, I realized how Adam and Eve must have felt when they were turned out of Paradise. Gustave Doré's monsters swam before my eyes, birds that were half reptiles floated down from the sky, fiery dragons raised their heads everywhere around me, and a chorus went up, as from the earth before the Deluge—

"The Mammoth! The Mammoth!"

It was Corliss speaking, and his daughter's voice brought me down to earth again. "Papa, once more I beg you—"

"It is use-less, ab-so-lute-ly, Eva. Le Fort, I presume that you accept the condition?"

His tone became harsh, and I gave way before the obstinate man of business.

"Why, yes, certainly, Senator. But it seems to me that I, an artist, am scarcely qualified for the enterprise. If I were a scientific man, now."

"That does not matter. You have only to go and search, and bring back what you find. You can hardly mistake a mammoth when you see him, I imagine. Oh, if I only had the time to spare myself, I would go myself, and keep my daughter for my own. But I want the honour of the discovery to belong to one of us, anyway. If you want to be my son-in-law, get me a mammoth. If not— Is it a bargain, Le Fort?"

I turned towards Eva, but she was not looking at me. She was looking through and beyond me at something which I did not see, which alarmed me.

"Very well, Senator," said I. "You shall have your mammoth, since it is essential to your happiness; but I warn you that you will have to pay dearly for it."

Can you imagine that he misunderstood my meaning? He answered rather sharply.

"Any price you like to name. Can I have been mistaken in you, Le Fort? Are you more practical in your ideas than you have led me to believe?"

Eva interrupted us with her entrancing smile.

"Very well, papa; may your will be done, and not ours. I invite you to dinner, and you, also, my artist. We will drink the health of the great beast that separates us—our mammoth."

The room re-echoed with her fresh young laugh, while an almost imperceptible tear nestled in the corner of a most attractive dimple that was new to me. Corliss and I unbent also, and how young we all were for a time. Some very good but dyspeptic people tell us that laughter is foolish, and a smile barely tolerable; but I maintain that a good open laugh is the wine of Paradise. The dinner passed off more pleasantly than I should have thought possible. After all, I was going to have an opportunity of picking up some sketches that would be positively unique—the unknown types of the Arctic Circle.

"Well, that's all fixed," said Corliss, at the end of the evening, just when I was beginning to forget all about it. "I will telephone to Cavanagh to be at your disposal tomorrow. You can begin your preparations at once, on whatever scale suits you. Understand, I pay for everything, without restriction. You ought to start in a week."

That night I dropped in to the Athletic Club. Of course, Hamilton was presiding over his usual decoctions.

"Freddy," said I, "in a week I am leaving for the Arctic circle, to look for a mammoth."

He did not seem to understand, so I enlightened him.

"A mammoth is a great beast that existed before the Deluge. I must find one, so that Corliss will give me his daughter, and I mean to marry Eva. I shall leave for Alaska on the first whaling-ship that is going."

Hamilton dropped his cobbler-shaker full of crushed ice, rubbed his eyes, looked at me attentively, saw that I was in earnest. Then he shook his head, and pronounced seven words—not one more.

"Very good! Have a 'T. C.' first."

Which I did; which we both did.

CHAPTER III
JOSHUA CAVANAGH'S REVELATION

Never take a cocktail before you go to bed. My sleep that night was one long nightmare. The Steel King and his daughter were confined in a lunatic asylum. At the risk of my life I rescued Eva, bribing the warders to put the Senator in a strait-jacket, and keep him out of sight. Already my beloved and I were climbing the gangway of an Atlantic Liner, when an enormous beast rose out of the water, overturned the steamer, and put his paw on my breast. And what a paw!

I woke up panting, but a cold bath revived my spirits, and as soon as I was dressed I went to ask for some breakfast from Mrs. General Monroe.

This staunch friend, whom I call my aunt, although she was really only a distant cousin, was kind enough to receive me as soon as she got up. I explained to her as well as I could the crisis in my life. She knew Eva, in fact had helped us to meet from the first hour of our acquaintance. But she did not grasp the idea of the mammoth in the least.

"You are going to paint an animal? Well, it will not be for the first time."

"I am not going to paint him, aunt, but to dig him up somewhere around the North Pole, to add him to the father's collection of fossils. If not—no mammoth, no daughter."

My aunt made me put out my tongue, had her maid bring me a hot cup of lemonade, and very quietly asked me to tell her all about the previous evening. She had never heard of the Corliss Museum, my face was feverish, and my symptoms alarming.

"I am neither ill nor off my head, my dear aunt, but I am very unhappy. Just let me tell you all about it."

When she finally understood the Steel King's extraordinary whim, my dear aunt burst out laughing. Her kind face, a little wrinkled, became like that of one of Gainsborough's beauties, whose proudly-curved lips seemed equally ready to express contempt or love. What a radiant glimpse of last year's snow, seen in a flash of lightning!

And she did not feel the least compassion for my distress of mind.

"Why have you not started already, my boy? What are you doing here? Is this the way you make love in the new century? You are not like the lovers of long ago, when I was twenty years old. It would have taken more than a mastodon to frighten them, even a hundred-million-dollar animal."

A fit of coughing seized her, and I took advantage of it to make my escape. I was furious, as those who have really been in love can understand. As for those who have not, I do not care. But evidently the die was cast. I must part from Eva, almost on the morrow of our betrothal. Unhappy me!

The first thing was to go and see the custodian of the Corliss Museum. He alone could give me some information about the favourite haunts of these prehistoric monsters, so dear to the Senator. The polar basin is easy enough to say, but it is rather a large order.

The establishment was extremely "comfortable," as the donor had put it.

Skeletons of all sorts of the strangest animals were arranged in handsome, welllighted rooms, while numberless bottles, in which hideous beasts swam in alcohol, stood on shelves on the walls. All at once, in the place of honour, in the essential rotunda, I saw the artificial mammoth. Surpassing in height all the other antediluvian monsters, the mammoth pointed its enormous tusks towards a bust of the Steel King, which stood on a pedestal facing it.

Under the bust was this inscription:—

"JOHN JAMES NICHOLAS CORLISS,
ONCE A GUTTER-SNIPE
NOW UNITED STATES SENATOR FROM NEW YORK
GAVE THIS MUSEUM TO HIS NATIVE CITY."

Between the mammoth's fore-feet was another inscription, brief and unhappy:—

"FAC-SIMILE."

The imitation animal was a very successful reproduction. This plaster mammoth was quite good enough for the purposes of the museum. There was not a soul in the vast halls, I was going to say tomb, of the Senator. *Vanitas vanitatum.* It would have been so easy for us all to be happy together without any other mammoth than this amusing cast.

A musty odour, a light shuffling step, interrupted my reflections.

Tiny, very tiny by the side of the monster, an old man, with a face like a mummy, was looking sharply at me. For a moment I almost mistook him for one of the exhibits, his skin was so like parchment, his body so stiff, and his movements so noiseless. But the skeleton came forward a step, and a monotonous voice said—

"Are you not that worthy French gentleman whose visit his honour the Senator notified me of?"

"I believe I am the person you expected, Mr.—Mr. Cavanagh?"

"Worthy young man," said the mummy, in a burst of enthusiasm. "Are you then to have the glorious honour of crowning the great work of the Senator and myself? This plaster humbug you will replace with the genuine bones; this vain pretense you will make into a reality, a true skeleton. My dear sir, permit an old man to clasp your hand."

And he seized my fingers in his fleshless hands, this detestable old fellow, doubtless the first cause of my misfortune, perched as he had been, like a zoophyte, for forty years on his horrible collection of molluscs, invertebrates, vertebrates, and what not. I cut short his outburst.

"My time is limited, my worthy custodian, and I wish to get certain information from you. That is the exact type of the mammoth that I am to hunt for, is it not?"

"Exact to the smallest detail, worthy young man. We are in the presence of an artificial gigantic mastodon, the forerunner of the 'primitive elephant,' commonly known as the mammoth, or Siberian elephant. Order of pachyderm. Family of proboscideans. Think, my dear sir, what the colossus must have been in its living splendour—"

"I beg pardon, sir, but I am in haste. In a week—ah, yes, I remember. I wanted to know exactly where they were to be found, your elephants, and mastodons, and so on."

"Why, all around the polar basin, in Siberia and in Alaska. All these ice-bound regions are one immense cemetery of these antediluvian monsters, especially of the Pliocene period. There are found there frequently fragments of their skins, tusks, bones, sometimes even a skull. Unhappily, complete skeletons are extremely rare. The Museum of St. Petersburg is the only one that has a perfect specimen. It was dug up on the banks of the Lena. Soon, no doubt, the Corliss museum will rival St. Petersburg, and even outdo it. For you will bring us the imposing skeleton of the primitive mammoth, and the equally imposing specimen of the Antarctic mastodon will, I firmly believe, be brought to us by that worthy German gentleman who set out the other week."

"What! How? Who? What are you talking about?" My heart jumped up into my throat. "There is a worthy—a German, who has gone to look for a mammoth—my mammoth?"

"Not yours, not yours. The original belongs to you. It is the Antarctic variety that the Count von Sickingen—"

My blood began to boil.

"What does he call himself?"

"The Antarctic mastodon."

"No, no! Not the mammoth, the Count?"

"Oh, that is a different thing. He is Count Ulrich von Sickingen. A most worthy young man and a splendid horseman."

"It's a little bit thick, it seems to me. And he has set out under the same conditions as I do, doubtless?"

Cavanagh put his hands to his ears, dropped his spectacles, and murmured, or rather I read on his lips—

"As a matter of fact, the Honorable Senator Corliss."

"Good morning, sir," I shouted from the door. But at the bottom of the steps, a feeling of doubt made me return to the rotunda.

"A last word, I beg of you. Are there others besides? Other primitive mammoths, other Antarctic mastodons, other Sickingens, other Le Forts? How many mammoths are there to be looked for, and how many special commissioners have been sent by Corliss to look for them?"

"Only you and the Count, my dear sir. Besides, there are only two important varieties of the great elephant. In the family of the proboscideans—great heavens, what is the matter? Where are you off to in such a hurry?"

Where was I off to? Straight to No. 241, Fifth Avenue, at the top speed of Rakib, whose shoes struck fire from the pavement, while the passers-by cried "Help! He's got the bit in his teeth!" and cabs collided, and policemen shouted, "Stop, will you! I say, stop!"

Bah! I stopped only when I reached the office of the Steel King, I, Le Fort, number two in the list of entries for the mammoth race—original elephant, Sickingen, Antarctic, well, one of us three must be insane.

Corliss was seated at his desk, with his famous notebook in one hand and a telephone in the other, dictating figures which were always amounts of more or less hundreds of thousands. He motioned me to be silent, which gave me time to recover my presence of mind. Two or three million dollars dropped from his lips, and then he closed his notebook and wheeled around towards me.

"I'm delighted to see you."

"Senator," said I, "I have learned some news which has annoyed me frightfully, I cannot understand—"

He silently pointed to his electric clock. Then I burned my ships behind me.

"Who is Ulrich von Sickingen?" said I, bluntly.

"Really, Le Fort, you surprise me. What has it to do with you? Sickingen is a German Count, of good family, received at the German Court, asked me for Eva, like a lot of other people."

"And what was her answer?" said I.

"Hum! Not enthusiastic, I must say. Quite the opposite. Not the same as in your case, by any means. And besides, they are less well acquainted. Oh! if I could only have gone myself. The whole facts of the case are that I have offered Sickingen the same terms as to you, and he has accepted."

"Then, if he brings back a mammoth before I do, you will give him—"

"I will give him nothing. I should not, on the other hand, have the least objection to have for a son-in-law a man who could accomplish such a task, and I hope that Eva would always respect my wishes."

"And you never told me about it! Why, it's a steeple-chase."

"No, a mammoth chase. Get there first."

"But the other one has started already. Where is he now? He has got an unfair advantage."

At last the Senator showed a little emotion. He certainly felt that he was to some extent in the wrong.

"You are quite right," he said, "although in such a long chase a few days more or less should not matter. But let us play fair. We will soon fix up that thing." And he took up his note-book. "Sickingen took his formal departure six days ago, on the 2nd of June. You will take your formal departure—when?"

"I can get ready in six days from now."

"Good. Now, Le Fort, I will give you until twelve days after Sickingen's return. If the Count gets back before you, with my mammoth, I will wait twelve days, to the exact minute, for my other mammoth, which you are to bring back. And further, we will decide, with Cavanagh's aid, which is the finest of the two animals, and I will acquaint my daughter with the decision."

"So then, I must get not only *a* mammoth, but the finest of the two. Very well, Senator, you shall have it, and have it before Sickingen's as truly as you ought to have been born in the time of Laban, father of Rachel and father-in-law of Jacob."

The Bible was, I believe, the only book he ever read. He smiled slightly, and I took advantage of this to ask a last question,

"By the way, where is this Sickingen now?"

"I've not the least idea. I do not expect any news from him or from you, until I receive an invoice of the goods. It's a bargain, is it, Le Fort?"

Corliss had already picked up his telephone, and I went, a little calmed down, to call on Eva. I will not say what passed between us, for it was our first lover's quarrel. I was in the wrong, of course, and ended by asking her pardon abjectly. Was there ever, in this fallen world, a more charming being? Was it her fault if one could not see her without falling in love with her, even if her father did have that queer twist in his brain? Ulrich von Sickingen had tried to win her, as had twenty others. He should not have her! None of them should!

And a fairy whispered something in my ear. Was it one that sometimes aided me in those inspired moments when I must catch the changing expression of blue eyes or black eyes?

> "Tender blue eyes, honest brown eyes, spar-
>   kling eyes of grey,
> Softening with love-light in Aurora's ray."

Or was it my aunt, Mrs. General Monroe? Like those hidden springs that one hears but sees not in the depths of the forest, whose murmur is neither lively nor mournful, but yet make one dream, I could gather the sense, but not the words.

And the whisper seemed to say—"Raoul, you must not—be away—too long."

I jotted down my story so far, more than a year ago, in a diary that I left behind me in San Francisco, at the same time that I bade farewell to the garments of civilization, that I hoped then to resume in a few weeks. Oh the charming confidence of lovers! How many months of my life have I lost since then?—year-long months of a life which was so miserable and fantastic that when I came to tell the story of it, it seemed to evoke fragments of another existence, which I had passed ages and ages before my terrestrial birth. And who would believe my story, besides? No one. I knew that so well that I should have said nothing about my experiences had I not wished to get rid of those annoying people who worried me every day, like the polar insects, and who, like them, would have driven me mad enough to be sent to an asylum. Listen to them.

"Well, old man, they say you have had some rough times among the Laps." (Samoyedes, Koriaks, Esquimaux, are all the same to them.) "And we thought you had gone under.

Is it true that you were the King of the North Pole?" "Was it King or Idol?" "Raoul, tell me about the women up there." (That, of course, from one of my fellow-country-men.) "And how about the mammoth?" "And the pigmies?" "And the sleeping city? Was that an opium dream?"

I will spare you some other badinage in still worse taste, and to conclude, Hamilton and I asked our friend Ames Bemire, a gold prospector with literary tastes, to tell the story of our Arctic expedition. You will see that he spared neither of us. Let people get his story and leave me in peace. Those who do not believe it can interview Freddy, who left an ear up there, poor fellow; and my publisher has in his possession a note-book so greasy with seal-oil, so stained with whales' blood, with such a frightful smell of Esquimaux about it, that the most incredulous will say when they see it—

"Yes; he tells the truth, does Raoul Le Fort, even though he did travel so far . . ."

CHAPTER IV
ULRICH VON SICKINGEN

From the day when he landed in New York, Count Ulrich von Sickingen studied, with his practical German good sense, that Almanach de Gotha of New York where were to be found, with complete descriptions of their coats of arms and ancestry, the names of hundreds of titled democrats, like, for instance, the Princess of Tees in England, or the Duchess of Borough; or Lady Grey Reed; or the Countess de Santillane in France, or first of all, that Vicomtesse d'Henri, Parisienne to her finger-tips, who in other days had galloped her unbroken colts over the prairies of the Far West; and the Princess d'Elvire, and her of Augsbourg, and all those that came from Canada.

"I have every right to be particular," said Ulrich, whose pride was as lofty as his title; "for I shall bring to *her,* whoever she may be, what money can buy nowhere else, a Saxon coronet, with its standing at Charlottenburg. Always provided that I succeed in imposing on her."

The first "she" was Minnie Sandford, one of the beauties of the season. He had gone to the German Consulate, expecting to find an old college chum, Baron Schuster, an *attaché* of the Embassy in Washington. Unfortunately the latter was traveling and would not be in New York for some weeks. Meanwhile Ulrich began by utilizing some letters of introduction which had been given him by Isaac, the banker, who had more interest than any one else in the German Empire in seeing him successfully married. So,

from the very start, he found himself in the centre of the
most delightful society.

There were three of them in their Fifth Avenue Palace,
Minnie, Florrie, and Birdie Sandford, three very pretty
girls, anxious to get married, and resolved to carry off a
European title, and their remarkable talent for flirtation
would have turned a head less well balanced than that of
the Count. But his grey German eyes concealed a sound
sense of the value of the good things of everyday life. One
evening, as he came out of their box at the opera, he said
to himself—

"I am getting along too fast. I must find out something
about their property."

"The Sandfords? They have a royal fortune for this re-
publican country," said the clerk of the Waldorf-Astoria,
the palace hotel of New York, to Fritz, the Count's valet.
But such a general statement, which might have satisfied
a volatile French brain, was not precise and clear enough
for Sickingen. "Let me see," he said to himself, "they have
eight horses, and a single turn-out means twenty-five
thousand dollars of income. A butler, two man-servants,
four maids, and then the kitchen-staff—it looks well, but
I really cannot feel sure. I had better send a hundred dollars to a mercantile agency and get at the exact facts."

Schuster's opportune return spared him this expense.
Fine-looking, very intelligent, slightly conceited, the
attaché knew by heart all about the New York "Four Hundred." His diplomatic caution was dropped with his fel-
low-countryman, after a lunch at Delmonico's, where
some Johannisberger of the year IV., the genuine—only to
be found now in America—had brought the sparkle of its
sunshine into their brains.

"I have come for the purpose of making a match in the
New World," declared Ulrich. "You, better than anybody,
can save me from making a false step. Now, as an old
chum, what do you think of these people?"

He ran over a number of prominent names, and the Baron summarized in four words the income or fortune, family, actual position, or expectations, of each one.

Finally, Ulrich assumed an air of such entire lack of interest in the cares of this mundane sphere, that Schuster noticed it.

"And the Sandfords?" said Ulrich.

"The Sandfords? A chestnut," said the Baron. "Let us get on, please."

"What did you say?"

"I beg pardon, but of course you are not up in Yankee slang. 'Chestnut' means 'humbug.'"

Sickingen moved uneasily in his chair, which really was not of the softest, and said—

"Humbug? But the Sandfords live in a palace on Fifth Avenue?"

"Yes, but they had better make the most of it while the mother is alive, for when she dies, bye-bye."

"Impossible! Every one says that they are very rich, and their style of living indicates as much."

"It's very comfortable, as I can imagine, and so is the widow's annuity. Stop! Is it the J. S. Sandfords whom you mean?"

Schuster, with some suspicion, watched the Count narrowly.

"No, not at all," said the latter, while a cold perspiration stood out on his forehead. "Not J. S., but F. B.; yes, F. B. Sandford. Deuce take it, that's not the same thing at all."

Reassured, he drew a long breath, and his heart beat again at its normal rate. Alas! it was only for a minute.

"It is I who was mistaken," said the attaché, after a moment's consideration. "F. B. Sandford, No. 105, Fifth Avenue. He was a very rich banker, but Black Friday ruined and killed him. Peace to his ashes! His widow carries on with an annuity that the creditors were absolutely unable to get at. What a noise the affair made at the time!

But we live so fast here that yesterday, day before yesterday, a hundred years ago—it's all the same in New York."

"Then, when she dies—"

"It's all up, my boy. Not even a crust in the house."

Merciful heavens! If Ulrich's Saxon locks had not already stood up as straight as drumsticks from his forehead, they would have risen on end at these awful words. Ye gods! And that rascally Isaac, he must have known all about it!

Schuster took compassion on him. He had guessed the whole story.

"My dear boy," said he, "to make a successful deal in the American marriage-market, when one is a Count von Sickingen, two things are necessary. First, you must declare that it is your fixed intention to remain a bachelor; that opens every heart to you. Second, you must display all the cunning of a redskin. The Yankee always spends all his income, to the last cent. If necessary, he gaily dips into his capital. Add to that his mastery of the art of 'bluff,' and you can see the vast distance between a rich man in Berlin, who saves a third of his income, and a rich man in New York, who takes all the chances of absolute ruin or an enormous fortune. In ninety-nine cases out of a hundred, it is—"

"Ruin," said Ulrich, bitterly.

"Exactly. Excepting some great fortunes which are as solid as British Consols, like those of the Kirkpatricks, whom I mentioned at first, of Le Breton, Nicholas Corliss, the Les Fould, and some others, one never knows how much an American father is worth or how much he will leave behind him. Their daughters certainly make the sparks fly, although on the boulevards of Paris they might think them lacking in warmth. They act like millionaires before marriage, but afterwards you would not find a shilling in their trousseaux. And they know so well how to lead you on to marriage. Moët and Chandon is less intoxicating than their smiles."

Ulrich von Sickingen groaned.

"How have you been able to escape?" he said.

The Baron smiled complacently, readjusted his monocle, cast a knowing glance towards a mirror which returned it appreciatively, as much as to say, "what a good-looking fellow you are," and replied—

"How? I have never told any one my secret before, although it is very simple. Do you want to see my protection against marriage? This is it."

"Nonsense!"

"Not at all. When I feel myself in danger, I slip it on my finger, in the vest pocket where it lies near my heart, and then I defy them all." He raised his well-kept hand. "See; their first look is always at this souvenir-ring. I cannot really tell you the service it has done me. Without it, I should have had no resource but to go home and throw myself into the Spree. The laws here are absolutely ferocious. Always remember that, and may the gods be good to you."

And he went his way. Ulrich shut himself up in his rooms, and was still lost in meditation when he suddenly remembered that he was engaged to dine at eight o'clock with Minnie Sandford, her two sisters, and their mother, herself almost as young as her daughters.

Righteous indignation overflowed his heart like a geyser. The traitresses, cheats, five-cent adventurers. Five cent? There was not even a dry crust, as the Baron said, behind the deceitful appearance of luxury of their brownstone palace. And they were waiting for him in one of Delmonico's private dining-rooms, Minnie, and Flora, and Birdie—all that group of pretty pagans who had tried to entrap an honest German. Heavens, how ill it made him to think of them!

What time was there an express train for Newport? 8.35? Right. He had just time to catch it, and Fritz could come after him on the morrow with his heavy baggage. On his way to the station he could leave a card with his regrets at No. 105. Vade retro, Satanas.

It was a perfect hunting-party that Ulrich dropped into at Newport. There were an English duke, two French vicomtes, several German noblemen—in fact, Sickingen found that he was eighteenth on the list in the market where titles were to be sold, where the French are handicapped by their Republic, the Italians because they are reported to beat their wives, the Russians because those who cross the Vistula never return, but where the Englishman and the German shine with all the lustre of their Imperial and Royal Courts.

Thanks to the introductions with which Baron Schuster had furnished him, the Count von Sickingen at once found himself admitted to the most exclusive circles, and he laid himself out to make himself particularly agreeable to Miss Eva Corliss, whose name appeared in his revised and corrected memoranda as follows—

"Corliss; adorable; rated at 70 to 90 millions."

This appeared next on his list below.

"Sandford; very good; rated at four to five millions. (More accurate information desirable.)" This was still decipherable in spite of several hasty attempts at erasure.

As Isaac, in Berlin, was constantly urging him on, and as Miss Corliss, womanlike, was not averse to adding another handsome gentleman to the list of her admirers, he was not slow in inviting her to take a ride along the beach. He returned rather out of breath, as she had ridden as usual at the top of her horse's speed, and very red in the face. As they dismounted, she said, "We will not say good-bye now, will we? It would not be polite of you, as many of my friends wish to make your acquaintance. You know our proverb, 'while there is life—'"

"There is hope? Thank you, Miss Corliss."

"Oh, not in the sense in which you take it, Count."

"I beg of you, leave me under the illusion. By dint of wishing for it, the miracle may come to pass."

He bowed his most courtly bow and withdrew. Really he carried himself extremely well, this German Count, and he had the strong face of a man of action. This thought

also struck Corliss a few days later, during a private conversation which they had together.

"I am ready," said Sickingen. "I have two enterprises to
accomplish, and yours is not the most arduous of the two.
But I will perform them both at the same time. As they
used to teach us at school, 'Persistence achieves all things.
Genius hesitates, feels its way, wears itself out. Persistence
alone attains its end.'"

The next morning, in the express which did its mile a
minute, there was a twelfth-century Baron, who dreamed of
the happy times of long ago, when the great-great-grand-
father of the pretty Eva had paid tithes to his ancestors
(for the original Corliss had emigrated from a little village
in Swabia to America, to earn a bread less black).

How the times had changed, and what an arduous task
to regild the family coat of arms surmounting the draw-
bridge of the ancestral castle of Rüheldeck. "Crossed with
gold and sable, with two iron swords in saltire." And above
it the motto, "SICKINGEN TO THE RESCUE!" Really, it
was worth while to recall this war-cry before he plunged
into an undertaking from whence he should emerge with a
restored Rüheldeck, once more reflecting its lofty towers
in the blue water of the Elbe. The tithe would be in millions, and in addition he would have the most charming
wife in the world.

"Is not that worth the trouble of going on a hunt for
a pile of old fossilized bones? What an undertaking! But
when it is once plain sailing again, my pretty Eva, you
shall pay for your coquetries towards me as truly as I am
the fourteenth Count of my name." And he began to hum
softly to himself—

> "The fairest thing on earth to see
>   Is two bright eyes that beam on me,
>   A rounded form, a face so fair,
>   She draws me to her with her charms,
>   I long to clasp her in my arms,
>   My Charmer."

The Count's baritone was interrupted by the entrance
of a young lady into his section in the Pullman, preceded
by the negro porter with a dozen parcels; hat-box, muff-
box, dressing-case with silver-gilt corners, heaped themselves up around the Count, who was much discomforted
thereby.

"I beg a thousand pardons, sir," said his *vis-à-vis*, with
a charming smile. "These porters are so stupid."

She was a charming little person, with nose slightly
retroussé, with a vague odour of "Royal Lily" about her,
and gifted with the most superb self-possession. Stiffly
and silently the Count bowed. He was angry at the inter-
ruption of his dreams of Eva—and her money.

"If you would be so kind, sir—"

And again Schuster's warning words came back to him.
"Better throw yourself into the Spree, and the laws here
are so severe."

A girlish voice again broke in on his day-dreams.

"Would you mind changing seats with me? I cannot
bear riding with my back to the engine."

"Why certainly, madam."

The unknown had really a charming smile.

"Thank you; but not 'madam.' Miss, if you please."

"Mein Gott!" thought Sickingen. "Here's another five-
cent adventurer, another Sandford. It is just like my luck
to have such confounded adventures as these."

He hastily searched in his pocket for the souvenir ring
which he had bought the day after his lunch with Schuster,
slipped it on his finger, and exposed the finger ostenta-
tiously in sight.

"I am sure this party knows who I am," he said to himself. "Let us see."

"Are you going as far as San Francisco?" went on the
stranger, whose name, Clara Leslie, he now saw on her
copy of Tennyson. "I should like to know."

"Yes, madam, I am going there after my wife."

He bowed and fled to the smoker, followed by a peal of girlish laughter.

"Waiter," said Miss Leslie to the negro porter, "let down the table and bring me two pillows, a glass of ice-water, and an orange." Then she began to laugh again. "Really he is amusing. A thoroughbred German from his accent. Made in Germany. Ja, Meinherr. The real thing."

She settled herself down comfortably with her little tan boots on a cushion, pulled an absurd little handkerchief from her sleeve, poured a drop of "Royal Lily" on it, and was away in dreamland with Lady Clara Vere de Vere.

In the smoking compartment Ulrich von Sickingen smoked a cigar, watching the lights from the train as they danced over the sleeping country. Through the dark woods and their healthy odours of the night, the express rushed towards the unknown. The Count felt a momentary pang. Had he eaten too heavy a supper? Then his eyes gradually closed, while before them danced a flight of pagan names: Minnie, Flora, Birdie; Birdie, Flora, Minnie, Clara—no, Eva. He was asleep, dreaming on banks of forget-me-nots, on the blue waters of the Elbe—so far away. Hush! "Adorable—rated at 70 to 90 millions."

CHAPTER V
A MATCH

Some evil genius had condemned Fred Hamilton to live in a part of the city which had become the residence of the twelve or fifteen hundred doctors of New York. These gentlemen indicated their specialties on their doors, often accompanied by highly striking illustrations of their successful cures. When he went every morning to the office, where he made a pretense of business in connection with his inheritance—a hundred and fifty thousand dollars divided between five, of whom three were administrators—in spite of himself he spelled out each brass plate.

Doctor So-and-So, kidney and bladder troubles. Doctor So-and-So: eyes, nose, ears (with models of the aforesaid organs in unhappy-looking wax). Two blocks further on, no, for three miles, doctors for every possible part of the human system, from the brain to the toe-nails. Doctor This, Doctor That; even a dentist who treated animals, and where one heard yelps of distress. Perhaps there was hydrophobia near by. Quick, a cable to Pasteur!

For relaxation every summer, Hamilton was accustomed to go shooting in the Adirondacks with his friend Le Fort. Their temperaments were exactly opposed, so that they could not be apart, although they quarreled regularly at least once a day. The imagination of the artist enlivened the two hundred and fifty pounds of flesh and bone of the athlete, while the calmness of the Yankee was as quieting as Valerian to the excitable nerves of the Frenchman. The

latter shot with a light Marlin rifle, sighting as he raised
it to the shoulder. The former caught his aim on his heavy
Mauser-Winchester as he brought it down to the level. The
usual result was that one of them wounded the game and
the other killed it. Which was which? To decide the question it was often necessary to dissect the victim and follow
the track of the balls, when a heated discussion would end
in a sulky silence. But this never lasted long, when, if the
guide had been left behind, it was necessary to carry a deer
or a sheep to the camp.

"I will take it," Raoul would say.

"You! Go on! It is too heavy for you. Let me do it."

"Fred, are you not afraid of straining yourself?"

Almost bent double, the good fellow would make his
way through the woods, while Raoul would stroll along
studying a mossy bank, watching a squirrel nibbling a nut,
or a bird circling high in the air. The trees whispered to
him and made signs to him down deserted by-paths. And
in those magic autumn nights, when the woods sleep under the leaves tinged with all the glories of the dying year,
Raoul heard the voice of the Eternal talking to him of life
and death, of the day and the night which existed before
the Fall, and of which we get, sometimes, some shadow of
a remembrance as fleeting as the lightning's flash.

Then, when he reached the camp, Freddy would be
talking to the cook in front of a camp-kettle, wherein some
concoction of a pullet or a partridge whispered a gentle
complaint as it was being transformed into a savoury stew.
Then they must feel its pulse with a spoon, which each
tasted in turn. Too happy to last, such hours as these,
which are never known to those miserable beings who drag
out an existence within four walls.

A companion like this was indispensable to Le Fort's
expedition, so the young artist was in consternation when,
at the office where Fred pretended to earn his living, he
was told that Mr. Hamilton was at home ill and confined
to his bed.

Le Fort rushed there at once. His friend, in a dressing-gown, was seated by a round table covered with medicine bottles. His face was the picture of health, but his nerves were badly upset. The room reeked of iodoform.

"My poor Raoul, I am very low. Got a pain in my side, and the doctors talk of appendicitis."

Le Fort made him put out his tongue. It was in perfect order, his eyes were clear, and his respiration normal.

"You have no—" Raoul did not finish his sentence, for an inspiration came to him. He seized from Hamilton's hands a little red pamphlet, on the cover of which he read, "Dyspepsia, Diabetes, Gravel, Biliousness, Appendicitis, Tonsilitis. Who are you and what is the matter with you?" "Appendicitis be—Kaiser Williamed," said Raoul. "It's only your regular yearly low spirits. Let this horrible medicine alone. Have you got a cocktail?"

"Perhaps, in the sideboard," said Hamilton. "No, wait. Let me make it. There, you shall tell me the news. Really I am perishing with thirst. Have a T.C. So you really think there is nothing serious the matter with me?"

"Serious? Nonsense. The fresh-air cure and a shooting-trip is what you need. I want you to join me."

"I scarcely feel fit, my boy. And then the family property is in a very bad way. There is hardly enough in it for the administrators."

"We have got a free hand, Freddy. All that is necessary is a wire. Corliss, Fifth Avenue, pay to my order twenty thousand dollars, and the money is there. For once in our lives we shall be millionaires."

"I do not understand you at all."

"It is plain enough, though. I am going to take you with me to dig up a mammoth for Corliss somewhere in Siberia. Think what sport there will be! The elk with forty antlers—shade of St. Hubert, forgive me if I lie—reindeer in multitudes, polar bears, sea-horses, sea-lions of the north, even the great musk-ox with his enormous horns—all within range of our rifles, Fred Hamilton!"

The great athlete took another cocktail in absolute silence. Le Fort's rapid tirade had overwhelmed him, and the latter went on—

"*À propos,* do you know a German count who calls himself Ulrich von Sickingen?"

"Certainly. He was frequently at the club during the last two months, while you had disappeared under the pretense of working at Miss Corliss's portrait. I cannot say that I cared much for him. They said he was after a millionaire marriage, but I have not seen him for a week. I hope he has cleared out."

"Poor Eva!" cried Le Fort. "The beast! Now do you understand why we must get there first?"

Hamilton was non-plussed. "I don't understand a thing you say. We were talking of hunting. What is the connection between you, Sickingen, a mastodon, and Miss Corliss?"

"What connection? This Ulrich, whom you say has disappeared, is simply gone to look for Corliss's famous mammoth, between whose tusks he hopes to carry off Eva's fortune. The connection is clear enough, I think."

Hamilton jumped up, and medicine bottles and liqueur bottles rolled to the floor.

"What? Sickingen is after the animal too? Then it makes it a kind of match."

"A mammoth match, yes. It is stark lunacy, but it's the lunacy of John N. Corliss."

"A genuine match," insisted Hamilton, "where there will be a winner. And the winner will establish a record which will be positively unique, and which never can be beaten. The record of the mammoth!"

The cool-headed vice-president of the Athletic Club was beside himself. Le Fort had never seen him in such a state of excitement. The one aim of his life, to beat a record, no matter where, on land or water, with the pistol or with the gloves, had always left Le Fort unmoved. He scarcely tried to console him, if, by some deplorable bad luck, Hamilton came in second or third. But now the latter saw a chance for an overwhelming revenge on his friend's indifference, and already dreamed of his name as inscribed in letters of gold on the walls of the great hall of the club, as winner of the most sensational match of the twentieth century.

"Raoul, let me go with you."

"That's what I came for."

"Listen! When we find the mammoth, before Sickingen does, and bring it back to Corliss, before Sickingen does, you shall marry Miss Eva, before Sickingen does. As for me, Le Fort, my share will be the record—the record of the mammoth. Promise that you will not dispute it with me. Promise! It is the great chance of my life. This record no one can ever win from me."

The artist was too happy to get the aid of this comrade, on whom he had scarcely dared to count, to laugh at his enthusiasm. But he could not help murmuring, "Appendicitis."

Hamilton opened the window, out went the bottles. The iodoform fled, and the sun, the real elixir of life, came in.

"It shall be just as you like, Freddy."

"Promise."

"I promise, a thousand times over. Only let Corliss give Eva to me, and you will see how much I shall worry about the fossil."

"Then it's a bargain. From this instant I will go to work on the preparations for the trip."

"Would you like," said Raoul, somewhat disturbed by this sudden enthusiasm, "to get ready all the material part of the equipment, such as provisions, firearms, outfit, etc., while I will get together all the maps and documents we need, and study the different routes?"

"Right you are. I will begin at once."

When he was safely at the door, out of range of any possible missile, Le Fort turned back.

"By the way, Freddy—"

"Well?"

"Don't forget the necessary ingredients for making cocktails."

But Hamilton only replied seriously—

"I had thought of that already, Raoul."

CHAPTER VI
THE PRIMITIVE MAMMOTH

Le Fort had promised Corliss that he would be prepared in six days, and it was vital that he should keep his word.

There were a thousand details to arrange, and he quickly realized the value of Hamilton's assistance. Without him, he would never have been able to get through all the work that was crowded into one short week.

After having run through the library of the museum, and reduced Joshua Cavanagh's varied, but incoherent, suggestions into tangible shape, he had determined to make for the shores of Behring's Strait, so as to winter in Alaska and explore its ice-bound solitudes as well as the rigours of an Arctic winter would permit. Then, if, as he hoped, this scientific exploration resulted in the discovery of the desired antediluvian, he would get back to the coast and wait for the breaking-up of the ice and the return of the steamer that he proposed to engage for the expedition. If he had such bad luck as he did not like to think of, if he lost the winter in a fruitless search, he would pass over into Siberia, where there were also numerous remains buried under the snow. In the land of the Czar, the difficulties of transportation on his return would be most formidable, and it also meant not one year, but two; or perhaps even three, without Eva, or any possible news of her.

If he had listened only to the promptings of his French blood, that of a race somewhat enfeebled by the exaggerated care taken of it by its womankind, and which will only

be redeemed by the new offshoots of France beyond the
seas, where the Gallic strain will grow young again; if he
had been new to New York, Le Fort would have flown to
the Steel King and cried out, like the hero in a melodra-
ma, "Don't you realize the frightful cruelty of the exile to
which you are condemning me? Your daughter loves me, I
adore her. Drop this stupid mammoth business and let us
get married."

But not only did his pride restrain him, but also the
idea of giving in to the Count von Sickingen. No, he must
pursue the enterprise to the bitter end. For three days the
young man kept up a telegraphic correspondence with all
the steamship agencies and companies. Finally he had a
stroke of luck. A steam-whaler, the *Salvador*, which went
whale hunting from San Francisco every year to the Arctic,
had not been able to get off this year from want of means,
the captain, who was also the owner, having been made a
bankrupt. He promised to hold his ship in readiness for
the artist for a fortnight, on receipt of a handsome deposit
by telegraph.

Raoul closed the bargain at once. The *Salvador*,
equipped for his use, could land his expedition at the most
favourable point, and then go whaling along the coast, to
return and fetch the mammoth at a fixed date in the spring
of 1902. It seemed to be a decidedly lucky shot.

One question only preoccupied the artist's mind. What
had become of Sickingen? Why had he made such a mystery of the plan of his campaign, since, when the Steel
King had put down his engagement in his notebook, there
was no rival in the field.

Hamilton shrugged his shoulders when Raoul told him
of his misgivings.

"Sickingen was always close-mouthed and mysterious,"
said he. "He has probably gone to San Francisco, organized his expedition quietly and set out for the North.
Never mind; we may run across him, perhaps, but we will
get ahead of him and beat him."

There was a strange feeling of confidence about this man, who sometimes, as we have seen, let himself be overcome by purely imaginary maladies. His appendicitis, by the way, had taken flight, and his thirst, like his athlete's healthy appetite, seemed to increase in preparation for a possible season of short rations.

Raoul was less satisfied. It seemed strange that no sailings had taken place from any of the Pacific Coast Ports. The shipping telegrams left no room for doubt on this point. "No ship has left for the North for two weeks."

But there was scarcely time for useless guesses. It had been on the 8th. of June that he had broken the ice with the Steel King. On the 9th he had himself fixed the date of his departure. On the 13th he was ready. That same night Hamilton took the express for San Francisco to busy himself with the equipment of the *Salvador.* A crowd of members of the Athletic Club came to say good-bye to their Vice-President. All these gentlemen, in full evening dress, were surprised to see, at the end of the Pullman train, two freight-cars filled with crates of provisions of all kinds. On the doors stood out in big letters the words, "Arctic Expedition of Hamilton, Le Fort & Co." Then a third car of the same kind came along, with Fred in person on the roof, a gardenia in his button-hole, majestically directing the manoeuvres with his handkerchief.

"Would you believe it," he said, in response to the cheers of his friends, "they almost forgot our wine-cellar." In fact, through the grated doors, could be seen numerous casks and barrels.

"This is the first time that the Overland Limited has ever been turned into a freight-train," said a brakeman, almost in tears.

"What has it got to do with you, my man, if I pay for it? Oh, here you are, Le Fort. Awfully glad to see you. There are a lot of things short, but I can get all I want in San Francisco in the way of furs and other things. What I have here is only just our necessary stock of provisions."

"Freddy, you certainly do not imagine that we can load our sledges with the contents of three freight-cars? Be reasonable, can't you? It's all very well as far as the boxes of biscuits and canned meats are concerned, but all these barrels, my boy. You must have cleaned out the wine-cellar of the club."

"Merely a necessary sanitary precaution," retorted Hamilton. "There is nothing so unhealthy as the water you get by melting snow. Besides, we can establish depots at the principal stages. Don't worry. Corliss is paying for it, and it's all right. I don't mean that our expedition shall fail for the want of a drink, and I think that, as gentlemen, when we dig up Mr. Mammoth, we should drink his health in champagne."

"All right, Freddy. Let us find him first, and then we will celebrate. Remember, we meet on the 16th. And do not forget to find out all you can about von Sickingen."

That same night, Raoul shut himself up in his studio, where the portrait, that he was to abandon on the morrow, was carefully covered up. He gazed on it for a long time, and then set to work to make a sketch from it, which was striking in its resemblance to the picture. This he rolled up and placed in the hollow stock of his rifle, with some other loose sheets and some pencils. He wished that Eva's image should go with him through all possible catastrophes.

He had scarcely seen his dear Eva during these last few days of feverish activity, but she had promised to meet him in Central Park before seven in the morning.

When Raoul, at half-past six, turned the corner of the bridle-path near the lake, where they had first met, she was already there, as at their first meeting. As before, the swans came to greet her. Only the sun had not yet put in an appearance. Le Fort rode straight up to her; but this time, instead of running away, she waited for him, her face irradiated with delight, tempered with the sadness of parting. There are some things in this world that a hundred million—five hundred million dollars, cannot buy; some things that millionaires envy the beggar for; and it will be so, thank God, until time shall be no more. So, along the deserted pathway, in the blessed silence, they could hear their hearts beat in unison without thought of the future, and they lived the one supreme hour of their lives.

To the young man's great surprise, the Steel King and his daughter came to the railway station to see him off.

Raoul had notified him officially of his departure, adding some explanatory details of his plans, and Corliss had replied by telephone, "All right."

Raoul was stupefied at the sudden cordiality of his future father-in-law.

"You have surprised me, Le Fort."

"How so, sir?"

"By the activity and practical sense that you have shown in organizing your expedition. I had never supposed that you would get away in time. True, you should have gone yesterday with Hamilton—"

"It was my fault, papa," said Eva. She was more beautiful than the sunrise, and a charming blush tinged her refined features. The Steel King looked at her, and his face softened.

"I understand. I am glad to find that I was wrong, and that my idea of you was entirely mistaken. I thought that you only knew how to make pictures, and that very slowly. Possibly you are also able to undertake explorations, and not so slowly. I really believe, Le Fort, that you will find me a mammoth."

"I am sure of it," said a voice which could not help trembling a little in spite of itself.

The bell of the locomotive began to ring.

"Good-bye, my boy, and a safe return. Good luck to you, Le Fort," said Corliss, with unexpected friendliness.

"Come back soon, Raoul," said Eva.

Raoul could not speak. The train was starting. Eva held out to him a rose which she took from her corsage. He seized it, pressed it to his lips and closed his eyes. When he opened them again, the great arch of the Grand Central seemed to be nothing but a monstrous black speaking-trumpet, from whence came the words—

"Get me the primitive mammoth. Cavanagh prefers the primitive."

CHAPTER VII
FOR EVER AND FOR EVER

As soon as he reached San Francisco, Raoul made his way to Pier Fourteen, where he found Hamilton superintending the lading of the *Salvador*. The Vice-President of the Athletic Club was got up in the most correct costume for an Arctic expedition. He wore long thigh boots on his powerful limbs, a pea-jacket with a belt of Mexican stamped leather, and a Canadian cap of otter-skins, dressed with the hair on the inside. Freddy was almost stifled in this mid-winter equipment, but, like a true sportsman, he always dressed for his role.

"Raoul," said he, after the first greetings were over, "I want to introduce Bob to you."

A bundle of rags appeared from behind Hamilton, and a voice like the creaking of a rusty door said—

"Happy to meet you, sir."

"What in the world is this thing?" said Raoul, astonished at the appearance of this queer specimen whom Hamilton introduced so politely.

In fact, Bob was not pleasing to the eye on first acquaintance. He was not very old, was very sturdy-looking, but so dirty! He was dressed in a collection of nameless and shapeless garments, held together, sailor-fashion, by lashings of spun yarn, with a dust-coloured beard twisted around his neck with the twofold object of escaping the sparks from his pipe, and of taking the place of a collar.

Another pleasing little peculiarity was that he wore two pairs of trousers, one grey and one blue, and while he talked, continually unraveled the outer pair, although it was already up to his knees.

"Bob," said Hamilton, most politely, "this is Mr. Le Fort"; and as a triumphant climax, "Raoul, our friend Bob knows of a mammoth."

Le Fort looked at Bob with a sudden accession of interest.

"How, when, where?" he said excitedly.

"It's not so very near by, sure," said the man with the beard, "because, look here, I must tell you that I have been prospecting up there on all the coasts around the Pole, see? I was all through Alaska to Cape Prince of Wales, then through the interior and back, and then over to Siberia, seventy miles on an ice-floe, see? Then I strolled down into Kamchatka and over to the Aleutian Islands, and then—"

Raoul lost patience; "But the mammoth? the big elephant?"

"Well, wasn't I telling you? You know East Cape, the very end of Siberia, where Asia stands nose to nose with America? Well! There, a little to the west of the Cape, near the sea, I saw a mammoth's tusks sticking out of the ice, not three years ago. And it had ought to be the whole animal, because you could see that the tusks were fixed in the ice; and then I drove down eighteen feet behind them, prospecting for gold, and felt the bones. Perhaps we could find that same mammoth again—at a price—see?"

The sharp Yankee's eyes twinkled knowingly, and the artist was as taken with him as Hamilton had been.

"At East Cape," said Raoul, "we could station the *Salvador* somewhere near by, and by making haste, return this year. That would be too good! Never mind, keep your Bob and engage him, only wash him and dress him."

"I merely wanted to show him to you in his shore-going togs," observed Freddy.

"Quite right," said Raoul, "and what a lovely head for a study of a drunkard! Are you going in for art, too, old man?" and he sighed as he thought of his dear studio.

The big fellow grinned sympathetically, and said—

"Go and take a stroll along Market Street."

He could not have tried a better expedient to arouse Raoul from the lethargy into which he was sinking, as he got farther away from New York and Eva. For Broadway, New York, makes one feverish with its haste and bustle; the Boulevards of Paris, on a soft evening in May, make it a joy simply to be alive; Rome makes one dreamy; but Market Street in 'Frisco, from Lotta's Fountain to the City Hall, is intoxicating. The exhilaration of the Pacific breezes, bringing on their wings vague odours from mysterious lands; the alertness of the San Francisco people in whose veins runs the adventurous blood of the Argonauts; and then the array of all the goddesses of Olympus—Juno, Minerva, Hebe, and above all, the Diana of the New World, whom Lombard the sculptor has revived in marble; all the charms of the four quarters of the world united to sweep the artist off his feet and wing him up to the Empyraean.

Raoul, for the last time before making his wild adventure into the unknown, felt those purely artistic joys which are the best that life has to offer. He was forced to acknowledge to himself that the Senator's mad chase had its good side, after all, since he was sure, at the very end of the world, to gather fresh impressions, types yet unknown. A telegram broke his wings and brought him fluttering down to earth again.

"When do you start? Corliss."

He pulled himself together and went to find Hamilton.

"Have you heard anything of Sickingen?"

"Not a word," said Freddy.

"And the *Salvador?*"

"Is ready to start at a few hours' notice."

"Very well, I will go and telegraph to Corliss that we shall pull out to-morrow punctually at seven."

Raoul sent his message and went back to see how his friend's preparations were getting on. He found him on the pier, in the midst of a pile of boxes and barrels.

"Good heavens!" he said, "three freight-cars! Why, you've got a whole train-load here. I say, Fred, are you going to start a club at East Cape?"

"You must bear in mind," said Fred, "that it is a matter of provisions and general equipment to last us for a year. Just inspect the labeling and numbering of the boxes. I flatter myself that my arrangements are rather all right."

Fifty-two enormous packing-cases, exactly alike, stood in a row on the pier. Each one was marked, "Rations for one week."

The Vice-President of the Athletic Club pointed to them with a glow of pardonable pride, and said—

"Do you catch on? Instead of having one case of beef, one of mustard—"

"Mustard, Freddy?"

"Of course—likewise pickles, tomato sauce, oyster soup, and so on. Each case contains its due proportion of each one of the different items of the menu."

Raoul had not a word to say. Then his attention was attracted by a pile of fifty-two other boxes labelled "Liquids for one week."

"Those marked with a red star have champagne in them," said Hamilton. "Just keep your eye on them for a second, will you? Here, you fellows over there! Leave that alone!"

He rushed across the pier, disappeared amongst a labyrinth of packages, barrels, fishing-tackle, harness, dog-sledges, dog-biscuits, bundles of clothing and furs, and reappeared alongside a box painted bright red, and labelled "437. Fragile. This side up, with care."

A crowd surrounded it, who recoiled and fled at the furious rush of the colossus, who cried, breathlessly—

"Leave it alone, hang it all! Can't you read? Don't you dare to meddle with it!"

He seized No. 437 in his arms, rushed up the quarter-deck to the stern, and carefully stowed it away at the bottom of a lifeboat.

If Raoul had had the gift of second-sight, and could have foreseen the calamities that were to spring from this Pandora's box, he would certainly have stamped on the side labeled "This side up, with care," and thrown box and all into the sea. But he contented himself with the thought that it was probably only one of Fred's queer ideas, and went on board the *Salvador*.

He was somewhat surprised at the crowd on board the steamer, which he supposed he had chartered for himself exclusively. The crew consisted of thirty men, certainly more than were necessary, but the captain had probably counted on his powerful backer in New York, and spared no expense. And there were besides nine experienced miners—strong, sturdy fellows, specially engaged for the "Hamilton, Le Fort & Co., Arctic Expedition." But he could not understand the presence of a group of ragged prospectors, who were camped on the deck, nor that of fifty or more Chinese, crowded up forward, pigtail to pigtail, and evidently passengers of some sort or other. Raoul had a vague idea that a whaling-ship, if there was money to be made between San Francisco and Behring Strait, would boil down anything that oil could be got out of— whales, porpoises, or even Esquimaux; but he had not suspected before that it would be equally ready to land on the coast—given a hundred dollars a head, and a decently dark night—any number of unfortunate Celestials who had been kept out of San Francisco by the inhospitable Exclusion Act.

Raoul climbed up to the quarter-deck in rather bad humour. Captain Jones, short and fat, with a brick-red and dirty-white complexion, and a short pipe glued to his mouth, with a cap, once gold-laced, on the back of his head, welcomed him with cordial friendliness.

"Ah, you are the gentleman who is after the mammoth. I have met the other gentlemen already, and we have had a whisky together. Come and have a whisky."

"One moment, if you don't mind," said Raoul. "I would just like to know what all this lot is," and he pointed to the motley crowd on the deck.

"Oh, that's nothing," said the Captain. "Just some people that I'm taking along with me."

"But I chartered the *Salvador* for a special expedition of my own."

"That's all right. I am going to land you at Cape Prince of Wales, isn't it?"

"No, at East Cape, in Siberia. I have changed my plans. And later, if necessary, in the Gulf of Anadyr."

"East Cape?" said Jones. "Well, sir, I will land you at East Cape, and before I return for you and your mammoth, in the Gulf of Anadyr or the Bay of Sainte-Croix, there is nothing to prevent my making use of the *Salvador,* is there? Times are rough, sir, and one must do everything one can to earn one's daily whisky. These pig-tails," pointing to the Chinese, "are going to be landed somewhere along the coast. They won't have them in San Francisco. Anyway, they won't get as far as East Cape. As to the other crowd, they've all got private property in Alaska, where I shall land them, see?" He threw back his head so that he could laugh more freely, and added, "Of course, all the stern of the ship is kept for you—except one cabin, for—a friend of mine. See? Come and have a whisky."

Le Fort was not entirely pleased with these rather suspicious arrangements, and was about to make further investigations, when a frightful row broke out at the foot of the gangway. Twelve pairs of dogs, half hound and half wolf, were storming the ship, urged on by the whips of Hamilton, Bob, and the nine miners.

"They are thoroughbred Esquimaux," cried Fred. "It was only by a great streak of luck that I happened to get hold of—"

Here his voice was drowned by the despairing howls of the dogs, who knew too well to what horrible regions of hunger and cold they were being carried. And from all the highways and byways of the water-front and the Barbary coast, came innumerable stray mongrels, with mouths open and tongues hanging out, to yelp a farewell, and howl their sympathy to their unfortunate friends.

Raoul had had enough. He leaned towards Captain Jones and shouted—

"As quick as you like, Captain."

Jones interrupted the rhythmical breathing of his pipe, took a speaking-trumpet, and his voice rose above the tumult in three or four oaths in as many different languages. The crew rushed in every direction, the bewildered Chinese clucked excitedly to each other, the prospectors gave loud cheers. Half of San Francisco responded from the pier, where they had gathered to see the start of the "French Expedition," and the dogs yelped their loudest. Hamilton uncorked a bottle of whisky, and Bob pulled a couple of glasses from his pockets.

"Here's to the mammoth, old boy!"

"Here's at the mammoth, sir!"

"The mammoth, gentlemen!" shouted Captain Jones, through his speaking-trumpet, emptying the remainder of the bottle down his throat by the same road.

"Hurrah for the mammoth!" shouted 'Frisco.

"Bow, wow, wow," went ten thousand dogs.

The sea was already boiling under the propeller when a sharp whistle was heard. Hands were waved in the air and a man leaned over the end of the pier and threw something on board wrapped around a stone, shouting, "Telegram from New York!"

Le Fort caught it on the bridge. The telegram or rather telegrams were for him. The first, from the Steel King:

"Cavanagh insists on having the primitive mammoth.—
Corliss." The second contained only these words: "For
ever and for ever.—Your Eva."

The great copper cross of the church of the Franciscans,
which so many forlorn hopes have gazed at, loved, prayed
to, before going to their deaths in the North, had disappeared in the darkness; the frowning cliffs of the Golden
Gate had sunk below the horizon; men and animals had
ceased their tumult; one by one the stars came out in the
sky, while the water with its phosphorescent glow became
almost as milky as the Milky Way above their heads, where
White Vega shone steadily. And at this same hour, thousands of miles apart, both perhaps were joining in their
prayer to the same star; for they were no other, she and he,
than were the lovers of yesterday, than will be the lovers
of to-morrow—

"For lovers were but lovers,
A thousand years ago."

A soft breeze fanned the decks of the *Salvador* with
bracing odours of salt and oxygen, with whispers of tears
and of laughter, amidst which Raoul seemed to respire
the fragrance of a kiss. He roused himself, and the white
star, now near its setting on the horizon, flashed its last
message—

"For ever and for ever.—Your Eva."

CHAPTER VIII
AN UNINVITED GUEST

The saloon of the *Salvador* had never been as cheerful as
it was on their second night out. Hamilton had paid particular attention to the first dinner of the explorers, and
Captain Jones, who was necessarily one of the party, sig-
nified his approbation vociferously at the imposing array
of bottles. The *Salvador* did not pretend to be a first-class
passenger liner. Four cabins, called by courtesy "state-
rooms," surrounded the little saloon where the Vice-President of the Athletic Club sat in state at the head of the
table. He and Le Fort occupied the two rooms on the port
side, while Captain Jones had kept all the starboard side
to himself.

Through a half-open door were visible a pipe-rack and
a rack for bottles, as well as a cuspidor whose appearance
justified its presence. But the fourth room, that of the
Captain's "friend," remained constantly closed. Raoul, at
supper-time, had called Hamilton's attention to it; but
the latter only shrugged his shoulders. "Bah! something
contraband, I suppose." The artist had tried several times
to "draw" the Captain when he had been sufficiently mel-
lowed by Freddy's generous supplies, but the shrewd Yankee had evaded all his questions.

The evening went off pleasantly. Bob, who had been
invited in, told most enormous yarns about the discovery
of mammoths. To believe him, the coasts of Behring Sea

were planted with enormous tusks, as tall and as regularly aligned as the trees in Central Park.

Towards midnight, he confided to Jones that East Cape was really only one gigantic petrified mammoth, and the two friends wept tenderly on each other's shoulders. Raoul took refuge in his cabin, but could not sleep, and went up on deck. As he crossed the saloon, dimly lighted by a swinging lamp, he noticed that the door of the fourth cabin was open, and could even see that the berth had been slept in, while some handsome traveling-bags filled the nets. There was another passenger, then, on the *Salvador,* and a passenger who kept himself hidden? What did it mean? Jones was not in his cabin, and Raoul felt that he must find the drunkard, shake him, tear the truth from him. He felt disturbed, in spite of himself, and started for the bridge.

As he was climbing the first steps of the companion ladder, some one was coming down. In the moonlight Le Fort saw a tall young man, elegantly dressed, with a flowing blonde moustache and a monocle in one eye, who stopped short on seeing him. There was a brief silence. Then the stranger politely raised his hat, and in a most courteous tone said—

"After you, Monsieur Le Fort; and as we are, so to speak, in a foreign country, permit me to introduce myself. I am Count Ulrich von Sickingen."

Raoul was struck dumb by this titanic German cheek. So, after all, on this ship which he had equipped with so much trouble and expense to go in pursuit of his rival, the latter was calmly established as a guest. Raoul saw that he had himself organized his competitor's—his enemy's—expedition; and he guessed at the animosity which underlay the latter's imperturbable politeness. He had to make a violent effort to restrain his anger, but his tone was hostile, in spite of himself, when he finally succeeded in bringing himself to speak calmly to the Count.

"I presume, sir," he said, "that you can explain your presence here on this ship, where I am on my own premises, and where, I imagine, you have not the impertinence to continue your voyage further."

"I am deeply indebted to you for your hospitable reception," said Ulrich, "but I am very comfortable on board the *Salvador,* where, by the way, I am a little bit on *my* own premises."

His smile was too much for Le Fort, who burst out—

"Count, I do not care to continue the joke. Be so kind as to go with me to the Captain, as I insist on coming to an understanding at once."

At the words, "I insist," the Count lifted his eyelids slightly, and then, very politely again, replied—

"With all the pleasure in the world, sir."

Raoul burst violently into the pilot-house, where Captain Jones, with his arms crossed behind him, was studying the currents and tides of the Pacific. The man was a sponge filled with whisky, but no one had ever seen him drunk. At the sight of his two passengers he braced himself up against the table, and his pipe shifted from the left to the right of his mouth, as if he had been on the point of swallowing a quid of tobacco.

"Captain, have I or have I not, chartered your *Salvador* for a trip to the Arctic ocean? Answer."

It was Le Fort who spoke. Jones remained perfectly cool, and his attitude was as stiff as his pipe.

"Exactly so, sir. The *Salvador* was fitted out for you. It's a fine ship, too, you bet."

The artist turned towards his rival and said—

"Under these circumstances, sir—"

Sickingen interrupted him. "Captain, have I or have I not chartered the *Salvador* for a cruise along the Alaskan coast? Answer me that."

"Anybody who denied it would be a liar," said Jones, serenely. "You also have chartered the *Salvador*. You bet."

Raoul shrugged his shoulders, and without another word pulled out his pocket-book and produced the agreement, duly signed, sealed and witnessed, whereby Captain Jones bound himself to place at the orders of M. Le Fort, the steamship *Salvador,* equipped and all found, and to sail it whenever the aforesaid Le Fort might order in Behring Sea, in consideration of a sum of, etc., etc. He read over the terms of the contract, verified the signature of the old sea-wolf, scrawled half-way across the sheet, and held it out to Count von Sickingen. But as he raised his head, he was stunned to see his opponent hand to him an absolutely identical paper—with the same formula, same seals, same signature, same witness. One glance showed Raoul that he had been duped.

"Captain Jones," said he, "you are a—"

Jones began to swear. "By —, gentlemen, I am master here. Don't dare to insult old Jones on his own quarter-deck! By —, the times are hard, and one must do his best to earn his daily whisky, gentlemen." Then he put an empty bottle on the chart and went on. "It's all right, gentlemen. The *Salvador* is a splendid boat. You might say we are there now. It's beautiful weather and a smooth sea, and each of you gentlemen shall have his turn. Old Jones's word is as good as his bond; but don't insult him on his own quarter-deck, by —. Don't try that on—" and he walked out, with his head erect and his pipe firm in his mouth, as should do an honest Yankee who was in the right of it.

"Monsieur Le Fort," began Ulrich, "be kind enough to listen to me for a moment. Our situation is unexpected and a trifle odd, I admit, but perhaps matters can be made easier, at least for the present. We should only lose—"

"I will not accept your ingenious, I will even say suspicious, propositions in any shape or form," said the artist, violently. "We will get back to San Francisco, where you will at once leave this ship."

"Why?" said Sickingen, calmly. "And what gives you the right to give orders here? You forget that I have a perfectly legal contract with Jones, the same as yours; no better and no worse. What do you propose to do? To go to law and attack this ingenious Yankee? The summer would pass by in these ridiculous and useless discussions, and the season, the only one in which to try your luck, is far enough along as it is. You know there is no other ship to be got. I am too well aware of it myself, because, although I got here some time before you and investigated all the ports on the Pacific coast, I could not get hold of one, and was obliged to propose to this good fellow Jones—"

"To break his agreement with me!"

"No—to do for me just what he was to do for you on exactly the same conditions. Your preparations were all going on, my unfortunate luck prevented me from chancing on this one and only ship, the *Salvador*. It was vital, at any risk, that I should make a start and fight for my own hand, and I had no other choice. I might have tried to destroy all your chances of success by bribing this brave captain—"

"How do I know that you did not try?" said Le Fort, coldly.

"Well, the important point, as far as you are concerned, is that I did not succeed," retorted Sickingen, with perfect self-possession. "Really now, you had best resign yourself to make this first stage of our journey together. Once we are disembarked, if you still desire to continue the quarrel, I am at your service. Besides, the two expeditions will go in different directions. I have with me my own servant, a few men and some little outfit—not to be compared, of course, with your gorgeous cargo. Once on land, every man for himself and God for us all! While we are still on board, I beg of you to believe in my courtesy, and I think, Monsieur Le Fort, that I can count on yours in return."

Raoul did not need much reflection to see that Sickingen was only too much in the right, and that a return to port would be in every way disastrous. He saw that he must, at least for the present, put up with this ingenious fraud. The only lesson that he could give the German, after all the latter's underhand treachery, would be a thorough defeat. Until he had succeeded himself, his only possible attitude was one of indifference.

"Very well, Count," said he, in a contemptuous tone; "I will say nothing, for the present, about your proceedings, but I will consider you as my guest on board the *Salvador*. That is quite a sufficient reason why I should not express my opinion as an honourable man. We shall have an opportunity, and not very far in the future, I hope, to arrange this affair, as well as that of your friend Jones, but we will consider the sea as neutral ground. I only hope that our trip will be a short one."

"Amen to that!" said Ulrich, with a slight bow.

Le Fort bowed and returned to the saloon. Jones had shut himself up in his cabin; and, after all, what would be the good of a quarrel with the unscrupulous Captain? There was no one on board to take his place, and the success of the expedition depended on their speedy arrival at their destination. As he returned to his cabin, a rhythmic snore indicated that Hamilton had been happily ignorant of the events of this second night on board.

The following morning, at eight bells, Fred came to call Raoul to breakfast.

"Here's a queer start," he said. "The table is laid for four."

Le Fort was going to explain, when Jones entered, more beaming than ever, followed by Ulrich von Sickingen. The latter, after a brief nod to Raoul, held out his hand to Hamilton,

"Worthy Vice-President," said he, "I am most happy to continue our former pleasant relations of the Athletic Club."

Fred Hamilton jumped back, overwhelmed; then he looked in turn at Raoul and Jones, shook himself as if he had just waked up, and returned towards Sickingen.

"Count von Sickingen, I take your hand, like an athlete before a contest. In all fairness, however, I must tell you that in this match, where I think that our side already has a pretty good start, Le Fort and I are one."

"Gentlemen, let's have an eye-opener," said the Captain.

CHAPTER IX
THE ABOMINATION OF DESOLATION

In the midst of the comforts of civilization it is possible to imagine what an utter solitude is like; but the idea of being absolutely stripped of all the necessaries of life is difficult to grasp. When you read of unfortunates shipwrecked on a desert island you picture to yourselves a comfortable cave on one side, all the fruits of the season within reach, a spring of fresh water conveniently near, and in every direction varieties of game, almost tame, only asking to be killed for dinner. You also include in the picture the salvage from the wreck, which the waves land politely on the beach—to wit, assorted packages of tools, arms, and ammunition, and a full supply of provisions. Nothing is wanting to enable you to imagine the picturesque and comfortable surroundings of the Swiss Family Robinson, or ditto Crusoe.

But when you read of four unfortunate wretches dragging themselves along an icebound coast, with no other wood to burn than their only boat to warm themselves before striking into an unknown country, where they hope to find something to make a fire of, and something more to eat than one penguin among four in two days; when you hear that, besides a flint and steel, a rifle and a dozen cartridges, an axe, and a pipe without tobacco, they have absolutely nothing but soaking clothes sticking to the skin in the icy wind of sixty-five degrees north, can you realize the utter horror of the situation? Certainly not—any more

than you can imagine yourself being transported to some
other planet, naked as the day you were born, but with
your mind still active to remember what you once were.

In fact, the reader can scarcely be expected to realize such a thing, when the unfortunates themselves could
scarcely believe that it was more than a question of a couple of weeks of privations; for would the *Salvador* fail to
look for them along the windings of the Siberian coast,
where they shivered as they waited for her? "Shipwrecked"
they could hardly be termed—lost, rather, and that on the
very eve of their arrival at their destination.

This is how it happened.

For more than a month they had led a desperately monotonous life on the *Salvador*. Le Fort could not bear
the company of the Count von Sickingen, and his fists
clenched themselves involuntarily when the latter bowed
to him, with his unfailing politeness, as they met on the
quarter-deck. Only when they were at table could Captain Jones's serene cheerfulness maintain a little animation
among his hostile passengers. Happily, the day was near
when they were to disembark at East Cape. Hamilton was
in a fever for the match to begin, while Raoul, utterly
wearied out by his forced inaction, scarcely listened to the
continual chatter of Jones and the Count.

The *Salvador* had crossed the sixty-fifth degree of north
latitude, and was already ploughing the waters of Behring
Strait, when, one morning, the Captain rushed down into
the saloon, where Raoul was sitting.

"Mr. Le Fort," he said, "there is a d—d whale alongside
the *Salvador*, who is making fun of us. Fact! The other gentlemen have seen him already. The cussed animal has recognized old Jones, and he knows perfectly well that to-day I
am carrying passengers, like a cab-driver, instead of hunting
him. It's an everlasting shame. Come up on deck—quick!"

Raoul had never seen the old sailor so beside himself
with excitement. He went up on the bridge, where Hamilton and Sickingen were watching the evolutions of the

monster with great interest. They could see distinctly the double jet of water from his blow-holes, followed by a low rumbling, just as in the old style of artillery one saw the flash through the smoke, followed by the noise of the explosion.

Jones exhausted all the oaths in his extensive *repertoire,* and ended by a cry from the bottom of his heart—

"Gentlemen, I can't stand this! No man or beast has ever insulted old Jones on his own quarter-deck without paying for it. Besides, there is five hundred dollars' worth of oil in his carcass—"

"Nine hundred," interrupted Bob, who was perched on the starboard shrouds. "I know something about whales— you bet."

This was too much for the Captain.

"Gentlemen, the *Salvador* is a whaling-ship. Her passengers ought to be whalers. Let's all go and have a little talk to this cussed animal."

Le Fort agreed. The delay would be nothing, and a little distraction would do no harm. Besides, it was just as well not to anger the Captain, who was already growling out orders in his combined speaking-trumpet and funnel.

Two boats were lowered, and Jones took his place in one, with six of the crew and the artist, who brought his rifle in case he might get a shot at a petrel. Hamilton, very correctly got up as a whaler in a full suit of leather, jumped in at the last moment. The boatswain commanded the other boat, where Sickingen, much to his disgust, was joined by Bob. The two boats rowed in converging lines, so as to place the whale between the fires of their harpoon-guns.

The Captain, who was swearing a steady streak to urge on his men, was first to get within range of the enormous fish, which was floating at random, almost like a Yankee taking his after-dinner cigar in his rocking-chair. But what an awakening! Raoul, for his share, got a douche of water on his head which threw him to the bottom of the boat.

"Stay where you are!" roared Jones, who had struck the whale himself. "You'll be more out of the way than you would be bothering us." And he began to throw water on the bearings of the swivel, over which the line attached to the harpoon was running out.

Raoul, with his mouth full of foul air, feeling that they were traveling at express speed, raised himself to look over the stern; but all that he could see was a double line of foam, like a pair of converging rails on a railway on a prairie of the Far West.

The other boat fired its harpoon-gun as the great game went by. The harpoon flew with a sharp whistle, the line taughtened in a second, the flukes of the harpoon, barbed like fish-hooks, opened out like an umbrella in the flesh, and Sickingen also was following the chase—a chase far surpassing in excitement a steeple-chase or a royal hunt. Jones was in his element.

"This fellow is safe in the barrels of the old *Salvador*. Hold on tight, boys!" Suddenly he grew pale, and shouted, "Cut the rope! Cut loose!"

As the men, astonished, did not obey his orders quickly enough, he rushed up towards the bow, with his axe in the air.

Le Fort could see, far in front of them, a cloud of petrels, whose flight concealed the horizon. The sea boiled under their flying cloud like a line of breakers, but the breakers themselves were coming down from the strait. Down the wind came, a peculiar rank odour, the breath of the whales; and then, all at once, the whale-boat rose in the air, the ocean opened under him, and the frail boat turned upside down in a conglomeration of foam and viscous matter. A school of whales, coming with the current of cold water which flows out of Behring Sea, was charging by. From the deck of the *Salvador* they could see the immense crowd, whose flukes beat the water up and down. Many of them were gamboling along, balancing themselves, as if in play, on their side fins, turning on their sides or their backs, or rolling over and over like a mill-wheel.

Drowning people, in books, always hear a noise of a great rush of water, which is not surprising when the ocean is trying to find its way into their ears, and their entire lives pass before them in about a second before they lose consciousness.

Nothing of the kind happened to Raoul Le Fort. He did not even think of Eva! He said a last prayer, and then said to himself—

"You are not going to die like this! Swim for it! The other boat is somewhere up there." For he was going down, down, with the weight of his rifle in its sling, his clothes, and his boots. And God knows what a weight they all are when one is beginning to suffocate.

Hamilton, who had been a good second in numerous swimming matches, soon came to the surface. He saw a boat near by where two or three forms were visible, and was alongside in a few strokes. It was Ulrich and Bob.

"Come on, then," said Sickingen, sulkily enough.

"Count," said Hamilton, treading water, "I wish first to establish that, in this whale-match, I got there first, with Le Fort. Have you seen Le Fort?"

"No."

"Ah, excuse me just one moment, please."

The powerful fellow, as if by instinct, went straight to the spot where his friend was just coming to the surface, so near drowning, that he would have been dead in another second.

"Brace up, Raoul, we got the whale first. Let me hold you up. The boat is close by."

Raoul was inhaling with delight that marvelous champagne that one finds the air to be when one has been without it for two or three minutes. He floated easily on the sea, which was calm once more.

"Are you sure it has not gone, Freddy?"

"The boat? It is just here. One stroke more and we have it."

A plank, a genuine, solid plank, which did not give
way, met Raoul's fingers. An arm was stretched out and
lifted him into the boat. It was Ulrich von Sickingen.

The young Frenchman felt an instinctive repugnance
before he could say, "Thank you." As for Hamilton, he
hoisted himself on board with his own enormous strength,
exclaiming—

"We got the whale first!"

"Bother the whale," said the Count; "we must look for
the others."

"Right you are," said Hamilton.

The four survivors made a careful examination of the
scene of the shipwreck, but everything had disappeared.
The whales, the Captain's boat, which had probably been
shattered by some formidable fluke, and the sailors—all
were gone.

Ulrich had stuck to the thwarts of their boat, and Bob
had been the first to right it. The four of them, without
doubt, were the only survivors of the disaster. After an
hour's search, Sickingen proposed to return to the *Salvador,* which was visible, about four miles off, towards the
south-west. Bob seemed very anxious.

"Look at that stupid ship steering for us. You can see
she has lost her Captain."

"Well, it will be so much less way for us to go," said
Sickingen, who was pulling his oar sulkily enough.

"Yes, siree. And if the fog comes down, as it does every
morning and night in the strait, you'll lose your way sure
enough," retorted the old prospector. "It was risky enough
to look for the ship when we knew where it was lying, but
with no compass on board, and no sun showing—you'll
find the way a long one."

Hamilton struck his forehead. "When I go hunting
whales again, my outfit will include a pocket compass. My
yachting outfit has one of course. I'm sorry—"

"Well, the fog is coming down and going to eat us up,"
said Bob, bringing his oar on board. "It's no use tiring

ourselves out for nothing. Blind people can't go on voyages of discovery."

As they looked towards the northward they saw the fog driving down from the horizon, overtaking and blotting out their steamer, and filling all the air with white fragments, which danced up and down like snowflakes. Then it got more dense, like strips of cotton wool which joined themselves together. The air grew icy cold, the sun disappeared, and a freezing wind from the North Pole ushered in the night of Behring Sea. The four explorers found themselves shut up in this prison of fog, which the whalers call "hell before purgatory," it is so seldom that one emerges alive from it.

It did not take Bob long to take account of stock of the contents of the whale-boat, consisting of a coil of rope and an axe, which he found under one of the thwarts. Le Fort had got his rifle almost dry, and his copper cartridges had not suffered from their wetting.

There were a dozen shots to fire, but what was there to shoot? The sea was like a corpse under its white shroud, and if they were lucky enough to catch a fish where should they find water to drink?

All at once the artist cried joyfully—

"We are all right. Look at this box!"

It was the famous No. 437, "This side up with care," that Fred had stowed away in the boat before they left San Francisco. It was untouched, with the enticing label, "Open here," plainly visible in spite of the fog. On the other side, undoubtedly, they would find these cheering words: "Rations for one week."

"Give me the axe, Bob," said Le Fort.

Bob shook his head sadly, and Hamilton seemed for once to have lost his usual self-possession. Either the cold, or a sudden attack of shyness made him stammer.

"L-look here, Raoul, it's n-no use to open that case now. It c-contains something which w-won't help us to anything to eat or to d-drink, just now."

"What is it?" said the artist, impatiently.

"It's a d-d—" The rest of his explanation was lost in the fog.

"What?"

"It's a machine to make whisky," explained Bob.

"Yes," said Hamilton, "it's a small still to make whisky among the tribes of the Polar Basin. You see it would be a kind of circulating medium for us, and then I thought our provisions might give out, and so— Well, I'm awfully sorry it happened to be just this particular case."

Le Fort had no courage to answer, and Sickingen's comment was a sneering laugh. The arrival of the night made the dense fog more horrible still. Stretched out in the bottom of the boat, the four men shivered with cold in their wet garments and felt the first gnawings of hunger. They tried two or three times to hail the *Salvador,* but they could scarcely hear their own voices; as if Death, lying in wait for them, had already compressed their throats in his icy grip.

So passed hours and eternities, speechless and hopeless, in this frightful stupor of the Polar Sea, where one hears only some occasional vague sound, like the blowing of a whale or the crumbling of au iceberg. Towards morning, Bob saw the fog begin to move, and it was evidently on the point of clearing. He stood up, and the curtain lifted for an instant and then shut down again, but the interval had been long enough for him to see a dark line above the blue sea on the horizon, while the warm current which flows from the south to the north was carrying the boat with it.

"Hurrah, gentlemen; pull yourselves too-ether! I know where the land is! Take your oars."

They shook themselves together, and the light of hope shone in their eyes. The old prospector steered them against the current, but the coast, which must have been that of the Siberian peninsula, seemed to have disappeared entirely. At last, however, after half a day of heart-breaking work, the boat came to land on some flat rocks, half-covered with ice. The adventurers were utterly exhausted and lay stretched out on the ice, which they scarcely had strength to lick in order to quench their thirst. Bob, however, who had had this sort of experience before, went in search of game.

At the end of half an hour he came back with an old penguin, which, with its sharp-edged beak, had nipped his leg as he stepped over its nest.

"I had to cut off its head to make it let go," said Bob. "This is a mean country if you like. There's no game, and no wood. Now let's have something to eat."

One of the thwarts of the boat served for fuel, while Bob had to dry the flint and steel, which he wore round his neck like a scapular, before he could light it. Le Fort recalled those travelers' tales which relate how easy it is to get a light by means of two pieces of wood and a rotary motion—said motion to be continued until the rotator lost his breath.

The penguin's fat and the oily, half-raw flesh, gave new life to the three mammoth-hunters, and a council of war was held around the fire. Ulrich and Hamilton thought it best to wait on the coast for the *Salvador*. The fog had lifted and the smoke of their fire ought to attract the attention of those on the ship.

"But suppose we have gone off our course all night, and they think we have gone under like poor old Jones—do you think they will look for us? No, sir!"

His plan was to strike inland and look for something better than stones and ice. Raoul agreed with him, more to oppose Sickingen than for any other reason, and Fred came round to his side. So they agreed that next day they would strike due west. This coast should be that of Kamchatka or one of the neighbouring islands, and there were always stray tribes of Esquimaux in these latitudes in summer, whose tracks they might come across.

Sickingen was not at all satisfied with this plan of campaign.

"I beg you to understand, gentlemen," said he, with
his usual exasperating politeness, "that I had not the least
intention of embarrassing you with my company as soon as
we got to land. My one wish is to be free to act by myself,
but you must acknowledge that it is impossible for me to
leave you or to remain behind, with my pocket-knife as
my only weapon, while M. Lo Fort's rifle is the only thing
that can help us."

"Count," said Raoul, warmly, "it is out of the question
that we should part here. All rivalries must give way before
our common necessity. I cannot forget, besides, that you
aided me at the time we were wrecked—"

"To continue the match," said Hamilton.

"Match be hanged!" grumbled Bob. It's a question of
what to eat."

What to eat! The others agreed with him. To eat! This
is the word, the necessity, which is the motive force behind every savage animal, be he man or beast; and not
twice twenty-four hours had thrown Le Fort, Sickingen,
Bob, and Hamilton back ten thousand years, under this
same sun, which shone on them as impassibly to-day as it
had on the people of the Stone Age, the age of the mammoths—those thrice-accursed mammoths so dear to Senator Corliss!

CHAPTER X
NAROUTCHA

The next morning a dying sun shone on a deserted sea. The expedition did not require much preparation. Raoul's rifle and Bob's axe were the sole baggage, while Hamilton insisted on carrying his miniature distillery—Case 437. The boat was hauled up as high as possible and filled with stones, while a notice was scratched on the side with a knife—

"Four survivors from the *Salvador*
are exploring westward.
"Wait here for us for twenty days.
"Le Fort."

For they had decided to adopt Sickingen's idea, that one or two of them should return to the coast at the end of a week, whatever they found in the interior.

The beginning of their trip was scarcely encouraging. The rocks were succeeded by the "tundra," an endless plain of dry, soft soil, as arid as a sandy desert. The cold was less severe as they got away from the neighbourhood of the icy sea, and the sun was no longer half-frozen; but they made slow progress over the slippery surface, which gave way at each step, and they began to feel cruelly hungry.

Le Fort, who was walking at the head of the little procession, stopped short on hearing the short bark of a fox.

"Yepp-yourr! Yepp-yourr!"

He seized his rifle.

Sickingen cried excitedly, "On your right, on top of that great round stone! Fire quick, he's almost under your nose!" And he added a variety of guttural oaths mostly ending in *lich* or in *fel*.

The artist turned round quickly. "My sight is as good as yours," he said; "and, once for all, be kind enough to spare me your German imprecations. Look, Hamilton; wouldn't you say it was a tame fox?"

The snowy little animal was perched motionless on its pedestal. It was one of those tiny Arctic foxes, whose yellow eyes, full of intelligence, shine like stars through their snowy-white fur. Bob drew near him slowly. The fox wagged his tail like a dog, jumped off his rock and ran away a few steps and then returned towards the hunter; and his Yepp-yourr was followed now by an odd note, plaintive and familiar as a peacock's call—

"Li-ho Li-ho!"

And Bob answered, "Haia!"

The snowball began at once to trot on ahead of the prospector.

"Don't shoot, on your life!" said he. "It's one of those tame foxes that the Koriaks of Kamchatka train. I know the people, and I can talk to them. Let us follow him."

The three others followed him, their bad humour disappearing by an unanimous impulse. The fox, intelligent as a dog, was evidently going to lead them to some camp of the natives. After half an hour's march they came to the foot of a rather steep rock, on top of which were some slender birch trees and stunted firs. There was no smoke, nor anything to indicate the presence of human beings. But the white fox yelped more loudly and plunged into the underwood, where they could only follow his course by the trembling of the bushes. A carrion-crow rose into the air, hovered there for an instant, turned on his back like a tumbler-pigeon and recovered himself with a stroke of his wings, with the chuckling sound which indicates a full stomach.

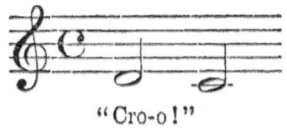

"Cro-o!"

"Hold on," said Bob. "We are there."

"How do you know? I do not see anything."

"Neither do I," said Bob; "but haven't you seen the crow show that it was one of his resting places? There is something to eat here, sure."

Bob had lived in the woods too long not to be able to recognize signs which civilized understandings would never notice, so his companions did not contradict him. A couple of minutes later they came out into a clearing, where, supported on four bushes as tall as a man, was a coffin made of interwoven branches of trees, through which they could dimly see something black, from which came a horrible smell. Underneath was crouched a very old Esquimau woman, whose head, surmounted by a mass of yellowish-white and frightfully dirty hair, was sunk in her hands. Curled up and sunk into herself, she was as motionless as the corpse above her head. Three dried salmon hung on an aspen behind them, by the side of a spear, a bow, and some arrows with points of bone.

The explorers were faint with hunger. They rushed on the salmon, and confessed to making the best meal that they ever remembered. The old woman did not move, although, perhaps, she was watching them through her fingers, while her tears fell slowly on the fox, which was curled up on her knees like a puppy.

When his hunger was satisfied, Bob tried his Tchouktchi.

"Tourou, miaserra. Friend—good."

He gesticulated wildly, stroked the fox, put his hand on his heart, and went on with his extraordinary gibberish. The fox barked again and the old woman dropped her hands, when Le Fort saw the most horrible centenarian

monkey-face that was ever dreamed of by a disciple of
Darwin in a nightmare.

He saw two holes in place of a nose, under two yellow, blood-shot eyes, set very far apart, with the eyebrows
turned up towards the temples; the brutal, bestial mouth
of the inferior races, with the lips scarred by three blue
lines; the whole framed by the wrinkles of a hundred years
of misery—such was Naroutcha, the old Koriak woman,
left there to die by the side of her eldest son; who was to
play such an important part in the existence of the explorers. Yet she was not entirely abandoned, for another
Esquimau woman, very fat and less wrinkled, came out
from behind a tree where she had hidden herself, and
crouched down at the old woman's feet.

"She is probably the wife of the dead man," said Le
Fort to himself. "Oh, Lord, who hast also created the
Egyptians, so enigmatic; the Greeks so pure, the symbol
of vitality—and my Eva—"

The fox fixed its suspicious eyes on him, and Naroutcha turned her eyes towards him; and the soul, human and
divine, revealed itself to the artist in the tangible, palpable splendour of one of the noblest lines in the French
language:—

"Les plus beaux yeux pour moi soot les yeux pleins de
larmes."*

This beauty, so sad, so superhuman since the Fall, those
eyes, where trembled, half-felt, a hope so full of anguish—

Bob interrupted this reverie.

"This is Miss Tuli," said he. "She can talk, anyhow. It's
a diabolical patois, but I understand it. They come from
Reindeer River, from a village called Ya-Thenaoddi."

"Ya-Thenaoddi! Haia-ha!" said Tuli, pointing to the
west.

* *La Samaritaine*, Rostand.

"I understand," said the prospector. "They are Koriak salmon-fishers, come from Kamchatka."

"Is it far?" asked Sickingen.

Bob stuck two bits of wood with a brand on top in the ground at each side of the clearing, and ran from one to the other, repeating—

"Ya-Thenaoddi! Ya-Thenaoddi!"

At the end of his fourth round, Tuli stopped him.

"It is four stages from here," said the prospector. "These people, who have either the sun or the moon over their heads all the time, don't understand our days and nights. You can't wonder at it. We should do the same in their place."

The mid-day meal consisted of the mice which swarm on the tundra. It was the white fox, Reka, who furnished the larder. Sitting straight up on her hind legs, the intelligent little animal watched the roots of the tamarisks. She was as motionless as a snowball, but her sharp eyes searched on every side, and at the least indication of movement in the bushes, two paws came down and another mouse was caught before it was seen. When they were toasted on the end of a stick, and eaten hot in their own melted fat, they were not so bad, in spite of an after taste of musk. Especially as there was nothing else.

After this banquet, when our explorers wished to start for the village on Reindeer River, Naroutcha and Tuli, who had become somewhat less wild, declared that they must remain by the coffin, where lay the remains of a famous fisherman. He had been a man who would launch his kayak in any sort of weather, and who would fasten the line of his harpoon to his belt. The stranger had eaten the fish which was meant for him on his journey into the Unknown, and he would call on Naroutcha and Tuli.

Sickingen lost patience, pushed Bob on one side, squatted down in front of the women, showed them his watch-chain—a large gold chain which was a curious contrast to his tattered clothes—and finally gave it to Tuli.

The effect was instantaneous. Naroutcha was delighted. Tuli, clucking to herself, placed the Count's hand on the oily chignon which surrounded her tattooed face, and started trotting away to the west, beckoning the others to follow. Bob opened his mouth to speak, but thought better of it, and shut it again, finally going off into a burst of silent but inextinguishable laughter, after the fashion of Leather-stocking in the "Last of the Mohicans;" and took up the line of march behind Sickingen, with Le Fort and Hamilton bringing up the rear.

It was now only a matter of finding supplies among the Koriaks, who, Bob said, were "good people, with rum ideas, but not bad-hearted."

In spite of their crooked limbs and the extraordinary rolling motion of their haunches as they walked, the squaws got over the ground very quickly. The explorers could scarcely keep up with them and followed in silence most of the time, for their common distress could not banish from the minds of the two competitors their passionate rivalry. Then, too, they were exasperated by this long delay in which, constrained by a temporary neutrality, they were forced to submit, side by side, to an inaction which was gravely compromising their possible success. At every halt, Raoul went off by himself and took Eva's portrait from its hiding-place, to contemplate and kiss it; and every time he felt his will to succeed grow stronger. But he read in Sickingen's eyes a cold obstinacy, as firm as his. From time to time the two men interchanged glances of such palpable defiance, that there seemed every chance of an open rupture.

Fortunately, at the end of the fourth day they came in sight of a river, free of ice, flowing through the plain a few miles away. Naroutcha and Tuli seized Sickingen's arms, exclaiming—

"Ya-Thenaoddi!"

CHAPTER XI
YA-THENAODDI*

There was no sign of human habitation on the wide plain, but a crowd of Esquimaux, aligned along the bank of the river, were fishing with wooden spears. Every time that a spear darted into the water, it was pulled out again with a great salmon struggling on the end, which was seized by the women, who opened and cleaned it, and hung it on a tree to dry. The Koriaks were laying in their year's supply of salmon.

"Do you see smoke?" said Bob.

"It is the smoke of dry wood on the ground, to dry the fish," said Hamilton.

"It may seem like the floor to you, but for these people it is the roof. Their houses are built underground, because of the cold. With ten people inside they are warm even in winter. What you see are their chimneys. I have seen villages like that not very far from East Cape."

Le Fort and Sickingen could not conceal their excitement—East Cape meant the mammoth and Eva—and each read the other's thoughts.

* "Ya-Thenaoddi," as they found afterwards, was a village of stationary Koriaks, in the midst of wandering bands of Tchoutkchis who brought them tobacco in exchange for furs.

91

A cry of fright attracted their attention. A squaw had noticed them, and women and children disappeared underground. The men looked up and brandished their spears, which had sharp points of bone, crying threateningly—

"Hihi! Yo! Nuya! Halloa! Stop! Hihi! Yo! Where did you come from? Get out!" And they slapped their legs with an increased noise as Naroutcha, Tuli, and Bob drew near them. The other three waited to see what was going to happen, Le Fort holding his rifle ready.

Bob finished his remarks in Koriak, by passing his pipe, which was furnished with a cord, around the neck of the biggest of the men. This piece of politeness was received with delight by the crowd, who withdrew their hands from their boots, where they carried their knives. Bob called out triumphantly—

"It's all right; come along. I've talked them over. And as you come, say, Yourou! yourou!"*

Tuli had been chattering away excitedly in the midst of her friends, and, with her gold chain in her hands, came back to Sickingen, whom the crowd surrounded with special indications of cordiality. The men, like the women, had round Kalmuck faces, with flat noses, and narrow slits of eyes, and wore their hair cut short, or rather grubbed off, in a circle around the head, like Dominican monks. They were dressed in seal and walrus skins, admirably fitted, with great boots of otter-skin, and fur caps. A terrible smell of fish, the reverse of fresh, pervaded the entire crowd, and the Count soon found reason to regret his sudden popularity.

Bob brought forward a solid athlete about forty years of age, with a fish-bone stuck in his chignon.

"Gentlemen," he said, "this is the chief, or, as you might say, King Toulouack."

* Friend! Friend!

"Toulouack! Hihi! Toulouack," said the savage.

"He's introducing himself," said Hamilton the punctilious; replying politely, as he struck himself on the chest, "Happy to meet you, Toulouack. I am Fred Hamilton, of New York."

The Koriak king seized the Vice-President of the Athletic Club in his arms, and vigorously rubbed noses with him.

"Phew! He's too polite altogether," stammered the victim, half-suffocated. "Here, Raoul, take your turn."

Some shouts of excitement were heard from the group which surrounded Sickingen, and Bob translated them by saying—

"They're inviting us to Naroutcha's house."

The procession, in more or less order, with the king at the head, followed by Sickingen, Tuli, and Naroutcha, wound among the dens which constituted the village of Ya-Thenaoddi. Raoul noticed appliances for hunting and fishing lying everywhere about, and that the seal-skin kayaks were pulled up high and dry under strings of salmon drying in the air. Evidently there was no danger of dying of hunger, and who could tell but that perhaps these hunters could help their expedition? It was rather vexatious that Sickingen seemed to be decidedly most in favour with the Koriaks, and that Toulouack invited him first to enter the "barrabora," or den, before which the procession stopped.

Like its neighbours, Naroutcha's residence was a hole five or six yards square, dug out of the frozen ground, with an entrance through a tunnel, which was scarcely thirty inches high, and perhaps twenty yards long.

Hamilton stopped short about five feet underground. His shoulders, which would not have disgraced a porter, could not get through where his companions had crept.

"Hulloa, Le Fort!" he cried dolefully; "for the love of heaven give me a hand. I'm stuck in this infernal tunnel!"

Le Fort pulled at his head, while Toulouack, in his turn, pulled vigorously at the artist's legs. On the outside,

Bob grasped the big fellow's feet, and the village, in a high state of excitement, assisted him.

"Pull—push—you're pulling me apart! May the Lord have mercy on your souls! Leave me alone, all of you!"

It would be decidedly improper to report the full-bodied language which streamed up from the tunnel until the moment when, by a supreme effort of his enormous strength, Fred Hamilton broke out of his prison, and like the god of earthquakes, stood erect among the astonished Koriaks.

"The Man-Whale! The Man-Whale!" they cried, scattering in every direction; and ever since this prodigious display of muscle, the legend of the Man-Whale has been told and will be told, to the farthest ends of Kamchatka, until the end of time.

In the interior, Naroutcha did the honours to her guests.

On the floor of trodden earth were heaped up piles of skins, which were inhabited by millions of insects that the Koriaks entertained at their firesides without the least annoyance, and by whose evolutions they were able, without going out-of-doors, to tell better than by a barometer, of atmospheric changes outside. Heaps of fishbones were piled up in the corners, and the only ventilation was a small opening in the roof, which served as a chimney, while on the stones, which did duty for a fireplace, smouldered some damp wood, which gave out an acrid smoke. In the semi-darkness of this pestilential atmosphere, Naroutcha sat in state, surrounded by a number of hideous little Koriaks, who were evidently her grandchildren.

Tuli even brought Sickingen a very small but densely populated little Esquimau, whom she wished to bestow in the Count's arms; but the latter, who was in a particularly nasty temper, pushed her away brutally. The woman uttered a sharp cry, and, after a string of violent remarks, addressed to Bob, who did not understand a word, she and her mother rushed out.

The three white men set to work to put the place in decent order, while Hamilton, outside, was working hard to enlarge the tunnel, plaintively lamenting to himself, "If I'd only saved my silk tent out of the wreck, with its patent ventilator and kerosene stove."

All at once the mansion was invaded by a crowd. Toulouack, escorted by two Koriaks, Naroutcha, Tuli, her children, her foxes, and a few particular friends, were trying to reach "the Russians." (So they called all white people without distinction.)

The king, with a severe look at Sickingen, came to Bob and made a long speech, during the progress of which the other two explorers saw the prospector's face fill with astonishment mingled with intense amusement. Finally he gave way to a burst of his peculiar inward merriment.

"What's up now, Bob?"

"It appears that you have married into the Koriak tribe, Mr. Sickingen, and they are wishing you good luck and a large family."

"Mr. Bob," retorted the Count, angrily, "I must ask you to leave off your ill-timed jokes."

"It's no joke at all, my dear sir. You have well and duly married Tuli, in the presence of Naroutcha, down below there at the dead Indian's grave, by giving her your watch-chain. That's quite enough ceremony for them. I wanted to tell you; but, to put it plainly, you have never been particularly friendly to me, and then I forgot it. It's a matter on which the Koriaks don't permit any joking, and if you don't look out there will be a row. You can see they don't look very pleasant while I am talking to you."

"I will never submit to be the victim of the stupid mistake."

The Koriaks were getting hostile at the evident hesitation of the strangers. Le Fort risked the suggestion. "Couldn't we arrange it somehow?"

"I will resign in your favour," replied Sickingen, violently, "and don't let us have any more talk about the matter."

The situation was growing embarrassing. Raoul proposed a substitution of husbands by way of compromise.

"My dear Bob—couldn't you—take the Count's place—and marry Tuli, since you are the only one that can understand her, and—"

Bob made a face. "Why should I, any more than the Count? Besides, she wouldn't agree to it. I don't look as if I was rich enough to suit her."

Toulouack's attitude was becoming menacing, and his bodyguards whispered in his ear. Tuli, in a great state of excitement, continued her complaints, displaying the chain, pointing to Sickingen, and calling on Bob, Le Fort, and Naroutcha as witnesses. Hamilton telephoned down the chimney that the crowd outside was increasing, and they could hear their cries of, "Hihi! Yo!" like the whistling of dolphins in trouble.

Raoul felt that the situation was becoming impossible, more especially so because Sickingen, swearing violently to himself, was on the point of attacking the king, and he took Bob to one side.

"Gain time, at any price," he murmured. "Make up some kind of a yarn."

The prospector cleared his throat before beginning a lengthy harangue, which appeared at first to be unsuccessful. Bob redoubled his eloquence, and little by little Toulouack's face cleared, and he solemnly slapped Ulrich on the leg, remarking—

"Yo! tserra!"

Tuli quieted down, and with a last fond look at the Count, went out, followed by all her relations.

"The king invites us all to supper," said Bob, recovering his breath.

"What kind of a yarn have you fixed up for them?"

"I told them that the gentleman was most happy to marry Tuli, but the chain by itself was not good enough for the widow of such a famous hunter, and that down there on the coast, the gentleman had left some boxes where he would go and get some more presents. When he had got those, he would have the pleasure of asking Tuli to share his house and home; so, until then, Sickingen," said Bob, in a tone which he made intentionally familiar, "you can consider yourself formally engaged to be married."

Raoul could not help smiling. The Count, angry and full of hate as he was, did not flinch, but a deadly rage struggled in his mind with the feeling of his ridiculous and humiliating position. Life in the wilderness is no respecter of persons, and from that moment he was no longer a rival, but an open enemy.

CHAPTER XII
YESTERDAY AND TO-DAY

The celebration of Sickingen's betrothal took place in the open air. Every one contributed his share of fish, as at a picnic. The main item on the bill of fare, of course, was salmon, crammed into the mouth and then shaved off even with the lips with nails, flattened out and sharpened on the edge like knives, that Koriaks called "Ha's"—probably got from some ship that had been lost on the Arctic coast; and some of them had knives made from walrus tusks. The dessert was supplied by pieces of whale-skin, which tasted like nuts, but which were as hard to masticate as the famous American chewing-gum. The amount of energy required from the jaws was about the same as that demanded from the legs in a thirty-mile tramp. The heartiest good-feeling prevailed amongst the guests, for there are certainly no people in the world as jolly and cheerful as those of far Siberia. There is no perfection in this world, and they are liable to fits of almost epileptic rage which pass away as quickly as the anger of a child. With their round flat faces, broad shoulders and slender limbs, Chinese eyes, and beautifully white teeth, they are the ugliest, the dirtiest, and the healthiest of mortals. These last two superlatives are scarcely in accordance with the scientific ideas of this present century of microbes, bacteria, sterilization, pure air, pure water, that try to induce the modern European to do away with his body, as being only a happy home for infectious germs, and turn over his bank account to the doctors. But Le Fort and Hamilton learned, after a variety of most unpleasant experiences, that the Esquimaux, perhaps by reason of their awful climate, are a living contradiction of all the theories of modern science.

Toulouack's monarchical status was quite different from European ideas. His privileges were limited to marching first in the line, when the tribe went hunting or fishing, to deciding on important expeditions, if they were willing to go with him, and keeping some of his poorest subjects in food, in return for the smallest possible amount of work. He was very well-to-do, having four wives, of whom the handsome Natiya was the chief, and a number of reindeer, which had been left to him by his father, who had been a famous *nakoot,* or medicine-man. Such was the extent of his autocracy, which was really more irksome than profitable, but which he would only have given up with his life; for in Kamchatka, as in Europe, one likes to hear people say as one goes by, "Look! There goes the king."

Toulouack's nautical achievements had also conduced to his being chosen by his fellows—not by universal suffrage, where the ignorant and the lazy would have been in the majority, but by the voices of those who knew how to hunt or to fish. When he tipped over in his kayak, or voluntarily turned bottom-side up in crossing a dangerous eddy, he was always able to restore his equilibrium with one stroke of his paddle. The Koriak youngsters, who were thrown into the sea in summer to teach themselves how to swim, to harpoon, or to manage the kayak, when they grew up could well appreciate all kinds of dexterity on the water, and not one of them would have dared to precede the king when they took up their march in Indian file across the tundras.

Such were the king and the people amongst whom were thrown, almost as naked as the day they were born, a fashionable portrait-painter of the prettiest women in America, the Vice-President of the New York Athletic Club, a great German nobleman, and the old prospector. But, however

great their distress, they must act, seek, find their object.
The first days were spent in enlarging their barrabora, the
zoological collection of which was expunged by fire, and
a sort of concierge's lodge was built at the entrance of the
tunnel for Naroutcha and Reka, her fox.

These building operations, carried on in the frozen
soil, which they loosened with wooden spears hardened in
the fire, took some time. Le Fort, as a preliminary to explorations in the neighbourhood, questioned Toulouack,
but he did not know the name of Anadyr, and all the rivers
he knew only by their Koriak names. He did not understand in the least any of the maps, drawn from memory,
which Le Fort showed him. Savages can recognize vertical
profiles, but any geographical projections are utterly beyond their comprehension. This, among other things, is a
sure test by which to distinguish voyages that have been
actually made, from those composed in a comfortable library, under an electric light, by the aid of a map and a
dictionary.

They still had one hope left—that of finding the *Salvador* cruising about waiting for them, after having seen
their notice that they had left on the coast. Sickingen,
who was the most anxious of them all, Bob, and Le Fort,
undertook a trip to the inhospitable shores where they
had been wrecked. Hamilton remained at Ya-Thenaoddi
to take part in the salmon-fishing and to complete their
housekeeping arrangements.

The three explorers travelled at their utmost speed, so
great was their haste to see their ship again, for one can
readily imagine that the wish was father to the thought,
and that Le Fort already heard the "Hurrahs" of the sailors at their sudden resurrection. They were sure to see
great fires lighted along the coast—God grant that we find
them!

On the fourth day he began to run like a boy. His companions did the same, and they came out on the tundra
after passing the grave of the dead Indian. The infinite

horizons—that of the great green and white plain, that of
the still greener sea—struck them in the face like a blow.
Their hearts fell as they stopped. There was nothing to
be seen of their ship—no smoke, not an animal, not a
man—nothing around them but that dead silence of the
far North which is so frightful that it forces one to cry
aloud to break it.

Le Fort started on again and they soon reached the
inscription on the boat, already half effaced by rain and
mould. Had anyone seen it? Had it been written there
yesterday or a hundred years ago? It seemed as if no living
soul had been there for eternities.

Ulrich and Raoul sat down on the half-rotten planks
which had cast them on this icy coast to sink to the level
of Esquimaux—or brutes. "Yesterday—to-day—to-day—
yesterday," seemed to say the waves which whispered at
their feet, with every swelling, every pulsation of the Arctic Ocean, with a murmuring which seemed to drive their
weary brains to delirium.

Bob continued to gaze further and further afield, and,
at last, shading his eyes with one hand, shouted—oh,
heavenly sound—

"I see a ship;" and then, "I think it is the *Salvador*."

The two others were on their feet in an instant. Bob's
eyes, undimmed by the artificial light of cities, gave them
extraordinary confidence. They could see nothing at first,
then a shade, a nothing, dancing on the water, seemed to
take form, to appear and disappear like a dolphin at play.
Sickingen ran into the water up to his knees, stretching
out his arms towards this long-dreamed-of apparition. Le
Fort joined Bob in his cheers and hurrahs, throwing his
cap into the air. All three were beside themselves, and in
all the glory of the sun at its zenith, the ship, for such
indeed it was, took shape with its sails, its masts, even
the smell of it, like a breeze wafted from Paradise. It was
coming up the straits and would be well in sight of them
if they lighted a fire.

"Help me break up these planks, Sickingen," said Bob, who was busily getting a bonfire ready.

"Count von Sickingen, my good man, if you please," remarked the Count, as he saw the ship drawing up the coast, "and for the future just drop your familiarity."

The prospector was overwhelmed. Then he turned to Le Fort, and said—

"What the devil does he mean, anyhow?"

"He means that he despises your friendship, my dear Bob," said Raoul, angrily.

Bob turned to the Count, who looked at him so contemptuously that the trapper raised his fist, swearing. Ulrich seized it, and Raoul was going to intervene, when these two madmen, about to fight in this lost corner of the world, stopped simultaneously. They were looking towards the sea in such terror that Le Fort also turned his head and saw the Arctic fog driving down from the Pole, rising from the sea, falling from the sky, blotting out the ship yet so far away, filling all eternity and annihilating them in its folds.

The sun disappeared, their ears were filled with terror, their souls seemed to leave their bodies for another world. And still, somewhere in this grey darkness the waves forever whispered—

"Yesterday—to-day—yesterday."

And the darkness of the tomb enveloped the three unfortunates.

CHAPTER XIII
PACKAGE NO. 437

On the 10th August, 1900—for every day at noon Le Fort scratched off a day from his calendar, which, perhaps, later on, preserved his sanity—on this day, in the morning, the village of Ya-Thenaoddi presented a scene of extraordinary animation. A file of Koriaks was aligned at the entrance of the hut of "the Russians," that was guarded by Naroutcha and Reka. The white fox had the sharpest teeth in the world, and everyone knows that a bite from them would putrefy the blood as quickly as the oil from a whale's tongue.

Toulouack headed the line, supported by his four wives, who intoned their customary chorus, "Hihi! Yo!" He looked like a Chinese doll with an unstable foundation, unable to stand straight without the support of their chignons. He was arguing with Fred Hamilton, of whom only the upper part was visible, by Naroutcha's side. The New Yorker punctuated with wild gestures his few words of Tchouktchi—

"Youngou! No, no! Haia! Get out!"

Raoul, Bob, and Sickingen hurried to the rescue, and found themselves hustled about by the Koriaks, embraced by the women, nose-rubbed by the men; and they found to their intense surprise that the whole crowd were blissfully, helplessly drunk—so drunk that for their lives they could not have told a salmon from a white fox.

The king was waving a reckoning-stick, while each of his subjects had some kind of a vessel in his hand, reindeer bladders, gulls' gizzards, or the hollow stones which were their domestic lamps. Some even held out their otter-skin boots, and a strong smell of alcohol pervaded the air.

"Fred," cried Raoul, in utter astonishment, "what on earth does it all mean?"

Hamilton gave a shout of delight. "Here you are! And not before you are wanted. Come and help me. It's all Tou-louack's fault. Bob, tell them to get out—that the king, officially, has drunk all there was left, and that they won't get any to-morrow if they don't bring me more of the red berries. It is my case No. 437, Raoul. Haia! Youngou!"

Bob disappeared underground, and each one got his bottle ready. He was one of themselves, anyway; his skin had not the sickly white of the "Russians."

When he re-appeared, this same complexion of his was of a lovely colour, and his nose shone as it was used to in the good old days of San Francisco. It made them warm just to look at him, and he began to distil the most elo-quent harangue that was ever heard by a Koriak tribe north of the Arctic Circle.

"Why did the king show a stick with only one notch instead of three? Weren't his subjects as thirsty as he? Why had he drunk all the rest of the fire-water that the Man-Whale had made?"

"*Will* you tell me what has happened?" said Raoul to his friend, behind the speaker's back.

"Well," said Fred, "I had the idea, while you were away, of distilling some berries. You see it was a good idea. This is my first attempt, and all Ya-Thenaoddi is beautifully drunk;" and he looked around with a highly satisfied ex-pression at the excited crowd. "Come and try the second lot."

Le Fort and Sickingen drank a swallow of the raw and villainous fluid, the distiller the while looking anxiously at their faces to see how they liked it.

"It is a bit dry," he said, "but we can mix it with pound-ed ice. Later on, I will take some bottles back to the club. With a lemon or two, some strawberries squeezed through a strainer, a sprig of mint and a drop of old Jamaica, we shall get the Toulouack cocktail. It will be a novelty, sure. Gentlemen, here's your very good health."

While this was going on underground, Bob, outside, had come to the end of his eloquence, rubbed noses with a dozen squaws who found him to be a fine fellow, and wept copiously on their shoulders. Meantime Toulouack, sulk-ily enough, took a party of his people to pick the berries, which at this time of the year ripened almost everywhere on the tundra.

This surprising reception, Hamilton's ingenuity, and, doubtless, also, his whisky at 40 or 50 degrees above proof, mitigated to some extent the terrible disappointment that the three companions had suffered; but the reaction was of short duration, and one day Sickingen took Le Fort aside.

"Monsieur"—for he always kept up his "monsieur," so absurd among shipwrecked people at the very end of the world—"monsieur, I would willingly spare you the trouble of my presence, if I had one chance in a hundred of not dying of hunger along the coast. Give me your rifle, with what cartridges you have left, and I will go. On my honour as a gentleman, I will send you word of the first ship that I sight."

"You would go to certain death," said Raoul. "Besides, I will not part with the only weapon that we have left."

"Death—rather death than this horrible Esquimau ex-istence. I cannot—cannot endure it."

"Do like the rest of us—wait and hope."

"Ach! I do not want anybody's sermons. Will you give me the rifle? Yes or no."

"No!"

The German looked at the Frenchman with the fero-cious eyes of one wild beast who would like to devour another. If civilized beings are thrown abruptly outside

of the pale of civilization, they become more savage than
savages. Besides, between these two fellow-unfortunates,
there was always an apparition which they would not have
mentioned for anything in the world, but which they saw
reflected in each other's eyes, at every minute of this forced
co-existence which was theirs, this community of interest
which is the basis of lifelong friendships, or, oftener yet,
of undying hatreds. Can you ever really comprehend Cain
unless you have lived in a desert side by side with someone whom you did not like? Antipathy becomes animosity;
animosity, hate; and hate ends in homicide. That the last
had not yet happened at Ya-Thenaoddi, was almost inex-
plicable, or rather it was due to Hamilton, who prevented
it by his perpetual good humour and his American energy,
which sometimes has that poetical vein characteristic of
simple natures, that Longfellow sung so aptly—

> "In the world's broad field of battle,
>   In the bivouac of Life,
> Be not like dumb, driven cattle!
>   Be a hero in the strife!"

It was just this "Psalm of Life "that Hamilton recalled
to Raoul, one day when the young artist seemed sinking
into the lowest depth of despair.

"What is the use of striving? But in order to succeed,
my dear Frenchman; and if we are beaten, we shall at least
'leave behind us, footprints on the sands of time,' which
'some other shipwrecked wanderer, seeing, shall take heart
again.' Ye gods! To understand him, you have got to be lost
at least once in your life, as we are at this moment."

"Much obliged," said Le Fort, stung to the quick. "Keep
your Longfellow to yourself. Every one isn't lucky enough
to have the heroic virtues necessary for a successful whisky
distiller."

The good-tempered giant shrugged his shoulders.

"You will have good reason to bless my distillery, all the same, and the time is near when you will wish I could turn out a hundred gallons at once instead of one. Now listen. For the last few days you have not deserved to be alive any more than Job did on his dung-heap, and then the poor old fellow did not have your iron constitution. Now I, who know what it is to be ill—"

Raoul burst out laughing. Hamilton began to get angry.

"Yes, I say, I, who know what it is to be ill, consider your discouragement shameful and ignoble. You make me tired; Why, even Sickingen is pulling himself together. He goes out fishing every day with that little bandy-legged Ervik, the future king, whose face, by the way, I don't much care for. But you—you get up to eat. Then you go to sleep. Then you wake up and eat some more. You've got a good, strong stomach of your own."

"But—"

"Now just hear me through for once in your life. Will the Past come back because you dream of it so much that you forget the Present? Can you guess the Future by thinking of it? We have only one hour of our own in all Eternity—the Present. It is the only hour that it is worth living in, as this country is the finest in the world, because it is the only place and time in the world that we are sure of. Come, old man, pull yourself together, wake your mind up, search here, dig there, find the animal, and—"

Raoul exploded. "You seven-storied humbug of a Yankee, you've gone too far! If either of us two is mad, it is not I! Find the animal! That's too easy. Where are you going to find him outside of your own whisky-soaked brain?"

"Not under your bed, for one place, sure, but somewhere in Siberia, where we are. Where did the St. Petersburg one come from? And that one at Ekaterinburg? If you want to dig up another of the family, you can have all the Koriaks you want to help you."

"That's easy enough to say. But how?"

"Out of my distillery, bless your soul! A bladder-full for a tusk, two for a leg-bone, four boots-full, brimming over, for a complete skeleton. That's the tariff that was published all over the town yesterday. Go out and look at some of the sample bones at the door. Houp-la! Here we are again! Have a cocktail, Raoul? Toulouack or T.C.?"

Raoul was too overcome to speak. He was touched to the inmost fibres of his being.

"Ah, you are a better man than I. Pardon, old boy."

Hamilton had settled down to his usual calmness.

"And you know, Raoul, if there is a bone or two missing, I'll make them myself to please your old fossil of a father-in-law. Come, let's get to work. There is time to make a success before winter."

From this day began the cure of the artist. He tried first to get some idea of the geographical situation of Ya-Thenaoddi. The only ideas of direction that the Koriaks have are derived from the winds at different seasons. The coldest wind blew up the Reindeer River, coming from the north. This river, Naroutcha explained, led to a great lake, on the other side of which land could be seen. Bob concluded from this that they were not far from the Bay of Koliutchin, and that, in following the bank to the north-east, they should finally make East Cape, because that was the point to aim at, unless they found another skeleton somewhere else. Unhappily, although numbers of bones were brought in by each expedition of the Koriaks, they were always defective teeth or fragments of leg-bones, from which it was impossible to reconstruct Corliss's execrable primigenius.

Sickingen passed all his time with Ervik, who was one of the few Koriaks who had met white men before, and who was silently hostile to the king. The Count had picked up enough Tchouktchi to make himself understood, and he could fish fairly well in a kayak, which is the most suitable craft in the world to give a novice all the pleasant sensations of a man who is drowning with his head under water and the remainder of him in the air if he has the misfortune to turn bottom-side up.

Le Fort and Hamilton preferred to hunt on land. Their rifle, contrary to expectation, had made but little impression on the Esquimaux. The noise of the explosion was not as loud as that of the cracking of the ice in a severe frost, or the crumbling of an iceberg. There was no smoke to puzzle them, and although the "hollow lance" shot to a long distance on land or water, it was not as effective as their harpoons. Christianity, therefore, cannot reckon on Ya-Thenaoddi for a good market for its old pattern guns.

The days passed slowly in a monotony which weighed down the spirits of the explorers. As for Bob, who was running the distillery, and whose complexion grew more and more brilliant underground, life had nothing more to offer. His three companions tried to put a good face on bad fortune, when an event occurred which electrified them all out of this lethargy of the Far North, which it is so difficult to combat.

It was during a tempest which was blowing all the snows of the North Pole over the village, that King Toulouack literally "dropped in" to the barraborra of his "Russian" friends, while behind him Naroutcha fastened the skylight which Hamilton had constructed when he started his distillery. Mournful yelpings burst out on the outside.

"Naroutcha! Naroutchina! Little sister, open the door, for the love of your white friends."

"Don't open it, Naroutcha," said the king and Sickingen.

The old squaw spit in the air, and the white fox bit a hand that came within reach. A chorus of insults floated down the wind.

"Old fool! Old one-eyed seal that nobody wants anymore! The Man-Whale says you smell of fresh fish!"

These remarks came from Natiya and the other three queens, who were in a disheveled state after a scrimmage with Toulouack, who had evidently had the worst of it.

When he got his breath again he sighed, as he sat by Hamilton's side—

"Oh, Lifa!" (This was Le Fort's Koriak name.) "Oh, Man-Whale! They say in your country a man has only one wife," and he began to weep, or, rather, howl. Bob noticed that his face was scarred all over, and rubbed it with whisky. The king wiped it off on his hands, which he licked delightedly.

"It's comfortable here. You are wise men. That is why I shall sleep here. You will help me to beat my wives. I have too many of them. Oh, my friends, I will give you anything you want. Mitourour!"*

"We don't want Natiya, not any of the others," said Le Fort, who was not pleased at the prospect. "Only give us this great animal."

He showed a sketch of a primitive mammoth, like that which one of our ancestors engraved upon a bit of ivory now in the Museum of Saint Germain, thousands and thousands of centuries ago, in the depths of those forests which were afterwards the home of the ancient Gauls.

When he saw the outline, Toulouack slapped his thighs.

"Hi-hi! yo! Oui-hi! Is *that* what you want?"

"Yes, that is the animal whose bones we are after."

"Hi-hi! Yo!"

The king took a long pinch of snuff mixed with pumice-stone (the Koriaks do not smoke), and went out to talk to Naroutcha. Their conference was so long that Bob grew suspicious, and was going to take part in it, when Toulouack reappeared.

"I have heard tell of a beast like that," he said. "Naroutcha saw one once, many days away from here. Will you give me all the fire-water I want?"

"Any amount of it."

"And you will stay here and make more?"

* Speak, quickly.

"Yes," said Hamilton, "you shall have enough for a lifetime."

"Then, after the storm is over, we will go. We must have as many of us as this," and he counted his fingers and toes.

"And I must sacrifice a reindeer to the Chaddi, because we are going to the country where a monster lies in wait to catch us if he gets a chance."

He stopped short at the reference to a mythical monster which is the terror of the Esquimaux, and from which the Chaddi, a gull's head smeared with blood, is the only thing that can save the hunter.

Then he stretched himself out perfectly naked on the ground. The Koriaks undress themselves completely as soon as they come inside their dens. To this precaution Hamilton attributed their remarkable freedom from consumption, coughs, anemias, colds, or rheumatisms, or any other of the diseases attributable to the blessings of civilization, disguised as Manchester cottons, or Lyons silks.

Whatever the reason, Toulouack snored the snore of the just. Bob carried the royal garments outside to give them a thorough freezing. The wind howled its loudest, in a storm suited to a witches' festival. Naroutcha washed herself in her peculiar fashion, to remove the smell of fresh fish.* And Le Fort and Sickingen dreamed of what the king had told them. This ignoble savage, curled up at their feet, was worth, to one, five hundred million marks, to the other, Paradise on earth.

* The Koriaks only like decayed fish.

CHAPTER XIV
MAMANTOU!

The night before the departure of the new expedition was very cold, but in the snow huts the heat was so stifling that towards one in the morning Le Fort went outside to get a breath of air. The sky was of a deep blue, with green tints, and the sun, very low in the horizon, seemed redder than usual. All at once it changed its colour, and assumed that hue of melted gold which dazzles the eye, while a vague perfume arose from the earth. It was morning.

Brilliant rays of light zigzagged in the horizon, crossing and meeting, weaving the web of a prismatic veil, behind which, on the background of a dark blue sky, a great cross of fire stood out. It had a sun in the centre, and three more at each of its upper extremities, while its base was lost in the plain. Each sun was surrounded by a double halo, while from their centres shone rainbows reaching from earth to sky, and filling the world with their light.

Some one behind the artist groaned, "Alas! alas!"

The young man shivered and turned round. It was Naroutcha, crouched down as she had been at the camp of the dead Indian, and between her knees Reka stared at the ten suns with her yellow eyeballs, which reflected them like so many convex mirrors.

"What is the matter, Naroutcha?"

The old woman, half woman and half animal, continued to weep, as wept before, and as will weep to the end of time, the millions of unfortunates whom bodily misery does not prevent from thinking more than does the beast. The ghostly suns faded away, and Reka barked once. Le Fort went into the hut where his companions were sleeping peaceably. Eight hours later the Esquimaux fleet was on its way. Toulouack, of course, led the van, with twenty of his subjects, dressed in their skin tunics made for traveling on the ocean, in which they were enclosed by their kayaks like a diver in his diving-dress. Each of them carried a spear to dig the ground. Following them were the king's wives with Naroutcha, Bob, Raoul, and Fred, in a great oomiak, a boat made of walrus skins stretched on ribs of white-wood and willow. They could see the water through the skins if they pressed them down with their feet. Hamilton, at the stern, steered with a long oar, and the rest, men and women, rowed in cadence with five words, always the same—

"Eh, yan, yan, yan, ah!" the *eh* when the oar was plunged into the water, the *ah* at the end of the stroke.

Sickingen had remained at Ya-Thenaoddi with Ervik, with whom he had taken up his quarters. He had simply shrugged his shoulders at Toulouack's revelations.

The weather was pleasant, the kingfishers flew ahead of the kayaks, skimming the water with their wings. There was life everywhere, and a tranquility from above which was very different from the numbness of the winter nights. Le Fort looked towards the north and began to hope.

After four days of traveling, they reached the open sea, with a coast like that where they had been wrecked on their disastrous whaling exploit. Soon the coast got steeper, and frowning cliffs, polished by the action of the waves, rose to a height of three or four hundred yards. The king stopped at the bottom.

The women set to work to prepare a meal. Bob, who was a particular favourite, as was shown by frequent nose-rubbings, hung a vessel of reindeer-skin filled with ice on three crossed sticks above a fire. This produced most delicious drinking-water. Toulouack, after having chewed a piece of whale-skin, made an invocation to the Chaddi to propitiate the spirits of the clouds. Naroutcha began to sing a death-song; but the king silenced her by saying—

"Be quiet! You will make *him* cold forever."

The Koriaks never speak of their dead by name. *"He"* was the husband of the old centenarian, and had, as Bob informed them, been killed while hunting, and now returned sometimes in the spirit to visit his widow in her dreams.

"Come," said Hamilton, "let us get on."

"She will not go yet. Tell the Man-Whale to stay by her side," said the queens. Then they set to work to grease the seal-skin coverings of the kayaks, which glitter in the sun when they are taken out of the water. Particular attention was paid to the oomiak, the walrus-skin covering of which had not been dressed like the stronger black skins which they used for their winter expeditions. Toulouack explained the difference between them to Le Fort, who was impatient to proceed, and said—

"Do you see that gap down there? We must get through there on top of the tide, which rises as high as that," pointing to the precipitous rocks. "Those of us who are in the kayaks can go anywhere, but you and the women in the oomiak—the salt water will cool you down a little, impatient man that you are."

On the following morning, Bob took his place in the bow of the canoe, so that he could guide Hamilton in steering through the narrow and tortuous fissure, probably formed by some volcanic action, where they were following the Koriaks. Very high above their heads they could see the stars above the sun, and at low tide a current of fresh water flowed down this dark canal. Le Fort remarked jokingly—

"The king is having a game with us."

Bob looked attentively at some black projections of rock twenty-five yards above him from which the water dripped slowly. He stretched out his hand and tasted the water.

"Sea water! Salt water!"

"What of it?"

"Hurry up, that's all."

It was easier said than done. The wind whistled across the precipice like a monster boa-constrictor disturbed in his sleep. The dark water from above, like a body without limbs, flowed down to meet the adventurers. Hamilton felt the oomiak stop short in an eddy, not gaining an inch, in spite of the frantic efforts of Natiya and her companions. Why was Bob urging them on when they are doing their best? He clung to a rocky point and shouted—

"Nuya! Enough! Rest a moment."

The outward current slackened and the green water from the ocean began to flow in the opposite direction.

"The rising tide is going to help us," said Le Fort. "Where are the others?"

Toulouack reappeared on the horizon as if they were viewing him through the small end of a telescope, and an immense lake or bay was visible behind him. He was making frantic gestures and shouting—

"Miatarra! Quick, quick!"

"He makes me tired," said Hamilton. "What's the hurry, anyhow? The women can do no more. Bob, what are you swearing at?"

"Sir—"

The prospector had turned round, and his face became as pale as death. Certainly he saw or guessed at something fearful behind them. Instinctively every one clung to a thwart, a paddle, or a gunwale, as he shouted—

"Hurry, hurry, hurry! There is a mountain of water coming up!"

Hamilton stuck to his tiller, while the women made the oomiak fly through the water. Panting for breath, with their mouths wide open and their eyes fixed on Bob, they paddled so fast that they were at the head of the canal, when a wave, coming up astern, seized the canoe, rolled under it and carried it along on its crest into open day and the midst of a raging storm, where the water boiled like the crater of a volcano surrounded by a ring of mountains.

Hamilton continued to steer straight ahead, while La Fort and Bob, streaming with water and perspiration, stopped paddling. The women did the same, and then they realized Bob's prediction, for another wave followed out of the channel that they had come up, a semi-circular Niagara, with a noise like thunder, with a concave wall of water, glistening with millions of glassy eyes, which shut out the sun. The breeze from it filled their lungs and their mouths, the oomiak was engulfed by a curling arch of foam, disappeared under it as it broke, and the wave swept on triumphantly. The circular lake, the narrow outlet of which was not enough to carry off its full contents at low tide, was filling itself with an extraordinary strife between the two currents—the one inside trying to escape, and the one outside trying to come in as the tide rose. Like the "prorocoa" at the mouth of the Amazon, a tidal wave came up from the ocean, filling the cleft in the mountains and breaking finally in the "Lake of the Last Judgment."* For by this name La Fort baptized this eighth wonder of the world, while Hamilton picked up the oomiak, and the queens rolled themselves on the sandy beach to get dry.

The artist stood motionless, gazing on the marvelous amphitheatre surrounded by mountains which lost themselves in the clouds. A thousand and one brooks and springs, and in some places torrents rolled down to the lake, which received them all and covered the clamour of their descent with its own roaring, except at high tide, when the lake became quiet once more, and a thousand and one cascades, illuminated by the sun, which centupled all their icicles and perishable and sparkling drops of

* This tidal wave in Alaska in Cook's Inlet, at the mouth of the Sushitna, is one of the most extraordinary phenomena in the world.— Amès Sémiré.

water, sung once more the great song of Eternity which an old Gallic monk once listened to for a hundred years and a day.

"Halloa, Le Fort! Dreaming again? Toulouack is a long way ahead of us."

Hamilton's voice awakened Raoul as he shouted down from the top of some natural steps of syenite, by the side of a stream, which the Koriaks were climbing. The young man followed with a sigh, and soon the party came out upon a plateau about five hundred yards long, a chaos of broken rocks, amongst which flowed a little river. This wound around until it was lost to sight in the midst of a well-wooded valley. On the horizon a volcano swayed its enormous plume of smoke and ashes, and sometimes threw up a brilliant light which reddened the eternal snows which clothed its base. The air was warmer at this altitude, for the valley undoubtedly owed to the neighbourhood of the volcano a temperature which was exceptional under the Arctic circle, but it was impossible to descend by the side of the river where the ground fell away, for the wall was straight up and down.

"It is here," said Naroutcha, who was leading the way, trembling all over. "King, we had better go back."

Toulouack appeared to think so himself, but a mouthful of alcohol gave him fresh courage. Bob did not recognize the ground at all. Certainly this was not where he had seen the tusks sticking out of the ground at East Cape. The Koriaks prepared their camp on the plateau, while Fred and Raoul induced the king to prolong their investigations without loss of time. Naroutcha led the way along a ledge of granite which ran the same way as the valley on the side of the mountain. They could not walk three abreast, but it would have been an ideal promenade for a hermit, if there happened to be one in this last corner of Siberia.

The old woman was silent now. After an hour of marching or rather climbing, she stopped on a projecting rock which overhung the valley at the height of a cathedral tower. Le Fore was looking for a stone to test the depth of the descent when Naroutcha became as white as a sheet.

"Lifa! Are you mad? Listen, listen!"

A distant rumbling was heard. Was it an earthquake, the explosion of a volcano, or the tidal wave of the "Lake of the Last Judgment?" Le Fort threw down a pebble, which fell into a round hole, cut out as perfectly as by an enormous punch, at the foot of the cliff.

Other similar holes were visible, looking as if they had been prepared for transplanting trees. Could it be that there were hermits at the North Pole otherwise than in the artist's imagination?

Suddenly the siren of an Atlantic liner in a fog off the banks of Newfoundland burst out under their feet, piercing the air and making the brain reel. From a cavern which they could not see from above burst out a fantastic beast. La Fort saw two immense tusks waving in the air, a monstrous mane behind a trunk or a serpent as long as the height of four men, and he lost if not consciousness, at least the use of his reasoning faculties for a time. When he came to himself Hamilton was gazing into the valley, Bob was struck dumb, and Toulouack flat on his stomach on the rock, was murmuring broken words—

"Mamantou! Mamantou! He lives underground; he lives for ever. Naroutcha's grandfather saw him look out!"

In a rush which knocked over three or four trees disappeared the mamantou of the old centenarian, the mammoth whose bones Le Fort had come to the end of the world to look for, and whom he found now, alive! Was he going mad, or had the hands of time been set back twenty thousand—fifty thousand years, and thrown him, Raoul Le Fort, back into the age of the dinotherium, the mastodon, the mylodon, and all those other Miocene or Pliocene monsters who had watched the dawning life of Quaternary man, and whose footprints he saw under his feet? Was the cave-bear, larger than the largest horse, about to climb up the rocks? Or were pterodactyls, with their long claws, ready to swoop down on the explorers, while an Atlantiosaurus raised his forty yards of flesh and bone towards the wall where they crouched breathless with fear? *

"Lifa, oh, white man!"

It was the old Naroutcha who called on him as she died, before the last spark of life was extinguished by the door which opened before her, the portal of the Unknown.

---

* It is interesting to mention in this connection that in this same year in which M. Le Fort has decided to publish an account of his adventures, a living mylodon has been found in Patagonia. The newspapers speak of the formation of an expedition to capture this antediluvian monster, hitherto supposed to be extinct. It is described as having four toes on each fore-foot, but only three on the hind feet, as having a head like a hippopotamus, a tail like a crocodile, and such remarkable strength that it can pull up full-grown trees by the roots to get at the leaves.— Amès Sémiré.

CHAPTER XV
BOB'S LITTLE JOKE

No one retained any very definite recollection of what happened after this extraordinary resurrection of a monster who dated back before the Deluge, who had made his appearance living, breathing, trumpeting, three or four hundred centuries after the extinction of his race; or of what occurred after Naroutcha's death. The only thing that was certain was that Toulouack got away into the camp at the top of his speed, and that Le Fort tried to follow with his friends; but what civilized muscles have ever been able to equal the speed of the savage when the latter takes the bit in his teeth? When they reached the camp, there was not a living soul there. The Koriaks, struck with a panic like that which once seized on Sennacherib's hosts in Egypt, had fled in the most admired disorder. Perhaps they had already embarked at the Lake of the Last Judgment.

"Let us follow them, in Heaven's name," said Le Fort. "If necessary, we will destroy their kayaks."

So saying, he flung down his rifle at the door of one of the huts, and started down the river with Hamilton. Bob followed reluctantly, looking at the sky, and grumbling, "We had better camp, gentlemen, and talk it over. I don't like the colour of those clouds—no, sir."

A cold breeze had got up, which was rapidly growing into a storm. The temperature grew colder and colder, and snow-flakes came drifting down from the north, which were as hard as hail, and stung the flesh where it touched it. The old prospector stopped.

"This child is not going any farther, gentlemen. It is going to be a blizzard which will last two or three days."

"A what?"

"A whirlwind of cold and snow, sir."

"Well, what then? It happens every day in this lovely country."

"Not this kind. This thing will shut your eyes and freeze you after it has blinded you. We must get back to camp in less than no time."

Without waiting for an answer, Bob started, almost at a run, for the plateau. Hamilton and Le Fort got close to each other, for the tempest drowned their voices.

"Bob is right, Raoul."

"In Heaven's name, what can we do without these brutes?"

"We'll see. For the present, we must look after ourselves."

"All right, I will go on alone."

Le Fort was beside himself. Hamilton looked him straight in the face. The artist's eyes shone like those of a madman, and his face was as deathly white as if it had been frozen. Then the giant seized him by the arms, threw him over his shoulder, and, in spite of his cries and his insults, followed Bob's tracks, which were already disappearing under the snow. The blizzard had broken out with all the fury of these northern latitudes, and the waters of the torrent were getting as solid as they usually were during the seven months of winter. The three took shelter under one of the Koriaks' huts, and Bob went around it to plug up all the crevices with snow and make it waterproof. All at once he stooped down and uttered an exclamation.

"Someone has been here lately; I can see their tracks." He kneeled down to examine the traces more closely, and went out.

"It's a white man."

La Fort instantly thought of his rifle, which he ought not to leave under the snow. He looked for it, and searched with hands and feet, the others aiding him, but there was nothing there. The rifle had gone. Someone had stolen it.

"*Someone* is Sickingen, I am sure," said Hamilton; and Bob agreed with him.

"You bet. He must have followed me with Ervik. I never thought much of that beauty."

"That is why they tried to find out which way Toulouack was going."

Le Fort sank down with his head in his hands. It ached as if it would burst.

"The Koriaks have escaped to the south, the mammoth has escaped to the north, and they've stolen my rifle. My God!"

Hamilton took pity on him.

"Cheer up, old boy! Let me get my hands on the man who sneaked it—"

"What does it matter to you? Oh, I forgot—your record? But for me it means Eva, so near and yet so far! Leave me alone!"

Bob and Fred went outside to talk it over. The violence of the storm had abated, or rather it was the calm which always exists in the centre of a cyclone; for there are cyclones in that country of ice and snow, whatever the savants say to the contrary.

"The tracks continue in that direction."

"We will follow them as soon as we can, Bob. Great Scott, how I would like to have a fight with someone!"

The prospector seized his master by the arm.

"Look, down below there."

"Well, what of it? It's only some rocks covered with snow."

"No. They are refuges. There are people underneath."

"Go on!"

"Fact! When they are caught in a storm like this, the natives dig holes under the snow, close them up hermetically, and wait until it's over."

"How do they breathe?"

Bob shrugged his shoulder. "I dunno. But I know they don't leave a single opening. I've often been in them myself."

When Bob began to talk in short sentences, it was useless to ask for fuller explanations. Fred Hamilton began to descend towards the hillocks, in spite of the prospector's warnings.

"Look out! Do you know who these people are?"

It made very little difference to the Vice-President of the Athletic Club, who gave a couple of kicks on the outside of the first hut.

"Halloa, you there!"

A sort of plug which served for a door flew out from the inside, followed by a savage. He was clothed in skins, and was much taller than the Koriaks. An iron ring hung from his lower lip, and four vertical lines were tattooed on his chin. At the sight of Hamilton he growled—

"Salakoua!"

Then, in place of running away, as one of Toulouack's subjects would have done, he seized the white man in his arms and tried to throw him.

The giant uttered a shout of delight that his wish for a fight should have been realized so soon. He seized his enemy's left wrist with his left hand, and passed his right arm around the left arm, twisting it upside down. His right wrist strained on his own left wrist, and with a downward leverage the arm of the savage broke off short, like a match.

"One!" said the New Yorker, without losing his coolness. "Anybody else want anything?"

But the other party were too numerous. They came out in a bunch, like a swarm of angry hornets. There was not a white man among them. Bob and Raoul were in time to rush in and bring off Hamilton, and force him to beat a retreat. It was evidently useless to attempt to force a passage through these nomads, who, besides, did not follow them.

"They are Tchouktchis of the south," observed Bob. "Toulouack told me that they came to Ya-Thenaoddi every year. You'd swear that they wanted to stop us."

"We'll go through all the same," said Le Fort, all whose energy was stirred up by the fight.

"Wait and see," said Bob. "They have spears and we have nothing, and in this cold a wound is sure death."

"We will come down at night."

"And leave tracks on the snow? It's better to be a bit foxy. Let's have something to eat, and then Bob will think it over carefully."

"He is right," said Hamilton. "The storm is beginning again, and we have nothing better to do. I was never so hungry in my life; all we need is a cocktail."

"Hasn't your fight been enough of an appetizer, Freddy? I heard your bones crack."

"Not mine, sure. How do you like my Japanese knot? I've never found an arm that would stand against it."

"Splendid! One never ought to lose courage while you are about."

The evening was short. The two friends slept side by side while Bob watched. In the middle of the night he stirred up the fire and went out. The snow continued to fall, but in very fine flakes, while the cold had increased to at least 50° below zero. The torrent had frozen over, except for one small opening, at the south-east of the plateau, from which a small stream was still flowing. The water smoked as if it were warm, and a hundred yards lower down it formed a moving glacier. A little lower yet, in a ravine, were the "snowballs" of the Tchouktchis.

"If I could only manage it," said Bob to himself, measuring the distance with his eye. "And if I have got time— well, let's have a try at it."

He set to work with a bundle of branches and his knife, which was the only tool that he had. After a couple of hours' work, he heaved a sigh of satisfaction.

"Good night, gentlemen! That will go fine. Take Bob's word for it." And he went peaceably to sleep by the side of his companions in misfortune.

The next morning the storm was over, the sky was a sapphire blue, and the sun brought back new life to this corner of the world which had been so dead and forsaken twelve hours before. Hamilton dragged himself outside in spite of the cold.

"Now," said he, "we'll hold a council of war before the battle."

"Battle!" said Bob, sarcastically. "What about?"

"Do you think we are going to take root here?" said Le Fort. "I suppose it's just what you'd like?"

"What prevents your leaving, gentlemen?"

"What? Why, the Tchouktchis; hang 'em!"

"Tchouktchis? Dunno. Where are they?" Hamilton looked towards their camp of last night, rubbed his eyes, and called out to Raoul—

"That's so. Where the devil are they? Am I going blind, or are they gone?"

Le Fort, utterly astonished, could see nothing but a long stretch of ice where his friend had fought the night before.

"They are not there," said he at length. "What does it mean, Bob?"

Bob drew himself up. He was taller by an inch.

"They are there all the same, gentlemen, only they are under the ice instead of on top of it. I turned the water so as to flow over them before it froze. See? It's Bob's little joke."

"Bravo, bravo!" cried Hamilton. "I should never have thought of it myself."

Le Fort was not so enthusiastic.

"And these poor wretches are buried alive?"

"Perhaps—very possibly. But they live a long time on their own fat, as the bears do."

"Le Fort, have you lost your senses? What difference does the fate of these brutes make to you? Besides, the sun will soon set them free. Now for the lake. Hurrah for Bob!"

It was the American who spoke.

Raoul joined in his congratulations so as not to hurt the old trapper's feelings, but at heart he shivered, in spite of himself, at the thought of the prison of ice which made him free at the cost of twenty lives; the French are so sentimental in war!

And no one, for the moment, remembered anything about the famous rifle.

CHAPTER XVI
THE SECOND RESCUE

Toulouack had had such a scare that, as he afterwards owned, his stomach was sticking to his backbone; but he was also happy in possessing one of the liveliest thirsts that a drunkard could wish for, and when his friends, the Russians, refound him at the Lake of the Last Judgment, he was between two horns of a dilemma—mamantou and fire-water, or Ya-Thenaoddi and whale-oil.

"What are you afraid of?" said Hamilton. "Isn't the mountain higher than the animal? Has mamantou got wings to fly up here with?"

And Le Fort backed him up. "You will be known as famous hunters. They will say everywhere, Toulouack's band killed the mamantou, and your wives will be afraid of you. Will you leave this enormous game to Ervik and the other white man—meat enough to last us all for a month, with nothing to do but to drink the Man-Whale's fire-water?"

His eloquence conquered their last hesitations. The king came forward, and said—

"I, Toulouack, son of Meigack, will lead the way against the enemy and aid the white *nakootl* Ouihihi."

"Hihi! yo! Ouihihi," agreed his subjects, slapping their hands on their thighs.

The little band started to climb the ledge leading to the "Happy Valley," as Le Fort had christened it. The three friends felt lighthearted again. The sun warmed the atmosphere, and even the Koriaks seemed full of energy.

A sudden thought struck the artist, and he stopped
short—

"Good heavens—my rifle!"

Fred, who was delighted at the prospect of this pre-his-
toric hunting-party, did not seem to be troubled.

"We'll worry along without it, that's all," said he. "The
Count, if he really stole it, has acted with absolute un-
fairness. He is not playing the game. Any referee would
disqualify him at once. I do not imagine that after this
rascality he will have the cheek to present himself at the
club. If he should, I'll insist on his expulsion.

"And in the meantime, old boy, we are at this wretch's
mercy. But, if I've nothing but this spear to attack him
with, I'll—"

"We're not after Count von Sickingen now," said the
ever-practical Bob; "we're after the mammoth. We're hunting game, not hunting hunters."

"Well, how can we hunt him, now?" said Raoul. "The
other fellow has got all the advantage of us, because he
can get up on top of the mountain and shoot away comfortably."

"That's all guesswork—besides, every bullet does not
hit. And when you have lost your gun, you have got to
use your ingenuity." Le Fort shivered at this reference to
"Bob's little joke;" but the latter did not notice it, and
went on, "Sickengen hasn't got the old mammoth's tusks
yet."

"Bob, we must succeed. We must—see? And I will
promise that the mammoth will be worth as much to you
as a gold mine."

"We'll make a scale of charges for him—by the pound,"
said Bob, cheerfully. "Just now we must keep Toulouack
sweet, for the least hesitation will scare him. Look at him
now."

The party soon got within half a mile of the cavern.
Hamilton made the Koriaks pitch their camp there, and
went to reconnoitre the field.

"The Happy Valley narrows a little further on," said he. "It's not more than one hundred and fifty yards at the most. What do you say to building a stone wall to shut him in, as the Siamese do with their elephants in their circular 'paneats' in Ayuthia, or the Cingalese hunters with their 'kheddahs'?"

"Your Chinese wall would take you two months to build, Freddy, and then Mr. Mammoth would knock it over in two twos, and you with it. And you don't suppose the Koriaks are going to shift immense masses of rock like that to please you, do you? No, we must invent something else," said Le Fort. "What do you say to lassoing him with our rope?"

"Good enough! Catching a mammoth with a rope! That's as good as your Count de Lacepede's yarn, where he tells us that they catch whales by driving wooden plugs into their blow-holes."

Hamilton was a living encyclopaedia of facts relating to hunting big game; but, try as he would, the mastodontal inspiration would not come to him.

"Let's look at the beast's cage," said Bob. "I have an idea; but take it easy, for he may be inside now."

Their route became very difficult; the hunters wanted to reach a projecting rock, nearer to the cavern than the first "balcony," and to do this they were obliged to utilize their ropes to get over some bad spots. At last, lying flat on their stomachs, they could examine the entrance to the den.

The ground in front was trodden down and swept as clean as an asphalt boulevard. Two pillars of basalt, detached from the main mass of rock, stood at the right and left of the entrance, like the posts of some gigantic, unfinished door. A great pile of dry grass and branches lay outside them.

The hunters were just inspecting these details when an extraordinary noise alarmed them. It was not the ear-splitting roar of a steamer's siren, but more like the

dull rumbling which precedes an earthquake. Below the
three men, and separated from them only by some yards
of rock, the mammoth primigenius was sweetly snoring.
His breathing seemed to shake the mountain. Almost un-
consciously the hunters flattened themselves out on their
perch. How small they felt themselves in comparison with
this monster, whose skin they were already sharing out.
Suddenly the opening of the grotto was blocked up by a
moving mass which came slowly out, and Le Fort, Hamilton, and Bob saw arise before them, in open day, this
enormous, fantastic survival of forgotten ages. He waddled
as he walked, his mane undulated like the snakes of story
and fable, his ears waved to and fro, and he breathed, not
through his trunk, but through his throat. When he saw
the sun, which he had worshipped for no one knows how
many long ages, he raised his trunk in the air and trumpeted two piercing cries—

"Brrrao! Arraho!"

His immense tusks curved up towards those who spied
on him, feeling like pigmies before this embodiment of
colossal power. Then the mastodon set to work to sharpen
his tusks on the basalt columns.

Raoul's first thought was, "Why should we kill this
wonder? He has never done us any harm." So feel the hunters who know the splendours of the dark forests, when
they are watching for the game to pass—the true hunts-
men who have seen the beauty of wild things at liberty,
these beasts whose minds, perhaps, are like ours, except
for our power of speech.

His second and more practical thought was—"If that
rascally German hadn't stolen my rifle, I could have shot
the mammoth in the eye from here."

"What did you say?" said Hamilton. "The skeleton!
Yes, it's a fine specimen. This primi-primigenius looks re-
markably well."

"See him walk, your skeleton," said the matter-of-fact
Bob. "He's a good deal better fixed up than we are just now."

The mammoth had strolled off without troubling himself to think of his enemies. He pulled up a birch tree with one sweep of his trunk, and stripped off the branches. The trunk of the tree cracked under the weight of his formidable feet.

"Couldn't we try to drop on this gentleman when he comes back?" said Freddy.

"I have a better idea than that, I think," said Raoul, who was looking carefully over the basalt pillars at the entrance of the cavern. "But it would take time, and we should need the axe. Bob, where is your axe?"

"At the plateau."

"Very well, we'll go back there, and if Sickingen comes while we are gone—"

"He will shoot, that's all. We can do nothing now, gentlemen. Just leave the animal in peace. Come along, gentlemen."

He then passed along the ridge, twenty yards above the mammoth, who was engaged in digging in the ground with his tusks, probably searching for roots. He was just in the narrow part of the valley, where Hamilton had proposed to construct his famous wall. The New Yorker was enlarging on his plan to the sceptical Bob when Le Fort uttered a cry of anger.

Just below them Sickingen made his appearance out of a cleft in the rocks. He had Raoul's rifle at his shoulder, took aim, and was about to fire when the Frenchman's cry, followed by exclamations from the latter's companions, made him raise his head. He saw the three leaning over above him, seemed to hesitate for a second, while the rifle shook in his hands, then he pulled himself together again. At the noise of voices the mammoth had raised his trunk, which reached to the height of a two-story house, and his little eyes shone as he stared at his enemy.

The Count fired. The noise of the shot was drowned by a frightful trumpeting which rolled through the Happy Valley like a thunderclap, and the mountain was shaken as if by a blast of dynamite. The mastodon had charged the rocks, which flew in every direction, and fissures appeared here and there.

A stone slipped under Sickingen's feet, and the solid rock crumbled away. He dropped the rifle, which the monster broke on a rock and then trampled underfoot. The Count, with his legs dangling in space, holding by only one hand to a projecting rock, found himself almost in reach of his enemy's trunk. They saw him try, by a last effort, to pull himself up on what remained of the platform; but his right arm, injured by his fall, hung useless at his side. He remained hanging by his left wrist, covered with blood. How long could he hold out?

"Well done!" said Hamilton.

"Fairly caught!" said Bob.

"Bob!" cried Le Fort, "give me the rope."

"What the devil—"

"The rope! Hold the end and let me down. Help him, Fred!"

The Frenchman was already letting himself down the steep, almost polished face of the wall. He reached the point that Sickingen was clinging to, just at the moment when the mammoth, with another furious charge, made that crumble in its turn; but he was in time to grasp the Count around the body, and both, hanging by the rope, turned slowly round in mid-air. Below them their foe's trunk sent out a blast of air like that which strikes you in the face as you stand on a bridge when an express train goes under it.

Hamilton, bent like a bow on the ledge above, braced himself with all his strength against a rock, and, aided by Bob, inch by inch they pulled up their heavy weight. Then the two broke out in a chorus of exclamations.

"Why the devil didn't you let him go under?" said Hamilton, while Bob's remarks could be expressed by "— — —"

Ulrich, who had seated himself without saying a word, raised his eyes—

"You would have done better if you had."

Then he was silent again. His hands were covered with blood, but he was not seriously injured. Le Fort stood before him.

"Count von Sickingen, you saved my life, willingly or unwillingly, when we were wrecked. To-day we are square. I wanted to settle up this old affair first; and now I tell you that I consider you a rascal, and at the first attempt that you make against me, or against this mammoth which belongs to me, I will kill you like a thief!"

Sickingen trembled with anger, but kept his eyes fixed on the ground and would not answer a word.

"Count," said Hamilton, who had recovered his breath and his coolness, "you don't play the game. You have lost the match. Leave the contest—you are disqualified. In the name of the New York Athletic Club, I declare your name expunged from the lists of amateurs of all America. Look out for yourself, if I ever find you among them again."

Bob said nothing, but his eyes followed the mammoth, who, with trunk erect and hair on end, was breaking through all obstacles as he lapsed into the infinite like the Overland Limited gone mad. After half an hour's silent walk behind the two companions, he shook his head and repeated—

"Why didn't you let him slide—"

CHAPTER XVII
HOW REKA STOOD AT BAY

The day after this theatrical performance, the explorer and the Koriaks returned to camp on the ledge above the mammoth's retreat, when Bob stopped and said—

"I hear something."

Toulouack listened, and said, "Yepp! Yourr! It is Reka, there, in that hole."

In fact, the fox's cry could be heard coming out of one of the numberless cracks that scarred the face of the mountain. The three white men started to search it, for the little animal's appeal had touched their consciences. Where was Naroutcha, and what could have become of the body of the brave old woman to whom Le Fort owed his mammoth, and whom, during these last events, he had forgotten as if she had never existed? How could her corpse have disappeared from the ledge? Had she had only a fainting fit, resulting from extreme excitement, instead of an utter collapse as they had imagined?

The crevasse, which widened as they advanced, terminated at the edge of an abyss which was lighted by a faint twilight. Another outlet probably communicated with the mammoth's cavern. Le Fort leaned over the edge in the semi-obscurity, and the horror of what he saw made his head swim.

"Look out, or you will fall!" said a voice in his ear. "Leave it to me. Come down, Bob, and bring two spears."

At the foot of the rock the little white fox was turning

139

round in her own tracks to face a circle of phosphorescent gleams which approached whenever her back was turned. A mob of other foxes surrounded her, with their teeth glaring and their great bushy tails straight behind them, waiting for a chance to spring upon old Naroutcha's body, which they had dragged there. Bob related afterwards that there was a collection of furs there which the hunters of the Russo-American Fur Company see only in their dreams: some of silver grey, others cross-barred, blues and reds with black stomachs, bays with two grey lines upon their backs, and even a black one—one of those famous Kenertorks, with reflections like a crow's wing, which surpass in silkiness the sables of Siberia, and that the great Chinese viceroys would ruin a province to buy.

The whole band were intent on Naroutcha and Reka. There was a deadly combat in progress, into which rushed Hamilton, Bob, and Raoul. The foxes vanished, and the three knelt by the side of the poor desecrated corpse. Reka lay upon her mistress's breast, and a despairing grief shone in her yellow eyes, as if she said, "How late you are!"

There was hardly a sign of life in her motionless frame, except in her jaws, which opened and closed with little convulsive tremblings; they had bitten too sharply and too well. In the middle of the back, under the skin, was a bunch as big as one's fist, like the ends of a broken spring.

"Reka's ribs are broken," said Bob. "How do you think she can live with a broken spine?"

Hamilton leaned over her as tenderly as a sick-nurse.

"It is true," said he. Then, after a moment's silence, he said, "It would be more merciful to kill her."

That was also true—horribly true. Le Fort's eyes grow dim. Reka gazed at him appealingly.

"Toulouack must do it," said Bob. "Not me."

And he went out, the others following him and feeling like cowards. They tried to close their ears, but they could not.

Who says that foxes do not cry out under the knife?

They buried the two in a cavity, covering them with great blocks of basalt to protect them from desecration by wild beasts—Reka with her yellow eyes, extinguished for eternity; Naroutcha with her black eyes, which will open again someday at the trump of the Archangel. Then she will call out, "Reka, little Reka! where art thou?" And Reka will not answer, for she will be as if she had never been. It is because animals know this mystery that almost all of them weep when they are dying. Watch closely the agony that shows in their eyes during the last convulsion, and you will see the escape of the vital spark which is their soul, an echo of the human soul. But what becomes of the echo of an echo?

CHAPTER XVIII
THE MAMMOTH'S REVENGE

Raoul, Fred, and Bob, perched up in their observatory, kept watch for three days, but nothing happened. It was inconceivable that Sickingen's single shot should have mortally wounded the mastodon; indeed, Bob was sure that he had seen the gleam of two little eyes of fire at the moment of his second attack, and they were the only point which were vulnerable by a Marlin rifle. Was it possible that the monster had been so frightened that he dared not return to what had been his home for a thousand years? Le Fort began to believe so, in spite of the cheerful confidence of the old trapper. Raoul had not imparted to his companions the plan of attack which he had mentioned when they were up on the platform above the cavern. Hamilton questioned him about it, but all that he would say was, "It is impracticable just yet."

They decided, therefore, to follow Bob's idea and try to catch the mammoth by means of a ditch, like a common quadruped. Of course, with the insufficient means at the disposal of the Koriaks, they could not think of digging a hole large enough to engulf the colossal elephant of the North Pole bodily; but Bob had conceived the idea of making two deep trenches, two yards wide, at the entrance to the cavern, and planting in them a number of sharp spears with the points up. Either coming in or going out the mammoth might get one of his enormous feet in the trap, and with the elephant the foot is the most vulnerable spot, next to the eye and the stomach. Once he was wounded or had a leg or two broken, the mammoth would fall a possible prey to these unarmed hunters.

Natiya and the other queens, perched on rocks from point to point, acted as sentinels in order to signal the return of Mamantou as far as possible, if he returned while the Koriaks were at work. Bob had left his rope still hanging, so that those who had not the time to creep into some crevice in the rocks, could climb up out of reach of the enemy's trunk or tusks.

The tribe went to work with zest, while Le Fort and Hamilton risked a hasty examination of the interior of the cave. It appeared to be very deep, and its walls dated from the earliest geological formations of the globe. They were of grey basalt, veined here and there with blue zeolites. There were numerous crevices among the prismatic masses of rock, where a man could hide himself; but what could he do in the way of a direct attack, having for all weapon a wooden spear hardened in the fire?

"And yet," said Hamilton, meditatively, "there must be traditions of sticking a mammoth like a wild boar."

"Sickingen's shot was a great success, too," said Le Fort, sarcastically. "By the way, what do you suppose has become of him?"

Hamilton's face darkened. "He must have got back to Ervik and his crowd, for there were no Koriaks among the Tchouktchis. That little bit of 'playing to the gallery' of yours is going to be an expensive business for us."

"Well, perhaps you were right and I was wrong, and say no more about it. Let us go and see how Toulouack and Co. are getting on."

The Koriaks had gone on strike. They had lost interest in their work after reaching the frozen ground under its covering of ice a yard thick, and to induce them to go on necessitated, not a double flow of eloquence but a double ration of alcohol, diluted with whale-oil, which they licked up delightedly from their hollow stone lamps.*

"We have got to hurry up," said Hamilton. "The kayak full of whisky that I brought from Ya-Thenaoddi is almost empty."

"Better tell Mr. Mamantou that," said Bob. "I wonder where he is keeping himself?"

On the evening of the fourth day, Natiya, from her elevated perch, signaled something fresh, but her comparative tranquility indicated that it was not the appearance of the mamantou, so that it was evident that something was going on in the Happy Valley. Hamilton and Le Fort hastened to Natiya's signal-rock, and from the top of a granite needle saw distinctly a camp fire some miles distant. It appeared likely that it was Sickingen and Ervik's troop, who had got down into the plain, either on the track of the mammoth, or perhaps looking for a route towards the open sea.

Bob was summoned, and the three held a council of war. Raoul did not think it fair to attack the Count after once letting him go, and Hamilton saw danger in stirring up Koriak against Koriak. But the question was, Would Sickingen be first in the field again after their prey? Bob thought that he would.

"But," said he, "you have seen already that we can do nothing against this animal in open fight, and only a madman would attack him with nothing but a stick in his hand. Don't let us move; we'll wait and see what happens. The one that is in the greatest hurry to start isn't always the one to get there first."

The Vice-President of the Athletic Club added.—

---

* The Koriaks, like other Esquimau; use hollow stones for lamps.—A fish, hung above the wick, details its oil drop by drop.— A. S.

"Mr. von Sickingen is not in the race any more, so we need not worry from that point of view."

A well-known trumpeting interrupted the discussion. Natiya disappeared underground like a seal sliding into the water, and the Koriaks set up a chorus of howls, until Hamilton quieted them with a few slaps, after which they also slipped into crevices in the rocks. Le Fort and Bob peered out into the darkness, which they would have liked to illuminate at any price, and gazed intently at Sickingen's camp-fire. Suddenly the cries of men in mortal agony mingled with the bellowing of the mammoth, and the fire was scattered as if a cyclone had struck it. The sparks from the embers flew around a black body, which disappeared in the night, and the cries redoubled, and then died out one by one. They could hear the low sound of a furious gallop on the ground. For a few minutes a burning branch, probably held in Mamantou's trunk, waved in the air. As long as the least trace of fire remained, they could judge of the repeated charges of the elephant of the ice, punctuated as they were by his formidable trumpetings.

And then night fell on the Happy Valley—and emptiness. Raoul and Fred looked at each other. What could be left now of Sickingen and his companions? Bob's voice, calm and satisfied, aroused them from their reflections—

"Gentlemen, the Count has 'got the experience, and we've got the money.' The mammoth is maddened by the sight of fire, and rushes on it as a bull does at anything red. Gentlemen, we'll bring the mammoth back home by lighting up his road with bonfires."

CHAPTER XIX
HOW MY LORD MAMMOTH CAME HOME

The next morning the prospector's idea was carried out. Raoul had intended at first to start the row of bonfires at the point where the mastodon had obliterated Sickingen's band the night before, and then they could also ascertain the extent of the disaster, and perhaps rescue some wounded Koriak, but they could not make Toulouack risk a descent to the plain. The queens were vociferous to go back to Ya-Thenaoddi, and it would be unwise to expect too much from the natives. The best that they could do was to profit by the terrible lesson that the other band had had.

The day was employed in arranging piles of wood about three hundred yards apart, the first bonfire being built at some distance from the entrance to the valley. Bob was confident that by lighting fires which were large enough and which would burn for a long time, they could draw the monster from his mysterious retreat. It was impossible to guess where he had taken refuge. The plain was strewn with masses of volcanic rock, overgrown with fir-trees, which had climbed up the rocky terraces, and the mammoth was hidden somewhere among them, and well hidden. From her rocky post of observation, Natiya kept watch on the Happy Valley without seeing anything.

So there was a general feeling of excitement when Le Fort, at the completion of all the arrangements, went to light the first bonfire himself. If the scheme succeeded, the mammoth would be sure to run to his old home, charging each bonfire in succession. Even in the cavern itself, just behind the trenches, in which Bob had ascertained that the *chevaux de frise* were firmly fixed, a last fire was ready to light by means of a train of dry leaves. It did not seem as if the monster could possibly escape the trap after his blind rushes.

And now, Raoul said to himself that the same night he would have in his grasp, perhaps, the price of Eva's hand, and that the traitorous Sickingen, annihilated somewhere out on the plain, was powerless to take her from him. Eva! Her dear portrait had been destroyed when the monster had trodden his rifle to pieces, but nothing could erase from his memory the words, "For ever and for ever, your Eva."

"Raoul, Raoul! Time's up! Wake out of your trance!"

Fred was waving a torch of lichen in the air. Le Fort set fire to the corners of the first pile of dry wood. High and clear the flame mounted straight into the air, fanned by a slight breeze. Hamilton and Bob stood on the watch at the second and third. The Koriaks watched the spectacle from a secure height on the ledge; no earthly inducement would have made them risk themselves below.

The hunters reckoned that the mammoth's charge upon the first bonfire would give time to light the others, and to fall back at full speed to their asylum. The last arrival was to utilize Bob's rope.

Their expectation was a prolonged one. The flame of the first bonfire, which they had built ten times as high as the others, illuminated a vast extent of the plain, but no living thing appeared in the desolate emptiness of the night. Le Fort, in his feverish anxiety, was already despairing, when a distant rumbling announced that the mammoth had waked up.

"Your turn, Freddy!"

Hamilton lighted his bonfire with the utmost calmness, remarking as he did so—

"A circle of loose powder, set off by an electric wire, would have been much neater. I must take care not to forget that when I am drawing up my notes for the Club. Bob, your turn!"

An avalanche shook the ground. The mammoth, doubled in size by the semi-darkness, charged into the circle of fire, rushed into the flames, lifted a blazing tree-trunk on his tusks, and, superb and fearful in his rage, began a mad circle around the bonfire. Bellowing with anger, he rushed on the flames and scattered them, becoming more and more maddened by the stinging of the fire which he thought he was destroying, but which sprang up behind him, and on which he charged again and again. Trees, rocks, and firebrands flew in the air; his trunk at times was like a fusillade of electric sparks, his mane shed fire like serpents spitting flames. There was never seen on this earth a more fantastic display of fireworks, and never while he lives will Raoul forget this fiery vision of the world before the Deluge. A second time Hamilton's voice aroused him.

"Great Scott, Raoul, what are you waiting for?"

Le Fort trembled, lighted the last bonfire, seized the rope, and climbed up to the ledge beside his friends. Ye gods! What was going to happen now?

The entire cavern seemed to be illuminated, and the light was reflected from the basalt rocks thousands of years old. The mammoth appeared to be easy in his mind once more, lowered his trunk, and sharpened his tusks on the doorposts as usual. The hunters already pictured him to themselves as being safe in their ditch, when he stopped short, breathed on the ground, and pulled up everything he found in or out of Bob's trenches. The trap had failed! The intelligent animal crossed it without trouble, placing his feet on the spots where he had pulled out the spears, and stamped out the fire inside as he began to trumpet again. Le Fort watched him disappear under the rocks. The antediluvian monster, safe and sound, and more formidable than ever, was going to rest by his own hearthstone.

"All the shots that are fired don't hit the mark, gentlemen, and all tricks do not succeed. Shall we have your idea, Le Fort?"

Bob's grumbling restored Raoul's presence of mind.

"Now, look here," said he, "pursuit and attack are both out of the question with the means which we have at our disposal. But there is a last chance left us. While the mammoth is inside there, and probably rather tired out for the time, why not shut him up in his cavern? If we can do that he will die of hunger, or we can suffocate him with smoke. Whatever happens, we shall have him, sure."

"Easy enough to talk about," growled Bob. "We ought to have a wall on wheels to close up the hole. Have you got one in any of your pockets?"

"It would have been a good idea to bring some solid steel cables and fix them up like wire-netting before the grotto," said Hamilton; and as his imagination was essentially retrospective, and as, forgetting how absolutely bare of everything they were, he lost himself in his ingenious combinations, he excused himself by saying, "Of course, you can't think of every little detail in a complicated expedition like this."

"Listen," went on Raoul. "I think that we can shut up the monster. Do you see these basalt pillars at each side of the cavern? They are solid beyond the possibility of a doubt, are they not? Well, between them and the solid rock there is a gap not more than a yard wide, which runs from one column to the other. This track of the mammoth's is not ten yards long, I should say."

"Eight yards and a half, exactly," decided Fred.

"Very good. Now, this is my idea. Between these columns, or door-posts, if you like, we will fit in whole trees, stripped of their branches, the strongest we can find in the valley. We can build up a barricade as fast as we can bring up the stuff and as high as we think best. Strong, prodigiously strong, as our enemy is, he cannot shatter the rock, and we can make buttresses of pointed trees, with their bases fixed in the ground, which will support the central part of the barricade."

"Not so bad, that," said Bob, "but you forget the game. He's going to take a peep out of his hole once in a while, sure; and do you think he's going to let you shut his door on him without taking a hand? You bet *not,* gentlemen. He would need a half-barrel of alcohol in his head for that, and we haven't more than a bladderful left."

"The devil," said Hamilton; "that's the worst thing about it."

"I quite understand," said Le Fort, "that we cannot do the work with the mammoth looking on, but the barricade will not take long to build if all the trees are got ready beforehand on the ledge, and we can distract his mind for a time with a little amusement. Fire exasperates and maddens him. Very well; let one of us take a stroll around the cavern with a torch in his hand. That will stir him up and keep him inside."

"And the amateur who is going to brandish his little candle under the old boy's tusks? It won't be Toulouack, sure, nor—"

"It will be I."

Bob and Hamilton looked at him dubiously. Then Fred said—

"Raoul, you cannot think of going to your death with a light heart, like that. You wouldn't be much better off, once you were wiped out. The referee would never allow such a risk, even in the most important match."

The artist smiled rather sadly.

"I shall go, all the same. I am not going to risk my life on a mad chance. You remember what the cavern is like inside, don't you, Fred? The walls are honeycombed with holes and corners and crevices where an adroit man can get round, appear and disappear out of his enemy's reach."

"Don't forget his trunk," said Bob; "it will pick you up ten feet away."

"I won't let myself be caught."

"That's easy enough to say. Why, his breath will knock you over fifteen feet off."

"I shall go," was all Raoul said. "Alone or not, I will try this last chance. But I know I can count upon you, my friends, can I not?" added he, already regretting this appearance of distrust.

"There will be two of us to run around inside and do the re-appearing act, as you call it, Raoul."

"No, my dear Fred," said Raoul, clasping his hand. "You are hardly the right build to sandwich yourself in a crevice, and besides that I want you to stay outside to do something just as dangerous. You and Bob will have all you can do to arrange the barricade and the buttresses. We cannot count on the Koriaks, can we, Bob?"

"When there is only one road, you've got to travel by it, even if it rains rocks," said the prospector, conclusively. "I will stay with the other gentlemen, and shut the door of the cage on this d—d bird. You can count Bob in."

CHAPTER XX
THE MAMMOTH'S LAST FIGHT

When night falls, and you are gathered around that domestic hearth so sacred to the Frenchman, in that "home" which the simple-minded Anglo-Saxon believes to be his national specialty, do you ever think of the Stone Age, when our ancestors, entrenched in their caverns, repulsed the attacks of the giant bears, the six-horned rhinoceri, the wild cats as big as lions? With jaws which projected beyond their noses and moustaches like those of the Ainos of modern Japan, armed with pointed spears of flint, they fought for their wives and little ones, who encouraged them from behind their protecting fireplaces.

Fire and the human voice are the two miracles which distinguish monkeys walking upright from their enemies, the animals which go on four paws. The savants tell us that we are 40,000 years from the Stone Age, but if we could traverse the Universe on one of those rays of light which travel 300,000 miles in a second of time, we should see before us the paleolithic man, exactly the same as the savage of Borneo or Japan or Australia, that the cinematograph shows us to-day.

Without the necessity of projecting himself into the infinite, however, Le Fort saw before him, at the extreme corner of Eastern Asia, a quasi-revival of the Quaternary Period. A troop of prognathous apes were scaling the cliffs, and with infinite pains were hoisting up the trees which they had felled at a respectable distance from the cavern. Bob, in their midst, urged on King Toulouack by that example which is better than precept; but in spite of all their efforts the work advanced very slowly, and by night-time scarcely half the number of trees that they wanted had been piled up over the cavern.

Raoul was afraid that the mammoth would come out in search of food and disappear again into the Unknown, and Hamilton had some trouble in convincing him that elephants, when their suspicions are aroused, can go for days without eating. They were reassured by the fact that the mammoth made no sign. All that they heard was some intermittent rumblings far underground, while the entrance remained always open.

At last, on the following evening, everything was ready. Thirty great trees were piled up on the ledge, and all that remained to do was to drop them down horizontally, so that they could pile themselves up between the mountain and the basalt columns. The Koriaks, each at his appointed post, were to guide their descent. Fred and Bob, aided by Toulouack, who had at last plucked up courage, were to adjust the buttresses, which would have Bob's trenches as a support. These trees, sharpened at each end, would fall into mortices made ready for them in the trunks which formed the barricade.

Raoul looked carefully to the two torches of moss and dry leaves which he had saturated with grease. Everything was ready. He raised his face to the stars, which shone with exceptional brilliancy in these cold latitudes. By his side, Natiya, leaning over the opening, was listening to catch the slightest noise.

"Do you hear anything?"

"No."

Le Fort leaned over in his turn to listen, but there was no sound. The stars are always silent. Then he went to sleep with his face turned up to them, and as if transfigured by their light.

In the morning, after a pretense of eating breakfast, they decided on their plan of attack. Raoul and Hamilton, with infinite precaution, glided around the left-hand pillar, and Bob concealed himself behind the one on the right. Toulouack, perched on the ledge, waited for the signal.

Le Fort made sure that his Koriak hunting-knife worked easily in its sheath, and took his flint and steel in his right hand, while he held his two torches in his left. Then he turned towards Hamilton.

"Now for it, Fred. If I don't—come back, you will tell *her* all about it, won't you?"

"Upon my honour as a gentleman," said Fred, who was more disturbed than he liked to show. "Shake hands once more."

"You will wait until I give the signal?"

"Yes, and God be with you."

The young man went around the column, taking advantage of the opening where the trees would fall, and got quickly into a fissure in the rock that he had noticed just inside the entrance to the cavern. There was just a little daylight penetrating the darkness.

On his right Raoul saw an impenetrable wall ten yards high. A little further on was something that looked like the opening of a grotto like Fingal's cave, the floor of which was strewn with leaves and straw. He debated with himself whether to run across, or to steal over silently so as not to alarm his foe, and decided on the latter course. He had almost reached the refuge where the darkness was complete, when he saw two gleaming lights eight yards above his head, which seemed to be following his movements. He trembled and darted behind a curtain of basaltic needles, where he took breath. He had not been deceived, for a few yards away the gigantic form of the mammoth stood out in relief against the dark background of the cavern, and the monster shook his tusks and trumpeted.

It was necessary to make haste. He struck a spark from his flint and steel and lighted his first torch, at the same time giving the whistle that had been agreed on. Two others answered him from without, or he thought he heard them, at the same time as he heard the first tree-trunk crash down among the rocks. Then he heard nothing more but the sharp trumpeting of the monster as he rushed upon the basalt columns which covered him, and made the stones fly even to where he stood.

The smoke of the torch blinded the young man's eyes, the ground shook under his feet, and his ears buzzed like those of an artilleryman in action; but his torch burned in his extended left hand, and he could see that the trees continued to fall, from the gradually diminishing light at the entrance.

Had the mammoth noticed it also? He ceased his rushes for a moment, and turned his trunk towards the outside; and as he did so, Le Fort distinctly heard Bob shout—

"Now for the buttresses, gentlemen—quick!"

The mammoth shook his ears and. lowered his head. He was going to charge the barricade! Raoul left his retreat at all hazards, lighted his second torch, and threw the first one at the monster's feet. The latter turned round, and his trunk almost touched the artist's head, as a gust of hot air threw him to the ground at the moment he was reaching his refuge. He seized his knife, struck at random, and, believing himself lost, recommended his soul to God.

But as he was going to annihilate this insect, the mammoth saw a dazzling light jet out under him. The first torch had set fire to the heap of boughs and dry grass in the cavern. Stung by the attack of this enemy, the red flower of the volcano, the only one that he had ever feared, and put to flight for the first time in his life, the great elephant of the Polar ice thought no longer of combat, only of flight, and, like an enormous catapult of flesh and blood, he rushed upon the barricade. The noise of the shock went through Raoul's head. The first time the monster was thrown upon his side. The second he charged with his eyes closed and his trunk bleeding, and the great trees cracked and bent. The third time they broke off short, and Raoul, leaning against a rock in the cavern, where he was almost suffocated—Raoul Le Fort, with staring eyes, saw his prey burst out to the open air, to liberty, to the ruin of his hopes.

Then he said only the word "Eva," closed his eyes, and sank to the ground. And the flames, drawing in around him, encircled him with a halo of fire from the nether world.

CHAPTER XXI
THE DIVISION OF THE SPOIL

"Rub his forehead with snow, sir. The gentleman hasn't got any bones broken. The d—d animal didn't catch him. If we only had a little whisky, the gentleman would be drinking our healths already."

"Raoul! Raoul! Do you hear me? And to think that I had a drug-store of my own once! Lift him up, Bob."

Le Fort, delightfully surprised at being still alive, was listening. He recognized Fred's voice, and Bob's. He made an effort and opened his eyes, and his return to life was welcomed with a joyful shout.

The young man was stretched upon a bed of leaves very near the grotto, which he saw to be wide open and empty. A little smoke was still issuing from it, and all around the outside twisted and shattered tree-trunks were lying on the ground. He only murmured—

"We are beaten again, and this time—"

"What are you talking about, old man?" said Hamilton's triumphant voice. "Turn round, or rather, let us turn you round. Now then, easy does it, Bob, old man."

With the utmost care the two hunters lifted up their companion with his face towards the valley, and Raoul, to his intense astonishment saw, twenty paces away, the mammoth, his own mammoth primigenius, who had almost crushed him with his powerful trunk, lying dead on the ground. A delirious crowd of Koriaks were dancing around the monstrous body. Raoul thought he had a night-mare, and closed his eyes, murmuring, "It is impossible! You have actually killed him—how? Don't deceive me."

"Hurrah! Raoul, wake up!" shouted Fred, who was also dancing with delight. "We've got him this time, sure. There's nothing for Corliss to do but to send you his com-pliments. Nobody will ever find another pri-primigenius mammoth. Come and see him. We've made an in-dis-put-able record."

"But tell me how it happened. I see that I am awake, and that the mammoth is dead there before me. But how did you manage it?"

"It was this way, sir," said Bob. "Everything was going all right; the trees fell into place as we wanted them, and the buttresses were properly fixed, when we saw the fire break out inside the cage. We said to ourselves that the gentleman was going to be broiled, and our trees as well, and that we were all safe to be 'done;' but we didn't have much time to think about it, for the d—d animal, driven by the fire, charged out on us. It was a great sight. It's a pity you were not here to see it."

"I was getting out of the way under a tree, and I heard Bob shout, 'Look out for yourselves, boys!'" interrupted Hamilton.

"I fell on my back in my trench," went on Bob, "and I saw the beast doing a dance over my head. Then we heard something like a mountain falling down, and when we got up we saw what you see now, sir."

"But I don't understand at all," repeated Raoul, more and more bewildered.

"Well, you can walk a little now. Easy—there. Look!"

Fred, supporting Raoul, brought him in front of the mammoth's enormous head, and there Le Fort saw a sharp stake—a whole trunk of a tree—driven a full yard into the monster's brain between his tusks.

"It's one of the buttresses," explained Fred. "The an-imal charged the barricade head down and shattered it, but at the same time he drove the middle buttress into his skull with all his force. He made two jumps and fell dead."

"We needn't have taken all that trouble," said Bob. "The best hunter is the game that hunts itself."

A tremendous noise re-echoed in the cavern. "Mamantou is dead! Mamantou toukou cohur!"

Bob added his hurrahs to the howls of the Koriaks, and on top of the corpse the Vice-President of the Athletic Club thundered out, in honour of his friend, an adaptation of the French hunting song—

> "The mammoth's met his death,
>   Conquerors we are;
>   I am out of breath,
>   I have run so far.

> "The fattest of his meat
>   Fairly earned have we,
>   And I know that sweet
>   And tender it will be."

Before Le Fort's eyes passed a dazzling vision, first Corliss, and then Eva, radiant with her lover's triumph, and saying, "I was sure of you!" with her great eyes full of love; it was an unexampled minute of happiness for the young artist, who was, for the first time, sure of success, and also absolutely forgot that he was shipwrecked six thousand miles away from Cavanagh's Museum.

His injuries were not severe. A semi-suffocation had overcome him more than had the attack of the mammoth, who had just failed of crushing him with his trunk. In a few hours he was himself again, and in spite of his fatigue he insisted on superintending the important operation of dissecting the monster, which had now to be undertaken.

It was a Herculean task. The primigenius was thirty-six feet high, and its tusks alone must have weighed fifteen hundred pounds. There were tons of meat to be cut off this colossal game, enough for them to eat forever, according to Toulouack. For that reason, before beginning to cut up the carcass, it was fitting that the occasion should be duly celebrated. "Mamantou toukou cohur!"

The *nakoot,* or sorcerer, manipulated his willow wands, and the king sprinkled his Chaddi with blood. The Koriaks dressed themselves in their finest clothes, knee-breeches of skin, and coats of bear or fox fur, with the tails of the animals hanging from their belts. They had cleaned the grease from their faces with shells, while the queens had done the same good office for each other with their tongues.

The faces of these ladies were framed in the skins of fawns, with black stones in place of eyes. They waddled along in style, dressed in beautiful white dalmatics, bordered with the skins of the grey lynx, the fox, the wolf, or the otter. Their hoods, like halos around their heads, bristling with the fur of the carcajou, were balanced on top of their chignons, which were knowingly brought back from the temples. Necklaces of different-coloured skins, passing from one ear to the other, hung under their chins.

Natiya surpassed them all in magnificence. She wore on her head the skin of a "mitchagatchi" bird, fashioned in the shape of a crescent, with two white aigrettes, and two long tresses of hair, which was certainly not black, fell to her waist on each side. Her eyes shone with pride between her narrow eyelids, and her smile and her whole bearing said—

"See this, and this! How do you think I look?"

"Oui-hihi! Where did she get it? What man gave it to her?"

What man? The jealous voices of the other queens might have said it a hundred times, and Le Fort and Hamilton would not have believed it, if they had not seen Bob without his beard, and much embarrassed thereby. His face was clean-shaven for a couple of inches above his chin, instead of being adorned with the beautiful long patriarchal beard which had before that kept his neck warm.

"She had done a lot of cooking for me—and she is a good sort, after all, sir."

The prospector stammered forth a few similar explanations, and Toulouack came and thanked him warmly. Hamilton turned away to conceal his delight, and the festivities began.

The queens, perched on the mammoth's back, began by striking two bones together, to the measure of their rowing-chorus in the oomiak—

"Ey, yan, yan, yan, ah!"

The Koriaks, hand-in-hand around the carcass, circled slowly, facing outwards. The king, who had on a cap of white bearskin, pivoted in his tracks in the opposite direction, in a movement like that of the earth around the sun. At intervals he would stop and shout at the top of his voice—

"Annah eya! Eya annah!"

And the others sang in a bass chorus—

"Hijo! Hijo!"

Natiya imitated the slightest movement of her lord and master, but as silently as a ghost. But occasionally she threw in a little side step, winking in time with her eyes—like the ballet at the opera in Paris.

After the ballet the queens climbed down, and Toulouack took their place on top of the mammoth.

"Who was it that killed thee?" he cried.

The Koriaks answered in chorus—

"It was not we; it was the Russians."

"Who will strip off thy skin?"

"Not we; the Russians."

The mammoth probably had his own opinion on that point. Then the banquet began. The menu, which will be handed down to posterity, was as follows:—

Dried fish sewed in fir-bark, *à la* seal oil.
Mammoth's blood boiled in reindeer dung
(which tastes like a swallow's nest).

Fire-water.
Whale's fat (ortchork) raw, *à la* lamp oil.
Salad of vegetables from the mamantou's stomach.
Fire-water. Fire-water.
Mamantou cooked in seal-oil
which has fermented fifteen in the sun
(which smells almost as bad as Limburger cheese).
Fire-water. Fire-water. Fire-water.

The whole was followed by raw mammoth, that is to say, the winding up of the banquet and the beginning of the division of the spoil. The Koriaks, already glutted with food, threw themselves on the carcass and pulled off the flesh in strips, in spite of Hamilton's attempted interference. They swallowed without chewing everything that came in their way, for fear someone else should get it. Their stomachs protruded and they rolled on the ground, crying, "I'm stifling! I'm choking! Oh, la la! Oui, hi-hi!"

Then the medicine man was called in, and if they had furs to pay for his attendance, he laid them on the ground and performed a primitive massage cure by walking on their stomachs. But it is quite impossible in a Christian country to describe at length one of these Esquimaux or Koriak feasts. The worst sufferer was King Toulouack, who died of a surfeit of mammoth. The waltz-step massage of the *nakoot,* their invocations to the Chaddi, even the smoke of the old boots which Bob burned under his nose, were unable to save him, and he expired three days after the festivities.

His subjects buried him with his face to the east, building a little circular wall around him to protect him from the evil spirits of the North. An opening was left for the spirits of the South, who are friendly to the Koriaks. His implements of hunting and fishing were hung up at the entrance, with a strip of whale-skin to show that he had been a king, and the inevitable salmon of the dead. His wives went to rub noses with other savages, and Fred Hamilton, Vice-President of the Athletic Club of New York, was proclaimed his successor, as King of Ya-Thenaoddi! Although he would not acknowledge it, the title pleased him, and he found that the Far North had something to be said in its favour, even in comparison with more temperate latitudes.

"Now, Raoul, I am going to order them to cut up our skeleton. The skin is unfortunately destroyed, but the bones are all right. We will take them to the Bay of the Last Judgment, near the sea. It will be easy to put them on board ship some day."

"Some day? It's a long way off, gentlemen," remarked Bob. "We mustn't forget to hang up some quarters of meat in the cave for this winter."

What the old trapper said was too true. The winter was coming on quickly to meet the conquerors of the mammoth, who were still prisoners on an unknown coast. It was necessary to look forward to winter quarters.*

In the meantime, the enormous skeleton was taken apart and divided into a number of pieces, fastened together with lashings of skin. After three weeks of assiduous cleaning, the mammoth was arranged on the ground in fifty packages. Le Fort made an exact plan of the collection, and numbered each section. The Corliss Museum was going to possess, at a near date, the finest specimen of the *Elephas primigenius* that could be desired, and it only remained, in the Steel King's words, to "deliver the order."

"Who knows but we may find some belated whaler coming down from the Arctic basin?"

---

* Le Fort and his companions were nearer Behring Straits than they supposed, as will be seen later. What they had supposed to be the Bay of Kaliutchin was in reality an unnamed bay near Cape Serdtze Kamen.—A. S.

Hamilton shook his head, and Bob remarked—

"It's a fine large game, but confoundedly bulky. The first thing to do is to get it down to the shore of the bay."

When the king broached the matter to his subjects, a strike broke out which had probably been brewing for some time.

"What is the good of our working? Look at our ribs! We are as thin as wolves in the winter;" and the ex-queens added, "Hihi! Bad luck is after us here. Yo! See what happened to *her* and to *him.*" (The Koriaks never pronounce the names of the dead.) "It is the vengeance of the enemy."

One of the king's lieutenants added, "No more fire-water—no more work."

The ultimatum could not have been more definitely put before his Majesty King Hamilton. This deplorable fire-water had made him at once king and prisoner, for the Koriaks would not leave him alone.

What was to be done in such a dilemma, if not to put a good face on against a revolution? Le Fort, who was distracted by this unexpected delay, had to yield to his friend's good sense.

"What should I gain if I smashed one or two of them?" said Hamilton. "The others would only run away, and we could get no other assistance. We are helpless by ourselves. The best thing to do is to go back to Ya-Thenaoddi and bring back an oomiak full of alcohol. Do you see any other way to keep these brutes at work?"

"No; but the mammoth?"

"Well, what about him?"

"Who will look after him?"

"He will look after himself. He wouldn't be very easy to steal. I ought to have included in our outfit a—"

"Fred, we will leave Bob here with half a dozen Koriaks, if it is only to keep the wolves away."

"All right, Raoul; you are right. That is, if we can find half a dozen to stay."

CHAPTER XXII
BOB TAKES AN OATH

The women of Ya-Thenaoddi, squatted around Aowena, Ervik's wife, were chewing birds' skins, turned inside out like old gloves, to make them white and to express all the oil from their pores. One of them, whose mouth was free because she had just taken out an eider-duck skin to scrape it with a shell, jumped up as she looked to the north.

"Kratsia! What a surprise! See, down there on the river, they have come back."

Her companions hastened to spit out their quids, which now perhaps ornament the pretty, perfumed shoulder of some Parisienne, and hastened to the bank.

"Toroa! Kratsia! You have come at last. Welcome!"

Their reception of their husbands was as amiable as their appearance was hideous. Their tightly fitting reindeer-skin trousers, their blouses made of the long-haired fur of the carcajou, and the hoods which protected their high chignons, often got by fraud from their husbands' hair, made a hairy *tout-ensemble* which placed them at the very foot of the animal scale. That had been Le Fort's first impression when he got back from the open sea, where he had seen hundreds of seals with human eyes who had growled, "Ho! ho! get out!" at him, and then slid into the sea with a friendly nod as he drew near.

But the wives soon proved that they were human. Their cries of "Kratsia" and "Toroa" changed into a chorus of reproaches, when they saw that there was nothing at the sterns of the kayaks.

"Fine hunters you are! Ouch! We want oil, and you bring us water. What fish shall we have to eat? Are you men? You've done well to go so far and bring back nothing. People that can't support their wives don't deserve to have any."

Hamilton and his friends made straight for their huts, which they entered with that inexpressible feeling of being at home once more that one feels in those regions where outdoor life is one long and painful struggle.

The Koriaks told their companions the story of their successes and defeats. The death of the mamantou was admirably described, as the ivory castagnettes imitated the successive charges of the monster. "Ra-ta-tat! -ta-tat!" then a silence of death, smoke, flames, ra-ta-tatatt, and at length "Baoum" went the bones. Everybody fell flat on the ground. Was the enemy really dead? Yes. When they felt quite certain, each one with the whole strength of his lungs sent up the shout—

"Mamantou toukou cohur."

Sickingen's treason, and his destruction along with Ervik's party, and at last Toulouack's death, were received with an explosion of astonishment which even reached the ears of the king underground, and he wondered if the Koriaks would ever return to the Happy Valley.

"There is our salvation," said Hamilton, slapping the still. "Raoul, we will start work at once."

The distillery accordingly opened its doors the next day. The savages needed no urging to bring in all the berries needed, and the worm ran night and day.

"If there were any petroleum springs here, as there are in Siberia," said La Fort, "we could produce ten times as much."

But Fred respected his new industry too much for that.

"Never!" said he. "My alcohol may be dry, but it is not adulterated. I shall take a sample of it back to the Club."

Tuli was inconsolable. At night she went out to mourn by herself on the tundra, for the enemy had bereaved her of the great white chief who had been going to marry her. Her sisters tried to bring her to reason by saying—

"Are the Russians our equals? Don't you know that they are the children of a grey dog and an outcast Koriak woman?"

Le Fort was astounded when he understood the meaning of these savages—he, who looked on them from the point of view of a European, the heir of twenty centuries of Christianity and civilization, and the celebrated phrase of one of Darwin's disciples sounded in his brain: "If we are better than the monkeys, we owe it mostly to Woman. She did not wish to remain in a grade of life which finally began to seem ridiculous."

In spite of these distractions, the time passed slowly in an impatience which, in the young Frenchman, became a high fever. "How long would it take to distil enough fire-water and get back to the cave of the mammoth?" Raoul asked himself one night, gazing in the direction where he had left Bob, alone with some natives, on guard over his treasure.

Very far in the north the sky touched the ice-fields. Suddenly it grew purple with the flames which were the fore-runners of the Arctic winter, changing colour like the Bengal lights of a vast firework display. Luminous globes sprang into the air, spread out into fantastic lotus-flowers against the blue-black of infinity, and melted away into space. Then came rockets, springing from the ground, chasing and interlacing and making a vast bouquet of sparks, and the lights came back to a dance of the will-o'-the-wisps on phosphorescent winding-sheets. Tuli, who had crouched herself down by the side of the white man, murmured—

"It is the dance of the dead; not up there, but down below"—and she pointed to the ground. "Look at the water which separates us from them. They are down there—waiting for us."

A shadow stood before the man and the woman. Tuli uttered a cry. Raoul stepped forward, and then recoiled with his hands before his eyes.

"Bob, in Heaven's name, what is the matter?"

It was, in fact, the old trapper—this phantom which had come from no one knew where, but so pale and changed in appearance that Tuli remained face downwards on the ground. She did not dare to look on death.

"Bob, speak, I beg you!"

Bob uttered a sigh, reeled, and fell stiff on the ground. Le Fort called Hamilton, and the two carried the prospector into the hut.

"Just a fainting fit, Raoul—a drop will bring him to. Raoul, restrain yourself. Look, you are trembling all over. The man has come back for provisions, that's all."

"Provisions! And the mammoth?"

This word waked Bob out of his stupor. He looked around him, saw the still, stood up automatically, and, before Hamilton could stop him, had thrown the machine on the ground, where it broke into a thousand pieces.

The smell of alcohol filled the air. Fred shouted out—

"Poor wretch, he is mad! Now, what shall we do?" and, putting him forcibly down on the furs, he sat on his chest. At length Bob spoke—

"You don't need your machine any more."

"How so?"

"The mammoth has gone away with Sickingen."

"Mad! quite mad!" insisted Hamilton, to prevent Le Fort from hearing him.

But Bob went on with renewed energy—

"Bob is not mad, and Bob is not drunk, but he was drunk when Sickingen came back on the third day after you left. He had some whisky, real whisky. We all had some."

"The miserable wretch! Then he wasn't killed?"

"Bob got properly full. When he came to himself, there was not a bone, not a mammoth, not a Count—only some tracks on the ground, some traces of white men—fellows from some whaler who came and robbed us."

The prospector began to curse between his teeth. The others said nothing. The deathlike silence of the Far North invaded their den. One would have said it was the end of everything. Then Bob stood up again, and Le Fort's fever seemed to have passed into his eyes. He took off his fur cap and held up one hand.

"In the name of the Holy Trinity, I swear never to rest until I have caught that thief—so help me God!"

Raoul went out of the hut, suffocated by the stifling atmosphere. Out on the waste of the tundra, he heard voices calling him from afar—

"Le Fort! Le Fort!"

Did they come from heaven or from earth—from below, where the enemy was lying in wait under the moss, or from above, where, on the clouds, the spirits of the dead were dancing? His mouth opened and his tongue protruded. He burst out laughing, and started off on a run. What a jolly time he had had, and what a good story to tell in the Club in New York, where the doors would swing open to receive him! and behind him the noises of a great city followed him, like a train which pursues you between two rails, two fences, two unscalable walls. Where were the whales gone? And the seals, who cried, "Ho! ho! get out"? Ah, how good it was to feel the cold air on one's dry tongue! The train—no, it was Mamantou who overtook him, and, as he fell, put his foot upon him, and on each side of him there was a splash of blood where his face had been. Mercy of Heaven! After that there was nothing left but to die, and he was dying.

CHAPTER XXIII
A LAST CHANCE

When you are knocked down and robbed at a street corner, you do not feel it much at the moment, but you suffer horribly when you come to yourself and realize your loss. Then death itself would seem preferable. So the sea whispered to Le Fort, on the banks of the Bay of the Last Judgment, where he had come in an oomiak with Hamilton, Bob, and Tuli. The latter was determined to follow her "Russian" to the end of the world, and the others wanted—what did they want? They did not know exactly what they hoped to get in this last desperate cruise in search of Sickingen, who was certainly stronger than they, if they had found him. As he thought of it, the artist looked at the water so despairingly that Hamilton was frightened, and said—

"Oh, Raoul, think of the *other thing!*"

But the American did not know that, beyond the Arctic fog, on the other side of the world, there were two black eyes looking at his friend, two eyes which Le Fort could not see distinctly, because before them or behind them he could see the diamond of a French king writing on a window in a castle on the Loire—

"Souvent femme varie—"

"Often—" What then? Oh, he remembered now! But it was false, of course; he lied, this French king. Why should one trouble about a lie?

"Raoul! Raoul, look at the seals? Aren't they amusing?"

The seals were dancing around the icebergs far and near, for the coming of winter was a joyful time for them. When they were tired, they held on to the edge of the ice with their long ivory tusks, and blew out a long breath like balloons collapsing. Those who were already on the ice-floes came and pushed them off, so that they could keep possession of their sunshiny corners, for the sun was soon going to disappear, sooner than the wanderers expected. They were camping on an unknown coast, which they were following without knowing where it would lead them. Raoul, sitting by a fire which Bob had scraped together, with his head in his hands, was dreaming of the *Côté d' Azur;* of Cannes so white, Hyères with its golden islands, Nice that shines, and Mentone that sparkles. He could breathe the odour of the jasmine, the violet, the myrtle, the laurel, and hear the songs of that Provence, the land of love and song, where he had hoped one day to go with Eva. Eva! He looked around him. He had fallen down the ladder of three thousand years of civilization. Was he still able to count? Was he really the creature of an almighty and beneficent God?

"Gentlemen! Le Fort, Hamilton, help! quick, quick!" cried Bob.

Le Fort rushed to the shore where his two companions were trying to haul their canoe up on the bank. A field of floating ice had come down from the North, surrounding a group of icebergs, which were crushing and falling over each other. Bob had seen them too late. The ice had passed under the stern of the canoe, seized it in a vice, carried it away from the unfortunates, and wrecked it in a few seconds. The three men had scarcely time to save themselves. A second shipwreck—was it not the end of everything for them?

When people are absolutely desperate, there is no need to discuss the matter. They had some pieces of the mammoth left, and Tuli might catch some fish. It was of no use to go back, and it seemed best to stake all on one throw and go on to East Cape.

"We'll get there sometime," said Bob. "Then we shall know what to do."

Le Fort did not even ask him what his idea was, because he could only think of the Count von Sickingen—of the thief's triumphant return to New York.

"We'll catch him," said Hamilton, who had got back all his old good-humour. "You Frenchmen have no perseverance. We've no boat? All right, we'll go on foot, that's all."

The little band marched on bravely for ten days, and then the cold became terrible. Their lips smarted as their breath turned into snow, and they were obliged to rub the corners of their eyes to keep them from freezing. But they kept walking on.

They had eaten their last bit of mammoth, and Tuli could catch no more fish, for all the animal life of this part of the world had fled to the South. There was nothing before them but the eternal bare beach, the waves which broke on the icy bank, and behind them the dead tundra.

In spite of his great physical powers, Hamilton was the first to give way to fatigue. He had a pain under his arms as if a knife had been stuck between his ribs. He could not see with his left eye nor hear with his left ear; and he lay down under an overhanging snow-drift.

"Let me die here," he said to Le Fort. "Go on, I know that you will pull through. As for me"—with a last attempt at a joke—"you will register my name and the record of the mammoth at the Club. I am paying in advance for my success."

"Leave you? Never! If you die here, I will die by your side," said Raoul; "and it seems as if it were all that is left to us. Shake hands, my dear old boy."

Then Bob chimed in, "Sir, it's all my fault, but I will make up for it. You cannot walk any further—well, let's sail."

"He's mad—quite mad!" said Le Fort to himself; and then aloud, "All right. Where is the boat?"

"The boat? One of these ice-floes. The current runs
to the east, towards the American coast. Bob told you in
'Frisco that he crossed Behring Straits on a piece of floating ice, and you thought that the whisky was talking. Now,
gentlemen, you are going to see how Bob made the trip."

Le Fort agreed. It was all the same whether they died
on land or on the sea, and there was always the thousand-
to-one chance of running across some whaler or some late
steamer from the Klondike.

Tuli brought some of the mice from the tundra, and Bob
got together some firs, a little wood, two spears and some
fishing-lines. Then he began to watch the ice-floes which
passed by continually, as they would strike an iceberg, re-
volve with the shock, and get into the current again. The
prospector let a number of pieces of ice drive down before
him, examining their size and shape carefully. At last he
made up his mind.

"Get ready. Lean on me, Hamilton. Quick, jump!"

Without any accident or the loss of any of their slender
stock of provisions, the three shipwrecked mariners of Ya-
Thenaoddi found themselves safe on their new domain, a
flat ice-floe thirty yards long by a dozen wide, which had
not given under their weight. Hamilton, lying on the furs,
got a little of his strength back as he drank some tea which
Le Fort and Tuli made out of lichens. Bob, stretched out
on his stomach, found to his satisfaction that the block of
ice went deep down into the sea, and seemed to be perfectly stable.

"Let us hope that our boat won't turn upside down," he
growled, as he scooped out a den in the snow. "Tuli, throw
the lines out astern."

Le Fort anxiously watched the drift of the ice-floes,
and was astonished and delighted at their comparative
speed. They could hope to get over nearly two miles an
hour on their improvised raft, and the direction was what
they wanted, being due south-east. What better could they
wish for in such an awkward corner?

In the morning, towards three o'clock, the whole sky grew white from east to west, as if the Milky Way had poured out the whiteness of its train of stars. The night was filled with a Biblical light, like that of the third day of the Creation before there was light, and in this floating whiteness appeared a queenly city, with its wide ramparts, its high buildings, its cathedral towers surmounted with the Roman cross—some capital city of another world. On its boulevards the tops of the trees pierced the fog which concealed the people in its streets. Le Fort seemed to hear music, singing, the murmuring voices of a crowd of people, and to get nearer to them he stretched out his arms. A hand seized him from behind.

"Sir, you are going to fall into the water."

"Oh, Bob, what is it up there? Am I out of my mind?"

"No, sir. It is the 'Sleeping City,'* that they talk so much about in 'Frisco. We must be near the Alaskan coast. Cheer up, sir!"

As he spoke the wonderful vision vanished by degrees as frost pictures melt away on a window-pane. Tuli, crouched at their feet, groaned—

"It is the vengeance of the Mamantou. Oh, Lifa, Lifa!"

* This extraordinary phenomenon, a sort of mirage, appears every year in Glacier Bay, in Alaska, and has been the subject of many discussions. It is asserted to be the reflection of the city of Bristol in England. The "Sleeping City" was photographed in 1889 by Professor Willoughby, of Juneau, Alaska.—A. S.

Coachwhip note: This footnote refers to Richard Willoughby's 'Silent City' hoax.

CHAPTER XXIV
HOW SICKINGEN CAME BACK VICTORIOUS

Seven gentlemen were holding a meeting around a table covered with maps. Three hundred years ago, as dukes, counts, or barons, with sword on thigh and helmet on head, they would have summoned their men-at-arms to their standards, and descended from their strongholds to ravage the people in the plains.

A hundred years—thirty years ago—as marshals, generals, commanders of army corps, they would have thrown their countless legions into the richest territories of their neighbours, where there is always glory and profit to be got, and where they will always fight, perhaps, as long as Europe shall endure. Now, in place of the loud-voiced heralds with their three knocks upon the castle-gate, or aides-de-camp with flags of truce, the telegraph ticked from one end to the other of the world which waited on these great and powerful millionaires, the lords paramount of the new age. A word, a luminous zigzag flashing across space which exists no more, a word of command to hundreds of thousands of mercenaries, and a twentieth-century war, of which the people pay all the expenses—a war of rates and rebates and tariffs, is declared between the great railroad companies. The lightning express of the world has scattered the years behind it, like the sand behind a railway train, but the times have not changed since men kneeled before the Golden Calf, as they will always kneel to the last day of their sinful race.

The directors of the Grand Central were separating after having approved the plan of campaign drawn up by their president, John N. Corliss. Their lines of rail were going to annex a country seventeen times as large as France, between New York and San Francisco. Their locomotives were to bind together the West and the East—to join London, Paris, New York, and the Atlantic, to the Pacific coast, whence five hundred and seventy-five millions of the Mongolian race were to draw their supplies.

And while the railway barons were taking their departure, dreaming of conquest, their chief, Corliss, was already at work. With a telephone in his hand, he was watching the tape of a stock-ticker as it rolled under his eyes. The quotations on the San Francisco Stock Exchange passed before him, and every now and then he shouted an order into his telephone. All at once the quotations were interrupted. Corliss, astounded, looked at his watch and wondered if the Exchange had become bankrupt. Then after some figures some words appeared. "Special urgent message—"

"There'll be one operator out of a job to-night," thought Corliss. "To have the cheek to break in on the quotations of the Stock Exchange—Great Scott!"

"From Count von Sickingen," continued the tape, "just landed from the whaling-steamer *Salvador* with complete skeleton of immense mammoth primigenius," leaning over the narrow strip of paper Corliss pulled at it to get it out quicker, "best regards Senator Corliss and Miss Eva—Los Angelos oil, 75; Colorado gold, 120," and the quotations continued on the tape. The Steel King took up his telephone again imperturbably, but the session of the Exchange had never been so tiresome to him. When he had given his last order, he hurriedly took down his domestic telephone and asked if Miss Eva would come down, and then, his calmness being exhausted, he exploded into a third mouthpiece—

"Hello! Corliss Museum! Cavanagh! Hurrah, Joshua! We've got our primigenius! Throw down that d—d plaster skeleton, old man—we've got a real one—the biggest in the world—real primigenius—hip, hip, hurrah!"

The telephone girls, who could not find enough receivers to go round, heard a feeble voice, almost like the breath of a ghost, which said—

"Worthy Senator—worthy young man—what a glorious day—now I am ready to die!"

Corliss cut short Cavanagh's transports as Eva entered. Since Raoul's departure the young girl had traveled about from Florida to the Adirondacks, from New York to Denver, without forgetting for a second the man whom she loved. The entire absence of any news from him had not discouraged her, for she had expected it, but at the same time it was beginning to distress her.

With his arms outstretched and his eyes shining, in the highest state of exaltation of which his nature was capable, Corliss greeted her with these words—

"The *Salvador* has come back with my mammoth, a complete specimen of the primigenius, the biggest on earth!"

"Ah, I knew he would come back successful!" cried the young girl, as she fell almost fainting into her father's arms. But it was a moment of happiness too bright to last, like all human joys. When she had recovered herself, she said, "Quick, papa! tell me all about it. Where is Raoul's telegram?"

Corliss started. "Who's Raoul? No, it's Sickingen—Count von Sickingen. He has come back with a complete specimen of the primigenius."

Eva stood up, with a face as white as the dead.

"Papa, didn't you say it was the *Salvador? The Salvador* is Raoul's—M. le Fort's ship."

"You're right," said Corliss, after a moment's thought; "and yet there is no room for doubt. The telegram is from Sickingen, and it is he who found the mammoth."

The young girl could not restrain her emotion.

"For mercy's sake telegraph yourself, and find out the truth!"

Before Corliss could answer a bell rang and the ticker started again. The Steel King motioned to his daughter to be quiet, and began to read the tape. At the first words his face grew dark and he opened his mouth, but dared not trust himself to speak. Then, taking a pencil, he wrote rapidly, and, without another word, handed Eva the following—

> "To complete my telegram from Exchange, have sad duty informing you that Le Fort expedition and part crew of *Salvador* were wrecked and lost while whale-hunting in Behring Straits. Found *Salvador* again, in charge first mate, cruising off coast to which my expedition had brought skeleton primigenius, of which have some fragments of skin, is unique specimen, thirty-six feet high. Taking special train for New York to-morrow. Respectful compliments Miss Eva.—Ulrich Von Sickingen."

Eva read the frightful news without at first understanding it. She steadied herself so as not to fall, and spelled out the words one by one, trying to draw some comfort from them, and hoping against hope.

"Lost!" murmured she. "Perhaps he is yet alive."

The despair in her eyes made her father turn his own away, and he made a vague gesture.

"Well, what did he want to get mixed up in a row like that for? That is not what he started out for. We've got lots of whales' skeletons in the Museum."

Eva burst out sobbing, and went away with the fatal despatch in her hand, while the Senator stood overwhelmed. He had forgotten to take this aspect of the question into consideration. He really loved his daughter, and her grief went to his heart; but a promise is a promise. The Frenchman was lacking in punctuality, rather a Bohemian, while Sickingen had succeeded—that was the vital point.

The Steel King picked up a telephone—Cavanagh first.

"Hello! What is the height of the St. Petersburg mammoth?"

"Thirty-one feet four, worthy Sen—"

"My mammoth is thirty-six feet high, Joshua."

"Worthy—"

Corliss sent to the twenty-seven evening papers the following notice—

> "An unprecedented success has crowned the efforts of Senator Corliss. The New York Museum will see in a few days, etc., etc."

The public was not obliged to wait even "a few days," for the next morning, while Sickingen's mammoth was on its way, a regiment of elephants primigenius, elephants Columbi, elephants of antiquity, not to speak of one dinotherium (δεινος, terrible; θηριον, animal) and four mastodons (μαστος, breast; οδους, tooth), descended on seventy millions of bewildered readers. The curator of the famous Smithsonian Institute wrote a pamphlet, "Ab Irato Calamo," to correct the translation of μαστος, which should be read "nipple," not "breast," and to protest, in the name of science, against this deplorable confusion of the Miocene periods (dinotherium and mastodon), with the Pliocene (Antarctic elephant) and Quaternary (mammoth primigenius). Such an ignorant vulgarization—

Bah! What headway could this feeble wail from a scientific man make against a deluge of articles, copied helter-skelter, anyhow from the encyclopaedias? There was only this one subject of conversation in the clubs, the saloons, under the electric lights of great cities, and the petroleum lamps of scattered villages, or around the

camp-fires of the Far West. The mammoth! Corliss's primigenius!

The crowds overflowed the stations through which the
train conveying the mammoth passed. The cowboys of
the Fleur-de-Lys Ranch, where once Sarah Bernhardt so
narrowly escaped abduction, those of Baron du Grancey's
ranch, and those of the T. O. T. and the S. N. J., stopped
the train at Green River, in Wyoming.

"Where is he? We'll see if he was killed this year or ten
thousand years ago. So much the worse for the Count if
he's fooling us!"

But the Count was not fooling them. The cowboys declared that the bones were still "green," in the name of
God and their revolvers, and after carrying Ulrich around
in triumph, replaced him in his Pullman car, with—

"Start her along, engineer! Now, boys, a grand salute—
fire!"

And so the mammoth of the Happy Valley sped across
the continent. Every quarter of an hour the telegraph sent
a report of its progress to New York, where the transpar-
encies recorded it all through the night, and as the hour
of its arrival drew near, the crowd, in a feverish state of
excitement, grew to such dimensions that half a million
people besieged the Grand Central Station, where, with
bayonets fixed on their Krag-Jorgensen rifles, the 37th
regiment of the National Guard of New York kept back
this enormous mass of people.

In this wild chaos, every member of the crowd was
talking of the extraordinary adventures that the hero of
the day, cool and disdainful as ever, had summarized for
the reporters in San Francisco.

"Having left San Francisco and been shipwrecked
with some hunters on the Siberian coast, near the Bay of
Anadyr, he had run across a tribe of savage fishermen, who
had told him of the existence of a gigantic monster in the
interior. Sickingen and his companions, guided by a native
woman, had followed the tracks of the mastodon and come

up with him in a rocky creek, where he, Sickingen, having attacked the monster several times at the risk of his life and with the loss of five men, had succeeded in lodging a ball in the eye of the giant mammoth, who had succumbed after a short but frightful struggle.

"After this success, which had come sooner than he had dared to hope for, the little band, reinforced by some of the natives, had with unheard-of labour, brought the packages of bones down to the coast, where Sickingen expected to be obliged to wait for a Norwegian whaling-ship that he had chartered for the following summer; but the *Salvador,* which had been cruising about at random ever since the tragic death of her captain and the unfortunate Frenchman, who had both been drowned while chasing a whale, had appeared on the coast, had seen their signals, and Sickingen had put his precious trophy on board. Their return had been very perilous, for the ice had thickened as the nights became more bitterly cold, and more than once they had been nearly wrecked in the floes. But they had got back in safety, and Count von Sickingen congratulated himself on the valuable contribution that he had been enabled to make to the cause of American science."

This story, had been enthusiastically received, for, in view of the unheard-of extravagance of this hunt after a prehistoric monster, nobody noticed the vagueness of some of the details of the statement. On the day after the arrival of the *Salvador,* twenty different accounts of this fantastic campaign appeared. An illustrated newspaper had already published a picture representing "the critical moment," with Sickingen, with his monocle in his eye, taking aim at the monster—the picture being based on some kodak snapshots taken by a member of the expedition! Two or three of the San Francisco reporters had been rather surprised at the disappearance of all the Count's companions, for all of them, whether seal-hunters or sailors of the *Salvador,* had disappeared no one knew whither, with their pockets full of money, within a couple of hours after the steamer arrived; but no one troubled his head over these petty details. As Corliss had remarked, there was one vital point—the Count was there surrounded by the packages that contained the precious skeleton.

What more would you have?

And on the rails which the special devoured as it sped on to New York, Ulrich von Sickingen congratulated himself that behind him, the impregnable barrier of the Polar ice guaranteed him for six months against pursuit. In six months he would be at Rüheldeck with Eva. Really, his luck had served him well so far.

His luck! The German thought of all that he owed to it. It was that which had brought him to Ya-Thenaoddi, which had saved him from the mammoth's mad rush which had blotted out all his companions except Ervik, who, like him, had taken refuge in the top of a fir-tree. For ten days they had wandered amongst the rocks, living on their slender stock of provisions, and accompanied by one frightened Koriak who had not dared to go back to Toulouack's people, especially after the disappearance of the Tchouktchis, their friends of an hour whom they had chanced to meet.

Only the hope of revenge had kept up the spirits of the Count and his hatred for Raoul, which was kept warm by his lonely distress. From the top of a hill, he, Sickingen, had seen Raoul's friends celebrate their victory and had witnessed the triumphs of his enemies, while he was half dead with rage and fatigue, to which he would have given way if his savage friend, who was always on the look-out, had not seen, one morning, the outlines of a ship cruising in the straits. It was the *Salvador*.

This sight gave him new life. A signal fire brought the whaler into a deep bay, where Le Fort, Hamilton, and their Koriaks could not see it. When he got on board, Sickingen persuaded the mate to anchor on the coast for a few days, to allow him to ship the mammoth that he had killed. To conceal from the people on the ship that he was going to rob his rivals, as soon as the last of them had disappeared in the direction of Ya-Thenaoddi, he had gone by himself to meet Bob and his men, had got them drunk with whisky from the ship, and stowed them away in the cave. Not a soul on board of the *Salvador* suspecting their existence.

The Grand Central Station in New York was gaily decorated with flags, and a brass band struck up, "Johnny, get your gun, get your gun, get your gun," while a hundred thousand—three hundred thousand—voices joined in the chorus, in honour of the hero. It was Jersey City, Brooklyn, Manhattan, and the Bronx—it was Greater New York, three millions of people, and victory!

Sickingen alighted from the Pullman under a rain of flowers. Senator Corliss, in evening dress, very grave and almost stirred to excitement, held out two hands—

"Count Ulrich von Sickingen, I thank you on my own behalf and on the behalf of New York."

"The worthy conqueror of science—the intrepid pioneer of paleontology," stammered Cavanagh, clinging to his arm.

The crowd pressed round them, some women fainted and had to be carried away, and the Chief of Police motioned the troops to advance, but the soldiers waved their bayonets in the air, with, "Hurrah for Sickingen! Hurrah for Corliss!"

The crowd invaded the platform and their shouts, under the great arched roof, became a Niagara of human voices. Sickingen felt that he had conquered fortune and glory, and a real emotion relaxed his impenetrable mask of steel, as he said—

"Senator, I am happy to have realized the dream of your life, as well as my own, which is to become your son-in-law;" and the ovation which New York gave them swept the two out, hand-in-hand. Yes, it was the triumph of Ulrich's life. "Hurrah for Corliss! Hurrah for Sickingen!"

CHAPTER XXV
"BUT IF—"

The next morning, after having received forty photographers and sixty reporters, after inscribing his precious signature in a hundred albums and accepting numberless invitations from learned bodies and universities, Count von Sickingen asked permission to present his compliments to Miss Corliss, but he learned to his intense disgust that Miss Corliss was "not at home to anybody." Since the night before, the non-appearance of his promised *fiancée* had disturbed him very much, and without delay he went to ask the Senator for an explanation.

The Steel King, after half a day spent in publishing his success far and wide, had got back to business, and was hard at work brewing fresh millions.

His reception of Sickingen was not as cordial as the latter thought he had a right to expect.

"Good morning. Why don't you look after the unpacking? Cavanagh has telephoned for you. It's a fine specimen, but the frontal bone is fractured."

"A big piece of rock rolled down on the head after it had been cut off," said Ulrich, chancing it. Naturally, he had not superintended the dismemberment of the animal.

"You made a mistake in leaving your skeleton in reach of rocks which might roll down," retorted Corliss, coldly. "Never mind, I am very much pleased with the whole outfit."

Sickingen's voice was almost harsh as he said, "When can I have the honour of presenting my respects to Miss Eva?"

Corliss became very serious.

"Eva," he said, laying down his pen, "has been deeply touched by the news of the death of Raoul Le Fort, who was at the head of Expedition No. 2. She was personally acquainted with this French artist, who was a nice fellow in his way, although he was decidedly lacking in punctuality. My daughter can scarcely resign herself to the certainty—well, to cut the matter short, she has brought to my notice the fact that Le Fort's expedition has a margin of twelve days in competition with yours. During these twelve days Eva wishes to be alone. She will doubtless be glad to meet you when your record is established beyond dispute."

"I can only submit to her decision, although I do not quite understand—"

"It is entirely in accordance with the conditions of the contest," remarked Corliss, who could not help noticing the anxiety on the young man's face, and he was resuming his writing when two light taps on his door preluded the entrance of a whirlwind of lace, surmounted by a Greuse face and two red lips full of animation.

"Miss Leslie!" said Corliss.

"The very same, Senator. Pardon me for my extreme cheek; but they told me that your conquering hero was here, and I wanted to pay him my compliments before I went up to see Eva—oh! oh!"

The young girl stopped short, looked attentively at Ulrich, and burst out into one of those joyous fits of laughter which were her specialty.

"Oh, but we are already acquainted!"

"I regret that I have not that pleasure," said Ulrich, with perfect politeness. "Are you not mistaken?"

"I? Look here. Don't you remember the overland express to San Francisco, where you were going to find your wife, as often happens in America?"

Ulrich von Sickingen turned pale with anger, and Corliss looked utterly astonished. Clara Leslie looked at the Count's hand.

"And your souvenir-ring? Left it over there? But it's none of my business. Excuse me, really. You have my best wishes for your success. Senator, I am going up to see Eva. Count—dear me! dear me!"

She disappeared like a whirlwind, as she had entered. Sickingen, who never lied more than seemed necessary, gave Corliss a short account of their meeting in the Overland, Limited. His embarrassment and humiliation would have been most comical in any other conjecture; but the Senator remained very thoughtful, and scarcely answered the Count. He evidently began to realize that the conquest of a fossil at the North Pole was not the only qualification necessary to assure his daughter's happiness, and that it would be advisable to make some investigation into this gentleman's past.

Ulrich could see what was in his future father-in-law's mind, and besides, the twelve days' delay disturbed the Count more than he would have been willing to acknowledge. He was afraid that Eva, whose faithful love for Raoul he could not but be aware of, would endeavour to find some survivor of the *Salvador's* crew, and get some details about the shipwreck. The only thing that reassured him was the brief margin of time. People do not return from East Cape in twelve days, and steamers are not to be found like tramcars at every corner of Behring Straits.

He was sure that his luck would stand his friend once more; that he would triumph over all obstacles, would marry Eva and her royal fortune, and go back to Europe, where a life of gorgeous enjoyment would enable him to shake off all these unpleasant recollections.

The Count tried to distract his mind by superintending the unpacking of the skeleton. Corliss had given orders to Cavanagh to install the real primigenius in eight days, in place of the plaster facsimile which had already been destroyed. The excellent curator was up to his eyes in work, surrounded by twenty naturalists who were helping him, and constantly referred to the Count for information. Sickingen was extremely embarrassed by these innumerable fragments scattered on the ground, and had not the least idea how to piece them together. Cavanagh's astonishment was unbearable.

"But, my dear Count, how is it that you, who have seen the animal alive, and taken him apart so scientifically, do not know where this articulation should go?"

Sickingen soon gave up risking an exposure of his ignorance, and left Cavanagh free to circulate among the cartilages and agitate himself about the articulations at his own sweet will. Somehow or other the primigenius grew, little by little, and in five days would be completely reconstructed.

These last days were like so many eternities to the young man. *Had* he escaped so many perils, broken through so many obstacles, risked his life on land and sea, and stifled the voice of his conscience, merely so that at the last moment a shadow, the memory of another man, should stop him on the threshold of his triumph? Eva's evident repugnance to him, Corliss's unwillingness to use his paternal authority to overcome her hesitation, and, above all, the astonishment of Cavanagh at the incomprehensible ignorance that he could not conceal,—all this disquieted and wearied Ulrich von Sickingen. Besides, they asked too many questions. When the first curiosity was satisfied, they wanted to be enlightened as to the minor details; and the Count was very much in need of some one who could enlighten *him*. Corliss also wanted to obtain the presence of his brave assistants, in order to associate them with the triumph of their chief; but it was impossible to find a single one of them—a fact which it was rather difficult to explain, even among a population of sailors in a seaport.

In another direction Sickingen had lost no time. He had been able to enlist in his cause Lady Frances Osborne, the female Ward McAlister of the Four Hundred, whose coats-of-arms, quartered in the first and fourth in azure, which is French, time of William the Bastard, and the second and third, d'or, which is English, constitutes the parchment aristocracy of the United States. The Count found out that the Duke de Lara, the year before, had subscribed two hundred and fifty thousand dollars to Lady Frances' heralds' college, and he telegraphed in cypher to his friend Baron Schuster, whose reply was rather enigmatical—"Duchess Lara, *née* Miss Blair, of Omaha, has had five million dollars as her marriage portion."

Some hours later—Sickingen was literally in a fever of anxiety—the parvenue who played so successfully at being a great lady, held out her finely shaped hand to the Count, saying—

"Count von Sickingen, let your mind rest easy."

These encouraging words helped him to be patient until the day of the inauguration. Punctually at the appointed date, the colossal primigenius reared itself, intact and majestic, under the dome of the Museum. His tusks threatened the bust of the former New York gutter-snipe. They had removed everything else from the rotunda, so that the monster should show in all his splendour, and Ulrich could not help a shudder as he remembered the frightful death from which Le Fort had snatched him, as he recalled those immense ivories and the great trunk uplifted in the air ready to seize him. The Steel King, evidently highly pleased, had assisted in person at the finishing touches, and he congratulated the Count and Cavanagh, saying—

"It is a very good piece of work. I accept delivery of the order."

And he at once sent out his invitations to the "Mammoth Ball," which, after having met Lady Frances Osborne in Eva's parlour, he believed to be an original idea of his own. The ball, in fact, for the world of society, was to be the celebration of one of the greatest scientific achievements of the twentieth century.

CHAPTER XXVI
THE MAMMOTH BALL

The ball was magnificent, one might say mastodontal. It was not confined to the Four Hundred of Lady Frances Osborne and the American Debrett, but opened its doors wide to a crowd of parvenus who had never even heard of William the Conqueror—an awfully queer lot, sprung from the Lord knows where, who were not the least impressed by worldly grandeur, and as likely as not to be ignorant of the difference between the insignia of American Benefit Societies and the official decorations of the rest of the universe.

These two thousand or so intimate friends of the Steel King had received invitations on vellum, ornamented with an artistic steel engraving, which reproduced the colossal profile of the mammoth, and which read: "John N. Corliss requests the pleasure of your company at an Arctic Ball, which will be given at the Corliss Museum, to celebrate the installation of the skeleton of a mammoth primigenius, discovered by Count Ulrich von Sickingen in Siberia (Corliss Expedition). Polar costume is requested. N.B.—The skeleton just acquired by the Corliss Museum is the largest and most perfect in the world. It stands thirty-six feet high, and the tusks weigh fifteen hundred pounds."

The invitation was an enormous success. At eleven o'clock the immense halls of the Museum were crowded with guests dressed in "Polar costume." Cavanagh's scheme of decoration was carried out on the same plan. Corliss had conceived the amusing idea of giving his dance among all these skeletons, these rows of bottles, in which swam all sorts of hideous shapes, these glass cabinets full of horrible remains. Thousands of electric lights and clumps of rare flowers decorated the anatomical specimens. The arrangements of the central rotunda were particularly magnificent. Bathed in a brilliant light from the arc-lamps in the dome, which showed him in all his immense proportions, the gigantic mammoth reared himself on an artificial iceberg, which was kept solid by a powerful freezing apparatus. Between the blocks of ice, paradoxical masses of bloom were furnished by quantities of white orchids. White bearskins covered the walls, icicles of crystal hung from the dome, and a white radiance sparkled around the Polar monster.

Under his tusks stood Senator Corliss, dressed in white fur, with a fur cap on which an aigrette of diamonds scintillated, receiving his guests. Eva stood at his right, a charming white vision in her dress of shimmering swansdown, while on his left everybody paid their congratulations to Count von Sickingen, who wore a complete costume of white leather, with the cordon of the Red Eagle on his breast. A dagger with a sheath of white morocco leather hung at his belt.

The master of ceremonies was a skeleton, the punctual Cavanagh, to wit, whose diminutive limbs were encased in a tight-fitting garment, whereon all the bones and anatomical processes were minutely detailed. He was beautifully hideous, and shone in the midst of the crowd, which agreed that only the absence of a label distinguished him from the real mummies. The throng included troglodites of the Stone Age, amber-coloured Sioux, Iroquois with three feathers in their crests, or Hurons with a bag of tobacco on their backs. New York, dressed in bank notes, gave its arm to Boston, which tinkled with copper, and to Chicago, fresh from a hogshead of lard.

At the rear of the main hall, the curator's rooms had been transformed into three salons in gold and ivory, the entrances to which were under arches of moss roses, and here the Four Hundred had taken refuge. At least one could breathe there, around the glittering fountains which sprung from bouquets of azaleas, free from the chorus of the rest of the crowd, whose burden, "business—dollars—money-makers," lapsed into silence, as the vain strife of mortals dies out at the threshold of Olympus.

The "Polar costume" was less favoured by the gentlemen, who were costumed like newly hatched European noblemen of the most brilliant periods of each country, than by the ladies, who appeared as Snow Queens, Polar stars, or Milky Ways. The occasion was favourable for a grand display of diamonds. They looked like walking constellations, and their brilliancy contrasted admirably with the dark garments, Esquimaux, bears, or seals.

The Steel King was stifling in his furs, but he was visibly triumphant at the evident enthusiasm of his guests. Eva let herself be carried away, little by little, by the extravagant animation of the scene, and Sickingen rehearsed his most tender speeches in preparation for the question which, very soon, was to definitely crown his success.

"Let us have a 'Boston' quadrille, please," begged Clara Leslie, who was radiant as Sirius, in a costume of pearls and muslin over a sky-blue bodice, with a similar train of satin, "a Boston for my share of Paradise."

An orchestra of Tziganes, hidden under a cluster of "oriental asparagus," struck up the waltz. Clara drew back her left foot, placed her right one behind it, and was off in the arms of a marquis of the time of Louis XV. Other couples followed, swinging and reversing, in series of two, six or eight pairs, forward and back. The young people were intoxicated with music and light—and the mammoth looked down on them impassively from his pedestal.

It was almost half-past eleven, and the string of new arrivals was lessening, when the liveried servants, who stood in a row in the entrance hall, saw a couple come in whose disguise was striking in its completeness.

The man had doubtless tried to disguise himself as a trapper, but his leather rags were so dirty, so worn into tatters, that one would have sworn he had been doing a three years' voyage on an iceberg. As for the woman, her complexion was painted, or rather lead-penciled; her short and greasy hair imitated that of a native of some Esquimaux tribe; and in her dirty clothes, which were as ragged as her companion's, there was a savage completeness which was absolutely genuine. The ushers were so struck with admiration that they permitted these realistic guests to enter without asking for their cards of invitation, the more so as the couple had reached such a pitch of perfection as to speak in a jargon appropriate to their costume.

The first steps of the new-comers provoked a joyful feeling of surprise, which broke out in a thunder of applause. It was impossible to do the thing more realistically. These two walking bundles of rags were certainly in the most exact "Polar costume," and the woman especially had been able to give her face the true Kalmuck type. It was admirable! Besides, what New Yorker would have been able to paint such wrinkles on her face, and what marvelous tailor could have constructed these unspeakable cast-off clothes? The guests crowded around, trying to detect the secret of the masqueraders; and for a quarter of an hour the man and woman, searching with their black eyes in every direction, without answering the banter which showered round them, could scarcely advance a step. At last, however, they reached the threshold of the rotunda, escorted to their hosts by peals of delighted laughter. When the man saw the mammoth with Eva, Corliss and Sickingen at its feet, he uttered a fierce shout and rushed forward, elbowing his way among fragile "Polar Stars" and delicate "Aurora Boreales." In three strides he was in front of Sickingen, followed by his savage mate, who brandished a gold chain with furious gestures. Then they heard, in excellent English—

"Thief! Pirate! Son of—"

The man raised his fist to knock down the Count. Twenty people seized and restrained him, while others kept back the woman, who was uttering incomprehensible cries of, "Youngou! Nuya! Nuya!" But the man continued to shout, "Thief! Robber! This man is a thief and an assassin! Send for the police!"

Sickingen shivered in every fibre of his being. He forced himself not to stifle the voice and stop the words which had not been spoken, but which were going to be. At the first cry he had recognized Bob, and with eyes gleaming with the light of madness, he glared towards the entrance door, where probably Raoul would appear next, with his vengeance ready to his hand. Sounds of intense excitement were heard amongst the brilliant assemblage which gathered in the rotunda.

"It is a madman—some drunken fellow," they said. "Drive him out!—he jostled Lady Frances Osbourne. The woman is epileptic—"

With perfect calmness Corliss signed to the servants, "Take them away."

The man calmed down at once and changed his tone.

"One moment! First ask Mr. Sickingen why he stole the mammoth which belonged to Messrs. Le Fort and Hamilton."

At the mention of Le Fort's name, Eva trembled.

"Papa," said she, "he has spoken of Raoul!"

The Senator turned to Sickingen. The latter, pale as a corpse after the rupture of aneurism, continued to stare towards the door with glassy eyes.

The Steel King began to feel vaguely suspicious.

"Let the man speak," he commanded. "What have you got to say for yourself?"

"What I have to say is, that I am Bob—Bob, Messrs. Hamilton and Le Fort's guide. I have to say that this animal

belongs to us, not to him," said the trapper, all in one
breath.

Sickingen tried to pull himself together. "This fellow
has drunk more whisky than he has ever hunted seals,"
said he, with praiseworthy coolness. And, turning to his
host, he went on audaciously, "Is this one of the items on
your programme, Senator?"

"Well, my good fellow," went on Corliss, scarcely noticing the Count, "you pretend to say that you were with
Expedition No. 2?"

"Yes; and that we killed the mammoth—our party. Yes,
sirree; and we cleaned the skeleton, and this thief stole it
from us; and this woman that he married up there will say
the same. Hey, Tuli?"

"That will do," said Sickingen, haughtily. "This man is
either drunk or mad."

"Yes, that will do," retorted the prospector. "Bob will
show you that he is neither drunk nor mad, and he will
prove it."

"Well, give us your proof."

"Sure! If it is his, this mammoth, he ought to know
what there is written up there; isn't that so, gentlemen? And
if I know, and he don't, it's my mammoth, isn't it, and not
his mammoth?"

The crowd realized the fairness of the argument. The
Count himself grew pale and a cold sweat stood on his
forehead. How should he escape the trap that Bob had set
for him?

Bob continued in the midst of a death-like stillness—

"Gentlemen, there is some writing on the left tusk, up
high, where the ivory is thickest. Look!"

"He is right. It is true. You can just see some writing
there—looks as if it was done with a knife," said some
voices; and under the tusks a hundred heads were lifted up
and a thousand pairs of eyes were fastened on the spot, but
it was hard to make out anything.

"Get a ladder, quick!" said Corliss.

"Count Sickingen, will you be kind enough to tell these gentlemen what is written on your mammoth?" said Bob, in a sneering tone.

The silence became terrible. All heads were turned towards Sickingen, and he felt that he was lost. He would chance it once more, and trust to his famous luck.

"I know," said he coolly, "and I am going to explain."

"What's written up there?" insisted Bob.

"Le Fort's name."

"It's nothing about Le Fort," shouted the old trapper in triumph. "There is no Le Fort written on the beast at all. What is on the tusk is this: 'Fred Hamilton, 1901. Record of the Mammoth. For the Athletic Club of New York.' I ought to know, I guess, because I scratched it there myself. Is that right, sir?" he called out to Cavanagh, who was climbing up a ladder.

The silence lasted for a few seconds yet, while the curator-skeleton adjusted his spectacles. Finally he said—

"It is the exact wording of the inscription."

A great shout filled the hall. It was finished; he had played, he had lost. All that was left to this handsome lord of Rüheldeck was to blow his brains out or to escape. But still unyielding to the storm, with his eyes haughtily fixed before him, he murmured—

"I will explain later on," and he started to the door, as the crowd, in some uncertainty, parted before him.

"Lebem sic wohl, Lustschosser! Adieu, my castle on the banks of the blue Elbe!"

Tuli followed him, and the two disappeared into the night. At this moment a flourish of trumpets is heard in the neighbouring hall. Midnight struck, and, according to the Steel King's programme, his two thousand most intimate friends were to celebrate, at this precise minute, the end of the match and the triumph of the hunter of the mammoth. A general feeling of uneasiness was evident at this celebration where there was nothing to celebrate. For the first time in his life Corliss felt embarrassed. He

looked at Bob, and Bob looked at him. Was Bob the only
survivor of the Le Fort Expedition, and the real winner of
the trophy? Was it he who had the right to be his future
son-in-law? The Senator turned towards Eva, who was trying not to faint. The overwhelming evidence impressed itself at last on her mind. Since he was not present to-night,
Raoul was dead—had died for love of her in this doomed
adventure. And the sight of all the gay company, this absurd show which covered a sinister drama, made her grief
only more poignant.

"Papa," she murmured, "take me home."

Corliss rushed to her, and she fell in his arms.

"Tell the man to come—and tell you—how Raoul—"

"How's Mr. Raoul?" asked Bob. "Beg your pardon, miss.
He's all right."

Eva could not restrain a cry of delight, and the Steel
King whirled round to the trapper.

"What do you say? Is the head of Expedition No. 2
alive? Where is he, then?"

"Not very far away, sir. He and Mr. Hamilton are at the
police-station. Didn't they tell you?" said Bob, calmly.

"At the police station? Why?"

"Well, it was this way: They had no money when they
struck 'Frisco, and they managed to borrow enough to
get the train to New York. We weren't looking first-rate,
any of us, and there were any amount of hard-luck yarns
among the crowd that had come back from the Klondike.
Mr. Hamilton had calculated that we would get here in
time, just within what he called the handicap limit of the
match, but when we struck here, just now, there was some
trouble about the old woman, who had lost her ticket. Mr.
Hamilton wished to stand for her—talked about his Club
and a lot of other things. The railroad people laughed at
him, and he got mad and knocked over a few. Then the
police came; they let Tuli and me go, and carried off the
gentlemen. They shouted out, 'Go and find Senator Corliss—to-day is the twelfth day—telephone to the Athletic

Club.' The police only laughed and said, 'All right, boys. You'll come to the Police Station Club first, and to-morrow we'll take you before some senators.' Then the gentleman told me to go as quick as I could to the Corliss Museum—something about the twelfth day that I don't understand."

Corliss interrupted him. "Cavanagh, telephone, ask for the police captain, from me. Get an electric cab. They can be here in ten minutes."

This unexpected climax astounded everybody. The guests crowded around Bob, as Eva, radiant with delight, asked the trapper about a thousand details, which they listened to with intense interest. A dozen reporters, dressed as seals or white bears, had got out their note-books, and were writing furiously. Others had rushed to the police-station; and Raoul and Hamilton, passing abruptly from the custody of the constables to that of their excited deliverer, had no time even to understand their questions, as they were carried off in triumph on a wave of sonorous hurrahs.

Le Fort and Fred, worn out by fatigue and emotion, scarcely able to stand, dazzled and half deafened, came into the rotunda, and there they saw the mammoth, "their mammoth," triumphant in the midst of his magnificent setting. Raoul saw Eva's star-like eyes, shining through her tears with anguish and love, death and life. The young girl held out her arms; the past and the future melted away, and there was no one in the world but she and he—he and she—and they realized in their first kiss the rapture of that terrestrial Paradise which no one has known since the fall of man.

The guests crowded around them. Hamilton rushed to the Steel King.

"Senator Corliss, what time is it?"

"Quarter-past twelve," answered Corliss, mechanically.

"Your time is fast. It is only three minutes to twelve by the clock at the police-station. These gentlemen who came for us will confirm it. I think that our record is incontestable."

"I think it is," said Corliss, in a conciliatory tone. "Cavanagh, tell them to strike up the *March of the Corliss Mammoth.*"

Fred Hamilton jumped in the air. His row with the police and his arrival at the ball had made him lose his usual coolness.

"*Your* mammoth! You mean *our* mammoth."

"How is that, sir? It seems to me that our agreement was perfectly clear."

"Perfectly so. You were to pay 'any price you like to name.'"

John N. Corliss took his famous note-book out of his pocket.

"Hurry up," said Hamilton. "You've not much more than a minute to decide in. If not, I keep my mammoth."

The Steel King's face grew red. They had not often opposed him like this, even on the battlefield of the Stock Exchange. He opened his mouth twice without speaking, then shut up his note-book again, and finally said—

"You are partly wrong and partly right. What is your price?"

"Two millions and a half. One for Raoul, one for me, and five hundred thousand dollars for Bob."

Corliss's fist fell on one of the monster's tusks, and the veins stood out in his forehead. Then Cavanagh took the risk of intervening.

"Worthy sir, the Count came much cheaper."

"Well he might! He stole it."

"In the name of science—"

"In the name of the devil, sir," said Hamilton. "It is not dear at the price. I left my left ear-drum up there. Will your science give that back to me? In forty seconds, if you do not take him, I will sell the mammoth to Russia, which wants to get him."

The big fellow triumphantly waved a telegram above his head, but let no one read it. Cavanagh fell into a chair and fainted away. The Steel King's face became injected with blood as if he were going to have a fit, and his jaws moved from right to left under his cheeks like the two jaws of a vice.

Hamilton pulled out his watch. "Senator, there are thirty seconds left. Yes or no?"

"Yes," burst out Corliss, adding a string of remarks which it is impossible to report—really quite impossible, and they were drowned, luckily, in a tempest of cheers.

"Hurrah for Corliss! Hurrah for the gutter-snipe! Hurrah for the Steel King!"

He quickly recovered his good humour. "You are the second, my boy, who was ever able to best Corliss—the first one died in an insane asylum. You have got a future before you. I'm sorry, really sorry, that I haven't another daughter. As to the head of Expedition No. 1, he stands convicted of robbery with violence. I will have my lawyer take steps against him."

Here Le Fort intervened. "Senator, Count von Sickingen has condemned himself by not daring to remain here with you and Miss Eva. I ought to have given him his deserts two months ago among the rocks of East Cape, but now that his intrigues are all exposed and his imposture is unmasked, I only ask you, Senator, to abandon him, now only Sickingen the adventurer, to public contempt. We need not trouble ourselves any more about this despicable character."

Raoul's words were received with universal approval, and the Steel King, after a moment's consideration, added in a low tone—

"Very well, Le Fort. Before we go to supper, shall I announce to my guests, who are personal friends of mine, your engagement to Eva? I believe that my daughter—yes? You both agree? All right."

He waved his arms, bristling with white fur, and his guests crowded around him. Not one of them will ever forget the novel excitements of this memorable gathering, to which a dazzling climax was added by Corliss's announcement—

"Ladies and gentlemen, I must announce to you that my daughter Eva is engaged to be married to Monsieur Raoul Le Fort, the true discoverer of the largest primigenius in the world. Ladies and gentlemen, it is a lovematch. Ladies and gentlemen, supper is ready. Cavanagh, the *March of the Mammoth.*"

MEN OF THE MIST

T. C. BRIDGES

(ILLUSTRATED BY G. HENRY EVISON)

CHAPTER I
THE COMING OF BART

Tea at Wasperton School was nothing but thick hunks of bread and margarine and an evil-looking black mixture served in huge metal teapots. The food was so bad that the boys could hardly eat it, but they dared not complain, not, at any rate, so long as they were under the hard eyes of their master, Mr. Silas Crayshaw. For his eyes were no less hard than his cane—and never a day passed but some of them felt the sting of that.

Among the forty or so boys who sat at the two long tables were a couple who somehow looked different from the rest. In spite of their shabby clothes and patched boots, there was an air of breeding about Clem and Billy Ballard.

As Clem took his place beside his brother, Stiles, the grimy old school porter, came along and dropped a letter by his plate. Clem glanced at the address, and slipped the letter into his pocket. Pendred, a big, sullen-looking youth who sat opposite, laughed unpleasantly. "Scared to open it, I suppose?" he remarked. "Don't want us to see the broad arrow on the paper."

Clem went oddly white, but Billy's eyes flashed and the colour rose hotly in his cheeks. Clem caught him by the arm. "Sit still, Billy. Don't pay any attention to him," he said coolly. "It's from Uncle Grimston," he added in a whisper.

Just then Mr. Crayshaw came in, and Pendred subsided. He was not going to risk a cut from the master's cane.

The meal went on in absolute silence, and the moment it was over the two Ballards hurried out. "Let's go down to the quarry," said Clem, and Billy, merely nodding, dropped into step.

Wasperton was near the big manufacturing town of Marchester, and the whole countryside was foul with soot and smoke. The two boys walked down a grimy lane, turned into a bare-looking field, and passing through some gorse and a clump of half-dead trees reached the edge of an old stone quarry, at the bottom of which was a deep pool of sullen greenish water. There they plumped themselves down on the grass. "What's he say?" asked Billy.

Clem tore open the envelope, and had hardly begun to read before he stopped with a gasp.

"What's the matter?" demanded Billy sharply.

"He—he—can't have us back, Billy! We—we've got to spend the holidays here!"

"What! Here at Wasperton?"

"Yes. That's what he says," Clem answered, with his grey eyes fixed upon the fatal sheet.

"Oh, he can't! He can't mean it!" groaned Billy.

"It's plain enough," said Clem bitterly. "He says he can't have us knocking about the place."

"He always hated us," said Billy fiercely.

Clem shrugged his shoulders. "Well, he's kept us since Mother's death. I suppose we ought to be grateful."

"What's the good of his keeping us?" cried Billy. "I'd sooner work as an errand-boy in a shop than go on like this. The school is a pig of a place; we don't learn anything, there are no decent games, and I hate the very sight of it, and of Crayshaw too."

In his excitement Billy sprang to his feet and went stamping up and down. "And the chaps jeering at us about Father!" he went on. "As if it was his fault or ours that they sent him to prison."

"Steady, Billy!" said Clem. "It's no good getting excited."

"But I can't help it!" retorted Billy. "It isn't fair. Everything's gone wrong since they tried Father for taking money which you and I know he never touched. And now to keep us in this place all the holidays! It's the limit, and I'm not going to stand it!"

"Look out!" cried Clem suddenly and leapt to his feet. He was just too late, for Billy had gone too near the edge, and with a deep crunching sound a great piece of turf had broken off and slipped down, carrying Billy with it.

"Billy! Billy!" cried Clem in horror. When he reached the edge he fully expected to see his brother plunged into the depths of the pool thirty feet below, and his relief may be imagined when he caught sight of him clinging to a narrow ledge only a yard or so down. In a flash he had flung himself on his face, and reaching down caught hold of Billy. "Hang on!" he cried. "Hang on, Billy! I'll get you up!"

But when he tried to do so he found that it was out of the question. The weight was too much for him to lift, and Billy could get no foothold. With a sinking feeling of horror, Clem realized that unless he kept quite still he himself would be pulled over the edge, and both would plunge to destruction in that noisome green water so far below.

"Help!" he shouted at the top of his voice. "Help!"

Clods of earth fell away beneath him. Another slip threatened. Billy looked up at him with agonized eyes. "Let me go, Clem!" he said. "Let me go! I shall only drag you down."

But Clem's teeth set hard. "No!" he answered curtly. "Hang on!"

More earth fell. Clem was slipping. Another moment and it would have been all over, when he felt a tremendously powerful grip on his legs. "Hang on, sonny!" came a cool, deep voice. "I reckon I can pull ye both up if ye'll hold still."

Such a pull! It was like that of a steam-crane. Clem's muscles cracked, but he held on, and next minute he and Billy were both safe on firm ground.

"There, that's all right," said his rescuer, as calmly as ever, and Clem, recovering a little, looked up into the face of a man of middle height, square built, and evidently of immense strength. His features were blunt, and tanned to the colour of an old saddle, but his eyes, of a singularly clear blue, held that curiously far-seeing look peculiar to men who spend their time entirely in the open air. He was dressed in a ready-made blue serge suit much too tight across his immensely broad chest.

"Thanks awfully," gasped Clem. "You saved us both. I say, you are strong!"

The other smiled, and it was a very pleasant smile which lit up his whole face.

"Glad I came along in time, sonny. But you're all right now. Well, I guess I'll be going. Good evening."

But Clem caught his arm. "Please tell us your name," he begged.

The big man smiled again. "Bart, I'm called—Bart Condon. And what's yours?"

"Ours is Ballard," replied Clem. "I'm Clem, and this is my brother Billy."

Condon's blue eyes widened. Clem almost thought he saw him start slightly. But all he said was, "I'm mighty glad to have met you. You're from the school, I reckon?"

"Yes," replied Clem. "I say, you come from America, don't you?"

"That's so, son. Say, I'll walk up as far as you're going."

So the three walked back together, but Clem had no chance to pursue his inquiries, for Condon did most of the talking. He asked many questions about the school, and by the time they reached the gates had got the boys to tell him practically all about it and about themselves. They had told him how their father had been put in prison for a theft he had never committed, how their mother had died of grief, and how their uncle, Mr. Robert Grimston, a hard, mean man, had taken charge of them, and put them at this wretched school, where they had now been for two years.

"But your dad escaped, didn't he?" asked Condon.

"Yes. But how did you know?" asked Clem quickly.

"Guess I read it in the newspaper," was the reply.

"Yes," said Clem. "He got away more than eighteen months ago, and they never caught him. They say he's gone to Australia. I do hope he's safe there."

"Mighty good place to get to, I reckon," said Condon. Then he stopped, and offered his hand first to Clem, then to Billy. "I reckon we'll meet again some time," he said, and, turning in his quick, quiet way, was gone.

"What a topping chap!" said Billy to Clem.

Clem nodded. "A real good sort," he agreed, "and he came just in the nick of time."

Billy nodded gravely. "I only hope Crayshaw doesn't hear of this. He'll stop us going down to the quarry, and it's the only place we can get to ourselves."

"Why should he hear?" asked Clem.

"Look at your clothes," responded Billy.

Just then a cracked bell began to ring.

"There's the bell for school!" exclaimed Clem. "We must hurry."

All the boys sat together in the large classroom for evening preparation. Every one was very quiet, for Mr. Gorton, the assistant master, was at the desk, and every one knew that his cane was as handy as Mr. Crayshaw's. The silence was broken only by the scratching of steel pens and the rustle of the pages of dog's-eared books.

And so the minutes dragged on until the hands of the big clock pointed to a quarter past eight. Only a quarter of an hour now, and then came bedtime.

The sound of the door opening made every one look up, and in came Stiles, the dingy old manservant, and went up to Mr. Gorton.

He gave a slip of paper to the master, and Mr. Gorton glanced at it. His big voice boomed out. "Ballard senior and Ballard junior."

"Yes, sir," answered the two boys, standing up.

"You are both to go to Mr. Crayshaw's room."

As the two left their seats Billy glanced at Clem. "What's he want?" he whispered to his brother.

"Probably he's heard from Uncle too," was Clem's answer. "Or else Pendred has sneaked about our going down to the quarry. He's always spying on us."

CHAPTER II
SEALED ORDERS

Mr. Crayshaw's study was a large, untidy room which reeked of tobacco, and Mr. Crayshaw himself was a tall, bony man who wore a tail-coat which had once been black but now was green, and a sort of fez cap on his bald head. He had bushy eyebrows and deep-set eyes. As Clem and Billy came in he was sitting at his desk. He looked up and stared at them.

"What's the matter with your clothes, Ballard senior?" he demanded.

Clem held himself very straight. "I had a fall, sir," he answered quietly.

Mr. Crayshaw grunted. "Fighting, I suppose, but you need not be afraid," he said. "Though no doubt you richly deserve it, you will not get a caning this time." He picked up a sheet of paper and. adjusted his spectacles. "I have a letter here from your uncle," he went on. "It seems he wishes to take you away from the school."

"Take us away!" echoed Clem, hardly able to believe his ears.

"Yes," snapped the master. "In my opinion a very foolish proceeding, but since he has sent a cheque in advance for next term's fees I have no choice but to let you go."

He went on talking, but the boys hardly heard. The one fact they realized was that they were to leave Wasperton, and this alone seemed too good to be true. It was also

215

utterly amazing, for the letter telling them they could not come home for the holidays had only just arrived.

"You will pack your things to-night," were the next words Clem caught. "You are to leave in the morning." He glared at the boys as though they had done him some injury, but it is quite certain that neither Clem nor Billy took the faintest notice of his expression.

The master turned again to his desk and picked up an envelope. "I am to give you this," he added, handing it to Clem. "It contains your tickets and money for your journey. You are not to open it until you arrive at the station to-morrow morning, where you will catch the eight-thirty train. You quite understand?"

Clem was almost breathless, but somehow managed to get out, "Yes, sir. Thank you, sir."

"Then good night, and good-bye, for I shall not see you in the morning. I only hope that you will both benefit by the useful tuition which you have received in my establishment."

He extended a large, cold hand, which the two boys shook in turn; then somehow they found themselves in the passage outside the study door. They were both gasping like fish out of water. Billy turned to Clem. "I—I say, Clem, it's a dream, I suppose. It can't be real," he said hoarsely.

Clem held up the envelope. "This is real, Billy. No, it's true. It's really true."

"B—but where are we going—back to Uncle Grimston's?"

Clem shook his head. "There wouldn't be all this mystery about it if we were," he answered. "Besides, his letter to me said he didn't want us at his house for the holidays."

"Then where?" demanded Billy.

"What does it matter? Anything will be better than Wasperton. Come on. Let's pack."

It was a job that did not take long, for one small box easily held all their worldly goods.

"And we don't even know how to label it," said Billy, when it was done.

"We shall know in the morning," Clem answered. "Now we'd better turn in."

Luckily for them, the rest of the dormitory were already in bed, and, barring a sneer or two from Pendred, they were not molested. But neither of them slept much that night. They were far too excited. Stiles called them at half-past six, and they slipped out like mice. The other boys were still asleep, and Clem and Billy were not sorry. But not until they were in a cab and on their way to the station were they able to believe that they were actually clear of Wasperton.

It was barely eight when they arrived, and except for a solitary porter there was not a soul on the platform. Billy seized Clem by the arm and dragged him into the deserted waiting-room. "The envelope, Clem—we can open it now," he said sharply.

Clem's fingers were not quite steady as he tore open the envelope. It contained a sheet of paper, two tickets, and five pounds in Treasury notes. "The tickets—where are they for?" demanded Billy.

Clem held them up. "Lime Street Station, Liverpool," he read.

The two boys stared at one another, but neither spoke. Then Clem unfolded the sheet of paper. On it were typed these words: "Your passages are booked for New York on the *Pocahontas,* sailing at 4 p.m. on Wednesday afternoon. You will be met at Liverpool. The password for which you will be asked is 'Potlatch.'"

There was no signature to this startling message, no address, no date. Clem and Billy stared at one another in mute amazement. "The *Pocahontas*—New York!" Clem muttered at last.

Suddenly Billy snatched off his cap, flung it in the air, and gave a whoop which made the solitary porter drop a large parcel he was carrying and turn quite pale. "Hurray!"

he shouted. "No more Uncle Grimston! No more Wasperton! Three cheers for America!"

The porter came up quickly. "Here, I say, young feller!" he said, in a scandalized tone. "If you wants to make a noise like that you better go out on the road and do it. This here's the private property of the railway, and lunatics like you ain't allowed here."

Billy turned a beaming face on the man. "I can't help it, porter. I'm not loony—only happy. So'd you be if you'd just got away from a place like Wasperton, and especially if you'd been there for nearly two years."

The porter's expression changed and became quite sympathetic. "Oh, you're from Wasperton, are you! Yes, I shouldn't wonder if you was glad to clear out. They do say as it's a sort o' 'Dotheboys Hall,' like Dickens wrote about." He paused. "I say, you ain't running away, be you?" he asked quickly.

"No, indeed!" replied Billy. "We're going to friends in America. See, here are our tickets to Liverpool."

The porter inspected the tickets and nodded. "They're all right. Now you'll go right through to Crewe and change there, and you'll get to Liverpool just after one o'clock. That'll give you plenty of time to get some dinner afore you goes aboard. Tell you what, I knows the guard aboard this train. I'll tip him a word to look after you."

"That's frightfully good of you," said Billy gratefully, and the good fellow stood chatting with them until passengers began to arrive and he had to get busy. But he did not forget his promise, and when the train came in introduced them to the guard, who put them in a carriage near his van, and was kindness itself.

It is quite safe to wager that two happier passengers than the young Ballards were not carried by any train in England that morning, and when they were swept away from the grimy surroundings of Marchester, and through the lovely hills of North Wales, their delight was beyond words.

Billy was constantly sticking his head out of the window to admire one thing or another, but in between he and Clem talked things over again and again. But the more they discussed the matter the worse puzzled they became. "It's no use troubling our heads," said Billy at last. "The paper says that some one is going to meet us at Liverpool. Whoever it is, we can ask him where we are going."

The train pulled into the big junction at Crewe, and the kindly guard saw the boys and their box across into the other train, and shook hands with them and wished them luck. Then they were off again, the express racing north for Liverpool.

It seemed a very short time before they reached the huge Lime Street Station, and there they stood on the platform beside their box, waiting alone in the midst of hurrying crowds, and, to say the truth, feeling a little lonely.

"Is your name Ballard?" Clem glanced up quickly, to see a quietly dressed, middle-aged man who looked like a lawyer standing beside him.

"Yes, sir," he answered.

"And the word?"

For a moment Clem wondered what was meant—but only for a moment. "Potlatch," he answered.

The other smiled slightly, and motioned to a porter to take the box. He led the way to a waiting taxicab, and they drove off.

Billy was the first to speak. "Where are we going, sir?" he asked.

"To get some dinner," was the reply.

Something in their new acquaintance's tone checked further questions, and presently the taxi pulled up at a small, quiet-looking hotel. Here the box was taken out and left in the hall, the taxi-man paid and dismissed, and all three went into the coffee-room, where dinner was quickly set before them. It was a plain enough meal, but there was excellent roast beef with Yorkshire pudding and baked potatoes, and an apple tart with custard.

To the boys, accustomed to the greasy, ill-cooked fare at Wasperton, it was delicious, and both had two hearty helpings of each course. Their new friend hardly spoke except to ask them about their journey, and somehow neither cared to question him. The minute the meal was over he got up and looked at his watch.

"Now we have some shopping to do," he said, "and since we have not much time we must hurry."

He waited them off bristly, and took them into a big department store, where he spoke to a shopwalker. They were at once escorted to a lift and whirled to an upper floor, where they found themselves in the tailoring department. Piles of ready-made garments of all sorts were on the shelves.

"I want two suits for each of these boys," said their guide, "one of plain blue serge, the other of rough tweed, thick and warm."

He knew exactly what he wanted, and got it. Thence he moved to another department, where he bought flannel shirts, underclothes, socks, collars, and ties. The third place they went to was the boot department, where each was provided with two pairs of new boots and a pair of slippers.

Then Clem and Billy were hurried to a dressing-room, where the blue serge suits were ready, together with complete changes of everything, including boots. "Ten minutes to change," said their friend briefly. "Meantime I will get each of you a travelling bag, an overcoat, and a cap."

When Billy stood up in his new clothes and saw himself in the glass he shook his head. "I don't know myself," he said slowly. "Nor you either, Clem," he added. "I'm sure we shall wake up presently and find it's all a dream. It's much too good to be true."

As he spoke the door opened, and in came their lawyer-like friend. "No," he said, "it's real enough." He looked at them, and there was approval in his eyes. "You do me credit," he said briefly. "Your things are all packed. I will take you to the ship."

An hour later Clem and Billy stood at the rail, waving to their friend on the wharf, while the big ship, in tow of a tug, began to move slowly down the river.

CHAPTER III
'THE BIG BRITISHER'

On the eighth morning after leaving England Clem and Billy came on deck to see the huge statue of Liberty towering in front of them, and beyond it the tremendous skyscrapers of New York outlined against a clear blue sky. They had enjoyed every minute of the voyage, but they were still as much in the dark as ever as to where they were going.

On the pier they found waiting for them a man from one of the great travelling agencies. He was an American, very brisk and cheerful. The Customs officials did not worry them much, and almost before they knew it they were driving through the roaring traffic of the capital of the New World to the great Erie Station.

"It's a real shame that there ain't time to show you boys something of this little old town," said their guide, "but my directions is to ship you right through to Seattle quick as you can go."

"Where's Seattle?" inquired Billy.

"A long way from here," replied the other with a grin. "You got to go clean across from the Atlantic to the Pacific, and that's a week in the train. Wal, here's the depot (station you calls it in England), and here's your tickets. I reckon some one will meet you at the other end."

"Who will meet us? Where are we going?" demanded Billy eagerly. The guide looked at him oddly. "If you don't know, I'm sure I don't," was all he said, and once more the

boys found themselves starting off on a new journey without the faintest idea of their real destination.

Everything was new to them—the great steel carriages,
so immensely larger than English ones, the big day coach,
the 'sleeper' with its chairs and tables, the clanging of
the engine bell, the negro porters, the boys who brought
round newspapers, books, and candy.

Their tickets, they found, included sleeping accommo-
dation, and the conductor had evidently been tipped to
look after them. Whoever was paying for their journey was
plainly not stinting money.

Over and over again the boys discussed the question of
who could be their unknown benefactor. They were both
quite certain that it was not their uncle Mr. Grimston.
Billy had suggested that it was possible they were going
right across the Pacific to Australia to join their father,
but Clem, older and wiser, had pointed out how unlikely
it was that their father could have made money enough
in less than two years to pay for all this. In any case, as
he said, it would have been far cheaper for them to go by
sea all the way. Clem's own idea was that it might be their
father's brother, Lionel Ballard, who had sent for them.
Neither he nor Billy had ever seen this uncle, who had left
England many years earlier. All they knew was that their
father had sometimes spoken of him.

On the sixteenth day after leaving England they reached
Seattle, where they were again met by an agent of the same
travel company, taken to a quiet little hotel, and ordered
to remain until called for. They stayed there a week, living
well and enjoying themselves immensely.

Then one evening they were just going to bed when
there was a knock at their door, and in walked a broad-
ly-built man with very clear blue eyes. Clem, who was in
the act of pulling his boots off, sat quite still and stared,
but Billy leapt to his feet. "Mr. Condon!" he cried in utter
amazement.

"Not Mister—just Bart," was the quiet answer, as Bart Condon shook hands gravely, first with Clem, then with Billy. He looked them over. "Well, to be sure, you have come on a whole lot! I reckon you're each seven or eight pound heavier than when I last seed you. You been weighed lately?"

"Weighed!" cried Billy. "We had something else to think of. How in the world did you come here?"

"Steamboat and train—same as you," replied Bart calmly. "Well, well, I'm mighty glad you're both looking so spry. How do you like this town?"

"The town's all right," said Billy, "and we're all right. But it's you we want to hear about. Did you know we were coming here?"

The blue-eyed man's expression did not change in the slightest. "Why, I won't go for to say I didn't," he replied.

Clem stood up. "Was it you took us away from Wasperton?" he demanded.

Bart shook his head. "No, sonny, it warn't me. But say now, I reckon you'd better get right to bed. The steamer leaves at seven to-morrow morning. Now good night to ye. I'll see as you're called bright and early."

He was as good as his word, and early next morning he and the two boys left Seattle aboard a small coasting steamer called the *John P. Wilkes,* and, working out of Elliot Bay, steamed north across Puget Sound, and so out into the Pacific.

The boys were wild with excitement, for now, for the first time since leaving England, they began to feel that they were getting out of touch with civilization.

Not that Bart told them a word of where they were bound. He would talk about anything except that. It was their fellow-passengers who made them feel it. They were nearly all men, and men of a sort which Clem and Billy had never seen before. There were Americans, English, Swedes, Norwegians, and a few French and Italians. There were also men whose dusky faces and sloe-black eyes showed that they had more than a touch of Indian blood in their veins. Almost all these men were big-muscled, deep-chested fellows dressed in thick flannel shirts and jean trousers, and wearing knee-boots, and handkerchiefs knotted round their necks in place of collars.

"Gold-miners, I believe," whispered Billy to Clem. "I say, do you think we can be going to the diggings?"

"The ship is bound for Dyea, in Alaska," replied Clem. "The purser told me. I say, Billy, look at those two who have just passed up the deck. Did you ever see anything like them?"

"Yes, I have. It was in a cinema," replied Billy as he watched them.

They were worth watching too, if only because they looked so rough and strange. One was a great big man with tow-coloured hair, hard, pale blue eyes, and a face that looked as if it had been carved out of stone; his companion was smaller, with a swarthy skin, a thick black moustache curled at the ends, and hair black as jet and clustering in tight ringlets all over his head.

By degrees the mixed company settled down, and by evening every one had found his place. The weather was very fine, and the ship ploughed steadily northward over a sea so calm that the brilliant stars were reflected in its placid surface. Supper over, Clem and Billy found the deck so crowded that they went aft and perched themselves on top of the emergency wheel-house. Here they sat silent, watching the sky and the sea.

All of a sudden they heard voices close by, and peeping over, saw two men standing and leaning over the stern, apparently watching the gleaming wake. They were the very same couple whom they had noticed earlier in the day.

Next moment the taller of these men spoke. "I take it, then, as you have some real information this time, Craze," he said in a low yet harsh voice.

"You can be very sure of that, Gurney," answered the other. "Surely you know me better than to think I should come all this distance on a wild-goose chase. I have it on good authority that the man whom they call 'the Big Britisher' is the one we want. There is a reward of a thousand dollars offered by the police for his capture."

"A thousand dollars!" repeated the tall man in a scornful tone. "You surely are not going to tell me that we are taking this trip for a thousand dollars! Why, that would barely pay our expenses!"

"I am telling you nothing of the sort," replied the black-haired man sharply. "There's ten times that money —maybe twenty—if we play our cards right."

"What do you mean, Craze?" questioned Gurney.

Craze leaned nearer, and spoke in a lower tone, yet the two boys were close enough to hear what he said. "Gold, Gurney. My information is that this man, who is a fugitive from justice, has struck it rich up there in the ranges. And once the police have him, what is to hinder us from restaking his claim?"

Gurney whistled softly. "That's a different story. Right you are, Craze. I'm backing you all the way through."

"What a beastly shame!" whispered Billy in his brother's ear.

But Clem pinched his arm hard. "Keep quiet, Billy," he answered in an equally low tone. "We must get to the bottom of this."

There was a pause during which nothing could be heard but the steady beat of the engine, the throb of the screw, and the rush of the broken water in the wake of the ship. Billy had dropped back close alongside Clem, and the two lay motionless, almost breathless.

The silence had lasted so long that Clem was beginning to be afraid that the men were not going to talk any more, when at last Gurney took his pipe from his mouth and spoke again. "What's this English chap's name, Craze? Know anything about him?"

"Not a lot," was Craze's reply, yet to the listening boys the words did not strike true. "I did hear as his name was Bandon, and that he ain't been up there a very long time. But he's got right in with the Injuns, and he's making a pile of dollars out o' skins and dust."

"And how do you reckon to track him down?"

"My information is as he's settled in a valley up in the Mammoth Range."

Gurney whistled again. "Gee, but that's a long way inland!"

"That's so," agreed Craze. "It's across the Liard River. But I reckon it's worth it."

Gurney nodded. "If it's as good as you say, it's worth a bit of trouble. But see here, Craze, do you reckon you can find the trail?"

Craze chuckled softly. "I got a guide," he said.

"What—one of the Indians?"

"No, he ain't an Injun. He's a white man. And—" he lowered his voice so that only the faintest possible whisper reached Clem's straining ears—"he's right here on this ship this minute."

Gurney started slightly. "Who is he?" he asked eagerly.

Before Craze could answer a sound of footsteps was heard, coming rapidly along the deck toward the stern, and Bart Condon's deep voice broke the silence. "You Clem, you Billy! Where be you?" Clem, caught hold of Billy's arm, and the two crouched closer than ever on the top of the deckhouse.

Bart called again, but as there was no answer, went away. But when Clem ventured again to look down over the edge of his perch Gurney and Craze had vanished. "Bad luck!" he growled in Billy's ear. "Just a moment more, and we should have heard who the guide was."

"It is bad luck," agreed Billy, "but I say, Clem, we've heard quite a lot as it is. And I say, isn't it rum that this 'Bandon' they talk about is a man who has got away from the police, just like Dad?"

"Yes, it is funny," agreed Clem thoughtfully, "Only perhaps he isn't innocent as Dad was."

"I don't care whether he is or not," replied Billy, quickly. "Anyhow, he's made friends with the Indians, so he can't be a bad sort. And whatever he's done, I don't see why these pigs of fellows should rob him."

"No. I'm jolly well with you there, Billy," agreed Clem. "We'd better go and find Bart, and tell him what we've heard. Anyhow, he's looking for us."

They slipped away quietly, and soon found Bart leaning over the rail, just by the companion.

"Say, boys," he remarked in his slow drawl, "hev you plumb forgotten as it's supper-time, or ain't you hungry?"

Clem looked round to make sure no one was listening.

"We had something to make us forget it, Bart," he answered, then told what he and Billy had heard. Bart listened without a word, merely nodding his head once or twice. When Clem had finished he nodded again, "I reckon I can tell you who the guide is as they spoke of," he said quietly. "His name is Condon—Bart Condon."

Clem and Billy gazed at him in speechless amazement. Bart raised his head, and they saw the shadow of a smile on his broad, pleasant face. "Only he ain't going to act, sonny," he continued. He was silent for some moments, then chuckled softly. "I knowed there was something funny doing as soon as I seed them two galoots aboard. But I hardly reckoned as they knowed as much as they seems to. Wal, boys, I'm mighty glad you heard what you did, for it gives me a chance to euchre them two beauties. But I'll hev to do a right smart bit of thinking if we're to get ahead."

Billy burst out. "Do you mean that those two men were going to track us wherever we are going?"

"That's jest exactly what I do mean, sonny," answered Bart deliberately. "But that's enough talk for this time. Come right down to supper. And don't worry. I'll fix them. Yes, I'll fix them proper!"

CHAPTER IV
A HASTY LANDING

"My goodness, Clem, look at those mountains!" exclaimed Billy.

It was eight days since they had left Seattle, and the *John P. Wilkes* was still nosing her way up through the maze of islands which border the coast of British Columbia and Southern Alaska. On this morning the two boys had come up early, to find a calm sea, a blue sky, and outlined against the east a most magnificent array of snow-clad peaks, "I suppose we shall have to climb over those one of these days," replied Clem.

"Maybe sooner than you think, my lads," came Bart's quiet voice behind them.

Both boys turned sharply, but Bart gave them a warning look. "You come along down with me," he said softly, and they followed him below to the cabin they all three shared. Bart closed the door carefully. "You pack your duds, boys," he said.

"What!" gasped Billy. "Are we going ashore?"

"That's so, but there's no need to shout about it."

"I'm sorry," said Billy penitently. "But when?"

"When I do," replied Bart quietly. "You watch me, and for the Lord's sake don't let on to a soul aboard."

It was not often Bart spoke so strongly, and the boys were much impressed. They packed their things, not in portmanteaux, but in bundles, and by Bart's advice left out everything not absolutely necessary. By the time they had finished the ship was steaming up a narrow fiord with high cliffs on either side.

"We stops at the mouth of the Taku River," Bart told them. "Some of the folk'll go ashore, but you jest stay around and watch me. And don't talk, and keep your faces straight. You get me?"

They did, and said so. When they went on deck again Bart locked the cabin door behind them. Presently the *John P. Wilkes* was slowing down into the mouth of a river, a river of medium breadth, which came down between lofty banks covered with gigantic forest. The great trees, which were mostly evergreen, grew to a height of fully two hundred feet, and beneath them was undergrowth thick as that in a tropical swamp. To the right of the river mouth was a plot of four or five acres, with several rough frame buildings. Some Japs and a few Indians were moving about. There was a landing close to the building with nets hung on it, and boats tied up. Stakes rose from the clear water in long rows.

"This here's the Taku salmon-cannery," Bart told the boys. "Now you jest set around and don't do a thing till I tells you."

Clem and Billy—Billy in particular—were quivering with inward excitement, yet managed to carry out their orders. With much splashing and backing the steamer worked in to the wharf and tied up; a gangway was got out, and a number of cases began to be unloaded. The Japs wheeled them up to the storehouse.

Presently Billy whispered to Clem: "Gurney and Craze are watching us."

"I've noticed that," replied Clem cautiously. Gurney and Craze were close to the gangway, and they hardly took their eyes off Bart and the boys. But as the three latter merely leaned over the rail, lazily watching the deck-hands at work, the two watchers seemed to become less suspicious.

A big man wearing his trousers tucked into high boots came down from the main building and crossed the gangway. He looked round, and his eyes fell on Bart Condon.

At once his big, sunburnt face lit up, and he strode across. "Why, Bart, you old son of a gun, be that you? I'm sure glad to see you!" he exclaimed.

Bart stretched out his hand. "Me too, Joe. I thought you'd be along."

"But ain't you coming ashore, Bart?" asked the other, as he wrung his friend's hand.

"Guess not," was the reply. "There ain't a lot of time," replied Bart. He turned to Clem and Billy. "Say, boys, shake hands with my friend Joe Western. He owns this here factory, and some day, when we got more time, maybe we'll stay over with him a piece."

As Bart spoke, Billy, watching him closely, saw one eyelid flicker, saw too that Joe Western seemed to understand something from this lightning wink. At any rate, the big man leaned against the rail, and began to talk salmon and nothing else. The packages were soon ashore; then some cases were brought down from the factory and stowed aboard. The boys began to feel positively ill with excitement, for they could see that in another moment or two the ship was due to leave.

The second officer came down the deck, and stopped opposite them. "We're right off, Mr. Western," he said. "Gangway's just coming up. Guess you better get ashore unless you want to come along with us."

"I'd like to mighty well," smiled Western, "but I reckon I've got my job to attend to. Wal, good-bye, Bart."

Bart walked with him to the gangway, the ropes of which two men were already beginning to loosen. "You better be sharp, boss," said one of them to Western.

"So long," said Western loudly. "I'm mighty sorry you all couldn't give me a call this time." Then, with a wonderfully light step, considering how big and heavy a man he was, he sprang lightly across the gangway and on to the wharf.

The gangway was actually being raised, and Clem and Billy were divided between despair and amazement, when suddenly Bart darted forward. "Here, what are you a-do-ing of?" roared the man who was casting off. "Want to drown yourself, or what?"

"Come on!" hissed Clem to Billy, and before the man could stop them they had both followed Bart, and with flying leaps reached the wharf. They turned to see Gurney and Craze make a dash for the gangway. They were too late. The gangway was already half-way up, the screw was turning, and the steamer beginning to move.

"Fifty dollars if you get us ashore," the boys heard Gurney say sharply to the man in charge of the gangway.

"You better go and ask the skipper," retorted the latter, who was not in the best of tempers. At this moment a man rushed to the rail, and two heavy packages hurtled through the air, to land with heavy thuds on the wharf.

"There's your duds, boys," said Bart calmly. "Take 'em up and carry 'em to the house. We've changed our minds, and are going to stay with Mr. Western a piece."

He waved his hand to the infuriated Gurney and Craze. "So long!" he said. "Better luck next time! And, Craze, when you wants a guide, you better fix up first to pay him, see?"

What Craze said cannot be printed, but Bart did not stop to listen. He turned his back and walked straight toward the house.

CHAPTER V
THE 'BORE'

Joe Western's quarters were rough, but comfortable. There were plenty of bunks and plenty to eat, and after as good a dinner as they had ever put away the two boys were turned loose to explore. "Only don't you go up in the woods, young fellers," warned Western. "Not onless Bart or me goes with you. You can go out in a boat if you've a mind to, but the woods ain't healthy for tenderfeet."

So Clem and Billy started off exploring, and the first thing they came across was a huge boatload of silvery salmon fresh from the nets being carried up into the factory. Here they were gutted and scaled by Indians, then packed into cans, which were placed in huge cauldrons of boiling water. When the fish was cooked the tins were allowed to cool, then soldered up, and after being labelled were packed in cases ready for shipment.

Afterward Sam, the Japanese in charge of the boats, lent them a canoe, and they went up the river a little way to look at the stake nets. The water was alive with salmon, which were running up the river to spawn. The afternoon seemed to pass like a flash, and it was only when they began to feel hungry that the boys remembered they must get back for supper.

Supper was as good and plentiful as dinner, and when it was over Bart and Joe Western pulled chairs out on the veranda, and Clem and Billy followed.

"Do we start to-morrow, Bart?" questioned Billy.

Bart shook his head slowly. "I reckon not, Billy. Ye see, we got to have carriers, and Joe here can't spare none of his Injuns until the fishing season's over."

Billy's face showed his dismay. "But, Bart, won't Gurney and Craze come back after us?"

Bart nodded. "Ay, they'll come back, but it's going to take them quite a while."

"But, surely, the sooner we get away, the better," said Clem seriously. "If Mr. Western would lend us a canoe, we could take our things in it all right, couldn't we?"

Bart nodded again. "Yes, sonny, we can take 'em as fur as the water'll let us. But that ain't where we're bound for. There's two hundred mile and more of mountains to cross after that. And it ain't as if you and Billy could heft a forty-pound pack over country like that."

"We could with practice," vowed Billy.

Joe Western spoke. "Five years' practice, Billy. No less. I guess you'll jest have to settle down to wait a piece. I'm mighty sorry, but it can't be helped."

His tone was so decided that the boys felt it was no use arguing. They got up and moved away toward the river. It was dark now, but the night was beautiful, calm and still, and a wonderful hush brooded over the great forests that sloped so steeply to the swift river.

"Hulloa, here's Sam!" exclaimed Billy. The Japanese, who was sitting in a boat busily sharpening a big three-pronged spear, looked up.

"You like go with me?" he asked in his polite way.

"Rather!" said Billy. "Where are you going?"

"I go hunt dogfish," he answered, lifting the spear. The boys tumbled in in a twinkling, and took the oars; then, under Sam's directions, they pulled out into the middle of the river, stopped, and let the boat drift. Sam pointed downward, and a wonderful sight met their eyes. The water was smooth here and clear as glass, and the depths were alive with huge fish, each about four feet in length.

These were outlined in gleaming phosphorescence, and were moving to and fro in the most curious and intricate patterns.

"They dogfish," explained Sam. "They hunt salmon. We hunt them." As he spoke he stood up, raised the spear, and suddenly dashed it down into the water with all his force. Next moment it was nearly wrenched out of his hand, but he held on hard, and up came a writhing monster like a small shark.

"You try," he said to Clem, and Clem eagerly took the spear. He waited, watching his chance, then struck hard, and instantly felt the barbed prongs fasten in a fish.

But he had not in the least realized the weight and strength of the creature. Sam made a snatch at him, but was just too late. Over went Clem, head foremost, and with a tremendous splash disappeared under the cold, swift-running water.

Billy gave a yell of alarm. "Quick, Sam, catch him!" he cried. "He can't swim!"

It was true. There had been no swimming-bath at Wasperton, and neither of the boys had ever had a chance to learn to swim. But it was too late for Sam to catch Clem, who, still grasping his spear, had gone clean under.

The plucky Jap did not hesitate an instant. He simply dived clean over the side and vanished in Clem's wake. Billy, left alone, did not lose his head, but turned the boat in the track of the line of bubbles which he saw rising. Suddenly the water broke, and to his intense relief he saw Sam rise, holding Clem by the back of his shirt.

Billy drove the boat alongside and Sam caught hold of the gunwale. "Help pull him in," panted Sam, who was evidently badly blown by his deep dive.

Billy sprang to obey, but in his haste knocked one oar overboard. He did not wait to recover it, but grabbed hold of Clem, and with a great effort managed to hoist him on board. Then he helped Sam into the boat. "I say, that was fine of you, Sam!" he said gratefully. But Sam, after giving himself one shake like a wet dog, turned his attention to Clem.

Clem had swallowed rather more water than was good for him, but otherwise was little the worse. His trouble was that he had lost his spear, and this he at once began to apologize for.

Sam cut him short. "We get back," he said in his good but curiously clipped English. "We get back quick. Give me oars, please."

"I'm sorry," said Billy, "but one's gone overboard. We shall have to drop down a bit and pick it up."

Sam snatched up the remaining oar, and pushing it out over the stern, set to sculling frantically toward the bank.

Billy was astonished. "Why, what's the matter?" he demanded. "What's the hurry?"

"The tide come," replied the other breathlessly. "Tide come quick."

Neither Billy nor Clem had the faintest idea what Sam was talking about, but they could both of them see that he was very much upset, and desperately anxious about something. Yet the sky was clear, there was no wind, the air was quite warm. They could not make head or tail of it.

Sam sculled with a sort of fierce desperation; but the current was strong, and the boat, a big flat-bottomed affair, was heavy and clumsy, and for every foot she got in toward the bank she drifted three downstream. As there was not another oar in the boat the boys could not help him. All they could do was to wait and wonder what the danger was.

They had not very long to wait. The boat was still quite fifty yards from the bank when suddenly the current which had been sweeping her downstream seemed to be stopped short. It simply ceased to exist, the effect being first as though great lock-gates had been suddenly closed. But before Sam could take any real advantage of this change there came a curious hissing sound out of the soft darkness in the direction of the sea.

In a flash Sam ceased his efforts to reach the bank, and with a mighty swing turned the boat so that her bow faced straight downstream. And still the boys stared blankly.

The hissing grew louder, and suddenly Billy pointed. "The wave!" he cried. "Clem, the wave!"

Clem stared, hardly able to believe his eyes. For there, racing up from the sea, was a wave at least eight feet high and filling the whole river from bank to bank. It was not the least like a storm wave, for it was smooth as glass, but the pace at which it travelled was simply amazing. It came pretty nearly as fast as a horse could gallop. What made it all the more startling and even terrifying was the phosphorescence which tipped this wall of water with a rim of bluish light.

"I know," gasped Billy. "It's a bore—a tidal wave." It was the last thing he said for some time, for next instant the wave was upon them.

The boat rose until it absolutely stood on end, and the boys were forced to clutch at the thwarts to save themselves from being flung out backward. The last thing that Billy and Clem heard was a loud shout from Sam: "Hold to the boat! Hold tight!"

Then the heavy craft was literally up-ended. She capsized, and all the boys knew was that they were under water, and ripping through it at a fearful pace.

Half-choked, blinded, chilled to the marrow, Billy hung on like grim death, and just when he felt that he could cling no longer, suddenly found his head above water. "Clem!" he cried hoarsely. "Clem!"

"All right. I'm all right," came Clem's half-strangled reply, and there, to Billy's intense relief, he saw Clem clinging to the opposite side of the boat.

"Where's Sam?" was Billy's next question.

"Don't know. I say, he must have been swept off!"

" HOLD TO THE BOAT !   HOLD TIGHT ! "

That was clear enough, for there was no sign of him anywhere.

"Do you think he's drowned?" asked Billy in an awed voice.

"He swims like fish," said Clem comfortingly. "I expect he'll get ashore. We weren't far off it when the wave caught us."

"And where are we going now?"

"Up to the head of the river by the look of it," said Clem grimly.

The wave was gone, or rather it was ahead of them, but the boat, and they with it, was travelling up the river with the speed of a steam-launch. Already the lights of the factory were a long way behind.

Presently Clem spoke again. "It's rotten, our not being able to swim," he grumbled.

"I'm jolly well going to learn," said Billy.

Clem did not answer. What he was wondering was whether he and Billy were ever going to have the chance.

CHAPTER VI
NIGHT IN THE FOREST

All this time the boat had been going right up the middle of the river, but now they were coming to a bend, and suddenly she swung to one side. An eddy caught and spun her, and there was a bump which nearly shook the two boys from their hold. "We've struck something," cried Clem.

"I could have told you that," replied Billy dryly. "It's a log, a big dead tree. I've got hold of a branch. I believe I can shove her inshore."

The boat was heavy, and even under the bank the tide rip was strong, but Billy pulled with all his might, and Clem helped. Good feeding had made a wonderful lot of difference to the two, and they were twice the boys they had been a month ago. Gradually the heavy boat yielded to their combined strength, and swinging again, bumped into the bank, ramming her blunt bow deep into the earth. "It's all right, Clem," said Billy cheerfully. "I've got my feet on the bottom. It's firm sand. Come on!"

"Wait," said Clem. "We mustn't let the boat go."

"She won't move. She's jammed. Let's get out of the water. I'm nearly frozen."

They climbed out on to the bank. "It's fine to feel firm ground under one's feet," said Billy, as he stamped about to try and get the blood moving again. Though the night was not cold the water had been cruelly so, and both the boys were fairly numbed.

"And what do we do next?" asked Clem rather glumly, as he looked round at the huge trees towering toward the stars.

"Walk back to the landing quick as ever we can," answered Billy. "We've got to find out whether poor Sam is safe."

"There won't be any very quick moving in this wood," returned Clem. "Did you ever see anything so thick? It's more like a tropical jungle than anything else. I never thought for a minute we'd find anything like this so far north."

"It's different once you get across the coast ranges, Bart says," replied Billy; "but let's try what we can do. If we keep close to the river we can't lose our way. And anyhow, we shall get warm."

Billy never said a truer word, for very soon they were both simply dripping with perspiration. The going was awful, and the darkness made it fifty times worse. Billy had a torch, but the water had got into the battery and spoilt it. Their matches too were soaking, for they had not yet learned the trapper's trick of keeping them dry in a corked bottle. The steep bank was simply littered with fallen tree-trunks, some of enormous size, and all grown over with moss and long grass and bush of every sort, mostly prickly.

Some trunks were still sound, but most were perfectly rotten, so that when they stepped on them they crumbled to tinder and let them down into wet and slime. Add to this that the ground was full of deep cracks and rifts cut by winter storms, and broken by boulders and jutting crags, and you may begin

to have some idea of the difficulties confronting the unlucky travelers.

"Don't wonder Joe Western said this brush was no place for tenderfeet," panted Billy as, for about the fifteenth time, he went blundering into a hidden pit. "I say, Clem, we'd better work uphill a little. It looks better than down here by the river."

Clem agreed, and they climbed the steep slope. Here the fallen trees were not quite so thick, but the undergrowth was thicker than ever.

Billy, who was leading, came to a steep place, slipped, and tried to save himself by clutching at a big, wide-leaved plant which stuck out dimly in front of him. Clem heard him give a sharp cry of pain, and caught him as he fell backward. "What's the matter?" he asked anxiously.

"Something bit me," replied Billy, in a voice hoarse with pain. "I—I'm afraid it was a snake."

For a moment Clem was so scared that his mouth went dry and he could not speak. But he quickly pulled himself together. "It can't be a snake, Billy. There are no poisonous snakes up here—not even rattlers. Bart told me so. You've been stung by something."

"It's something pretty poisonous, then," replied Billy, who was holding on tightly to his injured arm. "I say, Clem, it does hurt."

"Come down nearer the river. There's a bit more light there. Let's have a look at it."

Billy was quite sick and shivery with the pain, and Clem had to help him down the steep hillside. They found a little opening, but even there the light was very dim. Still, there was just enough for Clem to see a dark, inflamed patch on Billy's hand and wrist.

"It's a sting of some sort," he said. "Like a nettle, Billy, only worse. Come on down to the water's edge and dip it in the water."

Billy did so, and after a bit the cold water took the worst of the pain away. But the arm was swollen and almost useless, and Clem had to help Billy along. So progress became slower than ever, and in the next half-hour they travelled only a few hundred yards.

"If Sam got ashore he'd have been back at the factory long ago," said Billy at last.

"Not if he'd landed in this sort of stuff, Billy," replied Clem, but all the same he was very uneasy. They struggled on a bit farther, then both came to a sudden stop.

"What's that?" whispered Billy sharply, pointing to two dots of green fire which glowed through the darkness a little way up the hill above them.

"A wild beast of some sort," answered Clem, in a voice which he found rather difficult to keep steady.

"A—and we've got no gun," said Billy. "What shall we do?"

"Yell at him," suggested Clem desperately.

The noise which the two boys made between them was enough to scare the hide off almost any inhabitant of the woods. At any rate, the owner of the eyes removed them and itself abruptly, but without the slightest sound of its going.

"I wonder if it was a panther," questioned Billy.

"Just a wild cat, I expect," replied Clem hopefully. "But I say, Billy, let's get down close to the river again. I do hate this wood."

"So do I," agreed Billy, and turned downhill again. When they got well down to the river's edge they found themselves on the top of a steep bluff ten or twelve feet high, which dropped to a beach of sand and shingle. At this time of year, well on in August, the June floods were long past, and the autumn rains had not begun. So the river was at its lowest. At low water there would have been plenty of room to walk along under the bluff, but now the flood tide was beginning to cover the little beaches.

Billy stopped and looked over. "If we got down there on the gravel, we could shove along quite fast," he said.

"We should go an awful purler if we tried to climb down that bluff," Clem objected. "Let's go a little farther and see if there's a way down." Billy agreed, and they pushed on slowly.

A little point of land ragout into the river, and crossing this, they saw below them quite a broad strip of almost level shingle. They saw something else too. A little farther on, a figure was standing on the beach in a queer crouching position, bending over the water and apparently trying to rake something out of the river with one hand. In the dim starlight it appeared to be a short, broadly built man. Billy clutched his brother's arm. "It's Sam," he whispered.

"I'm not so sure," said Clem. "He looks to me bigger than Sam."

"Yes, he does look a whacking big chap," admitted Billy. "Come a bit nearer, and let's see before we shout."

As they moved forward, the man by the water seemed to grow larger. He certainly was enormously broad. By this time the boys had had such a fright that they were both getting nervous. Though they would not confess it, they each had a sort of suspicion that this might be a wild Indian. They reached a point exactly above the spot where the queer-looking fellow was still groping in the water, and Clem, catching hold of a branch, bent forward to get a better view. There was a sharp crack, the bough broke short off, and Clem, losing his balance, toppled forward and fell right over the edge of the little bluff.

Billy saw him land with a thud on the shingle. As he did so, the figure by the water reared up sharply and whirled round, and Billy was nearly frantic when he saw its huge, shaggy shape. "A bear!" he gasped, and forgetful of his injured hand and the fact that he had no weapon—not even a knife—made a flying leap down to the beach to Clem's rescue.

It was a bigger drop than Billy had supposed, and he came down so heavily that he pitched face forward on the shingle and lay half stunned. When he recovered Clem was kneeling beside him, anxiously asking, "Billy, are you hurt?"

"N—no," gasped Billy. "I—I'm not hurt, b—but where's the bear?"

"Gone. When you came down flop, like that, he simply hooked it."

"Hooked it?" repeated Billy in a bewildered voice. "I—I thought bears were dangerous."

"This one wasn't., You wouldn't have believed that such a clumsy-looking brute could travel so fast. He simply vanished." He paused. "But, Billy, it was awfully decent of you to come to help me," he added.

"Fat lot of good I could have done!" returned Billy gruffly. "I haven't even got a knife."

"That don't matter," said Clem. "It was a jolly plucky thing to do."

"Shut up, Clem!" growled Billy. "We've got to get home."

"I'd like to know how," said Clem ruefully. "Now, we've got down this bank, it's going to be a sweet job to climb up it again. And I'm just about fed up with that wood. I've a jolly good mind to camp here till daylight."

"Not good enough," replied Billy decidedly. "We're both as wet as can be, and we can't light a fire. We shall only get fever, or something nasty of that kind. Come on. It can't be very far."

Billy was so plucky that Clem felt a little ashamed. "Right you are," he said. "I'll give you a leg up."

Billy got to his feet. To say truth, he felt horribly shaky, and his arm was hurting abominably. But he set his teeth and vowed to himself that somehow they would get back.

Clem gave him a back, and he grabbed a branch and tried to scramble up the bluff. But the bough broke and let him down. He had another try, and this time got hold of a thick tuft of grass, only to have the whole thing come out by the roots and drop him once more to the shingle. "I've half a mind to do as you say and chuck it, Clem," he said at last. "There doesn't seem to be any foothold."

"We can't, Billy," replied Clem gravely. "Why not, I should like to know?"

"Because the tide's still rising, and in about half an hour all this shingle will be under water."

"That settles it then," grumbled Billy. "You—" He stopped short and flung up one hand. "Listen!" he cried.

"Hi—yah! Hulloa!" The shout came ringing faintly up the river out of the darkness, and both boys spun round, and stared breathlessly in the direction from which the sound came.

"Hi—yah!" came the call again, and Clem managed to collect his scattered senses and answer. His ringing "Hulloa!" sent the echoes flying weirdly up the steep hillside among the giant trees.

"It's Bart," said Billy sharply. "What luck!" Then he too shouted at the top of his voice.

"That you, Billy?" came Bart's voice.

"Yes, and Clem," answered Billy. "Here we are on the beach. Pull on. We're a good way up."

There was a splash of paddles, and soon a canoe paddled by two Indians came shooting up at a great pace. Billy thought that the sound of her bows grating on the shingle was the pleasantest he had ever heard.

"You all right?" questioned Bart as the boys came clambering in, and both of them could plainly hear the anxiety in his tone.

"Right as rain," answered Clem; "only Billy got stung by something. But Sam—is Sam safe?"

"Sam's all right. Trouble was, the tide swept him right across the other side of the river and it was an hour before anyone heard him shouting. Whar did you boys land up?"

They told him, while the two Indian paddlers drove the canoe swiftly back down the river. It was but a very few minutes before they were safe on the wharf again, where they were met by Joe Western. He took them straight to the house, and made them each take five grains of quinine, washed down by big mugs of steaming hot coffee. Then they had to tell their story all over again.

"Stung, was you?" said Joe. "No, it warn't no snake. I reckon it were that 'devil's club.' Let me see. Aye, that's it. Like nettle, only a sight worse, but I guess I got some stuff as'll take the pain out."

He went to a shelf, took down a bottle, and putting some of the contents on a rag, applied it to Billy's hand and arm.

"Why, it's wonderful!" exclaimed Billy. "It's taking all the pain away. But I say, I didn't tell you we met a bear."

"Met a bear!" repeated Joe. "What sort was he?"

"He didn't stop to tell us," answered Billy. "He simply cleared out."

Joe burst into a great laugh. "I reckon he was only a third-class bear," he chuckled. "But it might ha' been different ef you'd have met his big brother."

"Tell us," begged Billy.

"Not to-night, son. You get right to bed. I'll tell ye to-morrow, and mebbe I can show ye one in the daylight."

CHAPTER VII
THE COMING OF THE STRANGER

"What's the barrel for?" demanded Billy. Joe Western and Bart, together with the two boys, were tramping up a steep, narrow trail through the woods on the day following their adventure on the river, and Joe was carrying on his great shoulder an empty molasses barrel.

Joe laughed. "All in good time, son. I'm a-going to try to show ye a bear."

That was all the boys could get out of him, and anyhow they had not much breath left for asking questions, for the path they were following was somewhat steeper than the roof of an average house. It wound up the hillside among trunks of trees which were the biggest that Clem and Billy had ever seen.

They were mostly Douglas fir, and towered fully two hundred feet toward the blue sky. Some of the stems were so huge that it would have taken five grown men to encircle them with outstretched arms.

What utterly amazed the boys was that now and then humming-birds flashed like living jewels above the tangled undergrowth, while other birds that looked like canaries flitted in front of them. And yet they were farther north than the most northern point of Scotland.

At last, very hot and very blown, they came to more open ground above the heaviest belt of forest.

"Guess I've carried this here barrel about far enough," remarked Joe, and dumped it down just on the edge of the steepest part of the slope and under cover of a low, spreading birch-tree. Then he walked straight on without offering any explanation. His long legs covered the ground at a great pace, and Clem and Billy were both grateful when at last he stopped close to a big tree, and pointed to the trunk.

"See anything, Billy?" he asked.

"Yes," replied Billy, staring with interest at the tree. "The bark's all torn."

"My word, that was a big one, Joe," said Bart.

"A big what?" asked Clem.

"A big bear, Clem."

"You don't tell me that was a bear?" exclaimed Clem. "Why, the bark's all torn up to a height of ten or eleven feet!"

"It was a bear all right, son," said Joe. "What I calls a first-class bear."

"It must be a giant," said Billy in an awed voice.

"A 'silver tip,'" explained Bart. "Grizzly's the name the books give him. We get 'em mighty big here. Some of 'em is as large as an ox, and a sight heavier."

The boys could not answer. They only stared at the clawed trunk.

"Then there's second-class bears," said Joe. "Them's the cinnamons, and cunning chaps they are. The third class is the brown bears, same as you met last night. But set yourselves down," he continued. "We'll rest awhile and eat our grub."

He took a great packet of sandwiches from his pocket. They were of baking-powder bread with cold fried bacon and mustard inside, and very good indeed. While they ate he told them more about bears. "The Injun calls the bear his brother," he said, "and there's one thing you boys got to remember. If you're in camp with Injuns, don't you go mentioning 'bear.' It ain't good manners, according to the Injun way of thinking. You can talk of 'Fur-Jacket' or anything o' that sort, but don't say 'bear.'"

"But if we meet a grizzly, what do we do?" asked Billy.

"Walk right on and don't take no notice. Onless he's mighty hungry or got het up about something, he ain't a-going to hurt you."

Billy stared. He had always supposed that wild beasts went for you on sight.

"Same with all the rest o' the wild things," continued Joe. "They won't meddle with man onless they're in bad need of food. Only don't you leave your stores unguarded, for that's Mister Bear's chance, and he'll eat 'em all."

He stopped, and the boys saw that he was listening keenly. Suddenly he jumped up. "I said I'd show you a bear. Come right along. But quiet now. Don't you make a noise. Watch where you set your feet."

It was the boys' first lesson in woodcraft, and neither had ever had a notion how difficult it was to walk quietly until they tried to imitate Bart and Joe Western.

Joe led straight back to the spot where they had left the sugar barrel, then motioned them to a hiding-place among some shrubs. He pointed, and through a little opening the boys saw the oddest sight imaginable. A bear, a great big beast that must have weighed four or five hundred pounds, was busy with the barrel. He had turned it over on its side, and was lying by it, with his head right inside, licking the sides of it. They could hear him smacking his lips and grunting delightedly. He was evidently enjoying himself hugely.

Gradually, as they watched, he worked farther and farther in until his head and shoulders and forepaws were all inside the barrel. A very tight fit it was, but Mister Bear didn't seem to care. He was having the time of his life.

Now the barrel, as has been mentioned, had been left on a little ledge with a very steep slope below it. The bear, in his efforts to get the last lick of molasses from the bottom, had at last wedged half his body into the barrel, and in doing so had managed to turn the barrel right round, so that the butt of it projected over the lower side of the ledge. But he, of course, could not see his danger.

Suddenly the barrel went over the edge. Poor bear was far too tightly packed inside it to get out in time, and he went with it. Next instant barrel and bear were rolling downhill, spinning like a Catherine-wheel.

"Oh, he'll be killed!" cried Billy, jumping up.

Joe Western burst into a great roar of laughter. "Did you ever see the like of that, Bart?" he asked.

Bart's face was one great grin. "I never did, Joe. Say, let's see where he lands up."

Next minute all four were running helter-skelter down the hill in track of barrel and bear. For a wonder, this part of the slope, though steep, was fairly smooth, and they were just in time to see bear and barrel strike a patch of scrub fifty feet below and go through it like a shell.

"Gee, but old bear must be getting dizzy!" chuckled Bart as he went striding down the hillside. "Billy," he shouted, "don't you go too fur ahead. That beast'll be madder than a burnt cat when he gets loose again."

Billy didn't hear. He was ever so far ahead, racing along, jumping everything in his path. Clem was close behind him. Below the scrub was another sharp descent, ending in a sheer drop of ten or fifteen feet. The barrel and the bear whirled down the steep at dizzy speed.

"Clem, he'll be killed!" shrieked Billy as he saw the barrel whizzing toward the edge of the drop.

"So will you, if you don't stop!" yelled back Clem, flinging himself flat on the ground.

Billy would never have been able to stop if it had not been for a small tree which he was able to grab hold of. The barrel reached the edge of the little cliff, hurtled through the air, fell with a crash upon the hard ground fifty feet away, and instantly went to splinters. Staves flew in every direction, forming a sort of rainbow round the unfortunate bear.

Billy, gazing with all his eyes, was amazed to see the bear pick himself up and stand, shaking his head in a muddled sort of fashion, yet seemingly very little the worse.

"Lie down, Billy!" came Bart's voice behind him, curt and sharp, and Billy dropped like a flash. "He's mad as a hornet," muttered Bart. "He'll go fer anything as moves."

And just then something did move. Out of the trees, not twenty yards below where the bear was standing, a man appeared—a white man who wore knee-boots, blue jeans, and a dark blue flannel shirt.

"Look out!" yelled Bart.

It was too late. With a deep, rumbling growl, the bear lowered his pig-like head, and charged straight at the stranger. The stranger turned and ran for dear life. He was a long, lanky fellow of at least six feet, and the pace he made was surprising. So was that of the bear. You would never have believed that so clumsy-looking a beast could have gone so fast.

Clem and Billy stood at the top of the little cliff and stared. For the moment they were too surprised to do anything else. It was Bart who roused them from their trance. "The blamed fool! He'll be mauled!" he snapped out, and down he went over the ledge, climbing like a cat in spite of his heavy build.

Joe Western followed, and the boys were nearly as quick.

By this time the long man and the bear were both out of sight among the trees, but the others could still hear the crashing of heavy bodies through the undergrowth. Suddenly the sound ceased, but was followed by a terrifying growl from the bear.

"By gum, the brute's got him!" panted Joe Western, tearing onward at top speed. It was all that the two boys could do to keep up. All together, the four burst through the trees into another open space. The first thing they saw was the bear's hindquarters disappearing among the lower boughs of a small cedar, while up above the branches were being violently shaken.

Bart stopped short. "Treed!" he cried, and a broad grin spread over his jolly face.

"B—but the bear will catch him," gasped Billy, as he caught a glimpse of the long man going up through the branches at the rate of many knots.

Bart, however, did not seem seriously disturbed. "Guess there ain't much danger," he observed. "That there's no bear tree."

Clem look puzzled, but Billy's quick wits grasped Bart's meaning. "It's not big enough for the bear, Clem," he said. "The branches won't hold him very far up."

Sure enough, the bear, which was very fat and must have weighed all of five hundred pounds, had already reached a point where his weight was making the whole tree sag. It was quite a small tree, and under the combined weight of man and bear was beginning to bend right over. Quite near the top, the long man was clinging to the trunk, both legs and one arm wrapped tightly around it. He was scared to death and very angry, and the expression on his lantern-jawed face was so funny that the boys could hardly help laughing.

"But what are we going to do about it, Bart?" asked Clem. "It's all very well to laugh, but that beast is jolly near him. Look at him, reaching up with those great claws of his!"

"Help!" roared the man in the tree. "Don't stand there, a-laughing like ijiots! Shoot him, why don't ye?" As he spoke the bear made a blow at him with one great paw, but could not quite reach, and the stranger scrambled wildly another two feet higher, then stuck fast among the small twigs. The tree bent like a fishing-rod.

"Guess we'll hev to shoot him, Bart," said Joe Western, as he pulled a long-barreled pistol from the holster he wore at his belt.

"Don't you do it!" cried Bart. But he spoke too late. Joe's action in pulling the pistol and firing was all one— so quick that the gun was hardly out of its holster before the sharp crack of the report went echoing all down the hillside.

The bear, shot clean through the head, released its hold, and fell like a sack, crashing through the thick branches. All in a flash the boys realized why Bart had shouted, for the tree, relieved of the ponderous weight of the great beast, shot up like an uncoiled spring, and with such force that the long man was torn from his hold and flung into mid-air as if shot from a catapult.

"Ow!" His terrified yell rang through the warm air; then he vanished into a thick patch of scrub.

"That was a fool trick, Joe," said Bart, as he ran forward. "He'll be lucky if he ain't as dead as the bear."

Billy was the first to reach the spot where the stranger had fallen, and plunged into the thicket. "It's all right," he cried shrilly. "He's fallen in a mud-hole. He's not dead."

"Then he ought to be mighty grateful," said Bart dryly.

But the long man was not grateful at all. On the contrary, he was very angry indeed, and the language he used was not pretty or nice. Indeed, it was so bad that Bart shut him up pretty roughly. "You'd ought to be thanking your stars as you're alive instead o' cussing like that," he said, and the boys had never yet heard their friend speak so sternly.

The other shut up, but for a time was very sulky. It was not until they were nearly back at the landing that he recovered his temper and began to explain who he was and where he came from.

CHAPTER VIII
THE DEATH SLIDE

"My name is Pelly," he said. "Ed Pelly, come down from Juneau in a dug-out. Jest landed a couple o' hours ago. Thet little Jap feller o' yours, he told me I'd find you up the hill, so I walked up arter you. But I didn't reckon as I'd meet up with that there dratted bear a-rolling down the mountain like a pea in a drum."

He paused. Clem and Billy were aching to ask him what he had come for, but they had been in the North-West just long enough to know that it is the height of bad manners to ask personal questions.

Joe Western spoke. "You looking for a job?" he asked politely.

"No, sir. I got my job fixed. I'm a prospector, and a chap in Dawson told me as there's good gold in the ranges beyond the Liard. I got my grub stake, and I reckon to go up the river and get fixed on the ground before the freeze-up."

"Why, we're going up the river!" broke in Billy.

Pelly looked at him with interest. "Is that so? And when were you reckoning to start?"

"As soon as we can get Indians," replied Billy.

"Wal now, I got two Injuns," said Pelly, and turned to Bart. "Mebbe we could fix to join up fer the trip!"

"Mebbe we could. I'll let ye know," replied Bart, but though his tone was perfectly polite, it was not by any means cordial. Billy felt somewhat snubbed, and said no more.

They took Pelly to the house, and while Joe gave him food and drink, Bart took the boys out again. "Guess we better go and skin that bear," he said. "It'll be about all we can do before dark."

As they toiled up the hill again Clem and Billy noticed that Bart was even more silent than usual. They wondered what he was thinking about, but he gave no sign. When they got near the spot where the dead bear lay, Bart stopped short. "Seems someone has got ahead of us," he said dryly.

Sure enough, a man was squatting beside the carcass, and as he rose to his feet they saw he was an Indian. He was rather short, squarely built, and wore a pair of cheap store trousers and a flannel shirt. Yet Bart looked at him with interest. "A Stick Injun!" he remarked. "Comes from the inside country," he explained.

The Indian saluted them gravely. "Klahowya!" he said.

Bart answered with another word, "Tillicum!" and there was an almost pleased expression on the Indian's wooden face.

"Me Ahkim," he said. Then, pointing to the bear, "Hyas bear," he observed.

"Hyas fat," Bart agreed. "We want um skin. You take um fat and sinews."

The Indian actually smiled, but as Bart afterward told the boys, the Indian loves nothing better than bear-fat, while he uses the sinews for a dozen purposes. In a trice he was busy skinning the bear; when this was done, the four, between them, roped the carcass and hoisted it into a tree out of reach of wolves and foxes.

With the skin on his head, the Indian followed them down the hill, and on the way he and Bart talked, but the boys could not understand much of what was said. Bart, however, seemed pleased, and when they got back he told the boys why. "He's a-going up the river. He'll come with us. If we can get one more man I guess we shall do."

"Pelly has two," said Billy. "If we join forces, shan't we be all right?"

Bart frowned slightly. "Guess I don't know a lot about Pelly," he said briefly. And for all the rest of the evening he remained curiously silent.

Early next morning Clem and Billy were down by the river examining Pelly's dug-out when its owner came behind them. "She's a real good boat," he said, "but a mite too heavy for river work. I'm reckoning to trade her with one o' the Injuns fer a bark canoe."

He pointed out the difference between his boat, which was hollowed out of a single great log, and the light birch barks used for river work. They chatted a while; then Pelly said suddenly, "Say, I wish you boys was going along with me."

"I wish we were," replied Billy.

Pelly laughed, then shrugged his shoulders. "Your boss, Mr. Condon, he don't seem to trust me. Not as I blame him. He don't know nothing about me, and up here folk don't carry testimonials around in their wallets."

Not quite knowing what to say, the boys remained silent.

Pelly changed the subject. "Say, now, how d ye like to go hunting with me to-day? I got to get some meat fer my Injuns afore starting, and I was reckoning to shoot a moose or mebbe a sheep. They do say there's plenty up the mountain."

"Oh, let's go, Clem!" cried Billy.

"We must ask Bart first," replied Clem.

"Yes, you jest go along and ask him, then we'll start right off," said Pelly.

But Bart was not in the house. He and Joe had gone out together, and Sam did not know where they were.

"He won't mind, Clem," said Billy.

Clem looked doubtful. "Bart doesn't cotton to Pelly," he answered.

"He doesn't want to travel with him. That's all. You see, Clem, Bart won't tell even us where he's going to, and that's why he doesn't want anyone else with him."

Clem grunted. He was not sure that he himself quite liked Pelly. But he thought there could be no harm in going out for one day with the man; so after first leaving word with Sam, and getting some sandwiches, they started.

Pelly took them straight up the mountain, and by eleven o'clock they were far above the timber, with the snow-line, less than a mile away. The river was a mere thread three thousand feet below, the sea a flat blue plain, and the breeze had a winter edge as it blew above them. Still, they kept on until the snow was crunching under their boots.

"My goodness, Clem, this is a bit of a change!" said Billy.

Pelly swung round. "Hush, there! Don't either of ye speak above a whisper," he ordered curtly. "Jest foller me." They did, and presently realized that Pelly was following a trail. The prints of small hoofs were plainly visible in the dazzling snow.

The slope grew steeper. It was difficult to keep their feet. Presently they rounded a shoulder of the mountain, and both stopped short. Before them was a snow-slope steep as the roof of a house and blindingly white in the sun's blaze. It stretched down for four or five hundred feet, then broke off into a terrific precipice. So steep was it, so smooth, that it did not seem possible that anything on foot could cross it. Yet there, plain to see, ran the sharp prints of the mountain-sheep.

Pelly looked at the boys and grinned. Clem did not like the grin. "Skeered?" asked the man with a sort of half-taunt in his voice.

"Yes, a bit," replied Clem, and it took more pluck to acknowledge that he was afraid than to tell a lie and say he was not.

"Wal, I don't know as I blame ye," said Pelly. "But ef I'm a-going to get that sheep, I got to foller him. Yew better go right back an' wait fer me behind them rocks."

Billy broke in sharply. "No, we can go where you do, can't we, Clem?"

Clem nodded, and they followed. The snow seemed dreadfully loose, and Clem's heart was in his mouth as he picked his way across it. He could not help thinking what would happen if the snow started to slide. The only thing that comforted him was that here and there a jag of black rock jutted out through the dazzling surface.

Suddenly Pelly raised his hand and motioned them to stop. He pointed, and high above them they saw a brown creature with great curved horns standing upon a crag. Pelly raised his rifle, aimed carefully, fired, and the 'big horn' toppled over and fell with a thud from its lofty perch. It landed upon the slope and came rolling down, and as it came the snow began to move. Pelly's face went like chalk. "Look out!" he gasped, and made one wild rush toward the nearest rock, leaving the boys behind him to fend for themselves.

CHAPTER IX
THE LAST REFUGE

Pelly reached the projecting rock in safety, but before Clem and Billy could do the same the snow they were standing on had begun to move. Both struggled desperately and for a few moments gained upon the slowly sliding sheet.

Billy, who was just ahead of his brother, got to within a yard or so of the rock. "Give me a hand," he shouted to Pelly, but Pelly, clinging with both hands to the spike of rock, was so slow about it that before Billy could grasp his outstretched hand the sliding snow had carried him out of reach.

Still, he and Clem fought hard to reach safety, but all in vain. The pace of the snow-slide was increasing every moment, and to fight it was like trying to climb a treadmill which turns under your weight at every step.

"It's no use, Billy," panted Clem. "There's another rock. Try for that." He pointed as he spoke to a second crag, which rose black against the creeping white sheet. It was lower down than the one Pelly had reached, but farther away.

"Right!" answered Billy, and he made a fresh dash.

But the snow was slipping faster and faster. The whole great sheet, two hundred yards or more in width, was sliding rapidly downward, and long before the boys could reach the other place of refuge they were carried helplessly past it.

Billy looked down toward the edge of the precipice, over which the snow was already pouring like a river over a great fall, and his very heart froze as he thought of the appalling drop that awaited him and Clem. He could hear the roar of the avalanche, like distant thunder.

Clem slipped and fell, but Billy jerked him to his feet again. "One more try, old chap," he said hoarsely. "Our only chance is to go across, not against it. Look! There's one more rock showing below us."

Clem merely nodded. He was too blown to speak, and, holding each other's hands, he and Billy made a last attempt to save themselves. The snow was rising in waves, and the little peak of rock which was all that stood between them and a terrible death was almost hidden by the white masses which surged over it.

The roar of the fall was now deafening. It seemed that half the mountain-side was peeling off and dropping into the abyss. Yet Billy kept his eyes fixed upon the rock that was their last chance, and somehow he and Clem fought their way across the great snow-slide toward it. They were just above it, when a snow-wave caught them and swept them off their feet. But it did not break their hold one of the other, and the next thing they knew was that they had been carried right across the rock, one on one side, one on the other.

"Hold on!" shrieked Billy as he felt the strain. The snow surged over them like water. It seemed to grasp them with icy hands and try to drag them from their hold. It covered their heads and blinded them. The weight of it was so great that they felt though their arms were being torn from their sockets.

Yet, since both knew that to let go meant certain death, somehow they managed to cling, and after what seemed an age, but was really only a couple of minutes, the strain lessened, and they were able to draw themselves up and then get hold of the rock itself.

"Never—thought—I—could—do—it," croaked Billy. Clem did not answer at once. He was looking round. The rock which had saved them was within five yards of the edge of the precipice, a sheer drop of such depth that the great trees below looked like toys out of a child's Noah's ark. On either side of the rock was glare ice swept perfectly smooth by the rush of the avalanche. He shivered. "How are we going to get out of it?" he asked in a low voice.

Billy whistled softly. "It's going to be a job," he admitted. "Pelly hasn't got a rope, so I don't know what we shall do."

"You kids all right?" came Pelly's voice from above, and looking up the slope the boys saw that he had managed to cross the narrow strip of ice that separated him from the edge of the slide, and was standing in safety on a ledge beyond.

"We're alive," replied Clem rather dryly. "But it would be stretching it a bit to say we are all right. Can you help us off this rock?"

"Not without a rope," answered Pelly.

"Do you mean you'll have to go all the way to camp for one?" asked Billy sharply.

"That's about the size of it," Pelly replied.

"Then for goodness' sake be quick," said Billy. "This isn't the healthiest place to spend the night."

"Serves you right fer not keeping your eyes open," growled Pelly. "You'd ought to hev been watching out fer the snow moving."

Clem spoke up, and his voice was sharp. "Seeing it was you who started it, I don't think you need blame us," he answered.

Pelly scowled. "You keep a civil tongue in your head," he retorted, "or mebbe I'll leave ye there longer than ye like."

Clem was going to answer back, but Billy pinched his arm. "Shut up, Clem! No good making him in a wax," he whispered.

"I'll be back some time," said Pelly sourly, and, turning, began to climb the mountain, for in order to get back to the harbour he had to go right round the top of the broad ravine where the slide had taken place. The boys watched him, and it was nearly half an hour before he was out of sight.

Clem shivered. "It's horribly cold, Billy," he said.

"It's not what you'd call warm," allowed Billy. "I've got about five pounds weight of snow down my back, and it's melting slowly."

Clem shivered again. "So have I. My clothes are full of it. I say, we're dreadfully near the edge."

"Don't look down!" said Billy sharply. "It's enough to make a squirrel giddy."

The day was drawing on, and as the sun sank lower the breeze, always keen at this height, gained a sharper edge. Clem's teeth were chattering, and as for Billy, he felt his legs and arms growing numb. His hands were becoming like lumps of ice, and the unpleasant thought came to him that if help did not reach them soon they would get so chilled that they would be unable to hold on to the rope. The same thought had evidently occurred to Clem, for presently he asked,

"How long do you think Pelly will be, Billy?"

"Well, we took three hours to climb up here. Even if he hurries I don't suppose he can be back in less than four or five hours."

Clem looked straight into his brother's eyes.

"Then it won't be much use to us, Billy," he answered quietly.

"Keep your tail up, old man," said Billy.

"I'm not particularly scared, if that's what you mean," Clem answered. "I mean I'm not afraid of dying. All the same, it seems rather rough to be wiped out just as we are beginning to enjoy life."

Billy looked at the ice on either side. "I wonder if we could cut steps," he suggested.

"Yes, if we had an axe," answered Clem.

"I've got my big clasp-knife," said Billy.

"You'd never do it with that, old chap," Clem told him.

"Then I'll tell you what we will do, Clem," said Billy. "We'll cut a hole big enough to hold us and keep us from slipping. The work will keep us warm, too."

"Right-o!" replied Clem. "I'll help."

Both got out their knives and set to work. It was a slow job, for each could use only one hand. With the other he had to hold on to the rock. Still, the hole grew slowly, and, as Billy had said, the work kept them from absolutely freezing.

Each bit of ice, as they cut it away, slid rustling down the steep slope and dropped over the tremendous cliff beyond. And all the time the shadows were lengthening, and the wind which came down from the great snow-fields above grew colder and colder.

They had made a hole more than a foot deep and big enough to hold them both, when suddenly a loud shout echoed across the mountainside, making them both start violently. They looked up and saw two men coming rapidly across the snow toward them. Billy gave a yell of delight. "It's Bart! Bart and Ahkim!"

"We're all right, Bart!" he shouted at the top of his voice. "Have you got a rope?"

"I got a rope all right," answered Bart. "Hang on till we come across. We won't be long."

CHAPTER X
INTO THE UNKNOWN

Bart was always better at doing things than at talking about them, and in an astonishingly short-time he was round the head of the slide and on the side of it closest to the boys. The rope whizzed through the air, and at the first cast dropped clean across the rock.

Billy caught it. "You first, Clem," he said, and though Clem protested Billy insisted.

Clem was hauled across the smooth ice in a twinkling. Then came Billy's turn, and in a very short time both were, safe on the rocks beyond the slide. The first thing Bart did was to give each of them a nip of brandy and water. Then he examined their fingers and ears. "Mighty good job neither of you's froze," he remarked curtly. "How the mischief did ye come to get in such a fix?"

"Didn't Pelly tell you?" asked Billy quickly.

"Pelly? I ain't seed him," was the astonishing answer.

"Surely you met him on your way up!" exclaimed Billy. "He went to fetch a rope."

"Mebbe he did, but we didn't see him. I brought the rope because no one but a born ijiot or a tenderfoot would come a-climbing up in a place like this without one."

Billy felt snubbed, and stayed quiet.

"You ain't told me how you got here yet?" continued Bart.

Clem explained, and Bart's square face hardened as he listened.

271

"You mean to say as Pelly was in the middle o' this here snow-slope when he shot at the sheep?" he demanded. Clem said that was the fact.

"Then he must be plumb crazy," retorted Bart. "I reckon I'm a-going to tell him so when I sees him. But come on. It's a-getting late, and we got a long ways to go."

It *was* a long way, and the boys were pretty tired before they came in sight of the cannery. They were also much puzzled because they had seen nothing of Pelly on the way. Reaching the house, Bart flung open the door and marched into the living-room, where Joe Western was sitting waiting for supper, "Joe, where's Pelly?" demanded Bart.

"I ain't seed him, Bart," Joe answered.

Bart's lips tightened, and turning, he went straight out of the house and hurried down to the wharf. He was back inside a couple of minutes. "I thought as much," he said grimly. "He's gone."

"Gone!" repeated Joe.

"Aye, him and his Injuns. They've took their canoe and I reckon gone right up the river."

Clem and Billy simply stared. They could make nothing of it.

"But he went for a rope, Bart!" Billy managed to get out. "Surely you don't mean that he would have gone away and left us to freeze to death on that ledge? Why, it would have been murder!"

Bart shook his head slowly. "I ain't going to accuse any man of a thing like that," he said. "Likely, he may have seed me and Ahkim a-going up the hill to look fer you boys, and so knowed it was all right. I hopes he did." He paused, and his expression grew grimmer than ever. "But I'll tell you boys right now that Ed Pelly's a bad one."

Billy's eyes widened. "How do you mean, Bart?" he asked.

"I mean as he's a friend o' Gurney and Craze, and that he've been acting as spy for them."

"How do you know that?" questioned Clem.

"Ahkim told me. Seems he seed Pelly up to Juneau last year along with them two. So fur as I can judge, they got word to him off the steamer to come down and try to go along with us, him leaving a trail so they could follow."

"Then why didn't he go along with you?" put in Joe Western.

"Because I wasn't fer it. I never did cotton to him, and last night, when he put it to me to come along, I turned him down."

The two boys looked at one another. Both had a sudden chill, uncomfortable feeling. They had begun to see that there was more behind this expedition of theirs than they had hitherto realized.

"I wish you'd have told me about that this morning, Bart," said Joe Western slowly.

"I wish I had," admitted Bart. "But it's too late now to be sorry. Only thing to do is to get off as quick as may be and try to beat Pelly up the river."

"But I thought you said we couldn't go without Indians?" said Billy.

"Injuns is all right. Ahkim's brother Passuk is a-coming along. He's here right now. Ef you kin fit us out with a canoe and grub, Joe, I reckon we'll move at sun-up in the morning."

Joe nodded slowly. "I can fix you. Now you three have your supper and get right to bed. I'll have all ready for you before morning."

The Chinese cook had already brought in supper, and they sat down to it. In spite of their worries the boys were sharp set, and they did justice to the hot bread, fried bacon, and big dish of stewed fruit. Bart ate well too, but he was very silent. When they had finished, Billy ventured a question. "Bart, I don't quite see what good it will do Pelly to get ahead of us. If he's on in front, he can't be tracking us."

Bart smiled faintly. "That's a fact, Billy, but the trouble is you can't tell what devilment he'll be up to. F'r instance, he might throw trees across the river or raise the

Injuns on us. Ye see, he knows we got to go up the river. And even if he don't try tricks like that, then mebbe he'll hide up somewheres in the ranges and watch which way we're a-going. Guess you knows by this time we don't want to be follered."

Billy nodded. "Thank you, Bart. I understand better now, and I see that we must get ahead."

"That's it, son," said Bart. "But mind ye, it means mighty hard travelling, fer Pelly's got a real light canoe, and he and his Injuns is good paddlers. We'll need a big craft fer the five of us, and it's going to be days afore you and Clem can do your whack at paddling with the rest."

Billy did not answer. Since his arrival in this far northern country he had begun to realize that a *chechahco,* or tenderfoot, however willing, is precious little use.

"And now you go right to your bunks," said Bart. "And make the most of 'em," he added dryly, "fer it's going to be a mighty long while before the next time you sleeps in a bed."

Next day the dawn had not yet greyed the sky when the boys were called from their bunks. Breakfast was ready as soon as they were, and it seemed that they were hardly awake before they were on the wharf.

Below lay a long, narrow canoe. It was Joe's best, but given unhesitatingly to his friend. In it were the stores, well lashed and packed, and in it sat the two Indians, Ah-kim and his brother Passuk, paddles in hand, their broad faces stolid as if carved in wood.

"Good-bye, Bart," said Joe. "Good-bye, lads, and the best of luck to ye." Then they were all three in the canoe, and had cast off.

The tide was racing upstream, and driven by the Indians' paddles the canoe shot away at great speed. Looking back, the boys saw Joe Western's tall figure looming through the morning mist. He waved his hand. Then they whirled round a bend, and lost sight of him and of the cannery. The journey had started in earnest, and they were off into the unknown.

CHAPTER XI
THE FALL OF THE GLACIER

For the first three hours the voyage was a swift and easy one; then they came to the head of the tidal water, and found the current against them. The boys noticed that the Indians at once drove in close to the bank so as to dodge the full force of the stream.

As for themselves, they were so taken up with gazing at the amazing scenery that they had eyes for little else. With every mile the mountains gained in size and majesty, and, high against the blue, vast snow-clad peaks shot up in every direction like sugar-loaves. Just at the head of the tidal water they saw their first glacier, a cliff of blue ice two hundred feet high, from the base of which a torrent roared, white as chalk.

But presently Bart set them to paddling. "You got to learn sooner or later," he told them. "And I guess you won't get no better teachers than Ahkim here and Passuk."

At first the boys did more harm than good, but Billy soon got the hang of it. Clem was slower. Clem did not learn quickly, but once he did learn he never forgot.

They stopped for dinner where a big point of smooth rock ran out into the river. Ahkim speared a salmon, and Bart showed the boys how to split, clean, and grill it over hot coals.

An hour's rest, then on again. The river was getting swifter all the time, and about four o'clock they came to a place where it narrowed between towering cliffs of black rock. From the dark recesses of the cañon came a hoarse, terrifying roar. The canoe rounded a curve, and the boys saw the river, heaped up in white foam, thundering down in a terrifying rapid.

Billy gasped. "I say, have we got to go up there?" he exclaimed.

A slow smile spread over Bart's face. "Onless ye goes round," he answered. "Shucks, Billy, you'll see worse'n that afore you're a lot older. Ship your paddle, son. Me and the Injuns'll handle her."

The cañon curved so much that the river struck the left-hand cliff. It struck the cliff with such force that it was actually heaped against it in great leaping waves.

Ahkim and his brother drove the canoe to the right, and began edging up with short, sharp strokes. Bart, in the stern, did the steering. The roar was appalling. The boys sat stock still. They were both pretty badly scared, but even more frightened of letting the Indians see that they were scared.

Yard by yard the canoe was worked up close under the cliff, until it reached a spot where the cañon made a snake-bend. Here was a bit of slack water, and the Indians held the canoe a few moments while they recovered breath.

Bart gave a sudden sharp order, the paddles dipped, and suddenly the canoe was shooting right through the central rush. Spray flew in sheets, the light craft quivered like a living thing in pain, and for a few seconds the boys were convinced that she must be swamped or battered to pieces. Then, almost before they knew it, she was close under the opposite cliff, and again edging steadily onward.

At the second curve the same manoeuvre was repeated, and presently, very wet, but quite safe, they were out of the rapid and the cañon.

They passed no more rapids that evening, and just at dusk made camp on a sandy beach. Before the light failed Bart walked the whole length of this beach, and the boys saw that he was closely examining the ground.

"Seeing if Pelly camped here?" suggested Billy.

"Jest so," answered Bart; "but since I don't see no signs I reckon he's gone farther." He paused and shrugged his big shoulders. "But who's to say? It's like hunting fer a needle in a haystack. Fer all I knows, we've passed him and left him hid up in the woods. Anyways, we'll hev to set a watch to-night."

Since the Indians could not be trusted to watch, the boys took their turn with Bart. But there was no sign of Pelly, and in the morning they were off again as soon as it was light enough to see. Clem and Billy ached in every muscle from the hard paddling of the previous day, but this soon passed off, and the air was so fresh and the scenery so glorious that, in spite of their anxieties, they enjoyed every minute of it.

Each curve of the river showed new marvels—terrific cliffs, fantastic rocks, giant glaciers, and everywhere wildlife. Twice they saw bears fishing for salmon, and once a giant moose drinking at the waterside. There were quantities of birds and beautiful butterflies.

Rapids added to the thrill of it all. Sometimes they had to paddle, but where there was any sort of beach they 'tracked'—that is, towed the canoe up with a rope, while either Bart or one of the Indians steered her. And always, as Billy noticed, Bart's eyes were on the banks, and he knew that he was looking for signs of Pelly.

But there was not a trace of him or his canoe, and at the end of three days' travel, when they camped, Bart told them straight out, "I guess we've passed him. He's seed us coming and hid his canoe somewhere in the woods."

Two more days passed, and on the fourth morning they started as usual at dawn and found the travelling easier. The river was deeper and not so swift. Just before midday, as they paddled up a long, smooth stretch, a sound like distant thunder came booming through the sunlit air.

It was so heavy that they could actually feel its vibrations. Everything seemed to quiver. It was followed by several other crashes, which lasted in all for a minute or more.

"My goodness, it sounds as if a mountain had fallen down!" exclaimed Billy.

Bart nodded. "You ain't a lot out, Billy. Only I guess it's an ice mountain."

"A glacier, you mean?" asked Billy quickly.

"Jest so," replied Bart calmly.

"One of those we passed this morning?" questioned Clem.

"I reckon so. The ice gets rotten with the sun this time o' year. I've seed a chunk big enough to fill this here valley fall off right in one piece."

"I wish we'd seen it," said Billy eagerly.

Bart chuckled. "Jest as well ye didn't, sonny. A fall like that'll make a wind as will blow away a forest jest like so much straw. I tell ye, a avalanche is a mighty good thing to give a miss to."

The thundering echoes died away, and before they had gone far a new excitement made the boys forget all about the fall. Ahkim, who had been staring at the hillside to the left, pointed. "Him caribou," he grunted, and, looking up, the boys saw a number of reindeer grazing high up on a mountain meadow.

Bart put his field-glasses to his eyes. "Good chance to get some meat," he said, and without a word the Indians drove the canoe toward the beach. Tingling with excitement, the boys jumped ashore.

Bart considered a moment. "Guess we'll need the Injuns," he said. "See here, Ahkim, pull the canoe out and cache her. No use to take any risks."

Ahkim, who rarely spoke, merely nodded, and he and Passuk dragged the canoe into a little backwater and cut branches, which they piled over her, hiding her completely. Then all five started up the hill in pursuit of the caribou.

The distance was much greater than the boys had imagined, and it was more than three hours before they managed to get close enough for a shot. Then Bart fired, and one of the caribou rolled over, stone dead.

While the Indians cut up the carcass Bart and the boys sat resting. It was getting late before they were ready to make their way back downhill. "Grilled venison for supper!" said Billy, smacking his lips. Just then they passed through some thick trees and came out upon a broad open space from which they got a view of the river.

All three pulled up short, staring wide-eyed at the extraordinary change which had taken place during their absence. For instead of the swiftly flowing stream which they had left some four or five hours earlier, there was now a broad, still lake.

Clem turned to Bart. "What's it mean? What has happened?" he demanded sharply.

Bart's face was graver than the boys had ever seen it. "It's that there fall," he answered. "The glacier's fell into the river somewheres below, and dammed her. And, boys, where do you reckon the canoe's gone by now?"

CHAPTER XII
BILLY'S FIND

How they ever got down the rest of the slope neither of the boys ever remembered. It was one wild rush through bog and brake, leaping over great logs and rocks, taking all sorts of risks and chances.

All three were breathless and dripping with perspiration by the time they reached the water's edge, and stood staring out across a wide lagoon, the edges of which were lapping high among the grass and trees of the forest.

"Worse'n I thought," the boys heard Bart mutter under his breath, and the look on his face frightened them. He began to move along the bank, searching the water with his eyes.

Billy turned to Clem. "Where do you suppose the canoe is?" he asked in a low voice.

"Goodness knows, Billy," replied Clem. "The little creek we hid her in has simply vanished altogether."

"She must have drifted out, unless she sank at her moorings," said Billy.

"That's what I'm afraid of—that she's sunk," said Clem. "With all those branches over her, she'd hardly float."

"Then that means she's at the bottom with all our stores," said Billy hoarsely.

"That's about the size of it," replied Clem.

"But Bart seems to think she may have floated," insisted Billy.

"If she has, it's all odds against our finding her," answered Clem.

"Oh, don't be such a Jonah!" cried Billy almost angrily.

"I'm not, Billy. We've got to face it, and the sooner we do so the better for us. If we've lost our canoe and stores, we can't go on. That's flat."

Presently Bart came back to them. "She's gone, boys," he said gravely. "There ain't a sign of her nowheres."

"Does that mean we've got to go back, Bart?" asked Billy, straight out.

There was a strange look in Bart's kindly eyes, a look which somehow frightened Billy. "How do you reckon we're a-going to get back?" he asked quietly.

"Why—why—we might make a raft," suggested Billy.

Bart shook his head. "We ain't got a axe left, son."

Billy gasped as if some one had thrown a bucket of cold water over him. He was realizing that as yet he had hardly begun to understand the terrible nature of the misfortune which had overtaken them.

"Besides," said Bart, "there's a mountain o' ice atween us and the mouth o' the river. How are ye going to get your raft over that?"

Billy was silent. He could find nothing to say.

It was Clem who spoke next. "Bart, I've read of things of this sort before. There's a story of a glacier that fell in Switzerland a great many years ago and blocked a river called the Ranz. The water went on piling up behind the ice till at last the weight of it broke the dam. Then, of course, all the lake went out in one big rush and left the river running again."

Bart nodded. "That's good sense," he said, "and I guess that's what may happen right here. But ye can't say for sure. It may be weeks afore the weight o' water is big enough to break through the ice-fall, and the freeze-up may come afore that happens; and, anyways, how do you reckon we're to live till the water goes out?"

"We've got our rifles," replied Clem simply. "And we've some meat and matches."

Bart brought his great hand down on Clem's shoulder, and for the first time since they had realized their misfortune there was a ghost of a smile in his grey eyes.

"Sonny, you're right. That's the proper spirit in which to look at this here job. I guess we've still got something to be thankful for. Anyways, let's get busy before it's dark and make a camp o' some sort."

Clem flushed with pleasure, for praise from Bart was worth hearing. Then they all set to work to make camp. The tent was gone, but that didn't matter much, for the nights were not yet cold. They picked a place high above the rising water, lit a good fire, cut hemlock-branches for beds, and presently were seated around the fire in the dusk with the appetizing smell of grilled venison in their nostrils. It was not pleasant to do without bread or salt, but no one complained, and anyhow they were hungry enough to eat anything.

Billy, who had been silent for some time, suddenly spoke. "Bart, do you think Pelly had anything to do with this business?"

"What—the ice-fall, son!"

"Yes. I suppose he could have started it with a stick of dynamite."

Bart pursed his lips. "It's a fact as he might have done it. But it would be a mighty big risk, Billy. And anyways, you got to remember as it would block the river so as he couldn't get no farther, nor any of his pals arter him."

"Yes," said Billy, "but he might have hurried on past the fall before the explosion. And perhaps he's calculating that the ice will go out before Gurney and Craze are ready to follow."

Bart nodded slowly. "You may be right, Billy. No one of us can say. Anyways, it don't make much odds."

There was silence for a little while. Then Billy looked up. "Bart," he asked, "what are your plans? What are you going to do?"

Bart fixed his eyes on the boy, and there was a twinkle in them. "Sleep on it, Billy," he answered, and lay back on his couch of branches.

It was all very well to talk of sleeping on it. Billy did so, but Clem, who was better able to realize the real perils of their position, lay awake till after midnight, turning things over and over in his mind. And as for Bart, he had got up again, and Clem watched him sitting by the red embers of the fire, hunched up, with his chin on his big fists, and knew that he too was trying to make up his mind what was best to be done. At last Clem's weary body forced his anxious mind to rest, and he fell sound asleep.

The rising sun was in his eyes as he woke, and he sprang up in a hurry, reproaching himself for having slept so long. Then all in a flash he remembered, and dropped back with something like a groan. Billy was already up, and stood gazing down the hill. He heard Clem move, and turned. "Clem, she's risen a heap since last night," he said.

Clem got to his feet and joined his brother. "You're right, Billy," he answered, as he stared down at the water.

A great lake now filled the valley, stretching to the west as far as they could see and fully two miles to the east. A faint breeze rippled the great expanse, and the sun, which had just climbed above the great mountains inland, turned the ripples to gold. The strong light showed hundreds of logs and branches, lifted by the rising water from the forest, floating down the lake.

Bart's voice broke in. "Have a wash, lads; then come to breakfast."

The two Indians were stolidly grilling venison chops over the fire. So long as they had plenty of meat they cared little for anything else. With the white members of the party it was different, and meat without salt or bread was a poor sort of meal.

The boys watched Bart, but asked no questions. They knew he would speak when he was ready. Presently he finished his food, and lit his pipe. "Billy," he said, "I guess we'll have to try your plan and build a raft. Then, when we gets down to the dam, we'll have to cross that afoot and build another the far side. With luck we'll be back at Joe's place inside of a week, and we'd ought to be able to kill enough meat to keep us that long."

For a minute or so the boys were silent; then Clem looked eastward toward the great dividing range. "No chance of being able to go on, I suppose?" he questioned.

Bart shook his head. "Too risky, son. I'm not saying as me and the Injuns mightn't try it, but it'd be too big a job for you lads. Straight meat don't suit them as ain't accustomed to it, and you boys would likely get ill. You got to remember as all our dried fruit is gone. Ef I'd got a dozen pounds o' prunes I'd say 'Try it,' but as things is, there's nothing fer it but to go back and get a fresh start."

Clem knew too well to argue. "All right, Bart," he said. "Then we'd better get hold of some of these floating logs, hadn't we?"

"Thet's it," replied Bart briefly, and presently they were all at work.

Hard work it was, for logs of the right size were not easy to find, and rotten ones were no good. Also the water into which they had to wade was bitter cold. Neither of the Indians would go into the water at all, so Bart set them to cutting the caribou-hide into thongs for tying the logs together.

Billy, in his usual eager fashion, went farther than Clem or Bart, and vanished from their sight round a little point of land running out into the lake.

All of a sudden Clem heard a yell which made him jump. "Bart, Billy's hurt!" he shouted, and he ran hard toward the spot the sound came from.

Then, as he got nearer, he heard his brother's voice again. "Clem! Clem! I've found the canoe!"

CHAPTER XIII
TREASURE TROVE

Clem's first idea was that Billy had gone stark, staring mad, but as he crashed through the bushes and came out on the far side of the little point of land, there was Billy fairly dancing with excitement and pointing—pointing straight at a canoe which was drifting idly some thirty yards out from the shore.

Clem pulled up short, hardly able to believe his eyes. "H—how on earth did she get there?" he gasped.

"I don't know and I don't care," replied Billy, and raced away down the bank. "But the wind is bringing her right in."

Away went all three crashing through the thick brush until they gained the spot to which the canoe was evidently coming in.

Bart stood staring at her. Then he spoke. "That ain't our canoe, lads!"

Billy looked round at him sharply, then fixed his sharp eyes again on the canoe. "No more she is!" he exclaimed in a tone of utter amazement. As for Clem, he could find no words at all. To him the whole business seemed too much like a miracle.

A puff of wind, and the canoe brushed against a bush and stuck. Bart's big hand closed on her gunwale and dragged her up the bank. The first thing they saw was that she was full of packages.

"Is—is she Pelly's?" cried Billy.

"No, she ain't ours, and she ain't Pelly's," replied Bart.

"Then where in the name of goodness has she come from?" demanded Clem.

"Maybe I can tell ye more when I've unpacked her," said Bart, and as he spoke began lifting out the packages, each of which was carefully cased in oilskin.

The first was a sack of flour, the next a side of bacon, and the third coffee in a big tin canister. Then came a large package of dried fruit, a tin of salt, and some smaller articles, including a case of medicine.

"Everything we want," exclaimed Billy.

"It—it's a miracle," added Clem.

Bart shook his head. "It ain't no miracle, Clem. This here canoe belongs to some chaps as have come up here a-prospecting for gold or platinum. There was two of 'em, and most like they've gone up in the hills. First, ye see, they cached their canoe like we did ours, only I reckon they hauled her way up out of the water, and didn't tie her. Then along comes this here flood, and floats her out. Thet's the whole story, so far as I can read it."

A look of dismay crossed Clem's face. "Then—then—?" he began.

Bart nodded. "Yes, son, that's whar the trouble lies," he added soberly. "The canoe ain't ours, and ef we takes it, why, we leaves its owners in the lurch, so to speak."

Billy looked absolutely dismayed. "Do you mean that we can't take her, Bart?"

Bart nodded. "Thet's a fact, Billy."

"B—but she'd have drifted away and been lost if I hadn't found her!" cried Billy.

"Ah, but ye see, ye did find her," replied Bart dryly. "Ye wouldn't want to leave other folk to starve while you got fat on their grub, would ye, Billy?"

Billy's face had gone rather white, and he stood quite still and silent.

Clem spoke up. "Bart, do you think we might borrow a little salt and coffee—just enough to take us back to the Landing? Then we could return it when we come up again."

Bart nodded. "Aye, I wouldn't mind doing that, Clem, but mebbe we could do better. Ef we could trail these here prospectors, likely as not we could borrer their canoe to go down in."

Billy's face brightened. "That's a splendid idea. Let's go at once."

Bart's smile was a little grim. "They ain't jest round the corner, son. Mebbe they're twenty or thirty mile off in the ranges. 'Tain't going to be no easy job to find 'em."

For a moment the boys looked rather blue, but Billy soon recovered. "Then we'd better start at once, Bart."

Before Bart could answer, the two Indians had come up, and for once there was something like excitement on their usually wooden faces. They evidently took it for granted that Bart meant to make use of this wonderful find, and it took a deal of explanation to convince them that this was not possible.

Ahkim was quite indignant. "Him no find dem men," he said frowning, waving his hand vaguely around the horizon. And Clem and Billy, gazing at the miles upon miles of wild forest and jagged mountains which surrounded them, felt their hearts sink. Any such search must be very like looking for one needle in a huge haystack.

But Bart was firm, and the first thing he did was to haul the canoe a long way up the hillside, to a spot where the ever-rising water would not be likely to reach her. The stores he also cached in a small cave some way higher up the hill, and when this was done he made the others help him to pile stones against the mouth. "Ef we don't make it good and tight," he explained, "the bears'll get the grub while we're away."

"Are we going to start at once, Bart?" questioned Billy.

"Right away," was the reply.

"But which way, Bart?"

"Straight up the hill. Ef we get on the high ground, it's likely we may spot their smoke. That's our best chance."

Billy nodded, for he saw the sense of this. They had a meal, packed the rest of their meat, and started. Barring that first night when they had got lost, this was the boys' first experience of travelling through virgin forest, and it was not a pleasant one. The going was simply awful, and but for Bart's woodcraft they would never have got on at all. But the old trapper had an almost uncanny knowledge, of the ground, and he kept out of the worst of the swamps and thickets.

It seems odd to talk of swamps on a hillside, but there were great pockets in the hollows where a man might sink in liquid black mud over his head. For the most part Bart kept them on more open ground, which was firm enough, but very steep and littered with loose stones which had a nasty way of rolling under them and plunging away down-hill, each starting a regular little avalanche as it rolled. It was desperately hard work, and it took them three hours to climb to the top of the first ridge.

When they reached this they found a wooded valley beneath them, and beyond it a second and loftier range of hills. Beyond this again rose a third range, the tops of which were white with snow. There was dismay on Billy's face as he turned to his brother. "Clem, this country scares me," he said. "It's too big."

Clem did not seem to hear. He was gazing away out across the wilderness, and suddenly he stretched out his arm and pointed. "Smoke!" he exclaimed. "Do you see it, Billy?"

"I guess you're right, Clem," came Bart's deep voice. "Aye, it's smoke right enough. But you got mighty good eyes. I never seed it myself till you pointed." He turned and spoke to the Indians, and Ahkim nodded and grunted.

The smoke was the merest feather of blue haze rising from the woods on the opposite slope, but not more than three miles away, and since the going was not so bad, they covered the distance in a little over an hour.

They walked straight into a little open glade, in the middle of which was a small shack. It was from the clay-built chimney of this that the smoke was rising.

"Hulloa!" shouted Bart, but there was no reply. He went across to the shack, and knocked at the door. There was no answer, so he opened and went in. The boys followed, but the little place was empty.

"Where on earth can they be?" asked Billy.

"Guess they're at work," replied Bart, as he stepped out again into the open. "Aye, there's the mouth of their adit," he continued, pointing to a small hole in the hillside above the camp, with a pile of raw earth and rock beneath it.

The boys ran on up the hill, and Bart followed. They shouted again, but still there was no reply. Billy reached the mouth of the adit and peered in. "Black as a hat," he said. "I don't believe there's anyone there."

CHAPTER XIV
THE BROKEN ROOF

Bart stooped down and entered the adit. He had to bend nearly double, for there was only about four feet head-room. He struck a match. Billy, close behind, heard him draw a quick breath. "What's the matter, Bart?" he demanded.

Bart turned his head. "Matter is as the roof is down," he said gravely. "A fresh fall, too. Ef there's any poor chap inside, I don't reckon there's much life left in him."

The boys were too horrified to speak, and for a moment there was silence. Suddenly Billy started.

"What's the matter, lad?" asked Bart.

"I heard something. It sounded like some one knocking," answered Billy breathlessly.

Bart went forward to the face of the fall, and taking up a stone rapped sharply on the rock wall of the shaft. There was a moment's pause; then, faint yet quite distinct, came the answer—three short, sharp raps.

"There's one alive, anyway," said Bart curtly. "And we got to get him out. Boys, run down to the shack and fetch any tools ye can find. Smart's the word."

He did not need to urge them. The boys fairly flew to obey. They found two shovels, a pick, and an axe. Then the work began in earnest.

A terrible job it was too, for it was no use just digging. That would only have meant the roof falling again and burying them, as well as whoever was inside. They had to cut logs and 'timber' the rotten roof as they went, and without Bart the boys and the Indians could never have done it. But Bart knew every least thing about mining, and with his help they at last cut through the fall into a little dark chamber behind.

The light of a flaring fir torch shone ruddily through the gloom and showed two figures flat on the floor, face down and very still. Bart shook his head. "I guess we're too late," he said gravely, but Clem was already on his knees beside the nearest, and had put his ear against the man's chest.

"No," he answered quickly. "He's alive. I can feel his heart beating."

"That's more'n you can say for this poor chap," answered Bart, who was examining the other. "A rock's got him on the head, and I guess it killed him right away."

Between them they lifted the living man out. He was quite a young fellow, with red hair, a pleasant freckled face, and a snub nose. And presently, when they had laid him down on the grass, his eyes opened and proved to be very honest-looking blue ones.

"He's all right," said Bart. "It was jest the bad air that caught him."

The youngster looked up at them in a puzzled way; then his face changed. "Where's Grayson?" he asked hoarsely. Before they could answer, "Oh, I remember now!" he groaned. "He was killed when the roof fell." He covered his eyes with his hands, and a sob shook him.

"I reckon he didn't suffer none," said Bart soberly. "Anyways, I'm glad we came in time to get you out."

The youngster sat up and gazed at Bart and the boys. "It's a miracle," he said. "We've never seen a soul here before—not even an Indian. However did you happen to come just in the nick of time?"

"'Twasn't just happening," said Bart gravely, and briefly explained matters.

The other drew a long breath. "And you saved our canoe and stores! Well, you're white, anyway!"

He said it as if he meant it, and old Bart reddened a little under his tan. "I'm mighty glad we was able to," he answered, "but I guess you don't need to give us too much credit. Ye see, the reason we come along up here was to beg for a loan of that there canoe."

"Loan of it! Why, I'll give it you—and gladly!" exclaimed the youngster. He looked up at Bart. "My name is Jock Scarlett," he said.

"And I'm Bart Condon," was the answer. "And these boys is Clem and Billy Ballard."

Young Scarlett rose to his feet and shook hands all round. Then he pointed toward the adit. "I guess we've got to bury poor Grayson," he said heavily. "After that we'll go down to the shack and talk things over."

The grave was soon dug, and when the mournful ceremony was finished, the party returned to the hut. Tired out, the boys were soon asleep, leaving Bart and Jock Scarlett chatting in low voices over the store.

Early next morning Billy and his brother went down together to wash at the spring.

"Jock's a real good chap—that's what I think," said Billy.

Clem nodded. "Yes, he does seem a good sort," he remarked. "And Bart says he'll come with us up country," he added quietly.

Billy gave a shout of delight. "That's topping. Then we shan't have to go back to the Landing for fresh stores."

"No, we're going straight on inland." Clem paused, and looked thoughtful. "Billy, *where* are we going, I wonder?"

Billy shrugged his shoulders. "I don't know, Clem, and I don't much care. So long as we go with Bart we're all right."

"I'm with you there all the way," agreed Clem. "All the same, the thing's a bit mysterious."

"You mean with these queer people on our track—Gurney and Craze and Pelly?"

"That's it. And just remember they're after this chap they call 'the Big Britisher.' I wonder if we are going to him, too."

Billy raised his head, all dripping, from the clear, cold pool. "I expect we are. I hope so's anyway. But this is the finest country on earth, and Bart's the best chap I ever met, so what's the use of bothering about anything?"

Clem smiled at Billy's enthusiasm. "That's the best way to look at it, old chap," he answered. "And now, if you've finished washing, let's get back to breakfast."

The shack was well supplied with stores, and all the party were pretty well loaded as they took the trail back to the lake. It was a glorious morning, but though the sun was hot a pleasantly cool breeze blew down from the gleaming snow-fields above them.

All were in good spirits except poor Jock Scarlett, who was naturally feeling the sudden death of his partner. But as the two boys chatted away to him his face lost some of its sadness, and he even smiled now and then as he answered their numerous questions.

He told them that his people were Scotch Canadians—that his father and mother were both dead, and that his only near relation was a sister called Maggie, who lived with an aunt in Vancouver. The aunt was very badly off, and Jock had struck north, hoping to find fortune in gold or platinum.

"But you're leaving your mine!" exclaimed Billy.

"I reckon we'd have done that anyway, pretty soon," Jock answered soberly. "It wasn't much of a prospect at best. From what Condon has told me, it looks as if I'd do a heap better up where you fellows are going."

"Did Bart tell you where we were going?" questioned Billy.

"No, he didn't. But he told me it was good country, and I guess he's one o' those chaps you trust right away."

"He jolly well is!" agreed Billy. As he spoke they were topping the last ridge, and Billy pulled up short. "I say, look at the lake!" he cried. "It's bigger than ever."

Jock Scarlett whistled softly. "My word, the river does look a bit different from the last time I saw it. I'm sure grateful you fellows found our canoe."

Clem, who had been gazing hard at something far down the lake, stretched out his arm and pointed. "I say, what's that?" he asked sharply.

Jock Scarlett took a pair of field-glasses from a case slung over his shoulder and focused them, "It's a canoe," he said presently, "And three men in her—one white and two Indians."

"Lend me the glasses," cut in Bart, as he came speeding up, and Jock handed them over. Bart took a long look, then lowered them, and the boys saw that his usually good-natured face had changed and hardened. "I thought as much," he growled. "It's that feller Pelly with his Injuns."

He handed the glasses back to Jock. "Come on sharp, the lot of ye. If Pelly finds our camp afore we reaches it there's going to be right serious trouble."

CHAPTER XV
PELLY SHOWS HIS TEETH

It had taken the party three hours to climb that hill on the previous day, but now, driven by the fear that Pelly might find their canoe and stores before they could reach them, they scuttled downward nearly three times as fast as they had come. But they were heavily loaded, the ground was as bad as could be, and when, badly blown, they reached a ledge some three hundred feet above the lake level, the canoe was no longer visible.

"Pelly's landed," growled Bart.

"Will he have found our stores?" panted Billy.

"I'll lay he has. I reckon our tracks was plain enough," replied Bart, and plunged forward again.

Near the lake the forest was thick, and so matted with undergrowth that it was impossible to travel very fast. As the party forced their way through the thick of it a great boom like the sound of a heavy gun fired in the distance came echoing up the valley. "Another ice-fall," thought Billy to himself, but he was too blown to speak.

Bart was ahead, Jock Scarlett close behind him. The boys, though doing their best, could not quite keep up.

Billy caught his foot in a twisted root, stumbled, and crashed on his face. Clem paused a moment to pick him up, and just then came Bart's voice. "Drop it, Pelly! Drop that stuff, or I'll shoot!"

The boys saw him stop and raise his rifle to his shoulder. Then from below came a harsh laugh. "Shoot as much as you've a mind to, Condon," Pelly jeered. "I ain't scared."

"He's right, Mr. Condon," said Jock. "It's no use shooting. The trees hide him, and the only thing for us to do is to try to cut him off before he can reach the canoe."

"That's jest what we can't do," groaned Bart, "for this here gulch stops us from getting at him, and before we can get across it the feller will be off."

Clem and Billy, coming up, saw at once what Bart meant. A deep gully, cut by the spring rains and running right down the hillside into the lake, yawned in front. It was twenty feet deep, and the sides were walls of rock almost as sheer as the sides of a house. The gully lay between them and Pelly, and the thick trees hid him and his canoe completely, though Bart's party could hear Pelly himself crashing heavily through the undergrowth less than fifty yards away.

"It's all right, Mr. Condon," said Jock. "I'll get across." And as he spoke he seized a bush, swung himself over the edge of the gully, and dropped. The boys held their breath, but he landed safely, and at once started to climb the opposite side.

"He'll never do it in time," groaned Bart. "And ef he does the chances are as Pelly will shoot him."

"And has he got our stuff?" questioned Billy;

"Looks like it," Bart answered, and neither of the boys had ever seen him more upset.

Clem cut in. "Come on down the gully to the lake shore, Bart," he said. "We might be able to see him from there, or the canoe at any rate. Then you can shoot if you have to."

"That's good sense," growled Bart, and all three went hurrying down the ragged edge of the gully.

It was a forlorn hope. They all knew it, for Pelly's canoe was some way above the gulch, and probably well hidden. Once Pelly got his cargo aboard, he could paddle right away up the lake or across and down it, and make his escape, before Bart's party could even launch their canoe.

Suddenly a hoarse shout came from among the trees a little way up the shore. "It's Pelly's Indians!" panted Clem in Billy's ear.

"What's the matter with them?" cried Billy. "It sounds as if they were scared to death."

"The lake! Look at the lake!" cried Clem, pointing to the water, which was just visible, through the trees.

Billy stopped shorth and stared for an instant, "W—whatever is the matter with it?" he gasped.

He might well ask, for the surface, a moment ago so calm and still, was now streaked with long lines of white, while all the logs and branches which had been floating peacefully upon its surface were rushing past the banks at a dizzy pace.

Clem seized Billy by the arm. "I know!" he cried. "The dam has gone!"

The sight was so surprising that for a moment the boys entirely forgot everything else in watching it. The water was racing out like a big ebb in Bristol River, and every moment it went faster and faster. As the boys ran forward to the shore the great logs were shooting away like straws, and the water dropping away from the shore with the oddest sucking sound.

Came another yell. "The canoe!" shouted Billy. "Look at it!"

As he spoke, Pelly's canoe came into sight. The two Indians were paddling like mad to reach the shore, but they had not a ghost of a chance. Even a motor-engine could hardly have forced the canoe against the terrific suction which dragged her outward.

"I say, what will happen to the poor beggars?" cried Clem anxiously.

"Don't you worry about them," advised Bart. "Injuns has got as many lives as a cat. They'll get out all right. It's Pelly I'm a-worrying about."

"But Pelly's on the bank," replied Clem.

"I knows that. And dangerous as a cornered cat. Now you go soft, young fellow! We don't want to have no accidents. Keep right back, behind me."

At its mouth, where it entered the lake, the gully was broader and more shallow. Bart scrambled down into it and up the other side. Then he began working slowly through the thick undergrowth beyond, the boys following cautiously.

Suddenly came a voice—or rather a snarl. "Stop right there, Bart Condon! Stop right still and put yer hands up, fer if ye don't, sure as I live I'll let daylight through you!" As he spoke Pelly stepped suddenly out from behind a tree, his rifle pointed straight at Bart, his finger on the trigger.

Clem and Billy felt cold chills crawl down their backs, but Bart stood coolly facing his enemy. "Steady on with that, Pelly," he answered quietly. "We don't want no trouble."

"It's you as'll get the trouble," retorted Pelly. "Jest remember as I've got the drop on you."

"I can see that right enough," replied Bart, as calmly as ever. "But you better remember as your canoe and Injuns is gone."

"I know that, so I'm going to have yours instead. Where is it?"

"Somewheres out there," replied Bart, nodding in the direction of the lake.

"You're a liar!" snapped Pelly. "I'll give ye while I count three to tell me the truth, and ef ye don't I'll shoot."

Bart's face hardened. "You skunk!" he said. "Ye wouldn't dare talk to me like that ef ye hadn't got the drop on me. The flood, which I reckon ye turned on us by dynamiting that there glacier, caught us unawares, and took our canoe off. That's the truth. Now shoot if ye want to."

Pelly stood biting his lip. He was clearly in a furious rage, and at the same time badly frightened. But, as Clem knew, it is just when a man of this type is really scared that he is most dangerous.

"Ye can't humbug me," said Pelly at length. "Now I'm a-going to count, and ef ye don't tell me where the canoe is, I'll shoot. One!" he began.

"What can we do, Clem?" whispered Billy in his brother's ear, in a voice that shook with horror and distress,

"Rush him!" Clem answered. But the words were hardly out of his mouth before Pelly gave a strangled cry. Two powerful hands had gripped him round the throat from behind and jerked him backward. His rifle went off, but the bullet whistled harmlessly into space. Next instant he was on his back, with Jock Scarlett kneeling on him.

CHAPTER XVI
THE SECOND START

Tied hand and foot, Ed Pelly sat upon a log glaring sullenly at his captors. Bart stood opposite him, and the boys hardly knew his face, so grim and terrible was it.

"Ed Pelly," he said, addressing his prisoner, and his voice was slow and measured as that of any judge. "Have you anything to say why I shouldn't turn ye adrift to starve in the woods, like ye was going to do to us?"

A quiver of fear crossed Pelly's face. "Ye wouldn't do that?" he whined. "Ye couldn't treat a white man that way!"

"White!" Bart's voice rang with scorn. "You call yourself white? Why, a yellow dog is whiter than you. You've been in the North long enough to know that to rob an outfit of their grub is the worst sin there is up here. I've seen men hanged for less. What did you do it for?"

Pelly did not answer. Bart stared straight at him, and his eyes were hard as stone. "Speak up. We treated you right. What grudge had you against us?"

"I ain't got no grudge against you," whined Pelly.

"Then who paid you to dog us like you have?"

Again no answer. "You better talk, Pelly," said Bart ominously. "Who paid you? Was it Craze and Gurney?"

Pelly nodded sullenly.

Bart shrugged his shoulders. "I knowed it," he said. "And, what's more, I knows more about them two than is healthy for them. Now see here, Ed Pelly. I'm a-going to give you jest enough grub to take you back to the Landing.

305

You ain't going to have any easy time getting there, but I reckon you can make it. And when you meet them two pardners of yours, jest you tell 'em that I knows what they're after, and I'm ready for 'em. Ef you or they ever cross Needle Pass or come farther than the Stone Man, you can take it you'll never get home again. You get me?" Pelly did not answer and Bart, after gazing at him for a few moments, turned away. "Start packing, lads," he ordered. "We've wasted more time than we can spare already."

Every one set to work, and the packing was soon done. By this time the whole of the water behind the ice-dam had gone out, and the river was running in its usual bed, and they had to carry the canoe quite a distance to float her. When all was ready Bart cut Pelly's lashings. "Here's your grub," he said. "Now git!"

"Ain't ye going to give me my rifle?" demanded Pelly.

Bart gave a short, scornful laugh. "No, we ain't," he answered curtly, and got straight into the canoe. The last they saw of Pelly, he was standing on the bank scowling at them as they paddled away.

Jock Scarlett was a capital hand with a paddle, and the boys were learning to be useful. For the next three days they travelled hard up the river, then came to water so swift, shallow, and broken with rocks that it was no longer navigable. So, carefully caching the canoe in a cave, they packed their stores into bundles, each carrying his share. Then they started afoot over the Divide.

It was terribly rough going, but up at this height the woods were not so thick. And since Bart knew the trail they got on pretty well. That night they camped high in the hills, and next morning found them tramping in single file along a pass so narrow that there was not room for two abreast. On the left was a wall of rock, on the right a sheer drop into a cañon so deep that the river roaring at the bottom looked like a silver thread.

"Don't you go a-looking over the edge," Bart warned the boys. "Ef you do you'll likely get dizzy. Keep your eyes to the left, and you'll be safe enough."

"I feel as if I was walking a tight rope," said Billy to Clem, who was just in front of him. "I say, I hope it doesn't get any narrower.

"It's not that I'm worrying about," Clem answered. "Look up."

Billy looked up. Three hundred feet overhead was a great arch of purest white on which the sunrays beat with dazzling splendour. It was the edge or 'cornice' of the snow-cap covering the peak above, and it projected over the pass like the edge of a great breaking wave. Here and there were ominous-looking gaps where large chunks had fallen away.

Billy whistled softly. "It would be a bit awkward if one came down on top of us, eh, Clem?" he said softly.

"Oh, Bart knows what he's about," replied Clem encouragingly, and had hardly spoken before there came a soft, crunching sound, a dark crack appeared in the cornice, and a vast mass which must have weighed many tons broke slowly away.

"Halt!" roared Bart. "Lie down! Flat on your faces, and hang on for your lives!"

It was lucky for Clem and Billy that they lost no time in obeying Bart's order, for next moment there came a thud which made the solid cliff tremble, and this was followed by such a blast of air as nearly tore them from their hold. Had they still been on their feet, nothing could have saved them from being swept over the edge of the pass into the terrific abyss which yawned beneath.

Two more lesser thuds, then things quieted down, and Billy ventured to raise his head. To his intense relief, he saw Clem quite safe just in front of him, and beyond, Bart and the others, all lying flat on their faces.

"We're safe, Clem!" he gasped out.

"Better keep still," replied Clem gravely. "There may be another fall."

Billy looked up. "It's most of it down," he said. "Look, the whole pass is blocked just beyond Bart. Wasn't it luck—its missing us?"

Bart rose slowly to his feet. "You're right, Billy. But it's luck as don't happen twice running. I didn't ought to have chanced it," he went on, "but I didn't reckon the sun was strong enough to bring the snow down like that."

"But what are we to do now, Bart?" asked Billy, as he glanced at the pass, which for many yards ahead of them was piled with hard-packed snow. "We can't get over that, can we?"

"You're right, son. It's us for the back track. I guess we got to go round by the Needle arter all."

"What's the Needle?" asked Billy,

"You'll see when you gets thar," Bart answered, and there was a grim edge to his voice which both Billy and Clem knew meant trouble.

Bart came cautiously past them, and led them back along the pass for some distance, until they came to a great crevasse or rift in the cliff, which they had already noticed in passing. Into this he led the way, and a very rough way it was. The rift became deeper, and so narrow that at the bottom it grew almost dark. The party groped their way among huge boulders.

"I wonder where the Needle is," said Billy to Clem.

"Where the Needle is—Needle is—" The echoes caught his words and sent them whispering up and down the vast, silent rock walls in a most uncanny fashion.

"Mebbe you'll see sooner than you like," replied Bart, and sure enough they had not gone another hundred yards before they did see.

Here the gorge was cut by a second gorge, only the second was far deeper than the first. The party found themselves on the edge of a gap at least a hundred feet wide, and of which the far side was much higher than that on which they stood. This gap was spanned by a bridge, but such a bridge as the boys had never seen before—never even imagined. It was one single stone, in shape not unlike the old Egyptian monument, 'Cleopatra's Needle,' which now stands on the Embankment in London. Only, of course, this was not smoothed by chisels, but all rough and jagged as it had split from the cliff.

"Thar's the Needle for ye," observed Bart dryly.

Billy whistled softly. "You don't mean we've got to cross that?" he said.

"Onless ye go back to the coast, ye got to. There ain't no way round," replied Bart.

CLEM TOOK COOL AIM AND FIRED

CHAPTER XVII
BIRDS AND BEASTS

Silent, hardly daring to breathe, the boys and Jock Scarlett watched Bart as he crawled up the slope of that terrible Needle. He had taken off his boots, and crept like a fly along its rough surface. Once he slipped a little, and Billy's heart was in his mouth, but Bart recovered and went on steadily.

He was about half-way over when there came a curious whistling sound.

"Hyas claw bird!" grunted Ahkim in evident alarm, and Jock Scarlett hastily opened the breech of his rifle and began thrusting in a clip of cartridges. "An eagle!" he cried, and looking up, Clem and Billy saw a huge wide-winged bird with hooked beak and golden eyes, dropping from the cliffs above straight toward the bridge.

For the moment Billy did not realize the danger, but Clem was wiser. He had heard from Joe Western that these great eagles of the North will attack anyone who approaches their eyrie, and he realized that the bird was swooping straight upon Bart. Also that Bart, who at the moment was on the worst and narrowest part of the bridge, was completely at its mercy. He saw something else, too, which was that Jock in his hurry had got his rifle jammed.

A moment earlier, Clem had been quaking in his shoes at the idea of having to cross that awful Needle, but now he forgot everything except that Bart was in fearful danger and must be rescued at any cost. In a flash he had leaped on to the Needle, and was running up it with the quickness and certainty of a cat. His eyes were on a spot a yard or two behind Bart, where a sort of spur stuck out, giving some sort of handhold, and before Billy and Jock had quite realized what he was about he had reached this spot, and flung himself down, with his left arm hooked round the spur. Quick as he was, the eagle was quicker and Clem felt the air about his head swirl with the beat of its great wings as it swooped upon Bart. With his right hand Clem drew from his pocket the small automatic pistol in the use of which Bart had trained him.

Bart was helpless. He was flat on his face, clinging with both arms to the Needle. The eagle struck, and Clem saw Bart's thick shirt split under the rending of its steel-like claws. Then, as the creature fluttered over its victim, beating the air with its wide wings, Clem took cool aim and fired.

At such close quarters the bullet ploughed right through the bird's body, and, turning over and over, it dropped like a stone. Clem watched it vanish into the black depths beneath. Then, as the excitement which had kept him up passed, a wave of dreadful giddiness swept over him, and he clung half fainting with his face close against the rough rock.

Bart's voice came to him, cool and steady, "That was a right smart bit o' work, Clem, and I'm sure obliged to you. Now, jest take three long breaths; then raise yer head and look at me."

Somehow Clem obeyed, and the sight of Bart's face, calm and clear-eyed as ever, gave him fresh confidence. "Now, you keep right on arter me," said Bart. "Ye can hold on to my belt if ye've a mind to. There's only this one ugly piece, and the rest is plumb easy."

Clem set his teeth and followed. How he ever managed to wriggle across those next few yards he never knew, but somehow he did it, and almost before he realized it, he and Bart were safe on the far side.

The rest was easy. Bart had carried with him a rope coiled round his body. One end of this he threw back to Jock, who made it fast, and with this as a hand-rail the rest soon crossed the stone bridge.

Billy drew his brother a little aside. "Clem," he said, and there was an odd little thrill in his voice, "I'm frightfully proud of you. I could never have done it."

Clem flushed a little. "Nonsense, old chap! I was in a most frightful funk."

"All the more credit to you," said Billy. Then Bart called them to come on, and once more they began to climb.

That night they slept in a cave near the summit of the Divide—and precious cold it was too—and very early next morning they reached the top of the pass.

Here Bart halted, turned, and stood with his hand over his eyes gazing back over a vast country of mountains, lakes, and forests. "Clem," he said presently, "can ye see anything?"

Clem stood silent for nearly a minute. Then he nodded and pointed. "Yes—smoke," he said.

Bart grunted. "I thought ez much. There's sure some chaps as never takes a warning. Wal, on their own heads be it."

Without offering any further explanation, he turned and went striding away downhill.

The next week was hard but steady travel, and at the end of it the little party found themselves clear of the big mountains and in a very different type of country.

"This is a bit different from the coast," observed Clem, as he and Billy tramped beside Bart up a lovely valley. "These woods are almost like England, and look at that brook! It might be a Devonshire trout-stream."

"It's a trout-stream right enough, son," replied Bart. "But I told ye that once ye'd crossed the mountains the country would be a heap different. Ye don't get the warm air off the sea here, and the winters are a sight colder and drier than over to the west."

"I like this a lot better," said Billy. "We've got out of all that nasty thick undergrowth. One can walk here without tripping up at every step."

"Yes, and the trees are all different," put in Clem. "Black pine and birch instead of those huge firs." He paused and looked doubtfully at Bart. "I say, Bart, have we much farther to go?"

Bart raised his arm and pointed to a range of blue mountains which lay like a wall across the sky to the east. Plainly they were very lofty, for their peaks were white with everlasting snow. "Them's what we're bound for, Clem," he answered.

Clem gazed at the mountains with intense interest. "How far are they, Bart?" he asked. "Forty miles?"

"Double that, and ye won't be far out," smiled Bart. And just then Billy broke in. "Bart, see those trees? All the lower branches are gone. Don't they look odd? It's just as if some whacking big bullock had been eating them off." He pointed as he spoke to a grove of biggish birch-trees on the hillside to the right.

Bart gazed at them, and there was an odd expression on his face. He bent toward Billy. "Don't you say nothing about it, Billy," he replied in a low voice. "I don't want them Injuns to notice it."

Billy was much puzzled, and so was Clem. They obeyed Bart, of course, but could not keep their eyes off the oddly lopped trees. Presently they heard a grunt from Passuk, and, turning, saw him pointing out the trees to his brother. They noticed at once that both the Indians seemed badly frightened.

Bart saw it too. "The jig's up," he grumbled. "Now we'll hev to watch out that them Injuns don't get plumb scared and make a bolt for it." He waited for the Indians to come up and spoke to them in their own language, at the same time patting his rifle encouragingly.

Billy could no longer, restrain his curiosity. "What is it, Bart?" he begged, "Do tell us."

Bart glanced at the boy, and there was the same queer expression on his face. "I guess you and Clem may as well go up and see. Jock and me will stay with the Injuns. But don't you waste much time, and ef ye sees anything alive don't meddle with it, but come right back."

Billy and Clem did not wait for a second leave, but were both off hot-foot up the hill, and it was not more than five minutes before they had reached the top. "Look at them!" panted Billy. "Something has been at them. The branches have been torn right off."

"Something pretty big, too," replied Clem. "There are boughs as thick as my leg ripped completely away."

By this time they were in the wood, and almost the first thing that happened was that Billy put his foot into a hole in a bit of soft ground—a hole two feet deep and about the same across. "Clem, look at this!" he panted. "What's made it?"

The two together stood and stared down at the great hole.

"It—it's a footprint!" said Clem, in a half-scared voice. "Look at the toe-marks!"

"But it would take an elephant to make a print like that," returned Billy. As he spoke there came a curious ripping, snapping sound from farther up the slope, and both boys started. Something which seemed as big as a small house was standing in the sun-dappled shadows not more than a couple of hundred yards away. Its monstrous form was covered with a mat of reddish hair, and to all appearance it had a tail at each end of its vast body.

THE GIANT CAME AT A SHAMBLING GALLOP

CHAPTER XVIII
THE BOYS' BLUNDER

The two boys were so paralyzed with amazement that they simply could not move. They stood perfectly still, hardly breathing, staring fixedly at the amazing monster.

Billy was the first to speak. "What is it?" he asked Clem in a hoarse whisper.

"I—I think it's a mastodon," replied Clem breathlessly.

"B—but they were extinct thousands of years ago."

"That one isn't," replied Clem, and the two fell silent again. The monster had not seen them, for it stood quietly, only switching its tail occasionally. What the boys had at first taken for a second tail they now saw was a trunk. This too the great creature swung at intervals.

"Let's go nearer," said Billy at last. "See those rocks over to the left? If we were to work up behind them we could get quite close without it seeing us."

Clem looked, and saw that Billy was right. The rocks seemed to give quite good cover. In their intense interest and excitement both of them had entirely forgotten Bart's warning to come back if they saw anything living. Another minute, and they were behind the rocks, and creeping cautiously up the hillside.

The rocks were big glacier boulders covered with lichen and half sunk in the ground, and there was a deal of rough undergrowth all round which made a good screen. At any rate there was plenty of cover, and within a very few minutes the two had gained a spot almost opposite that where

the hairy giant was still standing under the cool shade of
the big birches.

Billy stopped with a gasp. "You're right, Clem," he
breathed in his brother's ear. "It is a mastodon."

Clem did not answer. He simply could not. For there,
in full view, was a creature more wonderful than anything
he had ever dreamed of. It resembled an elephant, being about the same height as an African elephant, though
much longer in the body. It was covered from head to foot
with coarse reddish hair, and had the most tremendous
tusks. These were fully ten feet in length, and much more
curved than those of the elephant.

Clem felt half suffocated; he had a kind of feeling
that he and Billy had dropped back through a hundred
centuries into the dawn of the world. How long the two
crouched there neither of them knew, for they were lost
to all sense of time. What brought them to their senses
at last was a sudden movement of the gigantic beast. The
long hairy trunk went up, and he turned toward them. As
he did so the sunlight was reflected in his small, deep-set
eyes, which glowed red as live coals.

Suddenly Clem realized what they had done. They had
got to windward of the monster, and the faint breeze had
taken their scent down to him. He clutched Billy's arm.
"He's winded us. We've got to clear," he whispered sharply. As he spoke he ducked away again downhill, and Billy
followed. They had not gone twenty yards when the stillness of the great valley was broken by a scream like that of
half a dozen steam-whistles all opened at once. Then the
whole earth shook with the trampling of giant feet. Clem
leaped up. "Run, Billy! Run!" he cried, and together the
two raced away down the hillside with the mastodon in
full chase.

Clem glanced back over his shoulder, and saw the mastodon right on their track. The giant came at a shambling
gallop, which, however, ate up the ground at amazing

speed. His great trunk was lifted high above his head, and his little eyes gleamed red as blood.

Clem could hardly believe that what was happening was real, but felt rather as if he were in the grip of some dreadful nightmare. He and Billy ran like the wind, but inwardly both felt it was useless. They must be caught, gored by those fearful tusks, and trampled into the earth beneath those ponderous feet.

Immediately in front was a belt of thick, scrubby bush. Both hurled themselves into it; then Clem, leading by a yard or two, suddenly felt the ground give way beneath him. He was falling—falling! A thud that nearly stunned him, and he was lying flat in a deep bed of rotten leaves and twigs, and before he knew what was happening Billy was on top of him.

"W—where are we?" panted Billy. "Are—are you hurt, Clem!"

"No," answered Clem, struggling to his feet and glancing round. He and Billy were at the bottom of a gully some ten feet deep, a narrow place with bushes arching over it so that it was almost dark. To the right it opened out, but to the left it seemed to be narrower and deeper. "This way!" he cried, and seizing Billy by the arm dragged him away to the left.

They had not gone ten paces before the sky was darkened overhead, and right above them the huge form of the mastodon shot into sight. Impossible as it might seem, the monster had actually cleared the gully in his stride, and the bushes ripped with a noise like torn paper as he continued his headlong rush down the hill.

Clem leaned against the side of the gully for support. He felt suddenly weak, and was shivering all over. Billy's face was white, and his teeth were chattering. But he pulled himself together pluckily. "A close thing, Clem!" he said.

Clem recovered himself with an effort. "A bit too close!" he answered hoarsely. Then his face changed. "Bart!" he exclaimed. "Bart and Jock! The brute will be after them!" In a flash he was scrambling frantically out of the gully, and Billy following. Reaching the top, they were just in time to see the mastodon vanishing through the trees a long way downhill, and, sick with terror, they both ran after him as hard as they could go. But their late pursuer had a tremendously long start, and by the time the boys reached the edge of the wood he was ever so far away, and had nearly reached the brook.

"Where's Bart?" cried Clem, pulling up short. He and Billy looked all round, but could not see a sign of the rest of their party. Bart, Jock, and the Indians had all vanished completely.

"Perhaps they've hidden," said Billy hopefully.

"Where could they hide?" retorted Clem, looking down into the open, treeless valley.

"I—I don't know," answered Billy unhappily. "But the mastodon hasn't got them, anyhow," he added more hopefully.

"We'd better go and look for them," said Clem. "The mastodon seems to be going right away."

The giant beast was indeed half-way up the opposite slope, and still travelling nearly as fast as a horse would gallop, so the boys made their way downhill toward the spot where they had left Bart some half an hour earlier. But still there was no sign of any of their friends, and they were not only puzzled but both getting decidedly scared.

All of a sudden Billy gave a shout and started running. "There's Bart!" he cried, pointing.

Bart it was, his head just visible over the bank of the brook, and out he came, Jock following, then the Indians. They were all soaked through, and blue with cold. For though the sun was warm, the water of these Arctic streams has always an icy chill.

Bart's usually good-humoured face was decidedly grim. "I thought I told ye both to come straight back if ye seed anything," he said sternly.

Clem answered. "I'm awfully sorry, Bart. The fact is, we both got so excited we forgot all about it."

"Wal, ye see what ye've done," said Bart. "Jock and me have had to stand up to our necks in the river, and ez for them Injuns, they're so scared I don't reckon either of 'em will be much use the rest of the trip."

Clem and Billy hung their heads. They had nothing to say. Jock broke in. "They don't look as if they'd had too gay a time themselves, Bart. Did the beast chase you, Clem?"

Clem shuddered. "I should think he did. If we hadn't fallen into a gully he'd have got us, too."

Bart looked them over; he noticed their muddy, torn clothes and scratched hands and faces. He nodded. "I guess we won't say no more about it. But it'll be a lesson to ye both to mind what I say in future. Now I reckon we'll, hev to push on. I'd like mighty well to stop and light a fire and dry off, but them Injuns won't stay in this here valley onless we ties 'em. So ye'd better march."

CHAPTER XIX
THE STONE MAN

"Bart," said Billy, as they sat around their fire after supper that night, "did you know that wonderful beast lived in the valley?"

"Wal, I've seed his footmarks once before, and all them trees with the branches tore down. So I knowed he was somewheres around, but it's a fact I never seed him till to-day."

"But I can't understand it," broke in Clem. "The books all say the mastodon was extinct ages ago."

"Do you reckon the chaps as wrote 'em had ever been up here?" asked Bart dryly.

Clem smiled. "It's quite plain they haven't," he answered.

"No, and there's lots of things up here in the Great North as has never yet been set down in books."

"What sort of things?" questioned Billy eagerly.

"Wal, what would ye say to a beast as hops on his hind-legs like a kangaroo and is big enough to crunch a caribou up in his jaws?"

"Have you seen that?" demanded Billy.

"No, but I know chaps who have. Then there's the deer-bird as runs across the snow. He's nigh as tall as you, Billy, and the Injuns are scared stiff of him, though why I don't know. And thar's the big Dead Forest, and the flaming cliffs on the Arctic—aye, and heaps o' things as mighty few folk know about." He stretched and yawned. "I guess that's enough for to-night. Now we'll turn in."

For the next three days they marched hard and late. On the fourth afternoon after they had left the Valley of the Mastodon they reached the top of a long, bare ridge. In front was a wide valley with a big river at the bottom, a river which ran due north. It was bordered on either side by broad strips of curiously dark soil which was completely bare of vegetation. But Bart was not looking at the river. He had turned and was scanning the country they had crossed. "Can't see nothing this time," he said at last. "Kin you, Clem?"

Clem shook his head. "No," he answered. "You don't think Pelly is still following us, do you, Bart?"

"It all depends on whether he's met up with them other fellows," said Bart.

Billy broke in. "It's not likely we'd see them now, in broad daylight, but if we camped here, and if they really are following, we might spot their fire."

Bart nodded. "I reckon that's sense," he allowed, "and though we can't rightly spare the time I guess we'll do it." He considered a moment. "I got it," he said presently. "We won't waste no time after all. Dump your kit here, boys, under this here rock. Then we'll push on ter the river and come back here to camp."

The boys wondered much what Bart was after, but by this time they knew better than to ask questions. Down went their kit behind the rock, and the whole party marched briskly downhill.

There were woods between them and the river, and it was getting dusk before they got near the water. Presently they both became aware of a curious thin whistling sound which puzzled them greatly. They quickened their pace, and, as they broke through the belt of scrub which edged the river, saw a strange light shining through the gloom.

They pulled up short. "My goodness, look at that, Clem!" exclaimed Billy sharply.

They were standing on the edge of a broad belt of clayey sand, black as coal, bare and almost as smooth as a board floor. Half-way between them and the water spouted a geyser of blue flame which danced up and down, now quite near the ground, now shooting up to a score of feet or more. And as it spouted it whistled and crooned to itself in the strangest fashion.

"What in the world is it?" continued Billy.

It was Bart coming up behind them who answered. "Jest a gas-jet, Billy. There's heaps of 'em round here, fer these here is oil sands, and some day when this here country is opened up it's going to be the richest in the world. I lit this one myself last time I come along, and I reckon mebbe it'll go on burning long arter I've pushed on to another world. But we can't stop to watch it now. There's a job to do afore it gets dark." As he spoke he turned, dipped down among the bushes, and disappeared from sight.

Almost before the boys had started to wonder what on earth Bart was after, he was out again, dragging a canoe. It was a beautiful birch-bark, but in rather bad repair.

"A canoe!" exclaimed Billy. "Where in the world did that come from?"

"Out o' them bushes," replied Bart with a dry smile. "You didn't reckon we was going to swim the river, did ye?"

Billy flushed a little. He knew he had no business to have asked the question. "She'll want caulking," he said, to cover his confusion.

"Jest so. That's why I said we wouldn't be wasting time. The Injuns and Jock kin do it." He turned to Jock Scarlett. "There's pitch here," he said, "and ye kin use the gas fire to melt it. I reckon ye can finish in about two hours. Then come right back up the ridge to supper."

"Right you are, Bart," replied Jock cheerfully, and at once called the two Indians to help him carry the canoe to the fire. Then Bart and the boys turned back up the hill. Arrived at the place where they had left their packs, Bart picked a spot, well hidden on the river side of the ridge, on which to light the cooking fire. When this was done, and the kettle slung above it, he took the boys back to the top of the hill.

Almost at once Clem pointed. And far, far in the distance they saw a tiny point of light hardly larger than a star which glowed clear through the night.

Bart growled deep in his throat. "They're a-coming, and a bit quicker'n I reckoned." Then he laughed. "But not quite quick enough, I guess. You're up against it, Mister Ed Pelly—up against it good and hard. My, but I'd admire to see your face about this time to-morrer." He gave no further explanation, and the boys asked none for both had the most absolute trust in Bart.

Presently supper was ready, and a little while later Jock arrived with Ahkim and Passuk. "The canoe's good and tight, Bart," he said, in his pleasant voice.

"That's right," replied Bart, "for I guess we'll need her for quite a job to-morrow."

The boys went to sleep wondering what Bart meant, and were up even earlier than usual. Breakfast over, the packs were shouldered, and the party marched straight down to the river, where the canoe was launched and all the stuff stowed carefully in her. Then they got aboard and pushed off.

Reaching the center of the river, Bart turned the light craft straight downstream. Billy leaned across and whispered in Clem's ear. "Where's he taking us? He said the other day that we were going straight up into the mountains."

Clem shrugged his shoulders. "I don't know, Billy, but I expect it's some dodge for putting Pelly's crowd off the scent. Anyhow, we shall see before long."

For three or four hours the canoe travelled swiftly downstream. Then the river began to narrow, the black sand vanished, the banks grew higher, and soon they were in a cañon where the big river, penned in a narrow bed, rushed deep and swift between lofty walls of rock. They swung round a curve, and suddenly Billy stopped paddling and gave a sort of gasp. "Look, Clem! Look!" he cried, pointing to the right.

Hanging over the river was an enormous crag which had partly broken away from the cliff behind, and the shape of it was that of a huge head. It was impossible to believe that it had not been carved by human hands. There was the forehead, the great blunt nose, and projecting chin. There were the eyes and the mouth all startlingly perfect. The likeness was increased by a mass of scrubby bush growing on the top of the head and resembling hair.

Clem stared at it for a moment with a feeling almost of terror. "The—the Stone Man!" he said at last hoarsely.

"Aye, it's the Stone Man," answered Bart. "And I don't reckon Mother Nature ever carved anything more wonderful here or anywheres else."

"Wonderful!" repeated Clem, staring at the huge, amazing face, which had a stern yet not unkind expression. "It's the most wonderful thing I ever dreamed of."

"Wal, don't dream! Paddle!" said Bart dryly. "For you're a-going to see something a sight more wonderful afore you're many minutes older."

CHAPTER XX
THE HOLLOW MOUNTAIN

The canoe swept on beneath the sphinx-like face of the Stone Man; she drove round a second curve, and from both the boys at once came a cry of amazement. For right in front was a monstrous wall of rock, and at its base the black arch of a vast tunnel, into the gloomy depths of which the whole great river poured—and vanished.

"Set tight!" cried Bart. "It ain't as bad as it looks." He turned to the two Indians, whose faces were frozen with superstitious terror, and spoke to them sharply in their own language. It did not seem to do much good, but since the canoe was in the grip of the rapid and it was impossible to turn, the wretched men stolidly accepted their fate, and although they clearly expected nothing but instant death, obeyed Bart's orders.

The boys held their breath as the canoe, steered by Bart, shot straight into the center of the lofty arch. Next moment she was dropping at a giddy speed. The roar of the water penned under the rock roof was deafening. The sound increased to a deep thunder, and suddenly the canoe swooped downward with a feeling like that of descending in a fast lift. Then, almost before Clem and Billy had realized what was happening, she had steadied and was floating smoothly on a calm surface.

"And—and it's not dark!" came from Billy. "Look, Clem!" He pointed upward as he spoke, and Clem, looking up, saw, at an immense height above, a great opening, a sort of huge skylight through which the sunlight struck down in long shafts.

"Told ye ye'd see something funny," came Bart's deep voice.

"It—it's a hollow mountain," declared Billy.

"Ye've hit it in once, Billy. We call it Hollow Hill. I don't reckon thar's a bigger cave in all the North-West, and they do say Injuns lived in here once. Mebbe they do still for all I know."

The boys looked round with the most intense interest. The light from above, bright as it was, was not enough to show the whole of the cave, which stretched away on both sides into dusky distances where all was lost in shadow. As for its height, the roof seemed to be at least a thousand feet above them. The place was staggering in its immensity. Through the center ran the river, black as jet, deep, swift, but smooth.

"Give Pelly something to think about, eh, boys?" said Bart, with a deep chuckle.

"If it scares him any worse than it did me, he'll never recover," grinned Billy.

"If you was scared, you've got over it mighty quick," said Bart approvingly. "And now I'll tell ye there ain't anything more to be scared of onless them pesky Kaloots get arter us."

"Indians?" questioned Clem.

"Aye, bad Injuns. And we're a-getting into their country once we're out o' this. But I'm hoping as they'll be on the river catching salmon, and ef that's so mebbe we won't see nothing of them."

It took about twenty minutes to pass through the hollow hill; then the canoe shot a short, swift rapid, and glided out again into brilliant sunshine. There were still cliffs on either side, but not so lofty as before, and presently these dropped to wooded banks, and the river broadened again.

"Keep your eyes skinned," said Bart. "Ef ye sees anything, sing out quick."

A couple of fish-hawks wheeled overhead, but beyond these there was no sign of life; yet Bart slowed the pace of the canoe, and they paddled cautiously until they reached a pebbly beach on the right bank, with a thick clump of trees behind it. Here Bart steered the canoe ashore, and they all landed. Bart himself carefully chose the spot for caching the canoe, and when this was done the party shouldered their packs and struck inland toward the mountains.

It was not bad going, and by nightfall the little party was high among the hills, and had left the river miles behind. The boys hoped that all was well, but Bart did not seem quite easy. He picked a thick grove in which to camp, and would allow only a very small fire.

The night, however, passed quietly enough, and morning found them climbing again. The great mountains which they had seen ahead for nearly a week now towered above them in solemn majesty, and the air was colder than they had felt it since passing over the Coast Range.

They had been travelling for about two hours when Passuk suddenly pulled up and pointed to the ground. Bart stooped and examined the spot, and the boys saw that he was looking decidedly grave.

"Indians?" Clem ventured.

Bart nodded. "Kaloots. A hunting party. I only wish I knowed just which way they'd gone. Don't any of ye make a sound if ye can help it," Bart ordered. "It's a mighty still day, and a dry stick a-cracking under your feet kin be heard a mile off by them Injuns. So I just warns ye to be mighty careful."

The boys and Jock did their best to obey, but marching over rough ground is none too easy at any time, and the strain of doing it quietly became more and more heavy as the day wore on. They ate their dinner silently, hidden in a patch of thick-hush, and then went on as quietly as before, still climbing the giant slope, which stretched upward mile after mile.

The boys kept their eyes fixed on the ground, and every muscle in their legs was aching with the strain of going so soft-footed. It was all the harder because Bart carefully avoided all open ground, and kept to the thickest part of the woods.

Well on in the afternoon, when the shadows were beginning to lengthen in front of them, they came to open, park-like ground, with patches of trees scattered here and there. Beyond this, some two or three miles away, the mountains rose like a wall. Bart stopped and spoke in a low voice to Ahkim, who shook his head. "I believe Ahkim is scared of crossing the open," said Billy to Clem.

"But Bart wants to push on," replied Clem; "Billy, I believe we're getting pretty near the end of our journey."

Billy's eyes shone with excitement. "I believe too. Bart said it was in those mountains. I say, Clem, I hope we're going to keep right on."

Clem did not answer, for secretly he was feeling rather doubtful. If this Indian hunting party was about, here was just the country for them. Several caribou were visible in the distance, grazing on the rich grass. He looked at Bart again, and felt certain that Billy was right, for Bart had stopped speaking, and Ahkim was looking anything but happy. Next minute Bart turned to Jock and the boys.

"I guess we'll try and make it," he said. "It's risky, I'll allow, but in my notion it would be a heap more risky to stop here. Ye see, if the Injuns happens to hit our trail they'd slip upon us arter dark, and then there wouldn't be a dog's chance fer any of us."

"Just as you say," Jock answered quietly, and after a last careful survey of their surroundings the party started once more. Bart led the way from one clump of trees to the next, and they covered rather more than a mile without anything happening. Then, without the slightest warning, a figure rose into view on the crest of a little grassy rise some three or four hundred yards away to the left. In the clear air they could see that he was a man of middle height, wearing only a breech clout and moccasins, and that he carried bow and arrows. The low sun shone full on a streak of red paint across his face and on a tuft of feathers in his hair.

Bart stopped short, half-raised his rifle, then lowered it. "No," he said curtly. "I reckon we got to wait for them to begin. Boys, jest walk right along. Don't run till I gives the word."

The rest obeyed, but Clem's and Billy's eyes were on the Indian. Presently he was joined by four others. They stood for a moment or two, staring at the party of whites, then all disappeared again behind the crest of the knoll.

Bart quickened his stride. "Keep right close to me," he ordered. They had covered perhaps half a mile when Clem's sharp eyes caught a movement among some trees to the left. He told Bart. Bart looked and nodded. "Drop your packs," he said. "Drop everything except your rifles and ammunition. Ef we got to run, we'll run light."

CHAPTER XXI
THE BLACK GAP

At Bart's order all five loosened the straps of their packs and dropped them. Next moment, there came from the trees to their left a yell so hideous that it made shivers run down the spines of Clem and Billy. It seemed impossible that human beings could have produced such a horrible sound.

"They've seed us," said Bart. "How many is there, Jock?"

"Not more than a dozen, I guess," answered Jock Scarlett.

"It's enough," growled Bart. "Now see here. I don't want to shoot onless we has to. But ef they comes too close there won't be nothing else for it. Now foller me, and look slippy."

Dodging out of the clump of timber in which for the moment they had sheltered, Bart began running for the next. It was surprising what a pace he set, and the boys had all they could do to keep up with him. The Indians saw them, and yelled again. "Sounds like the Zoo at feeding-time," panted Billy as he raced along beside Clem.

Clem glanced back over his shoulder. "They're after our packs," he said. "That gives us a chance."

"Jolly lucky for us!" responded Billy, and he was right. The Indians, fourteen all told, had flung themselves on the packs like hungry wolves, and it was not until they had gathered up every single thing that Bart's party had left that they again took up the chase. But when they did really start to run they came like the wind, and gained rapidly. It was terrifying to see the way in which they ate up the ground.

There was one more clump of trees between Bart's party and the cliffs, and the Indians were not a hundred yards behind them when they gained it. Suddenly there was a faint hissing sound. An arrow rang on a stone within a yard of Clem and shot off at a sharp angle. Another thudded upon a tree-trunk and stuck there quivering.

"Guess I'll have to stop this," snapped Bart, and snatching his shotgun from Ahkim, who was behind him, he thrust in two cartridges and fired. Shrieks announced that the shot had reached its target. "That'll learn 'em!" growled Bart. "No, I ain't killed none—jest tickled 'em up a piece."

Dropping to the ground, the Indians lay flat among the tufts of coarse grass, and seemed to vanish like so many rabbits. Bart glanced through the trees toward the cliffs which rose, stern and forbidding, some four or five hundred yards away. Billy saw the look. "Not much help for us there, Clem," he whispered. "Nothing but a squirrel could climb those rocks."

"They do look pretty steep," allowed Clem, "but Bart must know some way up."

"And while we climb the Indians will pick us off with their beastly arrows," said Billy, scowling.

Just then Bart turned to them. "You boys slip along to the far side of the clump," he said. "Wait thar till I joins ye."

Clem hesitated. He hated leaving Bart like this. "Git, I tell ye!" said Bart, and this time there was no disobeying him. Clem and Billy got.

There was a pause of perhaps two minutes, then two loud bangs, and next moment Bart, Jock, Ahkim, and Passuk came running hard. "Foller me!" Bart ordered as he reached the boys, and then all six were racing together across the open. From behind them came the savage war-cry of the Kaloots, which echoed hideously back from the

towering walls of broken rock confronting them. Then
arrows began to whiz again. Clem and Billy heard them
strike the ground close behind with nasty quick thuds.
They ran with the rest, but both—Billy especially—were
feeling pretty hopeless.

For even if they did reach the cliff ahead of the Indians,
what was the good? True, they might turn to bay among
the scattered boulders at the base, but they had no food
or water—nothing but their rifles. Suddenly the air was
rent by another and much louder yell, and Clem, glancing
back, saw a sight which filled him with horror. "There are
a lot more Indians," he panted as he raced alongside Bart.
"Twenty at least. They're coming up from the left."

Without stopping an instant, Bart looked back. Clem
was right. Here was a fresh party of Kaloots, twice as strong
as the first, all running at full speed in a desperate effort
to cut off the white men before they reached the cliffs.

"Run!" roared Bart. "Run as ye never ran in your lives.
Make fer that Black Gap. If ye kin reach it afore them
redskins ye're safe."

The boys spurted for all they were worth. Their hearts
thumped, their legs felt like lead, but they kept well up
with Bart. Billy stumbled, and Jock Scarlett, who was
nearest, caught and steadied him.

Now they could see the point for which Bart was making—the Black Gap, as he called it, and that was just
what it was—a cleft so narrow as to be invisible at anything more than a couple of hundred yards. But that last
two-hundred yards was a nightmare, and how they kept
going neither Clem nor Billy ever knew. It was only the
knowledge that a terrible end awaited them if they failed
which kept them on their feet. They ran with their eyes
glued upon the spot.

"Fifty yards more!" Clem heard Bart mutter thickly.
"Keep up, boys. You're doing fine." The cleft seemed to
widen. It opened out so that Clem could see a passage
running deep into the cliffs. Again an arrow hissed past

and splintered on the cliff face. Clem felt Bart seize him by the arm; then he was suddenly in deep gloom, and as Bart let go he stumbled and collapsed flat on the hard ground. Not for all the Indians in Alaska could he have run another yard.

"Look out, Bart!" cried Jock Scarlett. "They'll be on us in a tick."

"I guess not," replied Bart dryly, "but ef they tries it I'm ready for 'em."

"Why shouldn't they try it?" demanded Jock. The words were hardly out of his mouth before there came rumbling down the gorge a roar like that of an explosion. It was so heavy that it made the solid ground quiver. It was followed by a tremendously loud, shrieking whistle which lasted for several seconds. Then came another roar, not so loud as the first, but still sufficiently heavy to resemble that of a good-sized waterfall.

"That's why!" replied Bart as soon as he could make himself heard.

"But what does it mean? I don't understand," said Jock.

"You'll understand when you've walked a bit farther up this here gorge," Bart told him.

Bart was still breathing hard, but he and Jock had stood the run better than the boys, who were still lying panting on the ground. Presently Clem managed to sit up. The first thing he realized was that all sight of the Indians and of the open country across which they had come was shut off. This was because the gorge did not cut straight into the cliff, but at a sharp angle. The next was that though the actual opening was narrow the part which they had reached was as wide as a broad street. Then he saw something else—that down the gorge was stealing a thick mist, rolling in soft grey folds, like the vapour from a giant kettle.

The roaring noise had stopped, but there was a curious gurgling in the distance. This, he thought, was like water running out of a great bath, and he could not imagine what caused it. Jock was standing facing the entrance of the gorge, his rifle ready in his hands, but as Clem watched he turned to Bart. "You're right, Bart," he said in a puzzled voice. "Not one of those Indians has shown up. I suppose they think the place is haunted."

"Something of that sort, I reckon," agreed Bart, with a twinkle in his eyes. "And they ain't so far wrong either, as mebbe you'll see afore you're much older."

Billy, who by this time had got his wind back, struggled to his feet. "Come on, Bart. Let's go and see. What sort of ghosts are they?"

Bart laughed outright. "I thought curiosity would cure ye, Billy. What about it, Clem? You ready to march?"

"I'm ready," announced Clem. "All I want is a drink of water. My throat's like leather."

"Ye won't have long to wait afore ye gets water and everything else ye wants," replied Bart comfortingly. "Now step lively. We got to get past her afore she blows again."

"What in the world does he mean?" Billy asked Clem, as they started off.

"I've no more idea than you, Billy, and it's no use asking Bart. But I suppose we shall see pretty soon."

Billy was so eager to solve the mystery that he hurried on at a great pace, giving Clem all he could do to keep up.

For wild magnificence the gorge beat everything they had seen yet. The cliffs were of a strange black rock, and towered to a terrific height on either side. They were fissured and seamed with deep cracks, and not even a blade of grass grew on their splintered faces."

As they went onward the gorge widened a little; then, rounding a curve, it opened out suddenly into a good-sized circular space. In the center of this was a round basin about fifty yards across, and its appearance was so strange that both the boys pulled up short and stared at it in amazement; for the rock of which it was made was white as snow at the bottom, and above that was banded yellow, red, and brown. In the middle of the basin was a small black hole. The great basin was soaking wet, yet there was no water in it, but over all still hung a soft cloud of thin mist.

CHAPTER XXII
THE VALLEY OF THE MIST

Billy swung round on Bart. "What is it?" he demanded eagerly.

Bart glanced at the big gun-metal watch which he carried in his trousers pocket. "She'll tell you herself inside of ten minutes. But I reckon we'd best be the other side of her afore she begins to talk."

The boys were simply bursting with curiosity as they hurried across the circular space. Beyond it the gorge ran onward into the heart of the hills.

"Guess we can stop now," said Bart, as they came to a spot some three hundred paces beyond the basin. He looked at his watch again. "She's due in jest two minutes," he remarked.

"What's due?" begged Billy, but Bart only grinned. Jock chuckled too, and it was clear that he understood. But even Billy could not persuade him to speak. Billy was getting quite cross, when suddenly a deep rumbling sound from the basin made him jump.

"Now watch her," said Bart.

The rumbling grew to a roar, the same roar which they had heard before, but now, since they were so much nearer, immensely louder. The ground trembled as if with an earthquake, and suddenly from the hole in the center of the basin up rose a vast spout like a giant fountain. Up and up it soared to a height of nearly a hundred and fifty feet, and with it rose great clouds of steam and vapour.

Then, when it had reached its greatest height, the huge spout curved over and fell thundering back into the basin from which it had risen. Clem gave a shout. "I know what it is. It's a geyser."

"Thet's what the books calls it, son," agreed Bart. "But we calls him 'Old Watchdog!'"

"Why?" questioned Billy.

"Because he guards the pass. There ain't no other way into the Valley o' the Mist onless ye passes the Watchdog. And onless ye knows jest when he's a-going off it's apt to be mighty awkward for ye."

"I should think it would be," cried Billy. "Why, you'd be boiled alive!"

"How often does it go off?" asked Clem.

"Every thirty-five minutes, to the tick," replied Bart.

The eruption ceased while he spoke, leaving the basin brimming and bubbling like a cauldron. Then the sucking sound began again, and the boiling water drained away into the hole through which it had risen.

Jock, who had been watching in silence, spoke.

"I don't wonder the Indians are scared of that," he remarked. "Look at Ahkim and Passuk." The two had fallen flat, their faces pressed against the ground. They were so badly scared that it took Bart some minutes to persuade them to get up again, and even then they were shaking all over, and could hardly stand.

"Lucky they haven't much to carry," remarked Jock. "They wouldn't get far with it."

"They wouldn't need to," replied Bart. "We ain't got above two miles to go."

"What!" cried Billy, in wild excitement. "Are we there?"

"Mighty near it," replied Bart, with the old twinkle in his eyes. "Half an hour's march, and then I reckon to show ye something as ye'd hardly expect to see up here in the mountains."

"Come on. Let's go!" begged Billy.

"Guess I'm ready," answered Bart. Then, as Billy shot ahead, he stopped him sharply. "You two boys keep right along behind me. It ain't reckoned healthy fer strangers to go running loose among the People o' the Mist."

Very unwillingly the two boys dropped behind Bart. They were both so excited that they had completely forgotten their dry throats and aching legs. "I wish Bart would go faster," grumbled Billy in Clem's ear. Clem did not answer. He was straining his eyes through the mist, which still lay thick in the gorge.

Suddenly Bart pulled up. "Say, boys, I'm a-going to show ye something," he remarked quietly. "Now shut your eyes tight."

Clem and Billy wondered, but obeyed.

"Ye'll keep 'em tight shut till I gives the word," said Bart.

They both promised. Then Bart took them by the arm, one on each side of him, and marched them along. They had a sort of idea that they were going round a bend, but both faithfully kept their eyes tightly closed, and so they went for about a couple of hundred paces.

Then Bart stopped. "Open yer eyes," he said. They did so, and found themselves standing at the head of a great slope which overlooked an immense valley—a valley so wild and beautiful that they had never seen or even dreamed of anything to match it. All around rose up mountains, like a great wall, soaring high against the blue sky. Their summits were white with snow, but their lower slopes were covered with thick forests which reached down to a great lake, the water of which was clear as crystal and blue as the sky above.

But the most startling part of the scene lay just below them. On the lake shore, at the bottom of the great slope, was a wide clearing, and in it was a village. Billy passed his hand across his eyes. "It—it's almost like England!" he said slowly.

"For a fact, it ain't a bad imitation," replied Bart, with a smile. Clem saw what Billy meant, for though the houses were of squared logs and the roofs were shingled, each house was surrounded by a neatly fenced garden full of flowers and vegetables. The houses bordered a wide street running all along the lake shore, and opposite was a landing, with canoes and boats tied to it. But what struck the boys at once was the house that stood by itself on the hillside, above the rest—a fine big house with a wide veranda and real glass in the windows.

"Whose is that?" demanded Billy.

"That belongs to the boss," replied Bart. "The 'Big Britisher' some calls him," he added, with twinkle in his eyes. "But you'll meet him mighty soon. Now keep right behind me, fer, as I told ye, there's them here as don't like strangers."

He started down the hill as he spoke, and the boys followed, full of wonder.

"Look at the people," said Billy to Clem. Three men were on the landing. They were Indians, but of a type the boys had never yet seen—tall, well set up men, as different as possible from the heavy, squat-built Ahkim and Passuk. Bart led the way toward the big house, and as they came near it the boys were more than ever struck by the English look of it all—the neat garden, with English flowers, and cabbages and potatoes behind.

"Watch out!" said Bart suddenly, and in a moment half a dozen great shaggy beasts came rushing out of the village, and made straight toward the newcomers.

"Wolves!" gasped Billy, but Bart shook his head. "Huskies," he answered. "Stand quiet, both on ye."

The pack came racing up. They were most formidable-looking creatures, with the long jaws and sharp-pricked ears of the true timber wolf, yet otherwise very like dogs. Yet the odd thing was that, unlike dogs, they made no sound at all, but came in dead silence. The leader was the biggest of them all. He stood thirty inches at the shoulder, and looked able to pull down a horse.

Bart waited till he came quite close, then called aloud, "Mikki!" The great leader stopped short; then with the oddest sound, half bark, half yelp, flung himself on Bart, and standing on his hind-legs put his paws on Bart's shoulders and began to lick his face.

Next moment came a shout from below. "Bart! Bart! Is it really you!"

At the sound of the voice Clem stiffened. He stood staring for a moment at the broad-shouldered, splendid-looking man who had just come out of the gate below, and then, with a wild shout of "Father! It's Father!" went tearing down toward him.

CHAPTER XXIII
LAKE FISHING

"So you never suspected who it was had sent for you?" It was Mr. Ballard who spoke. He, the boys, Bart, and Jock were sitting round the table in the great living-room of the big house, and enjoying such a meal as they had not seen for many a long day. Clem looked up. "No, Dad," he answered. "You see, we thought you were in Australia."

"The police thought so," replied his father, rather grimly. "And naturally I did not inform them to the contrary. As a matter of fact, I got away in a whaler from Dundee, and was landed up at Point Barrow, on the Arctic coast. There I had the great good luck to fall in with Bart Condon, and it was he who told me of this valley, where I have found refuge."

Bart looked up from his caribou steak. "David, you ain't told them yet," he said gravely.

Mr. Ballard flushed. "Do I need to, Bart?" he asked.

Clem understood, and spoke quickly. "Not that you're innocent, Dad. Billy and I know that."

"Thank you, Clem," replied his father quietly. "Still, I must tell you this much. It was my partner, Silas Wayne, who was the cause of all this trouble. Quite accidentally I had discovered that he was not playing the game, from a business point of view, and I spoke to him and warned him. The result was that he took a violent dislike to me, and set to plotting secretly to get rid of me. Like a fool, I never suspected it, and the first thing I knew of it was

347

when I was arrested for forging his signature to a deed. The signature was indeed a forgery, but it was the work of an accomplice of Wayne, named Gurney."

"Gurney!" broke in Clem. "Why, that's the fellow who was on the steamer."

Bart nodded. "Aye, he's got wise to where you are, David, but don't you worry. We've fooled him. But I'll tell ye after. Now go on."

"There is little more to say," said Mr. Ballard. "So cunningly had Wayne laid his trap that I never had a chance. I was found guilty and sentenced to a term of penal servitude. It is simply owing to the fact that I happen to be stronger and more active than most men that I managed to escape from the train. Luck was with me. I stumbled upon an empty house, found tools to get rid of my handcuffs and a change of clothes. Then I made straight for the coast. Luck was with me again, for I found a ship short-handed, and got a berth at once." He paused. "And here I am," he added.

"I think it was splendid of you, Dad," exclaimed Billy.

"So do I," agreed Clem. "But what about this horrid man Wayne? Can't we force him to own up? You see, Dad, you're always in danger until you are proved innocent."

"Exactly, Clem. There you have the root of the trouble in a few words. My chief ambition in life is to prove my innocence, but, there are terrible difficulties in the way."

Clem turned to Bart. "If we had only known that Gurney did the forgery!" he said sadly.

Bart shook his head. "Ye couldn't hev done nothing aboard the ship, Clem. My chief notion all through was to dodge that there son of a gun. That's one reason why I wouldn't tell you lads where we was going, nor nothing else about the trip. I warn't going to resk the chance of your even talking in your sleep."

For a while there was silence. Jock Scarlett, who had not yet spoken, broke it. "Mr. Ballard, it seems to me that the proper thing to do is to get hold of a first-class lawyer, put all the facts, in his hands, and see what he can do."

"Quite so," replied Mr. Ballard, "but that means money."

The boys stared. "But you paid an awful lot to bring us out from home, Dad," said Billy.

Mr. Ballard smiled. "I got that from selling a parcel of silver-fox fur, which Bart took down to the coast. Now I have heaps more furs here—perhaps two thousand pounds' worth. But the trouble is to get them to the coast. They are a big bulk, and you boys know the difficulty of the journey."

"It's plumb out o' the question to take 'em now," said Bart bluntly. "Not with Gurney and Craze and Ed Pelly lurking round."

"Just so," said Mr. Ballard. "We must think of some other plan."

He and Bart discussed the matter for an hour or more, but could not see any way out of the difficulty. At last Bart rose to his feet. "I guess there's nothing for it, but just to wait, Ballard. These troubles have a way of solving themselves if you wait long enough."

Mr. Ballard laughed. "Good advice, Bart. Good enough to sleep on, anyhow. Like you, I'm ready to go to bed."

A fortnight passed delightfully. Then one day Clem and Billy went fishing on the big lake which occupied the whole of the center of the valley.

Billy, who had been paddling vigorously, stopped and allowed the canoe to glide into a little bay. "This seems a good place, Clem," he said.

Clem nodded, and, pulling line from the reel of his fishing-rod, cast out his spinning bait. Flashing in the sun, it dropped into the ripples twenty yards away. "Now paddle quietly, Billy," he told his brother. "Bart says it's best to sink the bait pretty deep. The big fish swim a long way down."

Billy did as he was asked, and the light canoe glided easily through the water, the only sound being that of the tiny waves slapping her bow.

Billy looked back toward the village, now a long way astern. "I can hardly believe we've been here a whole fortnight, Clem," he said.

"No more can I. It seems like a dream."

"A jolly nice dream," grinned Billy. "I never had such a good time in my life. Wonder what old Grimston would say if he could see us now." Clem laughed outright. *"He'd* think he was dreaming. I say, Billy, what wouldn't you give to have introduced him to the mastodon?"

But Billy did not smile. "Don't, Clem!" he said quite sharply. "That was too much like a nightmare. I'm precious glad there are no beasts of that sort in the Valley of the Mist."

Clem nodded. "So am I. But, Billy, did you hear what that big Indian, Keesh, said about the next valley?"

"No," replied Billy. "He didn't tell me."

"He calls it the Valley of the Monster," Clem told him.

"Valley of the Monster?" repeated Billy.

"Yes, but when I asked him I couldn't get much out of him. Even these Piegan Indians of Dad's are superstitious. But from what he did say I got a notion it's something pretty big."

"A mastodon?" questioned Billy.

"No, for it lives on meat. He says it kills deer, and that it is as old as the hills. 'Very bad medicine,' he called it."

Billy shivered. "Sounds like that horrid thing Bart told us about—the creature that hops on its hind-legs and hunts caribou."

Clem nodded. "Well, like you, Billy, I've had enough of monsters, but this is what I want to know. If there's no way out of this valley except the one we came in by, past the great geyser, how did Keesh know anything about this beast?"

"He might have seen it from the top of one of these mountains," suggested Billy.

"I suppose he might," agreed Clem, "but I'm not so sure. See here, this is a jolly big lake, and quite a lot of streams run into it. How does it drain?"

"Haven't a notion," replied Billy, with a shrug.

"May be an underground passage like that Hollow Hill place we came through in the canoe."

Clem looked doubtful. "Anything is possible in this amazing country," he said, "but I'd like to know."

Billy did not answer. He was looking up at the sky. "There's a rum-looking cloud up in the north," he said presently. "I've a notion we'd better be shoving back."

The words were hardly out of his mouth before Clem's line tightened with a jerk, the rod tip bent, and the line went rattling off the reel. "A whopper!" cried Clem. "My goodness, Billy, it's the father of all the fish! Paddle! Paddle for all you're worth, or he'll break me."

The great fish had headed straight down the lake, and dipping his paddle, Billy drove the canoe after him at full speed. In a moment they were out of the bay, and the canoe travelling at such a pace that it seemed as if a tug was pulling her. The, two boys, intent on the great fish speeding onward deep in the clear cold water beneath them, never gave another thought to the monstrous black cloud which spread its dark wings over the mountain, never heard the low, moaning sound which filled the upper air.

CHAPTER XXIV
WHEN THE STORM BROKE

"What can it be?" gasped Clem, as he braked the reel and tried hard to control the struggles of the unseen monster. "It can't be a trout. It must weigh twenty pounds or more."

"Bart says there are trout quite as big as that in this lake," Billy told his brother. "He calls them 'Dolly Vardens.'"

"I can't do a thing with him," said Clem. "Paddle harder, Billy. He's still taking line off the reel. Oh, goodness, what's he doing now? I do believe he's going right down to the bottom of the lake."

"Hang on!" cried Billy, as excited as Clem himself. "Hang on! He can't go very much deeper. Ah, there he's coming up again! Reel! Reel for all you're worth."

Clem reeled in line as hard as ever he could go, and had gained ten or fifteen yards, when up came the great fish to the surface, and flung itself high into the air.

"It's a yard long!" exclaimed Clem, as it fell back with a resounding splash.

"And what gorgeous scarlet spots!" replied Billy. "It's a trout right enough, Clem, and we must have him."

"It's going to be a rare fight," panted Clem, as the big fish went off as fast as before. "I say, he's taking us right out into the middle."

Five minutes passed, and in spite of Clem's best efforts the great trout was still his master. Do what he would, he could get no more line back; indeed, he had lost some of

that which he had previously gained. Then, quite suddenly, the sunlight was cut off just as if a curtain had been
drawn across it, and the water, previously so brilliantly
blue, took on a dull leaden tinge.

Now at last Billy looked up. "I say, Clem, look at that
cloud!" he cried. "It's simply galloping up! I don't like it
a bit."

But Clem was too busy to turn. His rod was almost
double, and his whole mind was set upon the problem of
how long his tackle would stand this fearful strain. Just
then the monster trout jumped again, then made a fresh
dash, fairly ripping line off the reel. But this rush did not
last so long as the first, and presently Clem was really reel-
ing in. "He's tiring!" he exclaimed in triumph. "We'll have
him in a minute or two, Billy."

"If that storm doesn't have us first," said Billy uneasily.

The moaning sound came again, and this time both the
brothers heard it.

"Clem, there's a regular buster coming," said Billy,
quite sharply. "We must get back to the shore."

But for once Clem, usually the cautious one of the pair,
was too excited to think of danger. "In two minutes, Billy," he answered. "He's pretty well fagged out. Get the gaff
ready. You'll have to be jolly careful about getting him
into the canoe, or he'll upset us."

As he spoke the great trout, exhausted by its struggles,
was already on its side. He reeled in rapidly, and Billy
got the gaff ready. Slipping it deftly under the fish, he
gave one quick lift, and the splendid creature lay flopping
in the bottom of the canoe. "Isn't he fine!" cried Clem.
"Won't Dad be pleased. He loves grilled trout better than
anything."

But Billy did not answer. He had picked up the paddle,
and was driving the canoe back toward the shore as hard as
he could go. Clem looked up, and what he saw frightened
him. The sky to the north-east was black as night, and the
mountain tops were veiled in writhing mists, while the

upper air was full of an ugly moaning sound. He glanced at the shore, still quite half a mile away. Then he too snatched up a paddle and set to work. It was too late. All in a flash the storm descended upon the lake; it spun the canoe like a feather, and sent her skimming in the opposite direction. For a few moments the two boys worked like furies to keep her head into the wind. It was useless, and Clem saw it.

"It's no good, Billy," he cried. "We've got to let her drive."

The speed with which the weather had changed was simply paralyzing. When Clem had hooked his fish a warm autumn sun had shone on calm blue water; now a shrieking gale was lashing steel-coloured waves and sending the spray scudding across the canoe, while above the upper air was full of rushing grey mist.

Clem realized the danger to the full. "I was a selfish fool, Billy," he said bitterly.

But Billy would have none of it. "Nonsense, old man! You never saw. It was my fault. I ought to have told you. However, it's not a bit of good apologizing to one another. After all, it only means running down to the end of the lake and taking shelter until this is over."

"If we can—" began Clem, then cut himself short. "If we can ever do it," he had been going to say, but what was the use of scaring Billy? He knew what a sea gets up on these mountain lakes, and how frail a craft the canoe was, and he was desperately doubtful whether the canoe could live, or whether she would be swamped by the quickly rising waves. The only thing was to keep her going so that she would not be 'pooped'—that is, overtaken by a wave, and with that idea in his head he paddled like fury.

Driven by two paddles as well as the furious gale, the canoe fairly flew down the lake, but the worst of it was that the farther they went the higher grew the waves—very short waves, but for that reason all the more dangerous. They came hissing up astern, each one curling dangerously over the stern, and some breaking partly over her. Icy water began to lap in the bottom. "You'll have to bail, Billy," shouted Clem; and Billy, dropping his paddle set to bailing frantically.

Now the whole handling of the canoe was left to Clem; and it was almost beyond him. Yet he kept his head and stuck to it gallantly. Again and again he cast longing glances at the banks, but he had to realize that it was out of the question to turn the canoe one way or the other. If he tried it she would be swamped at once.

On and on they drove. The village was out of sight, hidden in the driving storm-haze and spindrift. All they could see were the dark waves leaping after them like hungry wolves, and the banks dim on either side.

It had turned bitterly cold all of a sudden, but this Clem hardly noticed. Furious paddling kept him warm enough. Presently he noticed that the banks seemed plainer to the sight. He knew what this meant—that they were getting near to the lower or western end of the lake. But this gave him no comfort, for here the banks rose into towering cliffs, and, even if it had been possible to drive across the wind, there would be no landing-place. Higher and higher they rose, and narrower and narrower grew the lake, until the boys were driving through a gut not more than five or six hundred yards wide. And here the wind was stronger than ever. Its whole force seemed to be concentrated in this funnel, and it blew with a shrieking fury impossible to describe.

Clem's heart went cold within him, for it seemed to him that they were in a trap from which there was no escape. The canoe would at last be driven to the very end of the ever-narrowing gap, and dashed against the rock face. The first blow would break the frail craft to match-wood, and he and Billy would be left to drown in the icy waves.

Billy too saw what was happening. "Can you shove her over one side or the other, Clem?" he shouted, above the roar of the wind and waves. "If we don't land soon it seems to me we shan't be able to at all."

"I'll try," Clem answered resolutely. "Bail hard, Billy."

Seizing his chance, he tried to drive the canoe to the right, where he fancied he could see a rock point projecting out into the waves. But the moment he began to turn her a wave top smashed in over her stern, leaving six inches of water washing about inside her.

"Straighten her!" shrieked Billy, and just in time Clem forced her back. Even then it was touch and go. If it had not been for Billy's desperate bailing the canoe would certainly have sunk. But he sent the water flying out of her, while Clem paddled like fury, and presently she was riding dry again.

But with every minute the gut through which they were rushing grew narrower, while on either side the dark cliffs towered up until they were lost in the mist.

"Where are we going, Clem?" cried Billy, panting with his exertions.

"I can't tell any more than you," replied Clem. "Still, we've kept afloat so far."

"Looks to me as if there was a bit of a curve just beyond," said Billy. "If we can get round that we shall be out of the worst of the wind."

"You're right. There is. There's a chance for us still," answered Clem.

The sight filled him with fresh hope and energy, and he paddled harder than ever. At the curve was a great shoulder of rock projecting out into the deep water, and the waves were leaping up it to the height of a man. With a last desperate effort Clem managed to drive the canoe round it, and the result was like a miracle. In the twinkling of an eye they were out of the terrible rush and roar of the wind and floating on long, smooth rollers.

CHAPTER XXV
INTO THE DARKNESS

"Oh, Clem, what luck!" cried Billy.

But Clem could not answer. Absolutely worn out by his terrific efforts, he had shipped his paddle and was lying forward with his head on his knees, panting for breath.

Billy remembered the little flask of brandy packed with their sandwiches in the basket under the stern. Bart had given it to them long ago, telling them never to go out without it. "A drop of good brandy has saved many a man's life," he had said. "And you boys jest carry it along with ye, in case o' need." Billy put about a teaspoonful in the metal cup, mixed it with water, and made Clem swallow it.

Clem choked a little, but the drink pulled him round wonderfully. His heart ceased to pound, and he began to breathe more easily. "You'd better have some too, Billy," he said, and made his brother take a dose.

It was just as he handed the cup to Billy that he noticed how rapidly the canoe was still travelling. The shoulder of rock was already fifty yards away, and the canoe was simply flying along at the foot of a tall cliff which rose like a black wall above them.

"Look, Billy! Look at the pace she's moving!" he exclaimed.

"Phew, I should think she was!" replied Billy, snatching up his paddle. Clem did the same, and they both set to work to turn the canoe and drive her back to the eddy behind the shoulder.

After four or five minutes of hard paddling they were exactly in the same spot. Their combined efforts were just enough to hold the canoe against the current. To save their lives they could not gain a yard.

"Clem, old boy," panted Billy at last, "I'm almost done."

"So am I," groaned Clem. "I say, what are we to do?"

"Let her rip," said Billy recklessly. "We shall have to do that sooner or later, and I vote we do it now, and save our strength for whatever is coming."

"I expect you are right. It's the only thing to do," Clem answered, and as he spoke he stopped paddling.

At once the mill-race current seized the canoe, and she shot away almost as fast as a man could run.

"Where on earth are we going?" asked Billy, as he stared, at the deep black water, now hardly wider than a canal, and at the huge black cliffs which towered on either side.

"Where *under* the earth, you'd better say!" replied Clem with a grim edge to his voice. "Look there! Look in front! This is where the big lake drains out, and if I'm not much mistaken it goes right underground."

Billy sat still as stone, staring. Clem was right, for a little way beyond the cliffs closed together, and the smooth black water along which they were helplessly speeding vanished beneath a tall, narrow arch. A vision of their driving helplessly down into those unknown depths made shivers, cold as ice, course down his spine, and suddenly he snatched up his paddle. "Paddle, Clem!" he shouted, and his voice echoed terribly up and down between the great walls of rock which compassed them.

"It's no good, Billy," replied Clem quite calmly. "Ten men couldn't hold her against this rush. Steady, old chap! Don't funk it. We've got to take our chance. Keep her well in the center and hold her to it."

As he spoke the canoe darted in under the lofty arch. Next moment she had tilted slightly, and was racing down into utter blackness at an almost incredible speed.

There was no roar, no sound except the faint hiss of water as it rushed between smooth rock. By this Clem knew that the channel must be deep and straight. In an instant, however, all light was gone, and they shot forward through intense and utter blackness. It was no use steering, for it was impossible to see anything to steer by.

"Sit tight, Billy," said Clem sharply. "Don't paddle. Just let her go."

"Oh, Clem, where are we going?" came Billy's voice from behind him, and the sound of it made Clem's heart ache, for he realized that for once Billy's splendid pluck had deserted him, and that the strain had become greater than he could bear.

"It's all right, old chap," he answered steadily. "We shall come out again. It's only another hollow mountain like the one that Bart took us through."

"But it's so dark!" groaned Billy.

Clem put his hand into his pocket, and his fingers closed on his small electric torch. Next moment its clear white gleam illuminated the blackness. It shone upon a narrow chute of smooth black water sliding endlessly away into the gloom, and on walls of black rock polished as if by hand.

"It's all right," cried Clem joyously.

"How do you know?" asked Billy thickly.

"Look at the walls, Billy. All polished! That's ice. And ice couldn't do that unless it found its way out at the other end." It was not really a very good argument, but it did a lot to comfort Billy. And then, before anything else could be said, the thin light of the torch was dimmed by a stronger glow. "Daylight!" shouted Clem, and almost before the words were out of his mouth they were out of the tunnel, and once more in a river which slipped swiftly along at the bottom of a monstrous crack in the mountains.

"What did I tell you?" said Clem.

"I was an idiot, Clem. I lost my head," answered Billy, in a shamed voice.

"Well, I jolly nearly did too," replied Clem. "So you needn't worry, old man. But I say, I wonder where we are going to land up."

"In that Valley of the Monster, I expect," replied Billy.

Then there was silence for a bit, while the canoe flashed onward. The situation was still desperate enough, but the boys were both so intensely relieved at getting safely out of the tunnel that they hardly gave a thought to the dangers that still threatened them.

So far, the river which carried them had been so deep and straight that its current had been almost silent, but now both became conscious of a low, deep roar.

"Look out, Billy," sang out Clem. "There's a rapid ahead."

The canoe tilted quite steeply, the roar increased, and suddenly they were shooting madly down a rapid so steep that it was almost a fall. Yet even here there were no rocks to break the surface, and Clem saw that so long as he kept the canoe in midstream there was no great danger.

Faster and faster they flew downward; then suddenly Clem saw beneath them a regular hill of water, a great smooth hummock laced with long streaks of snowy foam.

The canoe hit it, rose like a car on a switchback, and was safely over the center. She dipped again, her speed slackened, and she was floating in the middle of a broad pool with rocky banks and virgin forest all round.

"Topping!" cried Billy, his spirits rising with a bound. "You steered splendidly, Clem."

"Yes, but where are we?" said Clem doubtfully.

"Safe, anyhow. That's the great thing. Paddle on a bit, Clem. If we get out of these trees we can tell more about it."

Clem did so, and the canoe, passing out of the big pool, went gliding down a fair-sized river, which wound through the level bottom of a great valley. Behind them they could see the mountains bounding the lower end of the Valley of the Mist, and to the left was another chain of great hills. Clem glanced up at the cliff-like mountains behind them, and shook his head. "I say, Billy," he remarked, "we're going to have a sweet job to get home again."

CHAPTER XXVI
THE SOUND IN THE NIGHT

"We can't get back this evening," agreed Billy. "The best thing we can do is to camp, and wait till morning."

Clem nodded. "Yes, that's the only thing to do. The worst of it is that Dad will be in such a stew."

Billy agreed. "I'm afraid he'll be awfully worried," he said gravely. "Still, I don't think it's worth trying to climb those mountains to-night. It'll be dark in an hour."

Clem restrained a temptation to smile. It would not be an hour's but a full day's work even to reach the summit of those terrific cliffs. In fact, he had his doubts as to whether it would be possible to climb them at all. But he kept these doubts to himself, and beached the canoe.

"We've got the big trout still," remarked Billy. "That's grub for the present. And the storm seems to be over, so that's all to the good."

"It may be still blowing," said Clem, "but the mountains cut it off. How cold it's turned!"

"It is cold," allowed Billy, "but we'll soon have a fire. Luckily I've got my matches in a corked bottle, as Bart showed me."

"We'd better hunt for a cave," said Clem, as he dragged the canoe up. "I say, it's luck we've got a hatchet."

"And some sandwiches," answered Billy. "Come on."

Carrying their goods, they pushed their way through the trees up the steep bank to the left of the river, and started hunting for a cave. But this they could not find, and after a quarter of an hour's vain search they gave it up. "We must build a shack of pine-branches," said Clem. "Here's a good place. And hurry, Billy! The sun's down already." As he spoke he set to cutting branches.

By this time the boys knew all the tricks of camping, and the first thing they did was to choose two saplings about eight feet apart. They cut a pole long enough to reach from one to the other, and fastened it across at a height of about five feet from the ground. Then, after making a sloping framework with six other poles, they covered this tightly with pine-branches. Then the ground beneath was covered with a thick carpet of small branches and dry grass, and when all was complete they lit a big fire of dry wood in front.

The heat reflected from the sloping wall at the back of the shelter made it delightfully snug, and the two settled down to clean the trout and broil it over the coals. Since they had the remains of their sandwiches to eat with it, they both made a capital meal. Then they banked the fire well, and, curling up on their thick mattress of grass and pine-needles, went to sleep.

About one o'clock Clem was wakened by feeling very cold. He looked up at the sky, and saw that it was thick with clouds. There was not a star to be seen. He at once made up the fire, but as he lay looking at the crackling flames he did not feel happy.

It was now very late in the autumn, and Bart had told him that the long Indian summer which they had been enjoying might break at any time. It seemed to him that this was what was happening. But tired out with the long struggle of the previous day, he was soon asleep again.

When he next woke it was still dark, and Billy was shaking him by the arm. "What's the matter, Billy?" he asked, half crossly.

"That noise. Don't you hear it?" Billy whispered urgently.

Clem sat up. Somewhere in the distance there was a crashing sound, then a soft but very heavy thud. Then *thud—thud—thud*. It was as if some giant was pounding the earth with an enormous sledgehammer.

"What is it?" demanded Billy.

"I haven't a notion," Clem answered. "Not the ghost of a notion. Unless it's a rock which has rolled down from the mountain."

"It's not that," replied Billy decidedly. "I heard it before—the same slow thudding, and a crash or two. Clem, do you think it's the monster?"

"Bosh!" retorted Clem. "I don't know of any animal that could make that noise. Don't worry about it, Billy. It's probably something quite natural, and we shall find out in the morning."

Billy was silent, but Clem could see that he was not happy. Then the sound came again—the same ponderous thuds. But it was farther off. "Let's make up the fire," said Clem, trying to speak cheerfully. But really, like Billy, he was very uneasy.

There was plenty of wood, and the red embers crackled up again. As the flames leaped up, the boys saw that the air was full of fine white flakes. "Good gracious, it's snowing!" said Billy.

Clem's spirits fell with a bump. So Bart had been right, and winter was upon them. Clem had never seen a Northern winter, but he had heard plenty about it since their arrival in the Valley of the Mist, and he knew that this snow was going to make their climb back across the mountains difficult, if not impossible. But he was not going to tell Billy so. "Perhaps it won't be much," he said.

Billy was not listening to him. "There it is again!" he said sharply. Once more came the extraordinary thumping. It went on for some time, but was fainter than before.

"Whatever it is, it's going away," said Clem. "And we're safe enough, with our fire. Go to sleep, Billy: We must get all the rest we can, for we're going to have a jolly stiff climb to-morrow."

All the same, it was a long time before they dropped off again. When they awoke the next time the sun was up, and its frosty light shone redly upon ground carpeted with nearly three inches of snow. It was also freezing quite sharply. "Ugh!" growled Billy. "This is rotten."

"Might be worse," replied Clem. "It might be still snowing. Come on. Let's get some breakfast, then start. We must get over the mountains before we are caught by another snowstorm."

More of the big trout was grilled, enough to give them food for the whole day. Then the two started down to the river, launched the canoe, and paddled across. Caching her carefully among some bushes on the far side they walked up the bank. "Clem," said Billy, "I wonder what that row was last night."

"I'm afraid we haven't time to find out," replied Clem. "It was queer, certainly."

"The weirdest thing I ever heard," agreed Billy. "Some day we must come back here and try to find out." He broke off suddenly. "Hallo, look at that bush!"

"My goodness, it looks as if a mastodon had stepped on it!" said Clem, turning a little to examine it.

"So it has, I believe!" exclaimed Billy, running forward. Then he stopped short, his eyes fairly bulging. "Clem, this was bigger than a mastodon. Look at that footprint."

Clem stood silent, gazing at a footmark—If footmark it was!—so enormous that he could hardly believe his eyes. True, it was not so broad or deep as that of the mastodon, but it was of a length simply paralysing. "A yard and a half, if it's an inch," said Billy in an awe-stricken tone. "Clem, is it real, or is this a fake of some sort?"

"Not much fake about it," replied Clem dryly, "for see, here's another!"

It was true. About five feet away, and parallel with the first, was a second mark of equal size. The prints were somewhat dimmed by the snow which had fallen since they were made, yet there was no doubt about them, or about the monstrous weight which had crushed a stiff-looking bush quite flat into the ground. Billy walked forward. "Here are more marks," he said in a scared tone. "Just the same as the first."

Clem paced out the distance. "Nine yards, I make it," he said. "And, Billy, there's another mark behind the prints."

"I see. It looks like a tail."

"It is a tail," said Clem, in a tone of certainty. "Billy, do you remember what Bart said about a beast that hopped on its hind-legs like a kangaroo, and was big enough to carry off a full-grown caribou?"

Billy shivered. "He was right, Clem. That's what this thing is, and it's true what the Indian said about this being the Valley of the Monster."

CHAPTER XXVII
NO WAY OUT!

This time Clem could not contradict his brother. The evidence of the giant foot marks was too strong, and for the moment he felt as shivery and unhappy as Billy himself. But presently he pulled himself together. "The sooner we get out of this, the better," he said. "And particularly out from among the trees. Once we're up on the mountainside, we ought to be safe enough, A beast like that is too big to do much climbing."

Billy eagerly agreed, and they turned sharply uphill. But both went cautiously, and both kept looking about them, and listening with quivering eagerness for the sound of that terrible thumping.

They neither saw nor heard anything. Indeed, this part of the valley seemed quite deserted. Barring a few birds and some snowshoe rabbits, they saw no living thing, and soon they were clear of the trees and climbing a steep, bare slope.

Clem stopped and looked back, and his eyes roved across the great stretches of the valley, which lay white, silent, and inexpressibly lonely. "Nothing there, Billy," he said quietly.

"Nothing that we can see," replied Billy. "But it's no use pretending that the beast is not there. We've heard it and seen its footprints."

"Never mind. We're out of its reach," said Clem comfortingly. "Come on, Billy. The days are none too long, and we've got to be back in our valley before the light goes."

Billy merely nodded, and together they pushed on up the mountainside. The slope grew steeper and steeper, and the worst of it was that the higher they went the thicker lay the snow. Within an hour they were scrambling along ledges which were six inches deep in soft snow, making the going not only difficult, but horribly dangerous. They had to move very slowly and cautiously, yet even so they were constantly coming on places so difficult that they were forced to go back and try some other way. By midday they were hardly half-way to the summit, and both were a good deal more tired than they cared to admit.

They sat down to rest in a little hollow sheltered from the breeze, and ate cold trout. They had nothing else—not even a morsel of bread—and cold broiled fish without even a pinch of salt is not a very satisfying meal.

Billy, who had been very silent, gazing up at the cliffs, spoke suddenly. "Clem, I don't believe we can get up there," he said.

Clem started slightly. It was exactly what he had been thinking himself, but he had been careful not to say it for fear of discouraging Billy.

"You think so too," said Billy bluntly.

"It's a job, I'll admit," replied Clem. "Still, I don't see why we shouldn't manage it. Anyhow, we've jolly well got to try."

Billy looked back into the wild valley. He nodded. "I don't want to have to spend another night down there," he said with a shudder. "Come on, Clem." The next two hours were simply awful. The brothers crept along bare ledges, with hundreds of feet of empty space beneath them. They clung to the faces of great cliffs, hanging on with fingers and toes. The rocks were loose and shaly, and sometimes broke away, sending small avalanches thundering down the mountain face.

It was about three in the afternoon when they found themselves on a narrow terrace at the base of a sheer cliff. Clem stared upward, but the vast wall of rock was not merely sheer—it actually overhung the ledge. "That's done us, Billy," he said briefly.

Billy merely nodded. His face was very white.

Clem put his hand on his brother's shoulder. "Cheer up, old fellow! We'll find a better way to-morrow."

But Billy shivered again. "It's spending the night down there, Clem," he said hoarsely. "I tell you I'm scared, Clem—I'm scared!"

If the climb had been bad, the descent was worse. It had begun to freeze, and the ledges were like glass. When at last the brothers reached level ground again both were quite worn out. It was all they could do to crawl as far as their last night's camp and light the fire. Then they dropped down beside it, and lay there for an hour before they could summon energy to cook the remains of the big fish. This, and hot water boiled in their bailer, made their supper, and afterward they had to drag their weary limbs out again in order to collect firewood. Though they did not say so, both knew that fire was their one protection from the mysterious monster that stalked at night through this lonely and unknown land.

They made a huge fire, big enough to last till morning, and then lay down. Both were so utterly weary that they dropped off at once, and did not move until the cold dawn-light struck upon their faces.

"Good morning, Billy," said Clem, trying to look more cheerful than he felt. "The monster hasn't shown up again—that's one good thing."

"If there had been a dozen I shouldn't have heard them," replied Billy. Then, as he sat up, "Oh, Clem, I'm stiff!" he groaned.

"That will wear off, Billy. See here, I'm going down to the river to try and get a fish for breakfast."

"I don't believe they'll bite in this frost," replied Billy. "And Clem, I'm fed up with fish. It's meat I want."

Clem shrugged his shoulders. "Since we haven't got a gun I'm afraid we shall have to live on fish." He got up as he spoke, threw some wood on the red embers of the fire, and went off down toward the river. Billy followed, but after visiting the spot where they had cached the canoe, came back toward the camp.

Clem fitted up his rod, and cutting open a rotten log found some big white grubs called 'sawyers,' and started to fish.

It was abominably cold, and the fish most certainly were not feeding. Clem stuck it for an hour, and did not get a bite, and at last gave it up and went sadly back to the camp. He tried to put a good face on it, but was really dreadfully uneasy. If he and Billy could not get food they were done for.

As he came through the trees toward the camp he stopped and sniffed. "Smells like meat roasting," he said to himself in a very puzzled voice, and quickened his pace.

"Hurry up, Clem!" he heard Billy's call. "You're just in time for breakfast." And, coming out into the open, the first thing he saw was Billy, roasting a large rabbit over the fire.

Clem pulled up short. "My goodness, Billy, where did you get that?" he exclaimed.

"Shot it," replied Billy, grinning.

"Shot it? What with?"

Billy stooped down and picked up a bow. It was made of a stiff green sapling and strung with fishing-line. "Here you are," chuckled Billy. "I told you I wanted some meat, and that you wouldn't get any fish. Wasn't I right?"

"It was jolly smart of you," declared Clem. "How did you make your arrows?"

"Out of hard wood, and feathered them with parchment leaves from my fishing-book. Then I stalked Brer

Rabbit, and luckily he let me get within about ten paces. Anyhow, here's breakfast, so let's eat."

It was astonishing how good the meat tasted, and the meal did both the boys a wonderful amount of good.

While they ate they talked things over, and agreed that it was no use trying to climb the mountains back into the Valley of the Mist. "My notion," said Billy, "is to go right round and back by the way we first came in—past the geyser."

Clem whistled softly, "It's a long way, Billy."

"But the only way," answered Billy.

"And what about the Kaloot Indians?" asked Clem.

"We shall have to chance them, Clem. After all, I don't suppose they're camping there in this weather. The chances are that they have gone back to their village ever so long ago."

Clem nodded. "I believe you are right, Billy. Then the sooner we are off, the better."

"Can't be too soon for me," replied Billy. "As I told you before, I'm scared stiff of this place. Just wait till I pack up the rest of the rabbit; then I'm your man."

THE MONSTER LEAPT UPWARD AND FORWARD

CHAPTER XXVIII
THE MONSTER

Much to Clem's relief, the sky cleared, and, though it was still cold in the shade, the sun shone so warmly that the snow began to melt. The boys, keeping along the upper end of the valley at the foot of the hills, went on at a good pace, and midday found them eight or nine miles on their way.

After a short rest for lunch they tramped on. To the right rose the mountains, a regular wall two or three thousand feet high, their tops dazzlingly white, and to the left the valley sloped gently downward to a great central basin, where a large lake glimmered in the sunlight. The country was wilder than anything the boys had yet seen, for it was littered with great crags, which stood up grim and forbidding among thick clumps of gloomy-looking forest.

Soon clouds began to blow across the sky, and it became very dull and bitterly cold. Clem was again very uneasy. The big snow he knew to be due any day now, and, if it came, travelling without snowshoes would be impossible. He and Billy had no snowshoes, and would not have known how to use them if they had.

Deep in these unpleasant thoughts, he was tramping steadily along, when he was startled by a crashing sound among the trees to the left. It was followed by a thud, a sound which he knew in an instant to be the same that he had heard two nights ago.

"The monster, Clem!" he heard Billy mutter in a choked voice.

Clem took one swift glance to the left, the direction from which the sound had come. He saw something about half a mile away among the trees. The trees were too thick for him to tell what it was. All that he could see was that it was an animal of colossal size.

Then he looked to the right. About two hundred yards away the ground rose steeply toward the first line of cliffs. These cliffs were steep, but broken by deep fissures and great projecting rocks. He made up his mind in a flash. "Up the hill, Billy! Run like blazes!" he said.

As ill-luck had it, the ground they were on at the moment was quite open, There was no cover of any sort between them and the cliffs, with the exception of a few large boulders, which must have fallen in the past from the great mountains above. And he and Billy had hardly started to run before they heard a fresh crash in the distance, and then the tremendous *thud—thud*. And they realized that the monster had seen them and was in pursuit. Neither spoke, neither looked behind. Their one idea was to reach the cliffs and scramble to safety before this dreadful thing caught them.

Side by side they fled along, with the same horrible, regular *thump-thump* coming nearer and nearer at every moment.

Although the distance was so short, it seemed an age before they reached the base of the cliffs. Clem had seen a fissure, and that was what he had been making for. Whether it was a place that could be climbed or not, he had no idea at all, and when he and Billy reached it his heart sank, for it looked impossible.

But Billy's quick eyes noticed a tiny ledge about six feet up, and springing at it he caught it with both hands. Clem seized him and gave him a tremendous push. Next instant Billy was kneeling on the ledge and pulling Clem up.

Above was a slope dreadfully steep, but not impossible to climb, and although they had to crawl on hands and knees they went up it like two squirrels. Closer and closer came the terrific thuds; the very earth shook under the weight of the monster as it advanced with tremendous leaps. Then came a sound like a sudden explosion of steam, and a reek of foul air which made Clem feel deathly sick.

At that moment he and Billy both came to a dead stop. They were on a ledge beyond which the cliff rose like a wall. Clem scrambled to his feet, turned, and looked round, and the sight before his eyes filled him with a horror such as he had never felt in all his life before. For the creature beneath him, at the base of the cliff, was of a size so prodigious and an appearance so horrible that it did not seem to belong to this world.

Imagine a creature shaped like a lizard, but standing erect on its hind-legs like a kangaroo. Make it the height of a two-storied house. Give it a head not unlike that of an alligator, but with two horny lumps on the crest, and an upper jaw curved over like a beak. Cover this creature with a thick, warty hide of a drab colour, on which grow tufts of coarse grey bristles. That was the impression that Clem got at a first glance.

But even this was not the worst of it. It was the eyes, long, deep-set, red as fire, and glowing with an indescribable malignancy, which fixed his gaze. They fascinated him so much that his knees began to bend under him, and he felt a dreadful impulse to fling himself off the ledge down into the huge horny jaws which gaped to receive him.

Luckily for him, the spell was broken by Billy's voice. "Clem, we're stuck. We can't get any higher."

Even as Billy spoke the monster leapt upward and forward. Its huge hind-legs, armed with enormous claws, stuck upon the slope a dozen feet above the level on which it had been standing and its horned head swooped forward. But the loose rock was not equal to the weight of the

giant creature, and crumbled away beneath it. It was this
and nothing else which saved the boys from destruction.

Clem caught Billy by the arm and dragged him to the
right. All in a flash he had seen that, although they could
not climb higher, there was a ledge to the left which ran
deeper into the great fissure. It looked as if there were
some sort of a hollow at the end of it. Somehow the two
reached it, and, squeezing in through a narrow entrance,
found themselves in a tiny cave.

It was a dozen feet deep, but so narrow that there was
not much more than room for the two of them to stand
abreast. Just as they got inside, the monster leapt again.
This time it got some sort of foothold, and its croco-
dile-like head, with jaws wide open, drove straight at the
mouth of the cave. It reminded Clem of a great snake
striking.

The boys fell apart, each squeezing himself tight against
the opposite walls of the cave. The hideous jaws clacked
together with a sound like the snapping of a monstrous
beak, but they failed even to touch Billy or Clem. Then
the beast's foothold gave way again, and it fell back, foiled.

The boys stood, their hearts thumping, watching their
dreadful enemy. They were half suffocated by the vile reek
of its breath. For a moment Clem hoped it would give up
its attack, but not a bit of it! Its failure simply infuriated
it. Its red eyes glowed with a savage fire, and it leapt again
and again. Great rocks rolled under its clutch, and the
force with which its horny jaws struck the rim of the cave
opening actually knocked splinters of stone away.

Clem felt that same curious paralysis that one feels in
a nightmare, but, oddly enough, Billy, who earlier had
seemed much more afraid of the monster than Clem, was
now more angry than frightened. Suddenly he stooped,
snatched up a big stone weighing three or four pounds,
and as the brute leaped again, flung it with all his force
straight between the gaping jaws.

Seemingly it went right down the monster's throat, for the creature fell back, choking horribly. "That's one for you, you brute!" shouted Billy, and picking up more stones he hurled them furiously at the monster. He might as well have bombarded it with golf-balls, for all the harm he did it.

But the stone which it had swallowed had done it no good, and the creature seemed to have at last realized that it could not reach its prey by wild leaping. It crouched down upon the ground in front of the cave, watching the opening with malevolent eyes.

"You brute!" said Billy again, shaking his fist at it. "Oh, if only I had a rifle!"

Clem shook his head. "It would take a field-gun to kill that thing," he said.

CHAPTER XXIX
BILLY'S BRIGHT IDEA

The boys waited a little. "Do you think it means to stay there and starve us out, Clem?" asked Billy.

"I wish I knew. Luckily we've got the rest of the rabbit. We can stick it for a goodish while, and perhaps if we are quiet it will get tired and go away."

Billy gazed for some moments in silence at their awful gaoler. "What is it, Clem?" he asked at last.

"A dinosaur, I think, Billy. Bart told me that one was seen by two Frenchmen, one a missionary, about ten years ago right up in the far North."

"Ugh! I thought, when we saw the mastodon, that we had reached the limit," said Billy. "But this beats the mastodon."

"It's almost too dreadful to be real," agreed Clem. He looked round and noticed that the floor of the little cave was covered with loose rocks. "How would it be if we built ourselves in?" he suggested. "I don't know whether we could pile up any sort of breastwork that the monster could not pull down. But we might as well try. And anyhow it would keep us warm if we have to spend the night here."

Billy nodded. "It wouldn't be a bad notion," he agreed.

Working as quietly as they could, they began to pile up the stones, wedging them as tightly as they could in the entrance. The dinosaur watched them with evil eyes, and once or twice stirred uneasily. Yet it did not attempt to

attack them again. Before they had half-filled the entrance
the boys had used up all their material, and Billy began
pulling loose pieces away from the sides and roof. The
rock was very dark in colour, and here and there marked
with thin streaks of yellow. "Looks almost like gold," suggested Billy, but Clem shook his head.

"Mica," he said. "Bart showed me some just like it only
a few days ago."

"Be careful, Billy," he added. "You'll have the roof
down on us if you don't look out."

"I'll be careful," replied Billy, and turned to the back
of the cave. "Here's a big chunk loose," he said. "Give us
a hand, Clem."

The rock was almost as much as the two could handle between them, but after much tugging and straining
it suddenly came away and rolled with a crash on to the
floor. As it fell Billy gave a sharp cry. "Clem, we've broken
through! There's another cave behind." He pointed to an
opening from which came a faint gleam of light.

Clem stepped quickly forward, and pushed his head
and shoulders through the opening. "You're right, Billy.
There is another cave, and what's more, it's open at the
top. Wait! I'll get through."

It was a tight fit, but he managed it, and Billy followed. They found themselves in a rock chamber as large
as a good-sized room. The floor sloped steeply upward,
and at the upper end a gleam of daylight showed. Clem
gasped with eagerness. "If we can only find a way out!" he
exclaimed, as he scurried toward the light. Billy, hurrying
after him, heard him call out. "We can, Billy! I do believe
we can!" and found him scrambling up a sort of chimney
which sloped upward for a distance of some twenty feet.

Twice Clem slipped, but Billy pushed him from below,
and at last Clem got his fingers on the ledge at the top.
After that he did not waste much time in climbing out,
and in hauling Billy up behind him.

Looking round, they found themselves on a broad ledge fifty or sixty feet above the valley floor. Billy fairly danced with delight. "One for you, this time!" he jeered, and picking up a big stone flung it at the monster. As luck would have it, he hit it exactly on the tip of the nose, and this must have been the beast's tender spot, for in an instant it was up again, and with its hideous snorting whistle leaping wildly upward.

"You idiot, Billy!" cried Clem. "Why did you want to start him up again?"

"A jolly good job!" retorted Billy. "Keep on pelting him, Clem. Go on, I tell you! I've got a scheme."

Clem obeyed, and having plenty of really heavy stones at hand, succeeded in working the brute to a pitch of absolutely maniacal fury. It was really a terrible thing to see this creature, which weighed as much as a large elephant, leaping like a crazy kangaroo at the cliff face. Some of its jumps were twenty feet in actual height, and its terrific claws raked boulders weighing a ton or more off the face of the cliff.

"That's right, Clem. Keep it up!" cried Billy, and Clem, glancing round, saw his brother working desperately to shift a great boulder which lay poised on the very edge of the ledge. "It's no use," panted Billy. "I can't do it alone. You'll have to help me."

Clem saw what he was after, and put his shoulder to the rock. It tilted.

"Look out. It's going!" shrieked Clem, and sprang back. The big rock rolled slowly over, and even as it fell the monster made another of its appalling leaps. Clem stood breathless as the rock, striking the ledge, rebounded outward.

"It's got him!" shrieked Billy, wild with excitement. "It's got him! Watch!"

He was right. With a tremendous thud the boulder struck the dinosaur full in the chest, and, huge as the creature was, knocked it backward. For an instant the monster and the rock together seemed to poise in mid-air; then with an earth-shaking crash, the creature struck the ground, and rolled over and over down to the bottom of the slope.

"It's finished him! It's killed him!" cried Billy, in a voice hoarse with excitement. Clem was silent. For a moment he almost thought that it was true. He and Billy, side by side on the lofty ledge, watched the terror quivering and writhing on the ground.

"If we'd only got another rock," panted Billy, as he saw the creature's struggles increasing.

Clem caught his brother by the shoulder. "Lie down!" he said curtly. "Lie flat down. He isn't dead, but when he gets up again, if he doesn't see us, perhaps he'll go away."

Billy grunted, but obeyed, and they lay flat on the ledge and watched until the giant beast had slowly recovered and regained its legs. For some moments its vicious little eyes scanned the ledge, but the boys were out of sight. At last, after what seemed an age, it turned and bounded slowly and heavily away. It was not, however, until its giant form had vanished in the distant trees that either of the boys ventured to move. Then Billy rose to his feet. "It's gone, Clem," he said, drawing a long breath.

"It's gone," echoed Clem, "but where, and for how long?"

"I vote it doesn't find us here when it comes back," said Billy grimly.

Clem looked down. He shuddered a little. "Are we to go down there again, and chance it?"

"We shall never have a better chance," replied Billy, with a quietness which was in odd contrast to his previous panic.

Clem strained his eyes for sight of the monster, but there was nothing visible. He nodded. "All right, Billy," he said, and started back through the funnel of the cave. Billy followed, and presently they were at the bottom again.

It was now only about two hours to sunset, and those two hours were about the worst the boys had ever spent. All the time they were darting from rock to rock, and from one clump of trees to another. One eye they kept for any sign of the monster's return, the other on the cliffs, looking for a place of refuge in case of fresh attack.

But they saw nothing. The country seemed dead, and when dusk began to settle they were some six or seven miles farther on their way, and in country which under its pall of cold grey cloud seemed to be almost without life. "We must find a place to camp," said Clem at last.

"I can see one now," replied Billy confidently. "I spotted it ever so long ago." He pointed as he spoke to a long, dark streak on the face of the cliff. "It looks to me like a ravine or cañon," he added. "We ought to find a cave or shelter of some kind."

As it turned out, Billy was right, and Clem sighed with relief when they found themselves in a narrow ravine which, sloping steeply upward, ended in the mouth of a good-sized cave. They did not waste much time in reaching it, and very soon were standing under its arch.

"We shall be all right for the night, anyhow," said Clem. "Strike a match, Billy. Let's see how big it is." Billy struck one of their treasured matches, and its faint light illuminated the darksome depths of a long, narrow cave. But the light shone also on something else, something which brought a gasp of amazement from both the boys at once.

CHAPTER XXX
THE OUTCAST

It was the ashes of a fire that the boys saw before them, a fire so recent that red embers still glowed in its center. Near by was a pile of newly cut wood.

"Some one here," said Billy below his breath.

"Some one has been here," corrected Clem.

"Then he's coming back," replied Billy, "for there's his cooking-pot—yes, and his bed. Look in the corner."

Clem looked all round. "You're right," he said, "but what in the name of goodness is anyone doing in this horrible, haunted valley?"

Billy's match burned his finger, and he dropped it. "I don't know, and I don't think I much care," he replied recklessly. "Whoever he is, he can't be worse than that dinosaur beast. I vote we stay here."

As he spoke a gust of wind, cold as death, blew in through the entrance, making the red embers glow: Clem had been hesitating, but that icy draught turned the scales. "You're right," he said briefly. "We stay." And bending down he set to mending the fire.

Within a very few moments a cheery little flame darted up, and soon a delightful crackling blaze illuminated the cavern to its innermost recesses. The boys were crouching over it, warming their chilled and weary bodies, when steps made them both start, and, turning, they saw a man entering the cave.

The man stopped short, gazing at them, and they stared back, too astonished to speak. For the newcomer's appearance was as strange as everything else in this queer country.

He was a red man, an Indian, apparently about forty. He was very tall, with a fine face, though his cheek-bones were high. His eyes were keen as those of a hawk. But the oddest thing about him was his dress. Wild Indians wear skins in the cold weather, and the half-civilized ones any old cast-off white men's things. This man wore a pair of grey flannel trousers, a grey flannel shirt, and a tweed Norfolk jacket. Though his garments were old and much worn, they had evidently been made by a good tailor, for they were an excellent fit. More than that, in spite of the man's red skin and coarse black hair, there was something about him which made him seem different from the ordinary Indian.

He carried a gun and two rabbits.

Clem was the first to remember his manners. He rose to his feet. "Klahowya!" he said.

"Tillicum!" replied the new-comer gravely, yet with a curious twinkle in his eyes. Clem wondered what next to say, for he had only a few words of the Stick Indian language. Then he got the shock of his life. "Sit down," said the red man, in perfect English. "And if you are not too tired I should like to hear how you came here."

Clem heard Billy gasp, and he really felt like gasping himself. "You—you speak English?" he stammered.

"Why not? I have spent most of my life in the United States," replied the other. "Let me introduce myself. My name is Gerald Altemus."

"Our name is Ballard," Clem managed to say. "I'm Clem, and this is my brother Billy."

The other bowed, and Clem felt perfectly dazed. Indian looks and white man's manners made the most amazing mixture. "I am very glad to see you," said Altemus, "though I confess that I am much puzzled as to how you got here. But that can wait until we have had some supper. You look hungry," he added, with a smile which gave his harsh face quite a pleasant look.

He set to work at once, and the boys helped. The Indian produced flour, coffee, and sugar from a cleft in the side of the cave. He put the pot on to boil, and after skinning and cleaning the rabbits, gave them to the boys to grill, while he himself made flapjacks from flour and salt, frying them one by one in the pan.

It was such a meal as the boys had not seen since they had left the Valley of the Mist, and the Indian smiled gravely as he saw how they enjoyed it. He himself ate little and said nothing, but Clem noticed that he seemed to be listening all the time. At last Clem could stand it no longer. "Is it the monster you are listening for?" he blurted out.

The Indian turned and fixed his eyes on Clem. "You have seen it then—this great beast?"

"Seen it!" Clem shivered. "We only got away from it by the skin of our teeth."

"But we gave it something to remember us by," broke in Billy.

There came a queer gleam into the eyes of Altemus. "What do you mean? You have no gun."

Billy explained how they had rolled the rock from the cliff and—as they thought—damaged the creature severely.

"Good!" said Altemus. "That was very good indeed. Then it may be that you really have injured the creature, for every evening about this time it comes seeking for me up the gorge."

Clem looked at Altemus in amazement. "And you can stand that?" he exclaimed.

A curious expression crossed Altemus's face. "It is part of my punishment," he said grimly.

A question was on the tip of Clem's tongue, but he checked it. He had long ago learned from Bart the lesson of courteous silence.

Altemus seemed to sense the boy's intense curiosity. "I
will explain," he went on quietly. "When I was a boy I was
taken to the States by a missionary, and educated there.
I became a white man in many respects, yet in my heart
there was always a deep longing to return to my people.
Two years ago I came back. But the young men were hostile to me, and the elders would not receive me into their
council. Yet by degrees I made good. I have been trained
as a doctor, and I was able to give back health to some that
were ill and to save the lives of many children. The young
men became reconciled, but the old men were jealous.
Then the daughter of the chief fell ill of smallpox, and I
could not save her. She died. The medicine men accused
me of killing her by witchcraft, and I was sentenced to be
driven out into this wilderness of the beast. Here I have to
remain for a year, an outcast from my people, but if at the
end of the year I am still alive, I may return."

Clem and Billy had been listening with breathless interest. "How long have you been here?" burst out Billy.

"Three months," was the answer, "and already the monster has chased me a dozen times or more."

"I don't think he will do much more chasing," said
Billy. "He could hardly hop after that rock hit him this
afternoon. But, Mr. Altemus, can't you kill him with your
gun?"

The red man shook his head. "Not with a gun. With
a modern heavy-bore rifle it might be possible. But even
then one would require explosive shells."

"Dad's got some," cried Billy. "If we could only get
home we'd see you had a proper rifle."

The Indian nodded gravely. "In any case, I will do my
best to show you the road home," he said, "but I cannot
accompany you beyond a certain place, for it is a point of
honour with me not to leave this valley until my year is up."

"We shall be tremendously grateful to you if you can
put us on our way," said Clem. "We tried to climb back
over the mountains, but they were too steep."

The other nodded. "Yes, you can't climb them anywhere, so far as I know. The only thing is to go round.
But it's a long way and rough travelling, and you are not
safe from the monster until you are over the first pass." He
paused a moment, listening to the wind which moaned in
the gorge outside, and shook his head. "And the first big
snow is due any time now," he added.

"That's what Bart Condon told us," said Clem.

"It may come to-night, or not for another week," the
Indian answered. "Let us hope, for your sake, it will not
be yet. And now the best thing you can do is to get a good
sleep. You have a big march before you to-morrow."

Presently, as the two lay side by side on a good bed
of branches and dried moss, Billy spoke. "We're in luck,
Clem," he whispered. "He's a good chap, that."

But Clem did not answer. He was already asleep.

CHAPTER XXXI
THE INVADERS

On the second afternoon after leaving the Indian's cave the little party stood together on the bleak summit of a pass. Altemus had been as good as his word, and had guided them over country so difficult that by themselves they could never have found their way. And now at last they were on the summit of the divide. Behind them lay the great tract of wild and desolate country known as the Valley of the Monster, and to the right the lofty mountains which walled the Valley of the Mist. In front—that is, to the west—a long slope led down into rugged forest country.

Altemus stopped. "This is as far as I may go," he said gravely. "The rest of your journey you must make alone. But I do not think you will find it very difficult. All you have to do is to keep the mountains on your right, and a march of ten or twelve miles will bring you to the mouth of the Cañon of the Geyser. You are safe from the monster, and I do not think that wolves will trouble you, so early in the season. Now goodbye, my English friends, and do not quite forget me."

Clem grasped the red man's hand. "We'll never forget you as long as we live," he vowed. "We should be ungrateful pigs if we did."

"And we're not going to say 'good-bye' at all," broke in Billy. "We're jolly well coming back here first thing with that rifle. Can't you wait? We could bring it to-morrow."

The red man looked very kindly at Billy. "No, my friend. I will not wait," he said. "It is likely that the snow may come to-night, and I must return to my cave. But later, when the snow has fallen and you have learned to use the snowshoes, then, if you will bring me the rifle, I shall be very grateful. Now go quickly, for you must be at home before night."

A last handshake, and the two boys tramped away down the hill. At the bottom they looked back. The tall, upright figure stood lonely on the snowy hilltop. They waved, and he raised his cap. Then they were among thick trees, and could see him no longer.

"Isn't he a topper?" said Billy, in a rather choky voice. Clem merely nodded, and for a long time they went on in silence.

As Altemus had prophesied, they had no difficulty in finding their way. But the sky, which had been overcast all day, was growing steadily darker, and the light breeze bit like steel. Then all of a sudden the air was full of small, dry flakes of snow.

"This is the real thing, Billy," said Clem.

"Good thing it's not blowing," Billy answered, as he quickened his pace.

"It's lucky we haven't far to go," said Clem. "I don't think we can be more than three miles from the mouth of the gorge."

They plugged along as hard as they could go, but the snow came thicker and thicker. The ground was already covered with what had fallen three days earlier, but now the white coating thickened rapidly. Soon they were ploughing through it ankle-deep.

The worst of it was that they could not see more than fifty yards, in any direction. It was like being in a fog, only worse, and Clem grew very anxious. He knew that if they failed to find that narrow entrance they might wander until they fell over some precipice or else dropped and died.

All of a sudden the snow began to slacken. "It's clearing, Clem," cried Billy, in delight.

"It's great luck," Clem answered slowly. "Better wait a minute, old chap. It's awfully steep here, and we don't want to take a header into some cañon." They pulled up under shelter of a rock and waited.

They had been there for perhaps five minutes, when suddenly the ground beneath them seemed to quiver slightly, and through the snow came a sound like the shriek of a distant steam-whistle.

Billy gripped Clem's arm. "Old Watchdog!" he cried, in high delight, and almost as he spoke the snow ceased, and the sun low in the west broke through, flinging a lovely pink glow across the white world.

But this pink glow ended suddenly just in front of the spot where the boys were standing, and they both caught their breath as they realized that they were on the very edge of the cliff above the plain where they had been attacked by the Kaloots. Clem went cautiously forward to the edge. Next moment Billy saw him fling himself flat on his face. "Down, Billy! Get down!" hissed Clem in a sharp whisper.

Clem's voice told Billy that something was seriously wrong, and he dropped like a shot. Clem beckoned, and Billy crept forward, wriggling through the snow like an eel.

"Look!" said Clem in a low voice.

Billy found himself on the sheer edge of a tremendous precipice, and below this lay the great slope across which they had been hunted by the Kaloots on that day when they had first reached the Valley of the Mist. It looked different now, for its grassy surface was thick with snow, and the clumps of trees stood up gaunt and white against the desolation.

But it was not at trees or snowy plain that Clem was pointing, but at a long, dark line which moved cautiously beneath the cover of the nearest belt of trees. And Billy, watching it, saw that the line was a number of men, who were creeping forward in the direction of the clump of trees closest to the mouth of the ravine.

There was dismay on his face as he turned to his brother. "Indians!" he muttered.

Clem nodded. "Yes, and white men too."

Billy looked again. "You're right. I believe I can spot Pelly."

"And Gurney and Craze. Billy, this is a bad business. Somehow those fellows have managed to find the way, and they have raised the Kaloots against us."

Billy nodded. "That's what's up. But what a time to choose to attack!

"That's the cunning of them," replied Clem. "They know, of course, that Dad and Bart would never expect an attack so late in the season. So they count on getting in unobserved."

"But I don't understand," said Billy, frowning. "Bart said these Kaloots were scared to death by the geyser, and you know how they stopped that day we had to run from them."

"Yes, but now they are being led by white men I expect they will risk it," said Clem. "The chances are that Gurney has got hold of their medicine man, and got him to give them a charm or a spell of some sort. Billy, I'm scared of that chap Gurney."

"So am I, if it comes to that," responded Billy, "but you'd better remember that it's going to be something worse than a scare for Dad and Bart and every one in the valley if these fellows once get through the gorge. And it's up to us to stop them."

"We can't do that, Billy. What we must do is to get into the valley and warn Dad."

"It comes to the same thing," said Billy impatiently.

"Question is, how we are going to do it. From where we are now there's no way down into the gorge. A goat couldn't get down these cliffs."

"I know that," agreed Clem. "Our only chance is to go off toward the south and see if we can find a way down into the plain."

"And before we can find out those beggars will be through the gorge," snapped Billy.

Clem kept his head. "I don't think so, Billy. My notion is that they are waiting for night to make their attack. I don't believe for a minute that they'll risk an attack in daylight."

"I hope you're right," grunted Billy, who was very much upset.

"Right or not, it's our only chance," replied Clem firmly. "And I believe that I *am* right, for the whole lot of them have come to a stop in that belt of trees."

"Then let's get along," said Billy. "We've only about an hour's daylight, and I don't see myself climbing down that cliff in the dark."

As he spoke he turned and crept back from the edge of the cliff. Clem followed, and they did not rise to their feet until they were a good way back from the cliff and well out of sight of the Indians. Then both rose to their feet, and began to run in a southerly direction.

CHAPTER XXXII
THE RACE IN THE SNOW

From the slope of the tableland toward the south, it was only reasonable to suppose that the cliff would be lower in that direction. Clem, who was leading, kept on and on until they had passed a sort of projection which ran out from the cliff some distance into the plain, like a cape into the sea. Then at last he turned again toward the cliff edge. "That point will hide us from the Indians," he explained breathlessly to Billy.

"Yes, but shall we find a way down!" panted Billy.

Clem did not answer. He knew no more than his brother, and to say truth he was almost sick with anxiety. If they did not find a way down, it meant that these invaders would come driving into the valley in the dead of night, and what would happen then he hardly dared to think. The Mist Men would, of course, put up a fight, but what chance would they have, taken by surprise and attacked by superior numbers? Stories he had heard from Bart of the savagery of the Kaloots rose in his mind, and made his heart beat heavily with fear.

"No way here!" came Billy's voice. Billy had run on ahead, and was standing on the edge of the cliff. Next moment Clem had joined him and was staring down over the edge of a tremendous snow-slope to the plain three hundred feet or more below.

"It's not sheer," he said,

"No, but it's too steep for anything," replied Billy. "If you put your foot over the edge you'd never stop till you landed up at the bottom."

Clem did not speak. He went nearer to the edge. "Look out!" said Billy sharply. "Next thing you know you'll be overboard."

Still Clem did not answer. His eyes were fixed on that prodigious slope. It was steeper than any house roof, and ran, smooth and unbroken as a roof, clean down to the bottom.

"What are you thinking of, Clem? You can't go down there!" exclaimed Billy.

"I don't know so much about that," replied Clem slowly. "Do you remember how we used to toboggan at home in the old days down Devil's Coombe?"

"Yes, but good gracious, that was only about a hundred yards in all, and not half so steep! Clem, don't think of it. You'd be smashed to bits before you got half-way."

Clem's lips tightened. "It's the only way, Billy. I've got to try it."

Billy caught hold of his brother. "You're crazy, Clem. You'll only be killed."

"I don't think so," Clem answered calmly. "The snow is quite deep, and there seems to be a biggish drift at the bottom. You wait here, Billy, and I'll try it. If I get down safely you can follow. If not, you must go farther and try some other way."

Billy's face went rather white, but he made no more objections. He knew that, once Clem had made up his mind, he was like a rock. Nothing could turn him. He watched breathlessly while his brother buttoned his coat tightly and pulled his cap firmly down over his ears.

"Don't worry, Billy," said Clem calmly. "It's not as bad as it looks." As he spoke he sat down, and deliberately pushed himself off over the edge.

To the horrified Billy it looked as though a dark streak leapt the whole distance in a couple of seconds. One moment he saw his brother flashing downward in a cloud of snow dust; the next, he had vanished altogether in a white bank at the bottom.

Billy stood stiff and still as if frozen. All remembrance of Indians and everything else had vanished from his mind; his one thought was, "Clem is dead! Oh, Clem is killed!" He took a step nearer to the edge; he sat down. He must follow and try to help Clem. His brain was so dulled that he had forgotten all about Clem's order to go farther and try to find some other way down.

And just then the snow-bank so far below heaved and broke, and out of it Clem crawled, and, before Billy's amazed eyes, rose slowly and dizzily to his feet. Then he beckoned to Billy, and Billy, his heart in his mouth, pushed off and followed.

It was the swiftest travel that Billy had ever known. All he felt was one frantic rush through the bitter air, with the snow dust blinding him; then a thud, and he was deep in the drift at the bottom.

Clem hauled him out. "Not so bad after all," said Clem, smiling.

"Ugh!" sputtered Billy. "I'm full of snow to the neck."

"The under-layer of snow was frozen. It was lucky the drift was soft," said Clem. "But come on, old chap. There's no time to waste."

Billy, on his feet again, took a look all round. "But I say, Clem," he remonstrated, "we can't go straight for the rift. Those Indians will spot us the minute we get round the end of this point of rock."

Clem pointed to the sky. From the north-west another grey cloud was swinging up across the blue.

Billy nodded. "Another snowstorm. Well, the sooner it comes, the better."

"I don't think it will be long," said Clem, "and I want to be at the end of the rock point, ready to make a bolt for it, the minute the snow comes."

"Right!" said Billy briefly, and the two started. The rock point ran out about three hundred yards from the main cliff, and when the two boys reached the end of it they peeped cautiously round, and saw that they were something over a mile from the wood where the Indians lay hidden. And this wood, as they knew, was almost opposite the entrance to the gorge. Even as they lay there they could hear Old Watchdog shrieking away.

But the sun was still shining, and even under the shadow of the cliffs the snow was so white and smooth that anything—even a rabbit—would have been plainly visible. It would have been simply suicide to show themselves, so they crouched down and waited, anxiously watching the great snow-cloud, which crept slowly up across the blue. It was now freezing sharply, and since their clothes were full of snow they were both bitterly cold. Presently Billy stepped back a little behind the projecting rock and began stamping and beating his arms. "Don't make too much noise," Clem warned him. "Those Indians have ears like cats."

"They can't hear me a mile away," said Billy. "And if I don't get my blood moving I shall be too stiff for the run when the time comes."

Clem did not answer. His whole attention was fixed upon the cloud. "It's coming all right," he said presently. "The hills in the distance are blotted out already."

He was right. Snow was already falling over the hills in the distance, and the grey veil swept forward steadily. The boys watched it with trembling anxiety, for unless the storm came right over them they would be forced to wait until night fell, and then it might be too late. Clem fancied that the white men who were in command of the expedition would not waste much time in starting, once darkness fell.

At last a few soft flakes began to flutter down on the wings of the thin breeze. They thickened until the whole air was filled with them. Thicker and thicker they came.

The wood was blotted out, and in a minute or two more nothing was visible except the tall cliff looming dimly overhead. "Now!" said Clem below his breath, and they started away.

It was not easy going, for the snow was blinding in its thickness, and the two boys were forced to keep close under the cliff, for that was their only landmark. And the snow was already so deep that it clogged their feet and made running very difficult.

"We shall never get there," muttered Billy breathlessly, and just then, half smothered by the thick snow, came the muffled shriek of the geyser.

"Hang on, Billy!" said Clem in his brother's ear. "I don't think we are far from the mouth of the cleft." Billy sprinted again, but the snow was over his boot-tops, and loose as so much sand. Presently Clem slackened his pace. "Stop a minute, Billy, We mustn't over-run it," he said in a whisper, "I think we are quite near the mouth now."

Billy pulled up, panting, and glanced round. Next moment his fingers closed on Clem's arm. "There's some one behind us," he hissed in Clem's ear. "Look!"

Clem looked, and through the smother caught a vague glimpse of dark figures racing up behind them. In a flash the truth came to him. Gurney, or whoever was leading the Indians, had also chosen the cover of the snowstorm for his attack, and these were the Kaloots coming up behind.

"Run, Billy! Run!" he whispered back. "It's our only chance. These are Gurney's Indians behind us, and if we don't beat them to the cleft we're done for, and so are all the folk in the Valley."

CHAPTER XXXIII
IN THE CLEFT

It was all very well to talk of beating the Indians to the cleft, but the question was now to find the cleft. The boys knew that they were quite near it, but in this smother of snow it was impossible to see anything more than a few yards away.

The only thing was to run and chance it, knowing only too well that if they missed the cleft they were done for.

Still, the snowstorm was their friend in one respect, for it hid them from their enemies. But this was only for the moment, for suddenly there came the great roar of a voice from close behind. "Who's that? Craze, who are those two ahead of us? They ain't Injuns."

Clem's heart dropped to his boots, for the voice was that of Gurney. He sprinted again desperately, and Billy kept beside him.

"Where? I don't see nothing," came the answer from Craze.

"Straight ahead. Gee, but you're blind as a bat!" snorted Gurney, and his voice sounded so close that Clem almost gave up hope.

But just then Billy spoke in his ear. "The cleft! I can see it, Clem! We're saved!"

Billy was right, and Clem gasped with relief as he caught sight of the dark, narrow gateway to the valley looming through the whistling snowdrift just ahead.

"I know who it is!" roared Gurney again. "It's those boys! Stop 'em, some of you! Stop them, or they'll get ahead and spoil everything!"

Clem dared not look back. All his energies were concentrated upon gaining the mouth of the cleft before their pursuers could reach them.

A blast of wind cold as death came rushing across the plain, raising the fine snow in a seething, hissing drift which hid everything for a matter of moments. Before it passed, the two brothers had flung themselves past the tongue of rock which almost covered the entrance to the cleft.

Billy checked a little. "Done it, Clem!" he panted. "We've beaten them."

"Don't stop!" urged Clem. "Keep on! Gurney and Craze won't stop for the gorge or the geyser."

He was right, for next instant two tall figures came racing after them into the mouth of the ravine, and, glancing back as they ran, the boys saw that they were Gurney and Craze.

"I told you so!" cried Gurney furiously. "No, don't shoot, or maybe Condon will hear. Run, you fool! We've got to run 'em down."

Clem's legs felt like lead, and Billy too was failing, for they had come many miles already that day, and both were nearly worn out. They knew that they could not keep going much longer, while their enemies were probably still quite fresh. And then, just as all hope seemed to be gone, the ground shook, and next moment came the bubbling hiss which was the start of the great geyser's regular half-hourly outburst.

From somewhere behind there came a new voice—Pelly's.

"Gurney, Craze, what are you a-doing of? Come right back, or every one of these here Injuns'll be on the run."

Gurney's answer was a fierce oath. Then all other sounds were drowned by the shrieking roar of the Watchdog.

Clem, still running, looked back over his shoulder, and to his intense relief saw that their pursuers had fallen back. Evidently Pelly was right, and the Indians needed looking after pretty sharply to make them face the terrors of the gorge. "It gives us a chance," he said hoarsely, and just as he spoke Billy slipped on an icy stone and fell heavily.

Clem stooped and dragged his brother to his feet. Billy took one step and nearly fell again. "It's no use, old man," he said quite calmly. "I've twisted my ankle. You shove on, and warn the folk. I can look out for myself."

"Nonsense!" retorted Clem almost savagely. "Get on my back. I'll carry you."

Billy faced his brother, and even through the whistling snowflakes and the mist from the geyser Clem could see the set look in his eyes. "You're talking nonsense, Clem," he said quietly. "It would only mean we should both be nabbed. It's up to you to warn Dad and Bart, and you know it!"

Clem hesitated. His heart was like lead. To leave Billy to the tender mercies of Gurney and his precious crew was almost beyond thinking about, yet his duty was to warn the valley, and he knew it. "Let's wait a moment, and see if you feel better," he begged. "Anyhow, we can't go through the basin until the water is down again."

Billy shook his head. "It's nearly down now," he said, "and you may be jolly sure that Gurney is going to shove his Indians on the very minute it's stopped. Go ahead, Clem. It's your job."

"But Billy—Billy, I simply can't leave you to these awful men."

Billy looked round quickly. "There's a bit of a hole in the rock just over there," he said. "Help me to it, and I'll pile some snow up in front and lie doggo. Since it's nearly dark and the mist is thick, I dare say they won't spot me."

The cavity Billy pointed to was just a niche and nothing more, and gave very little shelter of any kind.

Again Clem hesitated, but Billy insisted, and in his heart Clem knew that his brother was right. He helped him to the place, then hurried on. He felt perfectly miserable. He had never hated anything so much in his life as leaving Billy behind. The only comfort he had was the thought of the way in which Bart and his father and Jock Scarlett would take it out of Gurney and his pack of marauders.

Fresh trouble was in store, for when he got to the basin he found that the edges of it, beyond the rim of the geyser cup, were one mass of ice. The spray had frozen on the rocks, and it was impossible to go fast. He hurried as much as he dared, but in some places he was forced to go down on hands and knees and crawl. He kept on looking back, expecting every minute that his pursuers would appear in sight. The worst of it was that the snowstorm was slackening. It had not stopped, but it was much lighter, and he could see plainly that it was not going to last much longer. The wind too was lifting the mist.

Sure enough, he was not half-way across the basin when he heard voices in the gorge behind him, and the tramp of feet. His pursuers were coming, and would be upon him before he could get clear. The Indians, wearing moccasins, could travel twice as quickly across the ice as he could in his nailed boots, and even if they could not actually catch him it was certain that they would shoot.

Once more Clem felt perfectly desperate. But there are some people upon whom this sort of thing acts like a tonic. The tighter the fix, the more quickly their brain works. And luckily for himself Clem was one of these. All in a flash it came to him that Gurney and Craze were depending on the space of time between two explosions of the geyser in order to get their superstitious followers through the gorge. At the same time he remembered that Bart had said something about stirring up the geyser and making it go by putting soap in it.

Well, he had no soap, but perhaps a stone might do. It was a chance, anyhow, and, so far as he could see, the only chance. There were plenty of stones, and kicking a good-sized one off the frozen surface he picked it up and went scrambling across toward the central basin. It was easier going here, for the heat of the boiling water had melted the snow and ice. All round the basin itself the ground was quite bare. And the misty vapour from the last out-burst still hung over everything. It was lucky for him that the mist was thick, for by this time the snow had almost stopped falling.

The central basin was surrounded by a rim of whit-ish rock, a sort of deposit left by the boiling water. He scrambled over this with the stone under one arm. Inside the rock sloped steeply toward the circular hole through which the jet rose. Down below he could plainly hear a bubbling like that of a great cauldron, while the whole ground trembled.

At any other time Clem would have been horror-strick-en at the idea of venturing so near to the very crater of the geyser, but now he hardly gave it a thought. His anxiety on Billy's account seemed to swamp every other feeling. He scrambled down a little way, found some sort of foot-ing, and flung the big stone with all his might toward the center.

It went rolling down with a sound like the beating of a drum, and Clem realized that the ground on which he stood was hollow. He saw the stone vanish into the central pipe; then without waiting an instant, he climbed back as quickly as ever he could. As he flung himself over the rim he heard voices through the mist, then the light thud of moccasined feet, and he realized that Gurney and his Indians were actually entering the basin.

Very nearly dead-beat, Clem went slipping and stag-gering away toward the opposite side of the great, cliff-walled pit. He knew very well that he could never reach the valley ahead of his pursuers, and that the only chance for his own people was the geyser. If the stone trick worked, all might yet be well, but if it failed—! Well, Clem could not bear to think of what would happen then. Once that horde of savage Kaloots was loose in the valley, it would be the end of everything.

CHAPTER XXXIV
WHEN THE WATCHDOG BARKED

The snow had stopped altogether, and the icy wind blowing through the gorge was rapidly sweeping away the mist. Before Clem could reach the entrance of the second part of the gorge he heard a shout behind him. "Thar's the kid! I sees him!"

The voice was Pelly's, and was followed by a sharp rebuke from Gurney. "Keep quiet, you noisy fool! Do you want to raise the valley before we get there?" Then came an order from Gurney in the Indian language.

Clem knew instinctively what it meant, and flung himself down. He was only just in time, for next moment a shower of arrows came zipping through the dusk, their flint-headed points rattling on the rock all around him. The moment the sounds ceased Clem scrambled up and set to running again. But his nailed boots slipped on the ice, and down he went again with a force that knocked all the remaining breath out of him. "This is the finish," he said dully, as once more he staggered to his feet.

But he was too worn out to run any more. He could only limp slowly forward. Again came the sharp order from Gurney, and glancing back over his shoulder Clem saw plainly a score of Indians standing just across the basin, and in the very act of fitting fresh arrows to their strings. Clem felt he hardly cared. He was so exhausted that he was almost beyond caring. Yet he dropped again to the frozen ground. Then, before the Indians could draw their bows, the ground trembled, and from out of its depths came the familiar gurgling roar.

Clem could hardly believe his senses, for by this time he had given up all hope of the geyser. The roar increased, and the ground began to shake like the lid of a boiling kettle. Clem saw Gurney and Craze dash forward in a desperate effort to encourage their men.

It was too late. At the very first sound from the geyser the Indians had wavered. Now they were one and all bolting back toward the cañon.

What happened after that Clem hardly knew, for next instant, with a roar twice as loud as usual, a gigantic column of boiling water shot up from the center of the basin. It rose to a prodigious height, sending out clouds of thick vapour. To Clem it looked as if the whole basin would be swamped by its fall, and, crawling on hands and knees, he managed to reach the mouth of the gorge leading into the valley. There he dropped, absolutely spent, with his head spinning giddily.

Down came the vast fountain with a sound like thunder. It was lucky for Clem that he had got as far as he had, for even where he lay he was splashed with boiling foam. Vaguely he saw the great surging, bubbling flood sweep backward to its source, but now the vapour was so thick that he could see nothing else. Then the thought of Billy came uppermost again, and he felt that he must make one last desperate effort to save him.

Somehow he got to his feet and went blindly staggering down the defile. He heard an outbreak of fierce barking, and suddenly was surrounded by the great wolf-dogs. They knew him and fawned on him. A light shone. "Clem— Clem, it's never you?" It was his father's voice, tense and cracking with emotion.

"Billy," said Clem thickly, "He's back there in the far gorge. Gurney's got him, I'm afraid—Gurney and the Kaloots. Save him, Dad!"

He staggered as he spoke, and would have fallen, but his father's arms closed round him and held him up.

Left alone, Billy, his back against the cliff, scraped up snow with both hands in an effort to hide himself. It was a difficult business, for there was precious little snow in the pass. The strong wind which constantly swept through had blown most of it away. He had hardly covered even his legs before he heard Gurney's voice, and next minute figures loomed vaguely through the mist and snow as the two white men, followed by a number of Indians, came running through the gorge.

There was nothing for it but to crouch back as far as he could into the little rift, and sit as still as a statue, hoping against hope that he would not be seen.

Billy's heart pounded as the dark figures swept past. Some were so close that by just stretching out his hand he could have touched them. It was a strong force. He reckoned there must be at least sixty or seventy of them in all, enough to destroy everybody and everything in the valley if they once got in. Last of all came the third white man, Pelly, who no doubt had been ordered by Gurney to bring up the rear.

Billy felt a hot thrill of anger run through him at sight of the treacherous scoundrel who, after first pretending to be their friend, had brought the enemy upon them. Another moment, and Pelly too was out of sight, and Billy breathed a sigh of relief as he realized that not one of them had seen him. The mist and the snow together had saved him for the moment, but the mist was clearing fast, and Billy knew well that he could not trust it to hide him much longer. If any of the Kaloots came back presently they would be bound to spot him, and his only chance was to find some better and more secure hiding-place.

The first violent pain in his injured ankle had sunk to a dull throbbing. Quickly unlacing his boot, Billy tied his handkerchief as tightly as possible round his ankle, but even so found he could not walk. The only thing to do was to crawl, so on hands and knees he started up the gorge in search of some hole in the cliffs big enough to hide him.

From in front he could still hear the thud of feet, and Gurney's harsh voice giving orders. Billy hoped intensely that Clem had escaped, and, knowing that he had had a good start, felt fairly sure that he would. Of course he knew nothing of the awful state of the ground around the geyser basin. His notion was that Clem would be in time to rouse the people in the valley, that there would be a fight, and that Gurney's Indians would be driven back through the gorge.

Billy had crept about fifty yards up the gorge, but without finding the hiding-place he so badly needed, when he heard the geyser beginning again. When the first whistling started, and the ground began to quiver beneath him, he could hardly believe his senses. He knew it was nothing like half an hour since the last outburst, and was, of course, completely ignorant of his brother's clever dodge. But there was no doubt about it. Next moment came the familiar roar, and the furious rush and hiss as the great fountain of scalding water leapt upward.

Then all of a sudden Billy realized what the result would be—that the superstitious Kaloots would make a bolt for it, and that their three white leaders would never be able to stop them. And here he was, right out in the open, actually in the very path by which they were bound to come. Small wonder that for the moment the boy felt a chill of fright. As quickly as ever he could, he turned to the side and crawled close up to the cliffs.

But just here the rocks were as straight and smooth as the wall of a house. There was not one atom of cover of any kind, and Billy heartily wished he had not left his former shelter. It was, however, too late for useful repentance, for next moment the thud of running feet came pounding along the gorge, and here were the Indians running for their lives, eager above all things to get away from the fire devil they had so rashly disturbed.

CHAPTER XXXV
IN THE HANDS OF THE ENEMY

Flattening himself against the foot of the cliff, Billy sat breathless. His one hope was that the Indians might be too scared to notice anything. And, indeed, the first lot passed at such a pace that it seemed as if his hopes might be realized. This first lot was composed of the worst scared and the best runners. Following them came older men, all in more or less of a panic, but not quite so terrified as the first lot. They ran in a bunch, filling the narrow gorge from side to side. Next instant the worst had happened, and one of them bumped right into Billy. Billy heard a grunt of surprise which changed to a cry of rage. Then a sinewy hand caught him by the collar, and he looked up into the fierce copper-coloured face of a Kaloot brave. The Indian's narrow eyes glowed with malice. He plucked a knife from his belt, and Billy saw him draw back his right arm to strike.

The next instant would have been Billy's last, when a powerful hand clutched the Indian's arm, and Gurney's voice rang out. "Drop it, you fool! Drop that knife, or I'll shoot your head off!"

Almost certainly the Indian did not understand a word of what Gurney said. What he did understand was the tone, and the threat of Gurney's pistol jammed against the back of his neck. He dropped Billy like a hot potato, wrenched himself free, and was gone.

"Craze!" Gurney's voice was full of ugly triumph. "The kid! I've got one of Ballard's kids! Here's a bit of luck!"

"Luck!" repeated Craze sourly. "We need a bit, I reckon, after what's happened to-night. What made that infernal geyser go off at the wrong time?"

"Didn't you see? It was this brat's brother. He chucked a rock into it."

"Hurray for Clem!" cried Billy. Then he gasped as Craze kicked him sharply in the ribs.

But his courage was not quenched. "Think yourself plucky!" he retorted, his small face white with pain. "If Bart Condon had been here, you wouldn't have dared touch us."

Craze said something which cannot be repeated, and raised his hand to hit Billy. But Gurney stopped him. "Want to kill the kid, you idiot?" he said harshly. "Don't you realize he's all that stands between us and our finish?"

"I'll knock his impudent head off!" roared Craze.

"You will, and I'll blow yours off," retorted Gurney, with such sudden fierceness that Craze quailed, and became suddenly meek. "He shouldn't cheek me," he said sulkily.

Gurney paid no attention to him.

"Get up," he ordered Billy. "Get up, and come with us, or I'll break every bone in your body."

"Think I'd be here if I could walk?" retorted Billy. "My ankle's sprained, or I'd have been out of your reach long ago."

Gurney glared at him, but saw he was speaking the truth. "Sling him on my back, Craze," he told his partner. "Sharp now, or we'll have Condon's crowd on our heels."

Craze muttered something under his breath, but did as he was ordered, and Gurney started away down the gorge at a sharp trot. As for Billy, he kept quiet. Young as he was, he had plenty of sense, and he quite realized that any attempt to escape was perfectly hopeless. The only thing to do was to wait, and hope that Clem would bring help pretty soon.

All the same, he was anything but happy as he found himself being carried rapidly across the plain toward the distant woods, and knew that every step was taking him farther from help.

Great burly brute that he was, Gurney had had enough of it by the time he reached the cover of the woods. He shot Billy off under a tree, and turned to look back toward the cliff. "They ain't in sight yet," he growled.

"Can't see 'em, anyway," replied Craze. "But it's too blamed dark to tell whether they're coming. What do you reckon to do, Gurney?"

"Find our tent and stop there the night. Old Condon's got more sense than to come tracking through a wood like this in the dark. Where's Pelly?"

As he spoke a tall figure came shambling up. He was breathing heavily. "Them Injuns is all gone, Gurney," he panted. "They run like old Nick was after them." Then he saw Billy. "What, you got one o' the brats?" he exclaimed.

"Only thing we have got," growled Gurney. "Pick him up, Ed. Carry him back to the tent, and watch him well. I reckon he's going to be mighty useful to us."

Pelly flung Billy roughly over his shoulders, and the three together made off into the depths of the wood.

The tent was pitched in a hollow cunningly hidden by thick hemlock. Billy was dropped again. By this time he was numb with cold and aching all over. But the hollow was well protected, and it was something to be out of the bite of the cruel wind. "Reckon we dare light a fire?" asked Pelly.

"We got to have one, or we'll freeze," said Craze.

Gurney, who seemed to have by far the best head of the three, looked round. "Yes," he said curtly, "we can light a fire all right. Condon and his lot won't come fooling round here to-night. They don't know the Indians have left us, and they'll wait till daylight to start out."

Billy felt a fresh chill of disappointment, but all the same realized that there was good sense in what Gurney said, for it would be sheer madness to attack in pitch darkness a wood that might be strongly held by Indians.

There was plenty of dry wood, and a good fire was soon blazing. In spite of his discomfort and anxiety, Billy was most grateful for the warmth. The three men, who were all silent and surly, proceeded to make a pot of coffee. But they did not cook anything. A tin of corned beef and some cold flapjacks formed their supper. Billy was cruelly hungry, but would rather have starved than ask these fellows for food. When they had finished Gurney flung him a flapjack, much as one would fling a bone to a dog, and Billy swallowed his pride and the food. He felt that he must do so in order to keep fit for what might happen next day.

Having finished supper, the men sat talking in low voices. Then one of them, Craze, got up, took his rifle, and went off, Billy thought he had probably gone to keep guard on the edge of the wood. He himself would have given anything to get away and tell his own people the real state of affairs, but since it was impossible for him to get away, or even to walk, he had to give up the idea and sit tight.

Gurney said something to Pelly, and Pelly got up. Taking a coil of rope, he proceeded to tie Billy's hands behind him and secure him to a tree. "Thar, I guess you'll stay where you be till morning!" he said harshly, and after making up the fire went and lay down in the tent, where he and Gurney were soon snoring.

The fire kept Billy tolerably warm, but the ropes cramped him so that he could not lie down. He was miserably uncomfortable and uneasy, and in spite of being so tired found it impossible to sleep. The night was the longest he had ever spent, and it seemed as if dawn would never come. About two in the morning Craze came back, kicked up Pelly, and sent him off to take his place as sentry. Pelly was very surly, but Craze took no nonsense from him.

At last the darkness began to get a little less thick, and Billy was able to see the outlines of the trees against a dull grey sky. The big snow still threatened, yet did not fall. There had been a shower or two in the night, but nothing very much. The fire was dying down, and Billy shivered miserably in the dawn chill. But the two men in the tent still slept heavily, and he himself was, of course, unable to put fresh wood on.

The wind had fallen, and the snow-clad forest was deathly still—so still that when Billy heard a slight rustle in the distance—it made him start quite sharply. At first he thought it was only a bird, or some loose snow falling from a branch, but presently he heard it a second time, and, screwing his head round, saw something moving in the distance. It was still too dark to see what it was. He could only make out some dark object which dropped behind a fallen tree and vanished.

Watching and listening intently, he realized that it was coming nearer. It was creeping and crawling along, taking advantage of every bit of cover. Billy racked his brain to think what it could be. It was not Pelly, for there was no reason for him to creep up like this. Then an idea flashed upon him. Could it be one of the Indians coming back, perhaps to wreak vengeance upon the white men who had led them into such a trap?

CHAPTER XXXVI
CLEM TO THE RESCUE

It was not a pleasant thought, and Billy's next idea was that he had better warn his gaolers. But he decided to wait. There was just the chance that it might not be one of the Kaloots, but a scout from the Mist Men of the valley.

This thought cheered Billy enormously. For the moment he forgot cold and cramp and all his miseries, and lay still as a mouse, watching and listening.

A voice made him start. Someone in the tent was speaking. At first the voices were so low that Billy could not hear what was being said. But presently Gurney spoke in a clearer tone. "Done! Of course we're not done, you chicken-hearted fool—not so long as we've got the kid to bargain with!"

"What good will that do if they get round us?" retorted Craze. "Mebbe we can bargain for our lives, but that's about all, so far as I can see."

Gurney gave vent to an angry exclamation. "You're pretty near the limit in fools, Craze. I only wish I'd got some one along with me who'd got a little sense. Seems to me there isn't much to choose between you and Pelly. See here! Ballard is dead nuts on his kids. I know that much, for I knew him back in England. Now we've got this younger one tight in our hands, Ballard can't rush us, for he can't know that all our Indians have quit, and anyhow he doesn't know just where to find us in this big belt of woods. My notion is this.

I'll go out with a white flag and see him personally and make terms. In exchange for the kid, he'll have to give us a safe-conduct, and a good bunch of furs into the bargain."

"Bet you he won't do it," growled Craze.

"He's got to do it. If it comes to that, we have another pull over him, and he knows it."

"The police job, you mean?" said Craze. "Seems to me that's all the more reason why he shouldn't let us go. Don't you see, once we're mopped up or prisoners in that valley of his, he's safe."

Gurney laughed, and it was an ugly sound. "I've a notion I can convince him that's not the case," he replied. "You leave it to me, Craze. I'll guarantee to handle it all right."

"You always were a 'cute one," admitted Craze grudgingly. "And anyway, Pelly and me, we haven't no choice, for we're sure up against it good and hard. You going now?"

"Yes. The sooner the better, for if we wait till full light there's always the chance that his Indians may find out that ours have quit."

Next moment Gurney came out of the tent. He scowled at Billy, then turned to Craze. "Take mighty good care of the kid," he ordered. "He's all that stands between us and trouble."

"You bet," replied Craze curtly. "We'll be here when you get back."

Gurney walked off and disappeared among the thick trees, and Craze came out and set to rebuilding the fire. While he did so, Billy anxiously watched the fallen tree behind which the mysterious prowler had disappeared. The light was increasing now, and he could see the trunk plainly, but the person who had been creeping behind it had utterly disappeared. There was not a sign of him or a sound.

Now Billy was mad to get away, for he saw that he was all that stood between these blackguards and defeat. As Gurney had said, once the three were prisoners, the danger to his father was over, for there would be no one to give evidence against him or even to identify him. Whenever Craze was not watching Billy pulled and twisted at his ropes, but they were too well knotted, and he could do nothing.

Craze went to a little distance to get some fresh wood for the fire, and Billy took the opportunity to glance once more at the fallen tree. Suddenly a head rose from behind it. Billy could hardly believe his eyes, for it was Clem who was looking at him—Clem, who made a quick signal with his hand, then dropped again like a shot and vanished.

Billy's heart beat so hard that he nearly suffocated. He had seen that Clem had a gun. If Clem could only get near enough to get the drop on Craze all might yet be well. Craze was alone for the moment, for Pelly was not yet back, and Billy had a notion that Craze was a coward at heart, and would give up at once if a gun was pointed at him.

Billy glanced at Craze, who was still picking up wood, then back at the log. He caught sight of Clem again, and saw that he had left the cover of the log and was creeping on hands and knees toward the hollow where the tent stood. He saw something else, which was that Clem had a dog with him. A great, black, shaggy beast which Billy knew in a moment for Pluto, one of the valley guards, the strongest and fiercest of them all. The dog crept after Clem, silent as a wolf.

Craze came back toward the fire, and Billy dared no longer look round. By this time the suspense was so acute that he could hardly breathe. He really felt as if he could not stand it much longer. The seconds crawled like minutes, and as each moment passed Billy's ears were straining for sounds of Clem's approach.

Suddenly a dead stick cracked, and Billy's heart was in his throat. Craze too heard it and jumped to his feet. "Who's that?" he snapped.

"Put your gun down, ye fool. It's only me," came Pelly's voice, and the man himself broke through the bushes and came striding down into the hollow.

Billy's heart dropped to his boots. Could there be more cruel luck? Now it was two to one, and Clem would surely not make any attempt at rescue. If he did the result could only be disaster.

"See Gurney?" asked Craze curtly.

"Yes, I seed him. He told me to come along back. Seems he's a-going to try some stunt with the Big Britisher."

Pelly's voice was a sneer; and Craze turned on him at once. "Don't you go talking that way., Gurney's the only one as can pull us out of this here fix."

"It's Gurney as dragged me into it," retorted Pelly angrily. "You and him, together."

Craze's dark eyes blazed. "Shut your head!" he snarled. "We've got the kid anyway. And so long as we've got him we're safe enough."

Pelly looked for a moment as if he were going to hit Craze. But the other man's appearance was so dangerous that he refrained. He swung round, and vented his ill-temper by kicking Billy in the ribs. Billy could not repress a cry of pain.

The result was startling. Next instant a great black beast leaped out of the bushes on the edge of the hollow, and with a terrifying growl rushed straight at Pelly and seized him by the leg.

Pelly roared with pain, and went down with the dog on top of him. Craze made a rush for his rifle, but as he snatched it up there came the crash of a heavy report from the rim of the hollow, and the rifle flew from his hand. A bullet had struck the barrel.

"Hands up, Craze!" came Clem's clear voice, and there he stood, with his rifle pointed straight at Craze's head.

Craze had more pluck than Billy had credited him with. He gave a yell of rage and leapt at Clem.

Clem's rifle spoke, but the bullet went over Craze's head, and Craze got Clem by the leg and pulled him down. "Ye brat!" he cried furiously, and then he gave a very different cry, for Pluto, leaving Pelly, had sprung upon Craze

and with the mere force of his spring knocked him sprawl-
ing. Before the man could do anything Clem had crawled
clear and jumped to his feet.

"Look out, Clem!" shrieked Billy, "Look out for Pelly!"

The long man was on his feet, and it looked all odds
that he would get hold of Clem. But Clem snatched up his
rifle, and, holding it by the barrel, swung it desperately.
The butt got Pelly on the side of the head, and down he
crashed as if he had been poleaxed.

CHAPTER XXXVII
THE TABLES ARE TURNED

"Hurray!" shrieked Billy, almost beside himself. But Clem kept his head. "Hold him, Pluto!" he cried, and, snatching a knife, slashed the cords that tied Billy.

In his excitement Billy forgot his aching bones and all his pains. "Give me the rifle, Clem," he said. Clem handed it to him, and Billy quickly glanced at the magazine.

"It's all right," said Clem. "It's loaded."

"Then you tie up Craze," said Billy. "I'll hold the rifle at his head to keep him quiet. Pelly's not going to move yet—not after the whack you gave him."

"Right!" Clem answered. "I'll tie Craze. But look out for him. He's a slippery customer."

"Don't you worry. I'm not taking any chances with him," said Billy. "Come off him, Pluto." Pluto, growling formidably, obeyed. Craze's face was purple, with fury and fright.

"Now, Craze," said Billy sharply, "the tables are turned, and you'd better realize that. If you try any more tricks I shan't hesitate to shoot."

Craze ground his teeth, but made no answer. Then Clem set to work. Billy kept the muzzle of the rifle jammed hard against his body, and Craze was forced to realize that it was of no use to resist. Inside a couple of minutes he was triced up so that he could not move.

"Better gag him," said Billy. "Gurney may be back, and we don't want him to get warning of what's happened to his pals."

Clem nodded, and gagged Craze with a handkerchief. Then he turned his attention to Pelly "Hope I haven't killed him," he said uncomfortably.

"Bless you, no! He's got a head like solid bone," returned Billy. "Tie his legs and arms."

This was soon done, and the boys had time to breathe. "Where's Gurney?" demanded Clem.

Billy told him that he had gone to make terms. "Didn't you see him?" he asked.

"Not I, I didn't see anybody. Pluto and I came on our own."

"Came on your own!" repeated Billy. "I say, Clem, you are a brick!"

"Nonsense! I couldn't leave you in the hands of these pigs."

"You came all that way alone in the dark?" said Billy wonderingly. "I'd never have had the pluck to do it. Why, you might have run right into the Indians! You didn't know they'd gone."

"I felt pretty sure of it," Clem answered. "I saw them running like fun when the geyser started up. But I say, old chap, you must have had a perfectly beastly time of it."

"It was pretty rotten," admitted Billy. "And, to say truth, I'm nearly all in. What about a pot of hot coffee?"

Clem laughed. "Some of theirs! This is turning the tables with a vengeance. All right. You sit still. I'll fix it."

The kettle was already on, and Clem piled small bits of wood round it. In a very short time it was boiling, and he made the coffee. "Keep your eyes open," he warned Billy. There was no answer, and looking round, he saw that his brother was lying by the fire, dead asleep. Clem's lips tightened, for he began to realize what Billy had been through. But this was no time to sleep, and very unwillingly he roused him and gave him some coffee. Billy drank it and revived. Then he ate some beef and flapjacks. Clem too had some food.

"There, I feel a heap better," said Billy, quite cheerfully. "What are we going to do next, Clem?"

"Sit tight, old chap. Gurney will come back sooner or
later, and we've got to collar him. He's worth much more
to us than either of these others, for he is the only one
who can clear Dad."

Billy nodded. "That's so. Yes, we must get him, Clem,
and once we have him it will be all right."

"Then we'd better keep quiet and out of sight. And
these fellows ought to be out of sight too. Can we get
them into the tent?"

"Afraid I can't help you with that," said Billy. "I can
barely stand up."

"I'll do it," said Clem. It seemed an impossible task for
a boy of his age, but Clem's muscles had hardened, and he
had filled out wonderfully during the past two months. He
managed to drag the men in. Then he and Billy took up
their positions under the lee of some bushes quite close to
the fire, and waited. They knew they could trust Pluto to
give them warning of the approach of Gurney.

Time passed. The sun was up, though the pall of grey
snow-cloud hid its light. It was broad daylight.

Billy grew uneasy. "What on earth has happened?" he
asked. "Gurney ought to have been back long ago."

"Hush!" Clem whispered back. "Some one's coming.
Look at Pluto."

The big dog's ears were lifting. It seemed certain that
he heard some one coming. But, strain their ears as they
might, the boys could not hear a sound. They crouched
down, Clem with his rifle ready, and the moments ticked
by.

"I don't believe it's Gurney at all," said Billy rather
breathlessly.

Clem glanced at Pluto. The big dog was listening keenly, but not growling. "It can't be," he whispered back.
"Pluto would know."

Again there was a pause. The waiting was dreadfully
trying. "Whoever it is, they can see the smoke of the fire,"
said Billy at last.

Clem got up quietly. He had his rifle in his hands. "I'll
crawl up through the bushes," he said, in a very low voice.
"Perhaps I'll be able to see them." Before he could move
a voice rang out. "Hands up, all of you! You're covered."
Instead of putting his hands up Clem gave a joyful shout.
"All right, Jock! We've got them long ago!"

Jock Scarlett's face as he stepped out into the open, followed by half a dozen of the Mist Men, was a study in amazement. "You, Clem! How in the mischief did you get here?"

"No time to explain now," answered Clem swiftly. "But
here's Billy all right, and Pelly and Craze are tied up in
the tent."

"You've got Pelly and Craze. My word, you're a miracle,
Clem! But Gurney—where is he?"

Clem's face fell. "I hoped you'd got him. Didn't he come
out to Dad, and offer terms?"

Jock's good-looking face hardened. "Yes, he came, but
his bluff didn't work. Your father flatly refused to bargain
with him. He told him that he should never have a penny
from him, but that if he touched Billy he'd hunt him down
if it took him the rest of his life."

"What happened then?" asked Clem.

"Gurney went off with a face like a thunder-cloud, and
Bart ordered me to take twenty of our men and try to find
Billy."

Clem nodded. "I see what's happened. Gurney must
have got the wind up, and cleared while the going was
good. I expect he heard me shoot when Pluto and I had the
fight with Craze and Pelly."

Jock nodded. "That's about the size of it. Then he'll
have gone to join the Kaloots."

"Not he! The Kaloots have all cleared. They're miles
away by now. And Gurney wouldn't be safe with them. I
believe they'd finish him in very short order."

Jock whistled softly. "Then where has he gone?" he asked.

"I haven't a notion," Clem answered. "The only thing to do will be to set our fellows on his track."

Jock spoke to one of the Indians, a tall, fine-looking man known as Black Eagle. He at once called to the others, and these went off quickly. Three Indians stayed with Jock.

"We must get the prisoners in," said Jock. "And Billy will have to be carried. Bart says the big snow is coming to-day, and the sooner we're back in the valley the better."

Clem agreed; the prisoners were brought out, and with their hands tied were marched away by two of the Mist Indians. The third took Billy on his back, and they all moved off rapidly through the wood.

Mr. Ballard and Bart were waiting in the cleft. When Bart saw Billy he gave a great roar of joy. As for Billy's father, he could hardly speak. To get both his boys back safe seemed almost too good to be true, and at first he paid no attention to the prisoners or anything else. It was Bart, with his strong common sense, who cut in. "See here, Ballard, the job's only half done. It's Gurney we want. You got to remember as he's the only chap as kin fix things so as you kin go back safe to England. Ain't that so?"

"You're right, Bart. We must get him if we can."

"I've sent Black Eagle and a party after him," put in Jock.

"Good for you!" said Bart. "Then wherever he's gone, I reckon they'll have him before dark."

"They will if the snow don't come," said Jock, glancing anxiously at the sky. "But it's not going to be long now."

The words were hardly out of his mouth when a blast came whistling across the great slope, a wind so cold that it seemed to pierce the thickest furs like so much paper. Then all in an instant the air was full of fine, driving snow-dust.

Bart caught Clem by the arm. "Come right along, sonny. Come on, all o' ye. It's as much as we'll do to reach the house."

CHAPTER XXXVIII
CLEARING UP

Ten days had passed. The blizzard was long over, and the weather fine, calm, and clear, but the air was tingling with frost. The lake was a vast sheet of ice, and the drifts were so deep that the Indian village had almost disappeared from sight. Even the big house was covered almost to the eaves, and they had had to dig out the doors and windows.

As for the boys, Billy's ankle was well, and the two had been spending the last few days in learning to travel on snowshoes. Already they were able to run for miles across the frozen surface of the great snow-sheet. At supper on that tenth night, in the big dining-room, with its roaring fire of pine-knots, Billy was very silent.

"A penny for your thoughts, Billy," chaffed Jock.

"I reckon he's thinking of that there Gurney," said Bart.

"Don't worry your head about him," put in Mr. Ballard quickly. "The man must be dead long ago. He could never have survived that blizzard. And I'm not worrying either. I shall be quite happy to stay here for the rest of my life."

Billy looked up. "You won't, Dad," he said with conviction, "but as a matter of fact I wasn't thinking of Gurney. I was thinking of Altemus. You know we promised him a rifle. Can we take him one?"

Billy's father looked rather grave. "Certainly he can have one," he said, "but there is no need for you boys to go. I can send it by Black Eagle."

"But we promised to go, Dad," pleaded Billy.

435

Bart cut in. "Don't you trouble your head, Ballard. I'll go with 'em."

Mr. Ballard's face cleared. "In that case I shan't mind, Bart," he said.

"Hurray!" cried Billy. "Then let's go tomorrow."

This was agreed, and as soon as it was light the three set out together.

The day was perfect and though the temperature was far below zero there was no wind, and the sun felt quite warm. They reached the top of the pass where they had left Altemus at about ten in the morning, and the very first thing they saw was the track of snowshoes on the smoothly blown surface. "He's been here," said Billy, frowning. "I say, what bad luck! He's been here and gone back again."

Bart nodded. "The tracks is fresh. I reckon he was here no longer ago than yesterday."

"And he was expecting his rifle," said Billy. "I say, Bart, do let's go on and give it him!"

Bart looked doubtful. "What about this here monster you been talking about?"

"I don't suppose he will bother us," said Clem. "You know we smashed him up badly with that rock."

After some discussion it was agreed that they should go on, and with the snow in good order it was only a little past midday when they found themselves in the Valley of the Monster.

"I reckon we'll keep the hills," said Bart dryly, as he looked round at the great, desolate valley. It was just as well they did so, for as they rounded the steep slope above Altemus's cave all three pulled up short.

"My goodness, there's the brute!" exclaimed Clem.

Bart stared. "I've seed queer things in my life," he said gravely, "but I'll tell ye straight, I never dreamed as a thing like that were still alive on this here earth."

Even the boys who had seen the beast before, felt cold chills creep down their spines. The giant brute was like a great black blot against the snow. Its hairy spine glistened with hoar-frost as it hunched itself, motionless, as close as it could get to the mouth of the cave.

Bart was the first to recover himself. "I reckon that thing's lived long enough," he said grimly, as he carefully thrust cartridges into the magazine of the heavy rifle which he had brought for Altemus. Then he lay down on the snow and sighted carefully. As his finger tightened on the trigger a sharp crack sent the echoes ringing, and was followed by a thud as the bullet struck the dinosaur.

Instantly the huge brute woke to fearful life, rearing up to its full height and roaring horribly. Bart paid no attention, but fired again and again. The range was only about a hundred yards, and every bullet got home. They were nickel-tipped bullets which would penetrate the hide of a rhinoceros, yet at first they seemed to have no effect on the huge body of the dinosaur. The monster leaped and raged in vain efforts to reach its enemy. "He sure takes a lot of killing," said Bart, as he fired for the sixth time.

"You got him in the eye that time," said Clem in a thick whisper.

"You've finished him!" cried Billy. As he spoke the monster made one gigantic leap high into the air, then fell back with an earth-shaking shock, and lay quivering. Bart, aiming more carefully than ever, put two more bullets into the giant beast's head. That finished it.

Next moment the tall figure of Altemus himself appeared at the mouth of the cave. "Hurray! I'm so glad you're safe!" shouted Billy. The Indian smiled gravely, and came climbing up to meet them.

"You have done me a very good turn, my friends," he said, in his grave, precise way. "We have been besieged for the past twenty-four hours, and my buckshot only seemed to infuriate the monster."

"'We'?" repeated Billy quickly. "Have you some one with you?"

"I have, indeed. I picked up a man in the blizzard, badly frostbitten. His name is Gurney."

"Gurney!" cried both the boys at once. "Oh, what luck!" went on Billy. "He's the one we told you about—the man who tracked us up here."

"And now he is dying," said Altemus gravely. "But come in. We have much to say."

They looked first at the monster, marveling at its tremendous size and strange shape. Then they followed Altemus into the cave. On Altemus's own bed lay a man. It was Gurney, but so shrunk and wasted that they hardly recognized him. Changed, too, for he no longer scowled at them. "I'm sorry to see you like this," said Clem quietly.

"You need not be," Gurney answered, in a voice so low and hoarse that they could hardly hear him. "If I had lived I should have done more harm than I have done already. Now that I know I am going out, I have come to look upon things differently. Altemus, there, has helped me. If his skin is red, he is the whitest man I ever met." He stopped, coughing dreadfully.

"His lungs are frozen," whispered Altemus. "I have done what I could for him, but there is no hope. He cannot last more than a few hours."

"Then can we ask him to clear Father of the forgery charge for which he was put in prison?" asked Clem.

"He has done it already," replied Altemus. "Yesterday he got me to write down the whole story, which he signed, and I have witnessed it."

Clem drew a long breath of deepest relief. "Dad will be very grateful to you, Mr. Altemus," he said. "And so are we."

Just then Gurney spoke again. His voice was weaker than ever. "Have you got Craze and Pelly?" he asked.

"Yes," Clem answered.

"What is your father going to do with them?"

"He was going to keep them prisoners. They are well treated and fed."

Gurney hesitated. The change in him was so great that it seemed beyond belief. "Ask him to let them go," he said hoarsely.

It was Bart who answered. Clem was too astonished. "I'll see to it, Gurney. We'll do the right thing, you can bet on that."

"I believe you will," said Gurney. Then he smiled. "I'm not going to apologize. If I had my life to live again, I should probably act in the same way as I have done. Unless, indeed, I had met Altemus earlier. Then I might have been different." He looked at Clem. "Altemus will give you the paper which will right matters for your father," he said. "I'm glad I could do that before I finished."

Clem felt dreadfully sorry for the man. Gurney had been a brute, and he had treated his partner disgracefully. But now that he saw him lying there with his lungs frozen, dying, all the old bitterness left Clem's heart., He bent over him. "I'll tell him what you have said," he told Gurney. "I—I—it will be all right," he ended lamely.

Gurney smiled. "Thank you," he said. "Would you— would you mind shaking hands?"

Clem flushed, but took Gurney's wasted hand. Gurney smiled again. "That makes me feel better," he said. "Now I'll sleep a bit."

Gurney did not wake again. He died quietly in his sleep. Next day the boys and Bart helped to bury him. Then they returned home, leaving Altemus alone in his cave home. But now that the monster was dead they were no longer anxious for his safety.

Clem himself handed his father Gurney's confession, and watched him read it. As Mr. Ballard did so the years seemed to roll off him. He became visibly younger.

He laid the paper down and turned to the boys. His eyes were shining. "We'll go home," he said. "We'll go home in the spring. Bart and Jock will carry on here."

Billy looked dismayed. "But not for good, Dad? You're not going to give up this jolly old place altogether?

"No, indeed!" answered his father smiling. "As soon as you boys have finished your schooling, back we come." He turned to Bart. "I'm a happy man, Bart," he said, "a very happy man."

ABOUT THE AUTHORS

Raymond Auzias-Turenne
1861-1940

Baron Raymond Auzias de Turenne left France (after refusing to serve in the military for the Republic) for the United States. Briefly operating a horse ranch in the Black Hills, he then moved to Canada. After marrying the daughter of the Minister of Agriculture of Quebec, he held a number of official positions, started businesses, became French consul in Dawson City during the Gold Rush, became a banker, and wrote numerous newspaper articles and stories. "Le Dernier Mammouth" was first published as a serial in *Lecture pour Tous* in 1902 and 1902, and as a book in 1904. It was translated into English for the 1907 edition. He wrote occasionally under the pseudonym Amès Sémiré.

The French edition may be viewed online at:

https://catalog.hathitrust.org/Record/012510022

Thomas Charles (T. C.) Bridges
1868-1944

Bridges, the son of a clergyman, was educated at Marlborough College (Wiltshire, England). After his schooling, he went to Florida to work on an orange plantation, unprofitably as it turned out, and he returned to England several years later. Turning his hand to writing, he became a popular freelance author. His main focus was the juvenile market (magazines, newspapers, and, later, books). Several of his novels involved 'lost worlds.'

For more information, see:

http://freeread.com.au/@RGLibrary/TCBridges/
    TCBridges-Bibliography.html

COACHWHIP PUBLICATIONS
CoachwhipBooks.com

COACHWHIP PUBLICATIONS
CoachwhipBooks.com

Bestiarium Cryptozoologicum

Mystery Animals and Unknown Species
in Classic Science Fiction and Fantasy

COACHWHIP PUBLICATIONS
CoachwhipBooks.com

zoologica
fantastica

COACHWHIP PUBLICATIONS
CoachwhipBooks.com

THE GOLDEN CENTIPEDE

LOUISE GERARD

FLORA CURIOSA

CRYPTOBOTANY, MYSTERIOUS FUNGI,
SENTIENT TREES, AND DEADLY PLANTS IN
CLASSIC SCIENCE FICTION AND FANTASY

COACHWHIP PUBLICATIONS
CoachwhipBooks.com

BOTANICA DELIRA

MORE STORIES OF STRANGE,
UNDISCOVERED, AND MURDEROUS
VEGETATION

COACHWHIP PUBLICATIONS
CoachwhipBooks.com

CETUS INSOLITUS

Sea Serpents, Giant Cephalopods,
and Other Marine Monsters in
Classic Science Fiction and Fantasy

COACHWHIP PUBLICATIONS
CoachwhipBooks.com

INVERTEBRATA ENIGMATICA
Giant Spiders, Dangerous Insects, and other Strange Invertebrates
in Classic Science Fiction and Fantasy

COACHWHIP PUBLICATIONS

CoachwhipBooks.com

Still In Search Of Prehistoric Survivors

THE CREATURES THAT TIME FORGOT?

Dr. Karl Shuker

Including Illustrations by William M. Rebsamen

COACHWHIP PUBLICATIONS
CoachwhipBooks.com

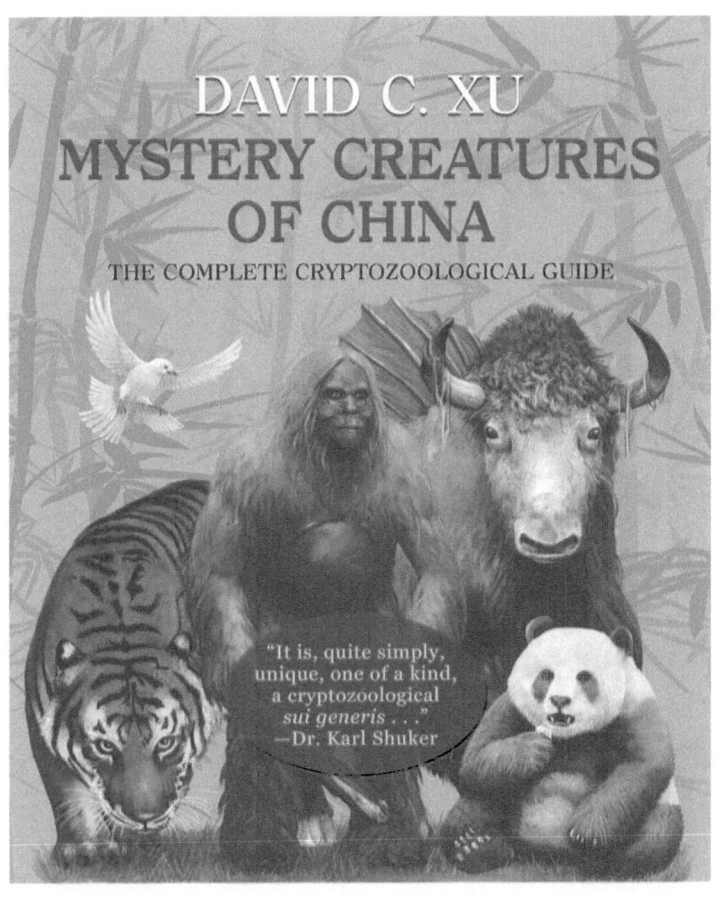

DAVID C. XU

MYSTERY CREATURES OF CHINA

THE COMPLETE CRYPTOZOOLOGICAL GUIDE

"It is, quite simply, unique, one of a kind, a cryptozoological *sui generis* . . ."
—Dr. Karl Shuker

www.ingramcontent.com/pod-product-compliance
Lightning Source LLC
Chambersburg PA
CBHW020502020726
47493CB00001B/143